ANDREW MOTION

Andrew Motion is the former Poet Laureate, co-founded the Poetry Archive and was knighted for his services to literature in 2009. He is a Fellow of the Royal Society of Literature and lives in London.

ALSO BY ANDREW MOTION

Biography and memoir

The Lamberts: Georgie, Constant and Kit
Philip Larkin: A Writer's Life
Keats: A Biography
In the Blood: A Memoir of My Childhood

Criticism

The Poetry of Edward Thomas
Philip Larkin
Ways of Life: Places, Painters and Poets

Edited works

Selected Poems: William Barnes
Selected Poems: Thomas Hardy
John Keats: Poems Selected by Andrew Motion
Here to Eternity: An Anthology of Poetry
First World War Poems

Fiction

Wainewright the Poisoner
The Invention of Dr Cake
Silver

Poetry

The Pleasure Steamers
Independence
Secret Narratives
Dangerous Play: Poems 1974–1984
Natural Causes
Love in a Life
The Price of Everything
Salt Water
Selected Poems 1976–1997
Public Property
The Cinder Path
The Customs House

ANDREW MOTION

The New World

VINTAGE

1 3 5 7 9 10 8 6 4 2

Vintage
20 Vauxhall Bridge Road,
London SW1V 2SA

Vintage is part of the Penguin Random House group of companies
whose addresses can be found at global.penguinrandomhouse.com

Penguin
Random House
UK

First published in Vintage in 2015
First published in hardback by Jonathan Cape in 2014

www.vintage-books.co.uk

A CIP catalogue record for this book is
available from the British Library

ISBN 9780099583783

Printed and bound in Great Britain by Clays Ltd, St Ives plc

MIX
Paper from
responsible sources
FSC® C018179

Penguin Random House is committed to a sustainable future
for our business, our readers and our planet. This book is
made from Forest Stewardship Council® certified paper

FOR KYEONG-SOO

The stars streaming in the sky are my hair
The round rim of the earth which you see
Binds my starry hair

Adapted from Jeremiah Curtin,
Creation Myths of Primitive America,
Boston, 1989

CONTENTS

PART III

THE RIVER AND THE SEA

Foreword

When one book is the child of another it is courteous to acknowledge the parent, so without delay I will say this volume continues the story of my life with Natty Silver, which I first brought to public attention a little under three years ago. I should also make clear at once that Natty is the daughter of Mrs Silver, formerly of the West Indies and in more recent times the landlady of the Spyglass Inn, Wapping, London; and of Mr Silver, better known as 'Long John' Silver on account of him having only one leg, or as 'Barbecue' since he used to work as a ship's cook. My own father Jim Hawkins was his companion on their celebrated journey to Treasure Island.

In my first instalment I described how I was persuaded by Natty to return with her to the Island in the summer of 1802; our purpose was to recover the bar silver left behind by Squire Trelawney, when he made off with the other spoils that Captain Flint had previously buried there in secret.

Nothing turned out as planned. Where we expected a primitive wilderness we found a barbarous kingdom, ruled by three villains the squire had marooned on the Island; when we thought to enjoy an easy and profitable return to England we faced a catastrophe. Our ship the *Nightingale* was blown off her intended course and back through the Bay of Mexico until she was smashed on the coast of Spanish America, in the part called Texas. In that disaster I lost a great deal, including the human cargo I had helped to liberate from the three maroons, and the promise of my own future wealth and comfort.

The fact that I am able to say as much proves I did not also lose my life. For instead of following almost the whole company of our ship into Davy Jones's locker, and never seeing the light of this world again, I managed to scramble onto dry land. Here, as I shall soon explain, I had good reason to think my Maker would have dealt more kindly with me if he had allowed me to die with the rest.

But I must not judge the events of my life before I have remembered them, and shall therefore now wind back the clock forty years and return to the waters of that savage coast. The *Nightingale* lies in pieces; the storm has abated; the moon is almost set; and the latest pulse of seawater has carried me onto a beach of black stones. I am exhausted – fluttering between life and death.

But I am alive.

I am alive.

The Hispaniola
1842

PART I

THE SHORE AND THE LAND

CHAPTER I

My Afterlife

When I approached the gates of heaven there was no brightness of the kind we are told to expect. No dazzle, no promise of homecoming, no rapture. There was only darkness, like a sky at night without stars or moon or cloud, and a mild but steady breeze blowing in my face, making me turn and look backwards over my shoulder.

Miles below me, dozens of miles but perfectly clear as if caught in the eye of a microscope, I saw – myself. My own young body stretched on a black shore, with my hair in my eyes, and my arms flung about, and my legs half-in and half-out of the water, and my skin puckered with cold, because . . .

Because why? Memory failed me, then sparked again.

Because of the hurricane.

The wreck.

My plunge from our ship.

The plunge, and the water rushing into my throat, and the wave that suddenly lifted me up. The smaller and gentler wave, that singled me out and brought me safely to land.

The lens of the microscope left me there and shifted back to the sea. Outlined in starlight was the miracle that had saved me – a rock-ledge jutting out from the beach, keeping the worst of the storm at bay. And beyond it, sixty yards off where the waves still surged and battered, with the first gleams of daylight brightening their white caps: the *Nightingale*. But not our home as she had been, never that any more. The *Nightingale* quite finished, with her two masts torn down, her sails billowing underwater, her hull smashed through, and deep at the heart of her wound – our treasure.

But the microscope would not let me see that. The microscope darted off once more, suddenly impatient with the sea and switching instead to the black cliffs that enclosed the beach where my body lay unconscious, scouring the rock-crannies and birds' nests, searching the clefts and cracks, before deciding it had done with them too and must turn instead to the shoreline.

Where at last it found what it wanted.

Which was Natty.

When I saw her there in the eye of the microscope, her bare feet stamping on the stones for warmth, I felt my grip loosen at my enormous height, and the breeze in my face strengthening, trying to shake me off.

But I was not yet ready to slip back to myself, my earthly self. I still hung at my distance, high and separate.

Except that nothing was separate now, because everything was Natty. Natty in her tattered white shirt and knee breeches, with the cliffs rearing around her, and the ocean roaring, and the moon dipping between clouds. When her head tipped forward I caught the sheen of her beautiful brown skin, and the gleam of her eyes. And her hair – the tight curls of her hair shining as brightly as metal as they blustered around her face.

What was she doing, though, staring at the waves continually and paying me no attention? I was lying no more than a few yards away from her! Had she not seen? Or had she seen all too clearly, and given me up for dead?

'I am here!' I called to her. 'Me, Jim Hawkins! Your Jim!' But I was not just a few yards away; I was still dozens of miles above her, and she did not notice.

I knew then I must find my way back to her, not wait for her to search for me. I knew I must tumble down through miles and miles of swirling air and rain and spray until I landed smack on the stones, the black stones.

Where she would find me and know who I was. Where she would fold me into her heart.

CHAPTER 2

A False Start

She reached me at once, hauling me out from the waves with the stones grinding beneath my heels. When I was clear she knelt down and rested my head in her lap; when she whispered my name there was no other sound I wanted to hear.

But I moved my head. I rolled it from side to side for pure pleasure, with life running warm in my veins again, and so I lost sight of her, finding the cliffs instead.

All through the hours we had floundered in ruins, with the *Nightingale* shattering beneath us, and her corridors flooding, and her cabins breaking open to the sky, and our friends dying, I had thought these cliffs were a blank wall. A vertical stop; the end of the world.

Now as they dizzied into the rain above me I saw they were

covered with scrapes and scratches – there, near the summit, where the first daylight was crawling across. Rockfalls I thought, my eyes blurry with salt. Gouges made by the rain and sea. But as the light grew stronger, much stranger than that.

They were teeth and tongues; but just for a blink because now a new ghost-mark had appeared. A fissure that ran from the crown of the cliffs in a zigzag down to the beach and ended twenty yards off.

A stairway.

I opened my mouth to tell Natty, to say she must see this too and help me to walk and climb and make our escape. But I only groaned, which made her whisper my name again.

So I forgot the cliffs. I forgot them along with the path and the stones and the storm and the wreck and the friends we had lost.

I'll sleep for a moment longer, I told her, or meant to at least. I'll sleep and we'll find our way home together, and heal ourselves in the old world we know, and be happy.

And I'll find my good sense there as well.

And my sentences.

But first I must sleep; I must sleep and dream.

CHAPTER 3

In the Black Bay

'Jim?' Her voice was so small the sea almost smothered it.

'Natty?' It was my first word and I could think of no better.

'I saw you,' she said. 'I thought you were . . .' She did not like to continue, but the word she had left unspoken hung between us in the half-light, until she placed her hands either side of my face and a flame sprang in my heart.

'Natty?' I spluttered. 'Who else is alive?' I felt like an infant, born for the second time.

She was adrift and not thinking of me, even while she brought me her comfort. 'Where are we, Jim?' she said vaguely. 'Where are we?' – then she lifted my head from her lap and floated away from me over the grinding stones like a sleepwalker.

When I propped myself on my elbow I saw her standing on the

shoreline with her back turned, staring out to sea. It was not the waves she saw; it was the dark shapes that weltered there, all life-less now.

I redoubled my efforts and sat up straight, then shuffled towards her and for a moment we were silent, waiting for the sunrise to show us the horizon.

'Is there no one else?' Natty said at length, and still with her back to me. 'No one at all, and no silver?'

This I could answer. 'There is no more silver,' I told her. 'Don't think about silver, Natty . . .'

'I meant for our friends,' she said, then twisted round to stare at the cliffs behind us, as if a voice had suddenly called out.

A moment before I had sketched a stairway there, and the begin-nings of faces. Now in the stronger light I discovered a kind of madhouse, with cats and dogs and creatures like freaks and devils all carved in the stone together.

'What are they, Jim?' Natty whispered. She was pointing towards a gigantic bear, a monster looming over the zigzag path with a mound of bodies heaped on his tongue. His eyes had almost popped out of their sockets with the effort of swallowing so much flesh.

'Who made them?' I said, more to myself than to her.

'Wickedness,' she said, as if I had asked a different question. 'But why here?'

'Why not here?' I said.

'This is the New World!'

'Wickedness is everywhere,' I said.

She glanced round then and I saw she was weeping. This was my doing, I felt sure of it, and gathering all my strength I stood up at last and caught her in my arms. I dare say it made a very dull sort of embrace, a kind of deadlock in fact, but for a second or two the world disappeared: the sickening surf, the gull-cries, the hiss of the wind. All I could hear was Natty's heart; all I could feel was her breath.

Then it was over and she was shoving me away. 'No, Jim, no!' she gasped. 'Look there in the water behind you!'

I expected – I don't know what I expected. Broken timber. A twist of rope. But when I dipped my hand in the surf whatever it was felt slick as a bolt of silk.

I almost choked, but I kept on looking and found a kind of mouth grimacing at me. A neck that was severed clean through.

I clattered away on the stones. 'Not yet,' Natty said, holding her ground; this was her old voice now, which I knew from London and the start of our life together. 'I need you to help.'

'Help you with what?' I asked, looking towards the skyline as if the answer might be shining in the distance; there was light everywhere now, with the purple gone from the clouds and a pearly brightness coming in.

'We must bring them ashore,' Natty told me; she had forgotten all her fear. 'We must bury them.'

'Who?' I said, still wavering.

'Everyone,' she said.

'Everyone?' I said, beginning to understand. 'But everyone is too many! We should leave them and look after ourselves, that's all we can do.'

Natty smiled her smile then, the same that had brought me from England, and so to the Island, and so to our disaster, and now had raised me to life again.

'We can think of ourselves soon enough,' she said. 'First there is this.'

She was so definite I simply nodded and stepped into the water; I bent over and found the monstrous thing that bulged beneath the surface; I felt the slithery skin and gripped.

Then we took the weight together, scrabbling backwards over the stones, and a second later I recognised it – recognised her I should say. She was Rebecca, the slave I last saw on the Island with a Bible pressed to her heart, the friend who read from the good book when we buried the captain. When her head jarred and twisted as we dragged her forward, and her tongue flopped over her teeth, I paused to straighten the body and give it some dignity; we only stopped for good when we reached the high-water mark, where we laid down our burden on a bank of seaweed.

A moment later I faced the sea again, the sea and the ship that was no longer our *Nightingale* but a graveyard. Not even a graveyard in fact; more like a death-spout, a fountain hurling up severed arms, and legs, and feet, and heads, and hands.

I dropped onto my knees with my eyes closed, and when Natty touched my shoulder I trembled to feel its weight.

'Thank you,' she said.

But I could not look up yet. Fifty more bodies, was all I could think. Fifty more bodies, if all the ship's company drift ashore.

Fifty bodies that will need fifty graves.

Fifty graves we must dig with our bare hands.

And no food to sustain us, and no shelter to cover us. And only rainwater to drink.

We would have managed somehow or other, I like to believe. In the event we never began.

CHAPTER 4

Savages

Up to this point I have been forced to collect my memories piece-meal; my sea-battering had scattered my wits. But I came to myself as we began our burial work. Salt and salt water drained out of me. Warm blood pumped into my toes and fingers. Exhaustion? Of course I was exhausted; we both were. But I could move, I could understand, I could speak – so I can tell my story more easily now, without always gasping for air.

After we had done our work with Rebecca, hiding her body beneath a mound of black stones, the next friend we hauled ashore was Mr Creed, who had fought beside me on the sand of Captain Kidd's Anchorage, beating away Smirke and his comrades. He was anonymous when I first caught hold of him, his face hidden by a rag of weed. As I pulled this aside and saw the pockmarks covering his cheeks and forehead, now all turned a peculiar clay colour by the water, I remembered how much his disfigurements had embarrassed him in life. He often used to dab at them with his handkerchief, as though one day he might manage to blot them away entirely.

Then Natty called me, pointing to the cliffs again. High up where the zigzag path began she had noticed creatures scampering towards us. Dogs, I thought at first – a dozen or so. But they turned into people. People squeezing around the faces carved in the black rock; people slithering over the rolling eyes and long fangs; people skipping and scrambling and rushing the last few steps onto the beach and huddling to stare at us.

I jumped to Natty's side and grabbed her by the hand. When I first saw Smirke and the rest on the Island I had felt terrified by their wildness. These men were not in the least bit wild; not savage at all in fact but very composed, standing stiff and straight with their weapons at their sides – bows, and axes, and arrows.

They were small, the tallest no more than five foot.

And young – twenty or so, the same age as ourselves.

With black hair combed away from their foreheads and slicked down with grease.

And clean-shaven faces decorated with swirls of green and red paint, which made their noses stand out like beaks.

With bare arms and legs but otherwise neat and tidy, wearing tunics of tanned animal hide, and moccasins.

And tucked into their belts, into every belt, a short knife with a bone handle.

'Who are they?' I was staring hard, as if this would keep them still or make them disappear.

'Red Indians,' Natty said, still perfectly calm.

I knew the words – I had heard them in Mr Clarke's schoolroom at Enfield – but Natty might as well have told me they had fallen from the sun.

'They must be Indians,' she said; she had made up her mind. 'What else can they be? We're in America.'

I stared at the ground thinking how the storm had blown us back past our Island and into the Bay of Mexico, how it had swept us north in the final part of its rampage, how this meant we must be – where in America, exactly? I remembered Mr Clarke again. I saw the map he had shown us. I saw the Bay of Mexico like a gigantic mouth, and on the northern shore the long spit of Florida, Louisiana with its marvellous big river, the desert of Texas.

Then I looked up. 'We are in Texas!' I said, like a conjuror producing a bird from his hat.

Was there ever a stranger geography lesson? We were guessing at territories, knowing we might be killed any minute.

'Which means . . .' I went on, 'it will be easier for us to get home.'

'Why on earth?' Natty asked.

'Because the English are in America.'

'The English are everywhere,' Natty said, as if our countrymen made no difference to anything. But I did not want to hear this. I felt so encouraged to know where I stood on the earth, I turned back to the Indians and lit up a smile.

It was well meant but not well done; it made them decide they had waited and watched long enough, and now should begin strutting forward – which they did while bunching closer together, and bulging their eyes, and wrinkling their foreheads, and sticking out their tongues. I thought the cliff behind them had come to life and its demons had leaped down to hurt us.

Natty was more sensible. Letting go of my hand, she picked up two stones from the beach and weighed them to show she was wondering which might be the better to throw.

This at least made the men stop still and give up their eye-rolling and tongue-waggling. Instead they began a strange chant: a very ugly sound, like wild dogs yowling for food.

'Natty.' I put one hand on her arm. 'We must show them we're friends.'

'But how, Jim?' Her calmness had all disappeared and she sounded faint with fear.

'By doing nothing,' I said, but she never heard me because the chant had reached its climax, which was a loud explosion of yelps, with the Indians shaking their bows above their heads.

Natty threw down her own weapons at once – her poor stones – and when they saw this the Indians finished making their noise and looked at us carefully for the first time, as though they were only now noticing the different colours of our skin, and our ragged clothes, and our bare feet, and our bedraggled hair and our bruises.

I thought they had taken pity on us and began hobbling forward, but this only made them lose patience. A moment ago we had been fellow creatures sucked from the ocean by the storm; now we were intruders and they felt free to hate us.

Two of the men stayed as they were, gripping their spears straight up at their sides like guards, while the other ten hurtled towards us screaming at the tops of their voices; the insides of their mouths were stained black as ink.

Natty and I raised our fists – ready for them, but in truth very pathetic. No matter, though; instead of knocking us down the men tore straight past; to my amazement they did not even glance at us; we might not have existed.

Were they like cats, deciding to murder us slowly? That was my thought, but when I turned to look – when I cringed and looked, I should say – I saw the men were still sprinting towards the sea, still ignoring us, and only pausing when they reached the water's edge. Here they made a huddle again, chattering urgently before breaking apart and scampering along the shoreline, one of them stopping every few yards until they stood at regular intervals around the whole crescent of the bay.

Was it the wreck they wanted to loot, was that all? And if so, were we free to leave? I glanced back at the two men left to guard us, but they were scowling and gripping their spears more tightly than ever. Daring us to run, I thought, so they could skewer us, then hack us to pieces.

The idea was so frightening we stayed perfectly still.

A minute passed and none of us moved, or took our eyes from each other.

Another minute.

Then suddenly our guards began strolling towards us, swinging their arms with insolent slowness, stopping only when their faces were inches from our own. I smelled fish on their breath and winced away, but they would not allow this and one of them seized my chin; he made me face him again and began fiddling inside my shirt, along the waistband of my breeches, pinching me and prodding me. The other guard did the same with Natty, and giggled as he touched her.

'Jim . . . ?' Natty's voice was trembling. 'What shall we do?' Both guards had finished their inspection and now they were leering at her, wiping their hands across their mouths.

'Nothing,' I said, still as steady as possible.

'Nothing again?'

'There's nothing we can do.'

'What do you mean? We have to do something!' Natty spun round to face towards the waves and I followed, thinking our guards would haul us back. In fact they seemed pleased, because now we had to watch the rest of their troop, the savages along the shoreline who while our backs were turned had all stripped naked and begun scouring the water, launching themselves forward whenever a body appeared. They did this very nimbly, gleaming through the waves with their warpaint fading along their arms and shoulders, seizing a prize, then wrenching it up the beach as though it weighed nothing at all.

The first two or three of our friends they landed in this way, including Mr Creed, were poor creatures who never owned anything valuable in their lives, not even a bracelet or an earring; their bodies were tossed aside as worthless. But when one of the men found the remains of Bo'sun Kirkby, who wore a gold band that remembered the wife waiting for him in London, he pulled the knife from his belt and sliced off the finger as if he was cutting a rose from a rose-bush.

As easily as that; the butcher had no human feelings at all. He slipped the ring onto the middle finger of his own left hand, then without pausing he lunged forward again to jerk the bo'sun's head from the stones and flourish his knife. Once he had addressed himself to his task in this way, with relish, he sliced around the crown of the bo'sun's head to strip the bald white skin from the scalp, pursing his lips to show it was a delicate job and required him to concentrate. Then he hoisted his trophy into the air; then he tucked it into his belt alongside his knife; then he turned back to the waves, looking for his next victim.

'No!' Natty whispered. 'What's happening, Jim?'

She meant me to comfort her but I was dumbstruck. I thought I had seen our own death. I thought it must come soon.

'Should we tell them about the silver?' Natty was desperate now, but still thinking more clearly than me.

'Why would we do that?' I spoke in a kind of trance.

'Jim. Listen to me.'

'I am listening.' I might not have been; I was looking towards the cliffs, but when I saw the stone creatures writhing inside their rock-prison I swung away again, scanning the gulls as they flocked above our wreck, or the sails of the *Nightingale* blooming underwater like colossal flower-heads, or the day's first weak sun-shafts lancing down through the waves towards our silver on the seabed, or anything except our guards.

Then they were stampeding forward again, spinning us apart and separating us. We staggered on the stones, we floundered, and a moment later we all stood in line: one guard, me, Natty, the other guard.

'Speak to him,' Natty said, meaning our leader who had turned to confront me; her voice was imploring. 'Be simple, Jim. Be kind as you are.'

I felt touched by this, and another time would have said so. Now I only cleared my throat, and said what had always been in my mind, speaking slowly and clearly.

'We come as friends.'

There was no reaction, no light in the hard brown eyes.

'We are your friends,' I said again, louder this time but still meaningless.

Meaningless and apparently outrageous, because my guard began chewing like a rabbit, pursed his lips, hollowed his cheeks, then cracked open his mouth and spat out a jet of disgusting black liquid. Some landed warm on my face, the rest on the tatters of my shirt so I felt it through the cotton.

Tobacco juice. I stood my ground, wiping the foul stuff away, although it clung to my fingers even when I smeared them on my shirt, my breeches, the stones at my feet. But this was outrageous too. So outrageous the guard spat a second time and then began to harangue me, spattering me with his saliva.

I withstood this tirade as well, but my heart froze inside me. I thought: when this is done he will murder me, because I have offended him so much.

But when his fury burned out he did not even reach for his knife. Instead, with a flash of his yellow teeth, which I suppose might have been a smile, he led us to the foot of the cliff, where he ordered us to wait for a moment.

Although Natty was standing behind me now I heard her distinctly. 'Goodbye,' she said, as a drizzle of pebbles blew down from the carvings above, and under my breath I finished what she had begun. Goodbye to the *Nightingale*; goodbye to our friends; goodbye to our fathers; goodbye to England; goodbye to the lives we had known as children; goodbye to each other.

Then the guards growled again and I set my foot on the path. We began to climb.

CHAPTER 5

On the Clifftop

The cliff path was hardly a path; it was shallow steps hacked into the rock, and so steep I soon dropped onto all fours, telling Natty she must do the same. Our climb was therefore very slow and painful, and also very frightening. Stones cut my hands, my fingers, my knees, my feet. Lunatic eyes glared at me. Bulbous lips puffed at me. Gusts of wind buffeted and blustered – the last gasps of the storm. Once I slithered so far into empty space, only a tuft of grass kept me alive. And all the while our guards never lost their footing, but skimmed over the ground as though their moccasins were skates.

I had no breath for talking and no inclination, except at halfway when I muttered 'Nearly there' to encourage Natty. The guard in front of me immediately whisked round and slapped my face; the sting of his hand stayed on my skin like a burn-mark.

'Silence,' he shouted – not that word of course, but his own ferocious yap.

After that, it would be too much to say I was thinking. I was too tired to think and too nervous. But I was not completely blank. I told myself that if cruelty was so natural to these men, we would only survive by convincing them we were broken, so they would lose their concentration and let us escape. Escape to what I had no idea; I thought freedom itself would be enough.

When I reached the end of the path I therefore made a pretence, humbly dragging myself over the last few yards, gazing wretchedly at the wounds in my hands, then flinging myself down with no more breath in my body.

The ploy succeeded after a fashion. When Natty collapsed beside me and seemed to be just as spent, our guards smiled at one another like smug farmers whose cattle have been driven safely to market.

In fact I was very relieved to lie quiet for a while, with the tangled smells of the earth filling my head, and the muggy breeze tousling my hair. I even let myself drift towards sleep for a while, or at least towards somewhere far distant, where I was not in danger.

But I had curiosity too; I wanted to know where we were, and a minute later hoisted upright again. Our clifftop, which was an arc enclosing the whole bay, was the only high ground for miles in any direction. A hundred yards to my left, and the same to my right, and the same facing inland, it sloped down to a wilderness where the course of our hurricane showed like the track of a colossal carriage. And either side of this track, where the country was still unscathed: grey sand with silvery meres and gullies. And beyond these: red-brown earth, and steam blowing here and there as if the earth had been molten lava only a moment before, and we were the first inhabitants.

As for our clifftop, the centuries had worn it bare, so I thought it would look clean and simple in good weather. Now it was a bump of chaos, littered with leaves and seaweed. Why had God landed us *here*, I thought, when anywhere else the *Nightingale* would have crashed into soft sand, and her cargo might have been saved? There was no explanation. What had happened had happened by chance, unless it had all been arranged by devils in the rock beneath us. Unless they had summoned us and we had not been able to resist them.

I scrambled to my feet and pulled Natty upright beside me. Her face was streaked with mud, and gashed across the forehead where a stone had struck her.

'The end of the world,' she said, staring around and reeling a little in the breeze.

'Or the beginning,' I said, putting my arm around her waist to steady her.

'How do you mean?' she said.

I glanced at our guards to see if they minded us talking like this, but they were already bored with their power, and had moved away to admire the work of their friends on the beach below.

'Because we are here,' I said.

'And that's enough?'

'It's everything.'

'It's all we have, you mean.'

'It's all there is.'

Natty spoke cautiously, as though our talk was a game and she could not decide which play to make next. In the end she gave up and broke away from me; for a moment I thought her strength had gone and she wanted to lie down again. But she was quite deliberate. She tested her balance, then walked carefully towards the edge of the cliff. When there were only a few inches of land left, she looked round and gave me a cat's smile, as if she knew a secret but would not say what it was.

'Natty!' I shouted, my voice drowning those of the guards who barked at her, then crouched down astonished. 'Get away from there! Come back!'

Her answer was to keep facing me and stretch out her arms sideways, so she hung crucified on the empty air, with the whole swerve of the bay widening behind her.

I found myself gazing at her calmly despite the danger. Why this should have been I cannot say – some part of my brain demanded it, as though I had grown so used to her company in the last weeks and months, I needed to remind myself what she looked like. She was beautiful with her slenderness, and her short black hair in its coils, and her liquid eyes, and her brown skin like river-water. But it was not her beauty that held me. It was her wildness. Her quickness that made her seem like a bird who had learned the ways of mankind, but might renounce them again at any moment.

I am not sure how long I rambled like this in my mind; for a second that passed as slowly as an hour. And when I came back to myself, I found that I was imploring our guards to help me rescue Natty and pull her away from the cliff-edge and save her.

All to no avail, because now their surprise had worn off and they no longer cared what happened. She was not so precious as she had seemed at first, not enough for them to risk their own lives, at any rate. When one of them knocked the other on his arm and grinned, I thought he was saying if she jumped she jumped: that was fate as well.

I took a deep breath and stepped towards her myself, with the shoreline opening giddily below me, and the *Nightingale* like a toy, and the waves scratching around her, and the scavengers scurrying over the stones.

'Why, Natty?' I said as gently as possible, looking away from the fall and into her face. 'What are you doing?'

She blinked at me. 'Surely you know the answer to that, Jim?' she said.

She was right; I understood perfectly well. She had put her life in the balance to keep herself safe. It was a way of saying 'I choose; I am still myself.'

'Very well,' I answered, still softly. 'But Natty, be careful.'

'Oh, Jim,' she said, with a curious drifting note in her voice, as if she was falling asleep. 'How I count on you – I do! You are always here to rescue me. You are always . . .'

Her voice trailed off, then wandered back again.

'Do you love me, Jim?' she said. She had never asked before, not straight out like this.

'I do love you, Natty,' I told her. 'You know that. I've loved you from the beginning.'

She gave a long sigh and the wind blustering up the cliff tore it away from her like smoke. 'From the beginning,' she repeated. 'The beginning's a long time ago now, isn't it.'

I thought she was trying to bewitch me and make me tumble alongside her down through the buffeting air. But I would not be tempted. 'Come away now, Natty,' I said, 'this is enough –' and reached out a hand.

Her expression changed at once, her dreaminess vanishing completely. 'Jim!' she hissed, turning away from me and pointing down to the beach. 'Look!'

I took a quarter-step forward, thinking a demon had broken into her mind and made her begin to imagine things – until I peered beyond, over the edge of the cliff, and saw what she meant. She had noticed another body on the black stones below. A lifeless body. And then, as the wave that brought it ashore drained away over the pebbles again, not lifeless. I saw a leg straighten and thrash in the undertow. I saw the body convulse and roll onto hands and knees. I saw it shake like a dog and stand.

It was Mr Stevenson, our watchman from the *Nightingale*. I had last seen him hours before with an ingot of the silver clutched to his chest, plunging towards the seabed as our ship foundered; now he was breathing again, and gasping, and wiping the hair from his eyes.

Our guards saw as well and they crept up beside us, nervous at first then suddenly careless, jumping about and chopping the air with their spears. What did they mean? To catch him, of course. To tell the scavengers to catch him.

'Mr Stevenson!' I shouted, but he could not have heard; the wind had risen again and the distance was too great.

Natty said nothing but seized my hand and gripped it tight. She wanted me to see that while the currents had stripped shoes and clothes from most of the bodies already washed ashore, Mr Stevenson was still wearing his blue sailor's jacket.

The mob swarmed towards him, all naked as the day they were born, and Mr Stevenson began to run, tugging at the pocket of his jacket with both hands. A pocket I now saw was bulging with something hidden.

A weight.

He tugged it clear and threw it behind him.

A bar of silver.

It thumped on the stones gleaming bright as a fish and the mob surged forward. '*Ooooh! Ooooh! Ooooh!*' they cried, their voices soaring across the cliff-face, then they rushed together and seized it and passed it from hand to hand in quick flashes and glimpses. Only when they had petted it like this for a while, crooning and ogling, did they remember to look up.

'*Plata*,' they sang out. '*Plata. Plata. Plata.*'

Whatever this meant I thought it would please the guards, but not in the slightest. They jabbed their spears towards Mr Stevenson on the beach below, hacking at the air.

I shall describe what followed very quickly, because I hate to remember it. After choosing one man to stay and protect the treasure (which he did by placing it reverently on the black stones, then standing directly above), the rest of the pack began sprinting along the shore, where Mr Stevenson was still struggling to escape. At this time I suppose he was a hundred yards away from them, limping and hopping with his blue coat flapping around his legs, and no idea where he might go, only that he must be as far away as possible. This made me think he was very brave when he turned to confront his enemies. When he heard them panting close behind him and dropped onto his knees to face them.

Mr Stevenson. I saw him then as I had seen him first on the *Nightingale* at her quay in Wapping, climbing into his crow's-nest to take a view towards the river Thames. For the next many days after that, in the rain as we blew along the south coast of England towards Start Point, then as we crossed the flowing green hills of the Atlantic and reached the calmer and warmer pastures of the Caribbean, I had heard him calling down to me – about the weather to come, about the weather we had avoided, about the chance of this landmark or that being our target. In particular, I could not forget the soft Scottish accent that coloured his verdict 'All's well, all's clear' as we came into the safety of our cove on the Island.

This good man had been the voice of our adventure as well as its eyes. Now the savages had bunched around him and set their bows and fired their arrows into him, all the while howling and yelping as if it was themselves they hurt. Mr Stevenson never made a sound, not even when most of these arrows pierced him in the chest and stomach, and a few punctured his hands, and more injured his face and head.

A single shaft, if it had been well aimed, would have been enough to dispatch him. This assault made him into a kind of hedgehog, which the savages then turned into a man again by all stepping forward to pluck out their arrows and wipe them on their bare skin and return them to their quivers. Once this was done they turned round and tramped along the beach to rejoin the guard they had left standing over the silver.

As I watched them go I realised I was still holding Natty by the hand, holding her so hard I thought I must be hurting her – and I loosened my grip. But I did not let her go. I was thinking one of the savages might suddenly remember some unfinished business, and return to Mr Stevenson to desecrate his poor body in the same way we had seen the bo'sun desecrated. In the event, after more rejoicing around the silver, only one brute went back to him – slapping his head like a forgetful schoolboy, then manhandling Mr Stevenson to remove his blue coat. When he had done this, and held it up to the sky, and seen it was spoiled with arrow-holes and blood, he put it on back to front.

Our guards watched this like the audience at a play, nodding approvingly from time to time and grunting, but otherwise in silence. Only when it was finished and the scavengers were all together again, fawning and gloating over their treasure, did they resume their shouting. Calling down orders to search the carcass of the *Nightingale* very thoroughly now, to see if it contained more of the same kind.

At last I let Natty go and heard myself breathing again, turning towards her to hold her in my arms. But now our guards had finished their entertainment they were impatient again, dancing along the cliff-edge without so much as another glance at the beach, and poking with their spears until we were back in single file. A few moments later we had marched off the high ground, and come to the edge of the plain that would take us to the interior of the country.

As we heard the air quieten around us, and felt its dampness and warmth, I gathered my wits enough to feel thankful the smooth ground made for easy walking in bare feet; it meant I was able to keep my head high and look about me, no matter what barbarous scenes continued to run in my head. Mr Stevenson on his knees. Mr Stevenson toppling forward onto his ruined face.

For the first two or three miles we tramped west along a narrow strip of sand that twisted between the coast and a shallow lake. The effect was very desolate, as the wind drooped around us in sickly swoops and plunges, and plucked at the debris our hurricane had left in its wake: boughs torn off trees and blown here from miles away; stinking clumps of seaweed buzzing with flies; mysterious root-clumps bleached as white as bone; and sometimes bones themselves – of birds, mainly, but also some larger skeletons of creatures that might once have been dogs or wild cats.

Even when this track ended we still walked easily enough, passing through stagnant marshes, then reaching sand-dunes covered in sea-lavender, where flocks of finches and sparrows sprang up like chaff, then fell down like grain.

Our guards paid no attention to any of these things, which they doubtless saw every day and thought quite ordinary; to my eyes they seemed almost miraculous, and for the first time since our capture I felt my spirits rally.

'They won't hurt us,' I told Natty, suddenly filling with hope.

There was a pause while she swallowed. 'You're a fool, Jim Hawkins,' she said at last, her voice cracking. 'If you believe that you're a complete fool.'

CHAPTER 6

The March Inland

Natty's reply hurt my pride but I knew it was fair.

I had deceived myself; I had let the earth deceive me.

For the next part of our journey, although the walking remained easy, and the wreckage of the storm fell behind us, and the clouds began to break up, and the deep blue sky reappeared, and clammy heat turned into dry heat, and our clothes dried out and became more comfortable, I would not be so foolish. I would accept things as they were. I would admit to strangeness and danger. And thirst. And hunger. I would see we had no authority over our own lives; no influence over where we went, or when, or how.

This was the lowest I had fallen since our wreck, because for the first time I accepted how much we had lost. 'Father,' I whispered to myself at one point, meaning not the Almighty but my own flesh and blood. 'Forgive me.' I had allowed myself to think of him once or twice since reaching dry land, but never before had I wanted his company so much.

At the same time there was Natty, and I knew we must cheat our fate together or not at all.

'Why is there no one here?' I said, just to make conversation. Our guards did not mind, but continued marching at the same steady pace, their moccasins pattering on the dry earth.

'Why should there be?' Although Natty remained out of sight behind me, it was clear she was not in the least interested. She touched me on the shoulder and pointed ahead, where our track now cut into different country again, sprinkled with small oaks and walnuts.

'You see?' she sighed. 'There's nothing here – just trees and grass. Nothing.'

I nattered on regardless. 'Where are their houses?' I asked. 'Where do they live?'

Natty sighed. 'Why are you thinking about houses, Jim? This is the wilderness. We're not in London now. We're not in England.'

'Very well,' I said; I knew I was making a fool of myself. 'Not houses, then. Whatever they make instead. Tents. Or whatever they find. Caves.'

There was no answer, just scuffling footsteps and another weary sigh.

'All right,' I continued, more wildly than ever. 'Not caves, then – I don't know, Natty. People must live somewhere, that's all I'm saying. There must *be* people here and they must live somewhere. People are everywhere.'

This provoked her so much she tried to laugh, a dry croak that made the guard ahead of me spin round and put a finger to his lips.

For once I was glad to obey him and fall silent; I had done my best and it had come to nothing. I had failed. For the next two or three miles I therefore kept my mouth shut and my eyes blank. I refused even to take an interest in my guard, let alone the seed heads that popped in the grasses as the heat of the day increased, or anything else in the country on either side.

In this vacancy I soon slipped back to childhood again and my father, who now appeared in a thousand scenes of kindness: showing me his winding tracks through the marshes near our home in the Hispaniola, asking me to help serve his customers in the taproom there, bringing me food when I was unwell, pointing out the boats and shipping that worked on the river, teaching me their names.

At another time these memories would have been delightful; now the weight of them made my chin drop onto my chest as if I had no more will to live. I felt the earth opening before me, and saw the darkness boiling at the centre; I decided I did not care any more if I toppled in.

What saved me was very surprising. We came to a hill-crest, a sluggish wave that rippled through the whole landscape, and when I looked ahead I found the earth suddenly opening into a valley. But not a valley like any we had seen before. This was very neatly shaped, and the central ground had been cleared to make fields, where rows of corn were growing between brushwood fences.

Our guards were certainly pleased to see it, and made us pause while they pointed out features they thought were especially admirable: the oaks that grew at regular intervals along the middle of the valley; the piles of stones that had been removed from the fields and rolled into heaps; and the smooth path (whitened by feet meandering to and fro) that led from where we stood and ended in a village.

A village. Not a collection of houses arranged as a street, such as we know in England, but twenty-five or thirty triangular tents – tepees, I soon learned to call them – which sprouted wherever their occupants had chosen to build them. Some looked like unlit bonfires made of sticks and logs; some had a framework of long poles covered with different kinds of skin; and some were shabby, with rubbish heaped around their entrances.

Beyond these tents, at the head of the valley, stood the greatest surprise of all: a large low house built of stones taken from the fields, with a shaded veranda in front and outbuildings to left and right. I knew at once it must be the home of their chieftain. Now, I thought, with my heart pounding; now he will appear to us and we will hear our sentence.

But nothing happened. Our guards continued their chattering; cloud-shadows swilled over the fields and darkened their yellow to gold; Natty touched my shoulder again, to show she understood what I was thinking, then her hand fell away. And that was all. The house was deserted. There was no smoke rising from the chimney, and no movement in the windows.

Was the chieftain dead or was he hunting perhaps, or fighting? I had no way of knowing, and therefore no reason to feel we were any safer than before. Yet at the same time I told myself we would not be killed at once, because the chieftain was not here to give the order.

The idea was soon knocked aside – by Natty, first, suddenly gesturing in front of us at a group of women working in the fields, then by the women themselves, who set up a great hollering when they saw us, and so brought everyone else in the village streaming out from their tents and up the slope towards us.

Very soon about sixty people had collected, all pointing and murmuring. Women with babies strapped to their backs in flimsy knapsacks. Children. Leathery old grandfathers and grandmothers. And all very inquisitive – darting forward, then back again, pointing and staring. And very suspicious as well. When one group of young boys ran up carrying bows and arrows which they fired into the ground at our feet, the rest of the crowd applauded them, because they could not decide whether we were humans or monsters.

Our guards did not like the idea that we might be hurt in this way and hurried us forward, but this only made the crowd surge around us more wildly than ever. The little children were the least afraid, often laughing at us behind their hands. The women were as scornful as the young men though more decorous, being dressed in animal hides that were stuck over with pieces of shell. I noticed that some of them had trophies dangling from their belts – hair, and wrinkled pieces of skin. And all of them, regardless of age and sex, had decorations painted on their arms and hands and faces – rusty reds and greens, the same as our guards.

The crush was so great we soon came to a standstill, whereupon a young child stepped forward, a boy of seven or eight; he approached very boldly, stretching out his hand with the fist clenched – and then, just when I thought he might be about to punch me, he pinched me, a sting like a mosquito, before breaking into a grin and stooping above the mark he had made, to see the whiteness in my skin before he scampered off again.

It was nothing in itself, a game, but I could not help feeling a little spurt of elation. I thought if the children of the village could make us likeable, our strangeness would be forgiven by the others and we might soon become friends. For this reason I then began to encourage them as much as possible, smiling and laughing when three or four others approached me, daring one another to pinch not just my hands and legs, but my nose, my face, and anywhere else they could reach.

Our guards soon tired of this and shouted at us to move again, which made the children scatter as quickly as they had appeared. It was a disappointment, I admit, and I felt it sharply – as though I had been banished from the company of friends – but I kept my chin up as we made our way forward, catching an eye here and there to prove I was made of the same flesh and blood, and showing as much curiosity as possible about their clothes and their tents and the whole arrangement of their village – until suddenly I found myself looking at things I wished I had never seen. Human heads, severed and sewn into a kind of necklace, that hung around the entrance to one of the largest tepees; and further off, a large circular area with a pit dug in the centre. The mouth of this hole was filthy with the wreckage of bonfires, and close by, collapsed between two stakes, lay a naked body, the skin so blistered it hardly resembled a body at all.

Our guards laughed aloud when they saw me noticing this, prodding me with their spears and seeming to congratulate one another. Only when we reached the chieftain's house did they become more sombre again, showing us we must stop here a moment, and admire the magnificent thing before us.

To tell the truth, the house was a very ramshackle affair when seen close up, with draughty holes in the roof and gaps between the stones of the walls. Yet it was also very mysterious and threatening. The shadows sprawling across the veranda looked heavy as marble, and the windows were empty squares of darkness. A curtain draped over the entrance dragged its hem in the dust as the breeze blew; it was dyed the colour of blood.

I looked – then looked away, and this time the guards did not prevent me. On the contrary, they seemed very anxious for me to take in the whole extent of the property, including the shelter and halter-rail that stood off to the right; it was obviously a stable of some kind, although there were no horses.

They were even more enthusiastic when I glanced away to the left, where a large pile of wood had been collected together, the timbers peeling and sick-looking. A woodpile for fuel, I thought – but what of that? Then I looked again and noticed a door among the timbers. Not a woodpile then. A cabin of some kind.

A prison. Our prison. Where we would stay until the chieftain returned.

We shuffled forward, Natty breathing quick and shallow beside me. That was the only sound I heard during our final seconds of daylight, and when I looked down all that I saw was the powdery dirt curling over my toes and against my ankles. It was nothing more than dust, but felt very precious to me because it was my last sight of the world. When we swung along the front of the chieftain's house, and one of our guards ran ahead to remove a wooden locking-pole from the prison door, it still danced in front of my eyes. And still danced when the door slammed shut behind us, and the log scraped back into place, and we were drowned in darkness.

CHAPTER 7

A Conversation in the Dark

I lost my balance, covering my face with my arms to shield myself. But there was nothing. Just pinprick lights and cobwebs tickling my skin – and stink. A warm, sweet, cloying stink of putrid flesh, and I did not like to think what else.

Then there was Natty, my fingers sliding through her hair and over her forehead and mouth, brushing her neck, the collar of her shirt, taking hold of her shoulders. I tugged her towards me and held her close; when I pressed my face against her cheek it was wet with tears.

'My love!' I whispered, and she leaned more heavily against me. Further off in the world, in the world that did not belong to us any more, footsteps retreated and a dog whimpered.

'I told you,' Natty said at last. 'They will hurt us – they will.'

I was too tired to encourage her any more; I merely straightened a little, then eased away from her.

'Where are you going?' she asked, in a flurry of panic.

'Nowhere,' I told her, and might have smiled. 'I'm looking.' I let my hands fall from her shoulders because my instinct, like an animal in a cage, was to see how far I could move in any direction. I could not think properly until I knew how much space we had, or how little.

'How can you do that?' Natty asked, more composed now. 'How can you look, when you can't see?'

'Easy,' I said, as if I felt more confident myself, and raised my fingers to the ceiling, poking them into a mesh of cobwebs.

I estimated it was seven foot high, then I groped my way from one side of the hut to the other.

This time, ten foot.

Then I started from the door – the one door, built in the wall that faced the village – and set off towards the furthest end of the hut. My eyes were adjusting now and I could see that the darkness was not absolutely black as I had thought at first; the cracks in the walls meant it was shot through with little darts and slivers of sun, which filled the whole cabin with an airy sort of twilight. I stopped in a narrow beam that showed the floor covered in silvery dust, scooping up a handful and holding it close to my face. It was oyster shells, ground into powder.

I walked on, but even more cautiously than before, because the stench in this further part was much worse. Fifteen paces. Twenty – then something brushed my bare ankle. Rags, I thought; something soft, anyway, ashily soft and then suddenly hard, with a burst of flies like fat in a pan.

'Ah!' I reeled away, my stomach heaving.

'Jim!' Natty called. 'What is it, Jim? Are you all right?'

'I'm not sure,' I said, struggling to keep from choking. 'There's something here.'

'What sort of thing?'

'I don't . . .' I staggered backwards another few steps, expecting to end up beside Natty again, but she did not want this. She was suddenly back in command of herself, and as I retreated she pushed ahead, floating into the gloom with her white shirt glimmering like a moth.

Then her breathing faltered. 'Come here,' she mumbled. 'I've found someone.'

Immediately, I put my hand over my mouth and went forward to kneel beside her. Although the light here was very dim I could see she was stooped over a man, though more a corpse than a man: lank hair, gaunt face, markings on both cheeks. By peering more narrowly, I saw these markings were painted in straight lines, not circles like the warriors in the village. This told me he must be a stranger, probably an enemy captured in battle.

I blinked once or twice, clearing my eyes as much as possible, and a clay bowl swam into focus – resting on his stomach with his hands clamped around it. Apart from that tight grip, there was nothing lifelike about him. His eyes were closed and his chin had sunk onto his chest; a string of saliva gleamed in the corner of his mouth.

'Why is he kept like this?' I asked, which was a stupid question. What I meant was: why haven't they killed him already?

Natty clicked her tongue against the roof of her mouth. 'You tell me,' she whispered. There was none of her mockery in this, just acceptance; we were both equally at a loss. 'But we might say the same of ourselves, don't you think? Why haven't they killed us already? What are they keeping us for?'

Her voice was steady, as though her questions had nothing to do with anything that mattered, and when I did not answer – when I could not think how to answer – she merely prised the bowl away from our friend and passed it over to me. Then she smoothed the hair on his head as if to say she would soon return, and led us back to our place by the door.

Here she told me to put down the bowl and sit side by side with her; she was breathing more easily now, we both were.

'He'll die soon,' she said, perfectly composed.

'And we –' I broke off as a large blue-fly droned towards us from the end of the cabin, circled heavily over our heads, then buzzed back towards the invalid and settled again.

'And we will die soon as well,' Natty went on. 'That's what you were going to say, isn't it?'

I paused again; the question was too enormous. 'It depends on their chieftain,' I said at last. 'He'll decide.'

Natty considered this. 'And when will that be?' she wondered. 'You saw his house – no one's been there for weeks. We've no idea where he is. We don't even know he exists.'

'Oh, I am sure he exists,' I said.

'Really,' she said, with a definite smile in her voice. 'We might be at home discussing our neighbours in London!'

The word 'London' sounded so strange in my ears that I could not help smiling myself. 'What else can we do?' I said, with a shrug.

But Natty's mood had changed again; now she was cold and matter-of-fact. 'Nothing,' she said. 'We can't do anything. You said so at the cliff.'

'I meant we should get their trust,' I said. 'I meant we should fool them and make them lazy, then try to escape.'

'Escape from here?' Her incredulity roused her a little. 'How will we ever do that?'

I ignored her question. 'I expect if we're not killed we'll be sold,'

I said. I had not wanted to seem angry. I wanted to sound cold like her, because I thought it was a sort of control. Instead I frightened her, and as soon as my last word sank in, my word 'sold', she suddenly pitched forward onto all fours and began scurrying around the perimeter of the prison, making a detour to avoid our friend but otherwise feeling along the timbers with her fingers, thrusting them into cracks, testing the foundations to see if they were well set in the ground, and eventually circling back to the door, which she banged and pounded until it creaked on its hinges. Then she collapsed beside me again, breathing quickly.

'Well?' I asked, still stubborn.

'Not possible,' she panted. 'Like you said.'

'Not by disappearing through walls, no.'

'How then, Jim?' she said, her voice high and desperate. 'How shall we ever escape? How?'

'Other ways,' I said, and when I heard how unhelpful this sounded, how mean-spirited, I knew I had hurt her. But in my unhappiness I did nothing. I hung my head and fell silent, listening to the life outside. I heard women summoning their children and arguing together, then men's voices giving orders until everyone stopped talking for a moment. And in that pause: birdsong, very brash and unlike our English birds, and the howling conversation of wild dogs beyond the village. The longer I listened, the more heavily every sound pressed down on me; each call, each growl and bark, crashing onto me like a stone, driving me into the earth.

I gave up and let my thoughts sweep me away. For miles in every direction, perhaps for hundreds or even thousands of miles, no one spoke our language or knew our customs. There were people, certainly: our fellow prisoner and our jailers and maybe other tribes scattered here and there. But no one we could appeal to for understanding. No one we could trust. The whole world was a wilderness.

I would certainly have continued in this way, falling and never reaching the end of my fall, if Natty had not saved me.

All her coldness had gone now, and her fear; the crackle in her voice, which was her thirst again, made my heart melt. 'There will be other ways,' she said – my own words repeated, but calmly and kindly. 'We will find other ways to escape from here, and reach England again.'

The words came to me like a blessing and I seized them in pure gratitude, stretching out my hand and laying it against Natty's cheek, curling my fingers into her hair and pulling her towards me. I kissed her, my mouth finding hers in the darkness and feeling her lips as dry as paper.

For a moment she yielded, relaxing a little, then turned away.

'Natty,' I said, my hand slipping down to my lap. 'Please, Natty . . .'

'Jim,' was all she said. 'We can't, Jim.'

'What do you mean?' I asked, my head spinning.

'Surely you know?' she said.

She was trying to protect me but I needed her to explain. 'What?' I asked her bluntly. 'You must tell me, Natty.'

She lifted her chin as though preparing for a struggle. 'Very well.' Her voice was a little louder now. 'If that's what you want. We are where we are – in prison. We have a dying man here. We are nearly dead ourselves. This is not—'

I interrupted her; I knew I would sound wheedling, but I could not stop myself. 'So when, Natty?' I said. 'When if not now?'

She hesitated, and even in the half-light I could see that her eyes were wet. 'I can't,' she said at length. 'I can't – that's all. And besides, we must be safe.'

'What do you mean, safe?' Again, I spoke despite myself.

Natty tipped her head backwards and bit her lip; she would not let herself weep. 'I mean they mustn't know anything about us,' she said. 'These people. If they know how we feel, they will hurt us all the more.'

She reached out and took my hand. 'Now, please,' she went on, more quietly still. 'Understand.'

She let go of my hand and looked away from me, facing the door of our prison; her shoulders were slumped as though she had used up all her strength.

Again I could not help myself, and when I opened my mouth the words that escaped me were not the ones I had meant to use. 'I will die of this,' I told her.

Five short sounds, but I regretted them bitterly. I hung my head in the darkness and waited for her to rebuke me.

'No, Jim,' she said. 'You won't die of this, not of waiting.' Then to show there was nothing to add she stretched herself out on the floor, as naturally as if it were her soft and familiar bed at home, folded her hands across her chest and closed her eyes.

A moment later I did the same, and the warmth of her body enveloped me as surely as if I held her in my arms. For a long time afterwards my voice continued buzzing in my head, repeating the same words over and over. How would I not die of waiting? How would I not die of waiting?

CHAPTER 8

Angels of Mercy

My dreams were all of shipwrecks. Bleached faces and mutilated bodies; wide-open eyes with crabs scrambling across them; bruised lips and bloated fingers; hair dandled like weed in a current. And Natty on the seabed beside me, weightless and silent.

None of them could scare me awake – and, when they ended at last, and I drifted back towards the surface . . .

A song.

A song that was beautiful at first and very faint, part of a different dream. Without waking Natty I crawled across the dust and pressed my face to a crack in the timbers by our door. No good. Not wide enough to see anything. Except there was a piece jutting out from the timbers, a loose strip of bark I could tear off and so make a peephole – an eye on the world that measured an inch wide and a foot long.

Our lookout place.

I blinked as the breeze streamed into my eyes and found a miracle waiting – sunset gilding the horizon, with russet mist drifting across the tepees in the village, and the cornfields glowing beyond. A young man was there, balanced on one of the little heaps of stone: the light made his body shine like gold; in the foreground a woman was grinding corn in a bowl.

They were watching too, but not watching the sunset. And when I squinted sideways I could see why. A party of men was winding through the fields, following the same path that we had taken earlier in the day, and all singing in unison. I knew them at once; one of their leaders was wearing Mr Stevenson's blue coat, still back to front with the tails flipping over his knees and the high collar covering his jaw.

The savages had finished their day's work and now they were swaggering home for food and congratulation, telling the village what they had found and showing them too: pewter cups from the captain's cabin; pans from the galley; a carved gilt picture-frame with no picture inside it.

Only the four men heading the party, including the one dressed in Mr Stevenson's coat, were carrying these bits and pieces. The eight who followed behind them had a much more significant task, and I thought would have swaggered much more boldly if they had not been so weighed down. If they had not been carrying two stretchers they had made out of sticks and rushes, and if these stretchers had not been stacked with our silver. Two large and heavy loads, glittering like an enormous catch of herring.

On the Island I had often troubled myself about the silver, thinking we should not call it ours. Yet when I saw it lugged along by these savages, and the smiles splitting their faces, and the other brutes rushing out from their tepees to gloat over it, I thought I had lost something I deserved to call my own. They might as well have broken into my father's house and robbed him while he slept. And robbed Mr Silver too, who in that moment I remembered as a reformed character, launching the *Nightingale* on her adventure simply to right a wrong and finish a story.

When they reached the chieftain's house opposite our prison they halted with a triumphant shout, and applause from the people now crowding around them. This noise finally woke Natty, who scuffled to my side. But we did not speak. We were too full of dread – and, if I am honest, of curiosity as well. The simplest actions seemed remarkable: the villagers returning to their tents and beginning to prepare for a feast – lighting fires, scouring pots, pouring oil, dropping in pieces of fish and meat and vegetable; the scavengers carrying the silver into their chieftain's house. Yet as each man disappeared with his load, or stepped back into the twilight empty-handed, smoothing his hair and straightening his tunic, he kept his eyes on the ground and never once looked in our direction. Even when the work was finished they still ignored us, leaving two of their tallest fellows as guards (who immediately lay down on the veranda of the house and fell asleep), while the rest carried away the stretchers they had made, and joined their families in the village.

As they withdrew, a woman and child broke from the shadows around the tepees. At first I thought they merely wanted to see the silver again, or to wake the guards who were meant to be protecting it. But when they reached the veranda they turned in our direction, drifting over the ground as if their feet hovered above the earth and did not actually touch it.

I signalled to Natty that we should shift away from our peephole, so they would not discover it and close it up again. This meant that when the door opened – after a little scuffle with the locking-pole

– we saw two silhouettes against the darkening sky, and could not read their expressions.

I wanted to say a friendly word and show we meant no harm, but as I was about to speak Natty put her hand on my shoulder. Our visitors kept silent as well, the child (a girl, no more than six or seven years old) staring and hunching a little, the mother more nearly upright and square-shouldered. So far as I could see, both wore the same sort of dress, made of hide and decorated with small stones. The mother's hair was pulled back from her face into a single long rope; the child's was worked into two smaller plaits that slid over her shoulders and swayed in the half-light.

Then the child stepped forward into the deeper darkness of the prison and towards our friend. I lost sight of her as she did this, but knew she had found him when I heard a grunt of pain – because she had kicked him or punched him. The mother chuckled, and when her daughter returned she nodded her head as a sign of approval.

I thought it would be our turn for some kind of insult next, but after piping a question to her mother, the child took from her two small bowls I had not previously noticed, and walked towards us very carefully, stopping a yard away; then she put them down on the ground without spilling a drop, before scuttling back to the doorway again and picking up the empty bowl we had left there.

I leaned closer to see what she had given us, but even this slight movement was too much for the child. She suddenly seized her mother by the hand and dragged her away from us over the threshold – at which our door banged shut, the locking-pole rasped into place, and the patter of their footsteps quickly faded. Although I was very hungry, and thirsty enough to have swallowed a whole barrel of water, I sat so still I might have been stunned; the turgid air of our prison swilled around us again, and the sour stink of our friend.

'They've gone,' I said after a little while, which was only to state the obvious.

'What is it?' Natty tipped onto her hands and knees and bent to sniff one of the bowls like a dog. 'Water,' she said cautiously. 'And this . . .' She dipped one of her fingers into the second bowl. 'This is porridge.'

'Porridge?' I almost smiled again. 'Surely you mean gruel?'

Natty sucked her finger-end. 'Acorns. They think we're pigs.' Then she sucked her fingers again. 'No, corn. Corn. Here.'

She was pointing to the water-bowl, meaning I should drink from it first. 'After you,' I told her, as if we were sitting at a table at home and minding our manners. As if, I thought in a flash, we were husband and wife.

Natty lifted the bowl to her lips and took two or three slow gulps, which made the saliva seep into my own mouth; then she passed it to me. The dusty liquid squeezed through my lips, over my parched tongue and sank heavily down my throat. I had never tasted anything so sweet; it almost knocked me unconscious.

'Jim,' I heard Natty say, which I thought meant she wanted more for herself. But when I gave her the bowl she climbed to her feet and disappeared towards our friend. I heard him swallow once, and felt the pang of not having helped a stranger myself; then she came back to my side and we shared the second bowl together.

She was right; it was corn, pulverised into a paste with some water added and foul-tasting as glue – but delicious all the same. When I had eaten a few mouthfuls, and Natty as well, I made amends for my neglect a moment before by taking the rest to our friend, and feeding him with my fingers; he was not able to swallow, and the mixture remained to harden on his lips.

I did not mention this when I came back to Natty, only placed the empty bowl beside its pair and sat down beside her again.

Another idea had occurred to me, which made me think the child and her mother were not angels after all. They had given us food to keep us alive – but not out of kindness. They had fed us like pigs for slaughter, so they could kill us whenever they chose.

CHAPTER 9

Black Cloud

When exactly does day become night? On the marshes at home I used to watch sunlight dropping from yellow to gold, from gold to purple, from purple to charcoal, all the time thinking that darkness would come soon – then glanced around to find it had fallen already. I had missed the moment of change!

In our new world the differences were more clear-cut. One minute the sun glared on the horizon, and a second later it had vanished completely. The darkness that flooded our cabin then was so deep, we might have been locked inside a stone.

'Natty,' I whispered, but she was asleep so I went back to my watching.

Very soon another kind of light sprang up, a bonfire blazing in the pit in the meeting-ground fifty yards off, and streaking the faces of everyone clustered around: women and children in the background, men closer to the centre.

Then a steady pulse began – tom-toms, played by a group of warriors sitting on the ground – and the remainder of the men began to dance. Not as we dance at home, in pairs or rows or columns, but rushing forward to make a ragged circle, jerking up their knees and pumping their arms like runners. As the smoke blew across them, making their bodies appear filmy and transparent, I thought they might have been lunatics in Bedlam, all screaming and yelping and lunging at one another with their spears.

Natty woke from her sleep at last, and so did our friend at the further end of the prison; we heard him whimpering like a puppy as if he knew the meaning of everything we had heard outside, and how it would end.

And sure enough, when the drumbeats began pounding more fiercely than ever, two of the dancers lurched away from their circle and raced up the slope towards us. After they had unlocked and opened our door, which made me and Natty scramble away into a corner, they stared around for a moment as if they really believed our friend might have escaped, which was merely a piece of cruel theatre, then plunged towards the end of the cabin and seized him and hauled him outside, pausing only to lock our door behind them.

As he sank down the slope away from us, I saw our friend forget his sickness and begin twisting between his guards like a wildcat – lurching and reeling, stumbling and rising, swaying forward and then heaving back. They dragged him straight to the meeting-ground and so to the fire, which had now sunk low in its pit and glimmered bright crimson, splashed with traces of pale ash.

All this happened so quickly I had no chance to feel any horror; I just stared in silence, even when the guards took our friend to the far end of the pit, where he faced the crowd and our prison on the slope above, then lashed his left arm to a stake driven into the ground beside the fire and swung on the rope to make it tight. Once this was done, they seized his right arm and tied it to a second stake planted nearby, which meant he was canted forward like a diver, teetering on tiptoes to escape the worst of the heat. But this was no help, because the guards simply heaped fresh brushwood into the pit and made the flames revive. Everyone watching enjoyed this; they clapped and moaned and sighed like the crowd at a circus.

Natty pushed away from her place beside me at our peephole. 'Jim,' she said, in a shaking voice. 'Don't look any more!'

I could not answer and I could not move.

'Jim,' she said again, but muffled now, and glancing round I saw she had curled into a ball, closing her eyes and pressing her hands over her ears.

I still did not move. I had the idea that I must see the worst, so I would be able to meet my own death more bravely when the time came, and looked back to the fire-pit again. The two guards were now standing either side of our friend, but a little behind him to escape the heat. The larger one was holding a knife – I saw the blade gleam – and I thought he was about to kill him. But the knife made only a casual sort of strike, a lazy stab and twist that left him still alive. Yet the wound was wide enough. Wide enough, that is, for the other guard to push his hand inside our friend's stomach, and ferret around, and catch hold of a piece of gut, and drag it out, and keep dragging it inch by inch like a fisherman pulling in a line, until it lay at our friend's feet in a slimy coil.

Our friend made no sound in his agony, not a single cry, and I continued staring.

I watched the guards take hold of a pair of wooden clubs given to them by others in the crowd. Then I watched while they began walloping our friend's legs and back. Then, when he could no longer cringe from the heat, I watched his body slump forward and the pool of his guts slide into the fire-pit and begin to roast.

Now at last I turned away and sank onto the ground. At the same time, I felt my mind expanding suddenly, travelling beyond the wilderness and the night-creatures around our prison until I came to the marshes near my home in the Hispaniola. I saw the moonlight there, quivering in creeks and gullies. I saw the flocks of white gulls sleeping on the mudbanks. I saw my father at home in his bedroom, with the Thames rippling beneath his window and the night-traffic of coal barges and other ships casting their shadows across the water. I did not spy into his face because I did not want to remember how unhappy I had made him. Neither did I want to catch myself in the room, because I knew it would remind me of how I had knelt beside the chest at the foot of his bed, and how I had betrayed him by stealing the map of the Island.

I wanted to be there, but invisible. I wanted to inhale the scent of the rush matting on the floor; to hear the lovely regular tick-tock of the clock, and the faint scratch of its minute hand passing round the dial; to remember the surprising tidiness with which my father laid out his clothes for the morning, like a boy nervous for his school-day. To find everything I had known from my own childhood, and would find waiting for me when I returned.

When I returned. If I returned. The words trampled on each other, and I shook my head from side to side in the silvery floor-dust.

'Have they finished?' Natty whispered, lifting her hands away from her ears, opening her eyes again.

'Yes, they've finished,' I said, which was the second white lie I had told her. I could not hear our friend, but I thought the savages must still be at work on him, slicing off his scalp and other parts.

Natty did not speak after that and neither did I. Maybe I slept. Maybe I stared at the ceiling in silence. All I know is that time passed and we were still alive when the sun rose, and still able to feel grateful when our door creaked open again, and our guardian angels flew in from the sunlight and put more food and water before us.

When I thought of these two standing in the crowd I had seen a few hours before, I knew they must be devils as well as angels – which should have made the food revolting. But it did not. Although Natty and I both rolled away into the shadows as they gave us our meal, we scrambled forward soon enough when they left us, and the door shut behind them again.

In this way our routine was settled; one meal after sunrise each day, one around sunset, and both always the same water and corn-paste. In between: nothing – for ten days, twenty days, a month. Splinters of misty dawn, bursts of bright sun, smears of evening, streaks of moon. Mosquitoes attacking when they were hungry, otherwise jigging above our heads. Laughter, or cries, or shouts from the world beyond. Dog barks and turkey gobbles. Goats bleating. Long vigils at our peephole, where I learned the ways of the village so well I might almost have been a part of it – watching the men and women set off to the fields, and mill grain, and make oil, and sweep and cook and quarrel and reconcile.

It felt almost like sympathy, and came with a consequence I never imagined. For the better I knew our enemies the more remote I became from my only true friend. From Natty, I mean. Over the long days and the longer nights our conversation stumbled and stalled. Our minds shrivelled. Even our small acts of kindness ended – holding hands while we fell asleep, lying in one another's arms. Our old selves, our original selves, wandered off from one another. We were separate now, together but separate.

And what was I doing when this wandering ended at last? Not planning my escape any more; not poised for action. I was kneeling in a corner staring at a spider as he worked in a crack in our walls, thinking how clever his web-making was; how ingenious. A fly was caught there, drawn in no doubt by the smell of our waste, which was bad however carefully we buried it in a corner under the dust. After a minute of buzzing and struggling he lay still, and the spider prowled forward to engulf him.

When I returned from this, it was to hear that a palaver had broken out in the village: boys shouting, footsteps running, children crying for their mothers, and mothers calling for their children. I left my spider to enjoy his meal and pressed my face to my peephole, brushing the hair from my eyes – my hair which was now long and matted. The tepees were all deserted, and so was the track leading back towards the Black Bay, yet the earth itself had a look of expectancy, such as I have often noticed while walking along a lane in England before a traveller appears. The dust seemed to be shivering slightly, readying itself. I knew at once who must be about to arrive.

The chieftain. Our judge and jury. Black Cloud, to give him his proper name, which I was soon to learn.

When he first strode round the curve of the path and everyone in the village surged forward to greet him, stretching out their hands to touch, screeching and hollering, I had only a general sort of impression. He was broad-shouldered, muscular, thickly covered in decorations, wearing moccasins and a tunic that reached to his knees. More strangely, I thought he seemed to *shine*; to glow with a faint and silvery light. Beside him was a smaller man, more compact, also wearing a tunic and moccasins, but with his face and arms and legs all streaked with red and yellow paint. And padding behind them, two savages I recognised from the Black Bay; they were leading almost identical brown ponies, which were smeared with sweat because they had been ridden hard.

Natty crept up beside me. We were both wide awake now and had to see everything; our lives would depend on it.

When Black Cloud reached the veranda opposite our prison, which meant he and the painted man were only some ten yards away from us, he turned towards the crowd and raised his arms; there was a gasp and then silence, broken by a dog yelping as it was driven away with a stone.

Now I saw why Black Cloud seemed to shine; why a luminous power seemed to hover around him. He was wearing a necklace that dazzled whether the sun struck it directly or not, and kept a pulse of light alive in his whole body. A necklace made of ten or twelve slim oblong silver pieces that were strung on a thin leather band. These pieces were longest at the centre, three or four inches, then gradually smaller as they spread outwards across his chest in a fan shape. When he lifted a hand to adjust them, a moan ran through the crowd and they knelt down and pressed their foreheads to the earth.

Black Cloud took his time, letting his gaze wander here and there as though he was counting everyone in the village, absorbing news of their existence since he had seen them last, allowing his power to flow out and weigh them down and return to him again.

Only when he felt sure of their devotion did he speak – a strangled roar consisting entirely of z's and x's, which I suppose meant something like 'dismiss', for the whole village then rose as one body, and meekly turned and went back to their tepees, many of them shaking their heads at the wonder they had seen.

The last men to disappear were the two in charge of the ponies; they now led them to the further side of the main house, tethered them to the halter-rail, fed and watered them, and rubbed them down with handfuls of dried grass before bowing to Black Cloud and slipping away to the village to join the others.

Black Cloud remained on his veranda, sometimes casting a glance in their direction to make sure everything was done as he wanted, mostly staring at the village and breathing deeply. He seemed absolutely content, absolutely fixed and solid. His companion beside him – whom I shall call the Painted Man, having never heard his name – was less . . . not less impressive, but less comprehensible. The decorations covering his body were not all one shade of red, as I had first thought, but many different colours, with dabs of yellow ochre and white and even pale green. In a different place he would have looked garish. Here he was sinister and important.

Black Cloud himself I could only see in profile, standing with his legs slightly apart like a massive statue and his thick arms hanging loose at his sides. His hair was pulled back from his forehead but worn much longer than his warriors', and criss-crossed into a single plait that reached to his waist; there were feathers worked into it, mostly white, but also bright green and blue, which must have come from some species of parrot. His costume was decorated with fragments of shell similar to those used by the women to prettify their dresses.

And the dazzle, the shimmer lifting off him? That was mainly due to the necklace as I have said, but also to the oil he had rubbed over his body. He had varnished himself like a painting, so the markings that covered his arms and face all came alive when he moved and showed the energy fizzing inside him.

When I had finished my inspection my heart was beating as quickly as if I had been running.

'Do you . . .' I began saying to Natty, but she would not look in my direction, and only put her finger to her lips; her hand was shaking.

I turned back to Black Cloud meaning to admire his necklace again – and I was immediately distracted, this time by the belt tied around his waist. It was plain enough, made of leather strips and fastened with a wooden pin, but there were trophies strung from it. Wood, I thought at first, then looked again. Not wood. Fingers and ears, in fact, and other scraps of flesh, some still caked with dark red blood. By the time I flinched away, I thought nothing would be impossible to Black Cloud. He would wreck and possess everything he wanted.

Then Black Cloud and the Painted Man began speaking about us. We knew this, because by pointing towards the horizon, then behind them into their house, they showed they knew about the silver, and if they knew about the silver, they knew about their prisoners. To judge by the way Black Cloud sneered at our cabin, while the Painted Man threw back his head and rolled his eyes, I thought they must already have settled how they would deal with us – but not yet. At their leisure. After glaring towards us once more, and scowling and stamping his foot, Black Cloud swung away and disappeared into his house, with the Painted Man following.

Natty and I let a few minutes pass, thinking they might make a quick recce of the treasure and then return to us. But when the silence settled more deeply, and a flock of sparrows landed on the veranda of the house and began picking about in the dust, and the shadows lengthened, we left our peephole and settled down by the wall again.

I felt so sure we had only a few more hours to live, perhaps until the evening, when we would be barbecued in the same way as our friend, that I found it astonishing my curiosity about the world should survive. Yet while we awaited our final judgement it was always the most ordinary things that caught our keenest interest. The heat and the mosquitoes. The faint squeak of the oyster-dust shifting beneath our weight. The spider, back at his butchery. Does every condemned man feel the same in the hours before his execution? I expect so, but to anyone who has not suffered in this way, the idea will seem very peculiar.

And this is how Black Cloud and the Painted Man found us, when they decided to give us their attention again. Not cowering in fright in the furthest corner of our prison, or kneeling as we made peace with our Maker, but lolling side by side as we had done every previous day, watching the sun-patterns in the cracks of our walls.

They tore our door open and stood on the threshold; although it was afternoon, the light dazzled me for a moment, then settled into a border of gold that clung around their silhouettes. Neither of them spoke. They stared – and after so many days spent living in dread, I found I was able to meet their gaze. If this was courage I have no idea, but it pleased me to keep my dignity and see Natty do the same.

When Black Cloud eventually broke his silence, he poured his voice very neatly into the ear of the Painted Man, pressing the open palm of his right hand against the necklace to make sure it stayed flat against his chest; I saw it gleam between his fingers. The Painted Man smiled, and nodded, then leaped forward and grabbed us by our shirt-collars, dragging us over the floor and flinging us down at his master's feet. Here, with what remained of the daylight shining directly into our eyes, Black Cloud examined each of us in turn.

He began by seizing my chin – his fingers smelled of charcoal – twisting my head first this way while at the same time running his free hand across my arms and shoulders, sometimes squeezing my flesh through the filthy cotton of my shirt. Although this alarmed me very much, I understood he was taking a rough measurement of my youth and my strength. When he had calculated these things, and no doubt put a value on them, he let me go – but only to grip me by my hair and tug me upright so that he could complete the process by fondling my legs and buttocks.

I lifted my eyes towards the roof of the prison and concentrated on the spiders and other crawling things that lived there, watching how they continued their spinning and eating without paying me any attention. Then I began to think I would keep better control of myself if I did some assessing of my own. I therefore looked down from the ceiling and stared directly at Black Cloud, as if he did not scare me in the least. Although I had scrutinised him as closely as possible when he first arrived in the village, I had felt rather blinded by his decorations and suchlike. Now I concentrated on the man himself.

He was twice my age and six inches shorter than me but much more strongly built, with a deep barrel chest and thick strong muscles like ropes in his neck and shoulders and arms. In England I had heard of athletes who were capable of running for hours at a stretch; this man looked as though he would gallop all day and never feel short of breath. There was a tirelessness about him, a machine efficiency, just as there was also something unnatural about the hardness of his expression. My stare seemed to bounce off his face like a pebble off iron.

The longer I looked, the more strongly I felt Black Cloud belonged to another species than my own, not merely another race. Especially when he decided he had finished with me, punched me in the chest so I staggered back into the shadows, and turned to Natty. Now he seemed even more heartless. After dragging her towards him he examined her as dispassionately as a surgeon, running his fingers over her face and hair, poking them inside her mouth to feel along her teeth, thrusting them inside her shirt to squeeze and pinch her there, then sliding his hands to and fro between her legs.

Because I was standing behind Natty at this point I could not see her face, only that she shifted her weight very nervously, and sometimes rose onto tiptoe to lessen the pressure of his touch. Black Cloud's face, however, was plain to see – when I wished it were not. His fleshy lips had broken into a gargoyle smile; his mouth was ajar and the tip of his tongue was flickering over his lips; his black eyes were glittering. When he thrust Natty away from him at last and gave a horrible grunt, it might have been the beginning of a laugh.

This was followed by a torrent of other sounds – words clashing together so angrily he had to wipe the spittle from his lips when he finished. At which point the Painted Man hauled me forward until I was standing beside Natty and close to his master again. I thought we were about to hear our death sentence. Instead, Black Cloud reached up and began thumping on our heads with his clenched fist. As we sank back onto our knees, with the power of his blows making stars shoot inside my head, he began to speak. Two words, which he repeated in time with his hammering. Two words, which resonated like the notes of a bell.

Black Cloud.

Black Cloud.

Black Cloud.

He had spoken in English! Although my head continued to reel and splinter as the massive hand kept pounding on my skull, I nevertheless clung to this thought. English! Why? Because he must have met traders from Europe, or other travellers such as missionaries and preachers. I could not keep the idea in place for long, but his words themselves burned in me very brightly.

I was right; Natty and I were not alone in the wilderness.

As soon as my beating ended, with Black Cloud breathing heavily and his arms swinging loose at his sides, I wanted to keep with this idea but could not. I was trapped again by the treasure around his neck; the colour, the glow, the weight were irresistible to me. All the more so when I noticed for the first time that each of the strips of silver was covered with carvings – of animals mostly: deer and rabbits and snakes and bear and horses all very delicately fashioned, with tiny blue stones for eyes and a border around each of them made of the same blue stones. On the largest pieces, at the centre of the necklace, these carvings were bold and definite; in the smaller pieces towards the edges of the fan-shape they were more intricate, even more skilful and marvellous.

I was part of the same world as these creatures – that is the notion I seized on then, and as Black Cloud eventually stepped away from us I knew I was not weaker but stronger than before. He had reminded me that if we could only escape our prison we had no reason to fear the wilderness. We could survive there.

For this reason I did not even flinch when he shouted his name once more, then whirled on his heel and stalked outside into the twilight. I think I may even have smiled when the Painted Man followed, slammed our door, locked it, and kicked it several times to show he would set about us himself when he returned.

CHAPTER 10

The Open Door

As Black Cloud retreated and Natty and I sank back into darkness, I felt sure we were safe for this evening at least. I even remained in good heart when our supper failed to appear, and a rumpus broke out in the village below. Listening to the yells and chatter, I told myself it must simply be the start of a feast: a celebration.

And so it proved. An hour after sunset Black Cloud arrived in the central meeting-place of the village, where drums were already pounding and women cooking over a fire, and sat down cross-legged on an arrangement of furs and blankets that made a kind of throne, with the Painted Man settled beside him. It was clear that all they wanted was to wolf down the next bowl of food their warriors brought them, and the next bowl of drink, and then the next, and then the next, and then the next.

I soon grew tired of watching and turned away from our peep-hole, but after I had dozed for a while I was awoken by the sound of shouting close to our cabin. Peering outside once more I saw that the meeting-place was almost empty, the fire a heap of embers, and the villagers wandering back to their tents. Black Cloud and the Painted Man were only a few yards from our door, with their arms wrapped around one another's shoulders; I knew from the way they both stumbled over empty air that they were very drunk.

Theirs were the shouts I had heard – oaths and snatches of song such as I knew from late nights at the Hispaniola, when men had sometimes lost their way home entirely and staggered into the Thames. There was no danger of these two disappearing for ever, however much I wished it, and however wildly they swung from one side of their track to the other; in due course they confronted the two steps up to the veranda with a solemn thoughtfulness, made their wavering ascent, and found the entrance to the house with another burst of singing.

After they had fallen indoors and the village was silent again, I left my place and lay down beside Natty. I thought she must be awake but we did not speak, only stared into the darkness and listened to one another breathing, while the night-wind swept across the country outside, sometimes rising to a moan as it passed through the cracks in our walls, and at others peppering them with dust.

As always at such moments, when I thought of the world now lost to me, I found myself slipping away to my childhood. The faces of my father, of school-friends, of Natty and Mr Silver, of his wife haranguing me in her wedding-cake dress, of Captain Beamish and the bo'sun, all appeared in succession, and I was able to stare carefully into each, and pay them due attention. Why was I so deliberate and particular? Because now that I thought my death was closer than ever, I wanted to say farewell to one and all, just as I also wanted to say goodbye to the country near the Hispaniola, which I did by wandering among the outbuildings where my father kept his puncheons for the taproom, and noticing how the muddy green levels beyond them were changed into lilac where they reached the horizon.

As I came to the end of these travels I was distracted by a change outside in the darkness. A very dim sound at first, like sand dropping through an hourglass. Then more definite, so I knew it was footsteps. Then stronger still, and turning into a dry little squeal as our locking-pole was pulled aside.

Black Cloud! That was my first thought. I had been wrong a moment before; drunk or not, he had come to finish us. But I steadied myself. When I had seen him vanish into his house he had been almost unconscious; every movement I could hear now was nimble and quick, so it could not possibly be him, who anyway had no reason to be secretive.

I craned forward to catch the least sound, and for a moment there was nothing more. I took a breath. Still nothing. Then another breath – which turned into a gulp as the air split with a hideous explosion (which was almost no noise at all), and the door opened, and the deep sky appeared, freckled with thousands of stars and a nearly-full moon burning at the centre.

'Natty,' I hissed, shaking her shoulder, 'Natty.'

She woke at once, but only to roll into a ball again with her knees up and her hands covering her face, because she thought the end had come, and blows were about to hammer down on us. From her groans, it sounded as though her bones might already be breaking.

'It's all right,' I said. 'There's no danger.'

She gasped and uncurled herself. She sat up, and reached out to squeeze my hand. It was the boldest sign of our feelings that either one of us had shown for a long time, and in that simple pressure I felt our lives flow back together. We had not been separated from one another after all. We had been living in parallel. Everything we felt for each other, our trust and tenderness, was still as it had always been.

'What?' she whispered.

'I don't know,' I told her.

'Who, then?'

This time I did have the answer, because a silhouette had stepped across our threshold. Thanks to the braids of hair dangling either side of her face, I recognised the child who had brought us our food and drink – until today. Did this mean she would now give us our ration, which she had not wanted to do during the daylight in case Black Cloud disapproved? I thought so until I saw she was empty-handed, and without her mother, and stepping forward more boldly than usual.

Natty and I were bolt upright now, both of us with our long hair in our eyes, and our clothes smeared with dirt and oyster-dust. The child was not in the least perturbed; it was only what she expected. She merely stretched out her hand to touch Natty's face and then mine.

As a sign of friendship this was very welcome, or should have been. In fact the child was extremely anxious, her breath coming in quick little gulps, so I thought she might fly away at any minute, bolting the door behind her.

'Shhhh,' I said, to reassure her.

The child stared wide-eyed, clasping her hands together.

'Will she rescue us?' Natty asked in a whisper; she was more and more like her old self, concentrated and eager. The light was back in her face and the warmth in her voice.

'Perhaps.'

'Let me see,' said Natty, and promptly became so skittish I almost laughed aloud. For instead of continuing to encourage the child with a soft voice and reassurances, she rolled her eyes and stuck her thumbs in her ears, waggling her fingers.

The child half-turned as if about to vanish, but in the second or two of delay she changed her mind. She smiled. She stepped forward and gripped Natty's hands, then slowly leaned closer still, until the tip of her nose rubbed against Natty's nose, when she spoke a single word that sounded like a growl but I thought must be affectionate.

The child then came to stand in front of me, where she repeated the same action and the same word; although the touch of her skin was almost too faint to feel, a charge passed through me that I suppose was gratitude – for the contact; for the kindness.

And after that, the greatest marvel of all. The child skipped away to the threshold, stretching out one arm and pointing at the sky.

There was no mistaking what she meant. She was giving us our freedom, although she did not want to stay and see us find it. As soon as she had raised her arm she let it fall again and melted into the darkness. This happened so suddenly she might as well have been swallowed by a giant or else not have existed at all; I could not hear her feet pattering down the slope to the village, nor when I scrambled upright and stared after her could I see so much as a shadow stirring. Everything lay suspended and silent under the huge bowl of the stars.

Natty loomed at my shoulder, softly closing the door of our prison behind us, pulling the locking-pole across, then whispering, 'Come on!' and turning down the slope towards Black Cloud's house. The sight of her darting ahead of me made my heart leap as I followed. This was the Natty I had known from the first, daredevil and free, her own self again. And our direction? I assumed we were going for the ponies, which had already heard us and were churning at their halter-rail – they thought we might feed them.

But as we reached the veranda I found Natty had something else on her mind. Something that came before anything, although she had never mentioned it.

She stopped running and began prowling. She began gliding. She began floating, until we had left the solid earth and come to the front entrance of Black Cloud's house, lifting aside the blanket that served as his door.

We crept inside as quietly as cats, and found ourselves in a courtyard that was open to the sky, with doorways on every side and a temple at the centre, well lit by the moon and stars. Carved wooden eagles were perched on the roof, facing north, south, east and west, and a low wall made of wooden stakes surrounded it, each crowned with a human skull. One was caked around the chin with ashes, and I thought must be all that remained of our friend.

I pushed the idea away and continued forward, entering another doorway off to the right which took us into a smaller courtyard. My eyes were jittery now but I told myself to keep steady, to keep paying attention, and a moment later I had my reward. The walls of the yard had been hollowed out to make cavities, all of which were filled with precious things: trinkets and ornaments; head-dresses; drums; spears with feathers tied around their necks. And in the largest alcove of all – our treasure. The silver pilfered from the *Nightingale*. All piled very neatly like a stack of bricks.

I felt no surprise. Of course they would keep it here. Of course they would think it was safe, guarded by a god who required the sacrifice of human heads, and who loved fire, and burning, and ash. Of course Black Cloud would keep beside him a man decorated like the Painted Man. Because the Painted Man was a fire spirit. A spirit of the god.

Natty glanced towards the silver but we said nothing; we both accepted that we would never have our treasure again. Besides, she wanted something else, and whatever it was she had decided it lay beyond this courtyard, in the furthest part of the house.

I followed her through the next doorway and stepped into a room with two large windows – both barred with strong pieces of wood – where the moonlight poured through in twin torrents. I was blinded for a moment – and then, when my sight cleared, dazzled again by a wonderful confusion. I saw embroideries with deer leaping across them, and hawks flying, and flowers coiling around one another; I saw rugs heaped on the floor and a rack of shelves with stones and shells strewn all over them; I saw glass bottles; I saw pieces of wood carved into grotesque horns and tusks.

There was no time to think what any of these might mean or where they came from. Immediately in front of us was a large wooden bed that appeared to be floating on the moonlight, and here Black Cloud and the Painted Man lay deeply asleep. They were face to face with their arms draped around one another's shoulders.

They would kill us if they awoke, I knew that; murder us and tear us to pieces. But for a moment my life was not my own, and I found myself creeping forward until I was leaning over them, gazing into their faces.

The Painted Man was still daubed with his red and yellow fire-patterns, but now that I stood so close to him I could see these colours were very cracked and thin. He was no more than a boy, his eyelids quivering as a dream slithered through his mind.

As for Black Cloud: I thought I was staring at Death itself. At my own death, which I would only control if I did not flinch. I therefore held my gaze as though I had all the time in the world, poring over the markings on his neck and cheek, and the gliding muscles in his arm, and the oiled shell of his ear, with a fragment of bone stuck through the lobe.

Was it brave, to look so long? Not at all, as I proved the moment Black Cloud rolled onto his back, blowing out his lips with a wet pop-popping sound. The hair lifted on my scalp in pure fear. But even then I stayed as I was, lingering over the sweat shining in his hair, and the violet veins in his throat, and the bulge of his Adam's apple.

In the end it was Natty who drew me away, whispering my name and wanting my help. 'I can't find it here,' she said, hunched over a wooden chest at the bed-end, sifting through its tangle of skins and other trophies. 'Where . . .'

At last I began my own search, my hunt for what we still had not mentioned to one another. And with a kind of magic I found it easily, by opening a plain wooden box that Black Cloud kept at his bedside. The necklace was shining up at me; he had laid it to rest for the night on a cushion of turkey feathers.

I felt my blood surge through me from head to foot as though my whole body had swollen. I did not hesitate for a second. I picked up the necklace and bowed my head and fitted it around my neck, with the knot of its leather tie resting on my nape. As the weight of the silver pieces pressed against me, and I ran my hand across the decorations, caressing the contours of the animals and the hard protuberances of their jewel-eyes and jewel-borders, I thought my skin began to shine.

Natty appeared at my side. 'Perfect,' she breathed, putting her face close to mine. She might as well have said I was perfect; she might as well have told me she loved me. I seemed to inhale the word rather than hear it.

'Perfect,' she whispered again.

I looked into her eyes and saw that the glow of the silver had carried into them; it was shining up at me like light reflecting off the bed of a stream.

'I know,' I told her, and wanted to say more. But she did not need any more. She dabbed her fingers against her lips, kissed them, and lightly touched the necklace, to show that she understood. Then she turned out of the bedroom and led me through the smaller courtyard, through the larger space where the eagles kept their vigil, and outside onto the veranda. It was astonishing to see our prison again, squatting on the rising ground to our right, and the village cradled in its valley. We had plunged so deeply into a different world, I thought the old one might no longer exist.

'Wait,' Natty told me, still very practical and busy, then doubled back through the entrance to the house. I could not think what else we might need, but stepped into the shadows of the veranda to wait for her.

We shall soon be away was all I could think, and away was everything I wanted. Away from Black Cloud. Away from the village. Away from lives that were never our own.

And towards . . .

But that would come later. For the moment there was only the wilderness stretching before me. A vast, flat, rolling ocean of grass and boulders and rocks and dust. Dust whispering when the wind rose, and dust lying in silence when the wind died.

Natty came back to me then. I had no need to ask what she had wanted, because she was already showing me: a hunk of flatbread; two pairs of moccasins; a water-bottle, filled with water by the sound of it; and a leather satchel. I clapped my hands when I saw them – but silently.

'Well, Jim,' Natty said. 'What did you think we'd live on?'

'I . . .'

'And walk on?'

'I didn't . . .'

'No,' she said, and then with a smile in her voice she added, 'But you'll have to keep me close now, won't you, to look after you?'

'I will,' I told her. 'And I will keep you safe, Natty.'

She smiled again – her wide smile! – then remembered we must hurry and made me take off the necklace, slide it into the satchel, and put the strap around my neck. When I had done this she dropped our flatbread into the other satchel, took charge of it herself, and said we should put on our moccasins.

We crept out from the veranda and towards the left-hand side of Black Cloud's house, the part that was shielded by the windbreak, where the two ponies were tethered to their rail. Once again, their fidgets told me they thought we might feed them, and this time I did collect a bowlful of grain from a barrel that stood nearby, so I could look around for a pair of bridles while they were munching; we found these easily enough, then chose which of the ponies we wanted as ours and got them ready.

The whole turnaround took no more than a minute, but I have described it in detail because of the pleasure it gave me. Every action felt like a proof that we were ourselves again. And not only that. It reminded me of my childhood, and of the pony my father had bought me then. She had been an affable old piebald who greatly preferred snoozing to any sort of exercise; these two ponies were chestnuts, very lean and quick-looking, with white blazes on their noses and black manes and tails. I had liked them at once, when I first saw them led into the village; now I could see they would suit us very well.

We jumped astride and I looked back to our prison on the further side of Black Cloud's lodge, thinking we would ride towards it and then turn into open country; where we stood now we were prevented by the windbreak, which was raised about four feet tall.

But as I began to tug at my reins and set off, a demon entered into Natty, the same that possessed her to steal the necklace in the first place. For instead of following where I meant to go, she turned her pony to face this windbreak, thrashed with her heels, and leaped over it almost from a standing start.

My own pony immediately twisted round and leaped forward as well, so that before I knew it I had also left the ground – and landed on it again in a clattery scrape. I shook myself, settled the satchel around my neck, and looked up.

The emptiness before me tore open then. Tore open and began to fly past, becoming fragments of green and brown and grey and wind and thorn and our own voices shouting without a care who might hear us, because our enemies – oh! our enemies would never catch us now, nor would they ever find us again.

PART II

THE WILDERNESS

CHAPTER II

Under the Stars

I had no idea how long we rode or how far; I was too excited. Too excited, too grateful to be free, too relieved, too astonished, and too frightened as well. Frightened more than anything, if I am honest. After weeks in our prison, after what might have been months, I had lost my sense of balance in the world, and careered headlong into the darkness.

In the end our ponies decided we must slow down, because they ran out of breath. And where were we then? Nowhere. A dry valley in an empty desert; a gully between walls of ragged stone. Logic told me it must be the dried-up bed of an ancient stream; now it was a natural trail where no one had walked before us.

'Still to the north?' Natty was breathless as well but her words swelled in the silence, echoing off the rocks.

'Yes, still north,' I told her, because I had managed to take a rough sort of direction from the stars.

'And after that?'

'Home,' I said.

Natty chuckled; she was already herself again. 'North is home, I suppose.'

'North-east,' I said.

'So precise!'

'Well, isn't home what you want?'

'And adventure as well.'

'I am sure that will come,' I said doubtfully. 'But home at the end – I hope.'

'Hope,' Natty said in a sing-song. 'Hope, hope, hope.' She was swaying in rhythm with her pony, still buoyant, still exultant. 'And north is as good a direction as any; wherever we go, it takes us further from Black Cloud.'

I let my reins droop in my hands. By mentioning Black Cloud at all, even so briefly, Natty had reminded me that our enemy could travel wherever he wanted, and equally well in darkness as light, because this was his world and he knew it minutely.

'What do you think?' I said. 'Will we find people to help us?'

The walls of our little valley had suddenly melted away and we were riding through open country again, with the wind blowing dust in our faces. 'Oh, friends are everywhere,' Natty said, and shielded her eyes to look around; I thought she expected faces would appear there and then, smiling among the dim rocks and shrubs.

'But how will we know they are friends?' I asked her doggedly.

'Because they'll be enemies of Black Cloud,' she told me. 'They'll be our enemy's enemy, you see? It's the same anywhere. We know what he's like. We know what he does to anyone not from his tribe.'

'But Natty, we don't,' I said. 'We saw the others, not him. We saw . . .' I could not finish what I had in mind, because I could not bear the memory of the fire roaring in its pit, and the punishment I had seen there.

'That's not the point,' Natty replied, and although her voice was still calm, it seemed tighter now. 'Black Cloud and his tribe are the same,' she said. 'That's why he must have enemies – thousands of them probably. The whole country must be filled with people who want him dead.'

'But where are they?' I went on. 'We haven't seen anyone.'

Natty pointed up to the sky and the stars blazing above us – a river of stars, a torrent flooding the whole universe of the sky. She had run out of patience. 'Jim,' she said with a sigh. 'Look. It's the middle of the night. In the daytime of course there'll be people.' Then she dropped her hand and slapped it against her knee, before adding one more thing.

'He'll come after us, though,' she said.

My hand darted to the satchel around my neck, touching the outline of the silver; I imagined it curled in its darkness like a dozing animal.

'What do you mean?' I said.

'He'll want the necklace back,' she said. 'And he'll follow us to the ends of the earth to get it.'

It was only what I knew in my heart, but it made me stop dead and for a moment the wilderness overwhelmed me. The barren land, the dry weeds scraping over stones, the little twisted trees – they were all different sorts of nothing. An immense nothing that renewed itself continually, and poured itself out continually over the whole surface of the world.

'Are you all right?' Natty asked; she had seen my head sink down, and now she was gentler again.

'I'm sorry,' I told her. 'But I was thinking – we've only tricked Black Cloud, haven't we? We haven't defeated him.'

'I dare say,' she said, not at all abashed. 'But it doesn't matter. We'll keep tricking him.'

'Are you sure?'

'To tell the truth,' she said, 'I'm not sure of anything – but that doesn't matter either, or not tonight. I'm sure we can find a way. We'll get home somehow.' Then she unhooked our water-bottle from around her neck and offered me a drink, and took the flatbread from her satchel and tore off a piece for me to eat.

It was the simplest sort of kindness, the sort any good friend might do for another, but in that desolate place at that desolate time, the effect was very powerful. I felt the wide horizons shrink closer, and myself breathing safely at their centre, and when I stared around me again I saw that the desert was not a barren wilderness any more, but dressed everywhere in sweet grass and sage and thyme. This is the beginning of my freedom, I told myself; the time I start to believe that I can live.

Half an hour later, when we had ambled forward another mile or so, I was almost lost again. We reached a point where our track took another turn between high rock walls, and because we could not ride two abreast in such a narrow space, we decided that Natty should take the lead while I followed behind. When this passage ended, we found ourselves in a natural enclosure surrounded by low cliffs – a shape like the crater a water-drop makes, when it falls onto a still surface. And in the centre of this crater we saw a cluster of rough stone lodges, arranged in a grid of streets. Apparently they were all abandoned, standing silent and empty under the moonlight. But then, as we continued forward, we realised they were not merely abandoned. They were ruined. Destroyed. Every doorway was scorched, every roof broken, every little garden or field trampled down.

I wanted to turn and run at once; we both did. But our curiosity pushed us forward, and soon we found what I already knew we must. There were corpses lying among the ruins. Indians. Two dozen perhaps, and by the look of them all just a few days dead. Young men who had been hacked down by knives or shot by arrows, with the scalps sliced from their heads. Women stripped of their clothes and left to rot among the thistles. Children butchered beside their mothers – one still holding her toy, which was a stick carved into the shape of a snake, with bright little beads for eyes.

I could not speak, only glance and then glance away, and when I heard Natty trotting back towards the entrance-place I followed immediately. I found her sitting straight and still in the passage between the rock walls.

'Black Cloud?' she said, her voice echoing softly.

I shook my head. 'It can't be him,' I said, with the same hollow sound shadowing my words. 'He can't have done so much, not by himself.'

Natty kept still, her shoulders slumped and her eyes gazing into the distance. 'Where were they, then?' she asked. 'What was he doing, him and that other one, before they came back to the village?'

'I don't know, Natty,' I said. 'But they weren't here. Think about it. There are only two of them and there are, what, twenty-five people here, thirty?'

But Natty would not answer me; she had decided Black Cloud was so powerful he could do anything he liked, and the longer her silence lasted, the more I began to doubt everything I had just told her. I remembered the scalps and other barbaric pieces I had seen dangling from Black Cloud's belt. Had he really collected them here? All of them? I touched the satchel around my neck, and his face appeared to me beside the Painted Man on their nest of blankets. My heart had softened towards him then, because I had seen their kindness to one another; now it shrivelled and shook.

'Are you coming?' Natty was suddenly impatient, kicking her pony in the ribs and expecting me to follow. At another time I might have felt this as a rebuke, because for a moment we had disagreed. Now, when I trotted after her and we headed towards the north again, I knew that her fears were the same as mine. Black Cloud was everywhere. He was racing in the star-rivers above us, and dancing behind us as lightly as the dust. He was the wind and the silence. He was the crackle of grass and the scuffle of claws.

He was here! On the crest of a small hill only a hundred yards ahead! But that was impossible. It was not a human shape – it was something even more astonishing. A building. A single tall room that seemed to have dropped from thin air. A room made of mud and straw with a pitched roof and a little crucifix above the door.

'A chapel.' Natty was the first to collect her wits, hauling on her reins and bringing us both to a halt. Her voice was full of wonder.

'A chapel?' I was much slower. 'Why here? There's no one to convert. There's no parish.'

Natty laughed at the word, at the very idea. 'No,' she said. 'But plenty of heathen.'

'You mean those poor devils behind us? There was no sign there of . . .'

'Conversion?' Natty slid off her pony and I followed. We took our animals by their halters and tethered them to a stump near the entrance. It loomed at me, a square of velvety blackness, and to show that I had not deserved Natty's impatience a little earlier, I pushed ahead of her and stepped inside.

After the cool breeze of the night, the air felt very hot – as close as our prison in fact, but with a sweet scent of sage and baked mud. And deserted. Not even an altar. Just a box of some kind, standing where an altar might have been, and lit by the moon shining in through the door behind me.

Then suddenly not deserted, because while I walked slowly forward the altar-box shifted, scraped across the floor, toppled over, and a wildcat scrambled out. A wildcat that turned into a rabbit, and I thought was about to streak past me and vanish into the night.

He did nothing of the kind. He advanced a few yards in ponderous hops and shuffles, then paused and looked at me with great curiosity.

But I was hungry and Natty was hungry. We had eaten nothing except bread and gruel for weeks or longer, and the sight of this plump animal was more than I could resist. I reached down to him, feeling his wet nose touch my skin. Then I closed my fingers around his throat and swept him off the ground, breaking his neck by swinging him like a rattle.

When I looked for Natty I found her in the doorway. 'We don't have a knife,' she said, very matter-of-fact. 'Or anything to start a fire.'

'We can make do,' I told her just as plainly, and squeezed past her to search outside. After rejecting several little stones because they were too blunt, or not stones at all but clumps of crumbly mud, I found something to do the job and got to work, slicing the rabbit along its belly, then dragging the body out from the fur. Once this was done I tore the flesh into pieces and divided it between us.

We sat side by side on a rock close to our ponies, who seemed to eye us very suspiciously as we chewed and swallowed the raw meat. It was the strangest meal, and we ate entirely in silence – in shock, perhaps I should say, because of the wilderness, and the massacre we had seen, and the chapel, and our exhaustion. For the same reasons, it did not surprise me at all that when we had finished and passed the water-bottle between us, we should lie down on the ground and still not utter a word.

Yet I could not just close my eyes and fall off to sleep.

There was Natty beside me, an arm's length away; I brushed the hair from her eyes, which was all I allowed myself to do, and broke our silence briefly by wishing her goodnight.

There were the stars overhead, except it was not the stars I saw, it was Black Cloud padding through the desert, scouring for our footprints.

There was the Painted Man following him, his body flickering like firelight, his quick feet stirring the dust.

And there was the dust itself. Tiny pieces of red rock, and grey rock, and white rock that once had been mountains stretching into the sky, and now stirred under my head where no one had ever touched them before, and might never touch them again.

CHAPTER 12

The Hunting Party

Next morning, in the second between waking and opening my eyes, all the comforts sleep had draped around me were instantly torn away, because the world had come to an end: the sky was full of devils raging and screaming and I was already a dead man, with a white cotton sheet pulled over my face.

Then this cotton sheet began to shake, ripped into dozens of smaller pieces, and I knew better. Fifty feet above me an immense flock of white birds was travelling inland from the coast to search for food. In England a naturalist might see a flock of a few hundred and think it was remarkable. Here I must have seen a thousand birds, maybe a hundred thousand, enough to hide the sun when they flew across it, and all crying constantly about where they were, and what they had left behind, and what they might find ahead, and in this way making their prodigious rumpus.

It was a purely natural thing – an abundance of life – but I felt I had seen another promise of God's kindness, and so felt able to continue my journey in better spirits. Natty felt rested, our ponies were refreshed by their grazing during the night, and the warmth of the early sun was pleasant on our faces. Even the chapel, which the previous night had been a box of darkness breeding all kinds of suspicion, now looked innocuous; its red mud walls and little tilting cross might have been a toy made for a child.

The next few hours passed very easily, our ponies picking their way over ground that was softened by a thin covering of weeds, with cacti sprouting here and there and also several large bushes covered in purple flowers that released a peppery aroma when we brushed against them. Then, towards noon, when the sun was hot enough for me to think we should take shelter and rest our ponies, I noticed some seagulls squabbling and circling above a patch of darker ground off to the west, and decided they must be competing for food. In the same breath I knew there must be a river nearby.

Our ponies, which by now were even thirstier than we were, since they did not have the warm dregs of a water-bottle to share, immediately thought the same. For a moment I wondered whether I should prevent them and stick to my original plan, which was to continue due north. But when I saw how eager they were to drink I let them be. We began trotting at a good pace, and only slowed down when the ground became more fertile, and we found ourselves in a little grove of orange trees, with their fruit glowing like lamps. I snatched one of these as we passed and bit into it, but the taste was very sour so I threw it away. I did not care; I could hear the river ahead of us now – a delicious rush, like the sensation of drinking itself.

Then the orange grove ended and we came into open ground again, and I saw footprints. I could not credit my eyes at first, but when I hung over the side of my pony there was no mistake. Human footprints, plain as day. One track alone to start with, and widely spaced so I knew it must be a man running; the feet were turned slightly outwards and the toes splayed. Then several together. A hunting party, I thought, and said so to Natty. But what kind? She did not answer, only signalled with her hand to show we must be quiet and move forward more slowly.

What if the men were not running in pursuit of something but away from something, an enemy or a ferocious animal? The idea was almost enough to make me turn tail and head for the desert again, but I could not. The thought of returning to that emptiness was too dispiriting; too like a defeat. Much better to trust that we were right, and would find friends soon.

I rode up beside Natty and we went forward together, entering another belt of trees. I did not know what kind these were but it hardly mattered; the cool shade they cast, and the light playing across their pale trunks and curiously extended roots, immediately quenched my anxieties and plunged me into a strange sort of contentment.

No doubt the noise of the river was partly responsible, soothing me as it floated through the leaves. Never loud, never roaring, but always a steady pattering ripple, broken sometimes by splashes as a part of the bank toppled into the current. In the same way I was also bewitched by – of all things – the moss we now found growing on the branches. Moss that was quite unlike any we have at home in England, which forms little pads or cushions. This hung down in swags as long as the beard of Jehovah: silvery and lime-green and lemon-green and grey-green and curiously crisp when it touched my face and hands.

The effect was so soothing, our ponies seemed to forget their thirst. And as for ourselves, we did not speak a word. We did not look at one another. We simply rambled and nodded, swaying sometimes to right or left, hearing the noise of our ponies' hooves change from a soft clip-clop to a scrape and slither when we reached stonier ground, feeling the air shake as the voice of the water grew louder, drifting in the flicker of sky and shadow.

Then we saw the river and were wide awake again. The river and a small jetty, with half a dozen savages crowded onto it and all facing away from us. But doing what? The confusion of bodies was bewildering. One moment they seemed knotted together, with their black hair plastered to their heads and mud flying as they hauled at a rope stretching into the river; the next moment the tension had gone from the rope and everyone was tumbling about separately, shouting instructions or warnings because any second now the demon they had lassoed in the water would rear up and eat them.

They had not seen us yet, although we were only fifteen yards behind them. Should we creep back into the trees, I wondered, in case they thought we were an easier kind of prey? There was no time to decide; Natty's pony suddenly gave a loud whinny, and the savages whirled round with their rope still bucking and shuddering in their hands.

They were like children – children surprised in a mysterious game that required them to remove most of their clothes and decorate their foreheads with a stripe of charcoal, but who very quickly recovered their wits and showed us with nods and shouts they would like to make us welcome but were occupied for the moment, and would we kindly wait?

I lifted my right hand in what I hoped they would think was a sign of friendship. Little as it was, the men seemed satisfied that this meant we would not hurt them, and went back to their work, hauling on their rope as before, while at the same time setting up a chant, a single word, which to my ears sounded like *'caiman'*, with the accent on the second syllable. As the volume increased and the rope became steadier in their grip, they braced their legs and leaned backwards, straining until whatever they had caught began rising towards them.

In the minutes before it appeared I saw several long snouts emerging from the water around the jetty, snapping their jaws together with horrible liquid crashes, and knew then what the men were after. An alligator. I had never seen one before, but the supple glistening backs, the gnarled skin, the yellow serpent eyes were all unmistakable.

I decided our Indians must be lunatics to want such a creature anywhere near them. But they were completely set on it and obviously expert, even though the river showed nothing for the next little while, except its own muddy colours churned into a fury. Then as I continued watching, a ghost slowly appeared beneath the surface of the water – black or black-green, with a texture like an oak tree. *'Caiman, caiman'*: the chant was gradually louder now, and when the snout broke the surface at last, and the jaws opened to show grey slanting teeth and mottled pink gums, and a great explosion of steaming breath rushed from the nostrils, and the water rattled like pebbles in the long exposed throat, then the chant ended and became a shout.

A bellow of triumph, but also of warning, because the creature that now lay near them was so full of rage, and so determined to scramble aboard the jetty and knock everyone into the water. Our ponies snorted and shimmied backwards. Natty seized my arm and whispered something but did not look away. Neither could I; the contest was too magnificent. Especially since the alligator, as the scrabbling front claws made contact with the timbers of the jetty, leaving deep pale scars, decided to switch its plan and launch forward instead of resisting.

It mounted the jetty in a scuttling dash, swinging its head from side to side and all the while gaping and grunting. The rope, which I could now see was tightened midway around the body, and gripped it behind the front legs, lay limp in the hands of the Indians, who did not flinch at all.

Then the head grew still. The yellow eyes made a lazy blink. The tail scraped until it lay in a straight line with the body. The thick legs tensed and lifted the body six inches from the ground.

Every inch of knobbly skin, every iron muscle, was braced to attack, and in my mind's eye I already saw myself galloping back through the trees and their mossy waterfalls, riding for my life. But the men were quicker. In the same second that the creature paused, exulting in its strength, the tallest of them stooped and picked up a spear from the jetty. He stepped forward until he was so close to the alligator he might have hit him on the nose. Then he leaped.

One moment he was among his friends on their flimsy platform, the next he was astride the alligator and facing us with his knees gripping its flanks, his face gaunt with excitement, hoisting his spear with both hands and aiming it exactly at one of the yellow eyes before plunging the point downwards; the eyeball exploded immediately, releasing a jet of dark blood that sprayed over his chest and face and dribbled from his chin.

Every time I had seen an animal killed – on the marshes as a child when a hawk knocked down a pigeon, or at farms nearby when pigs and cattle were slaughtered by their owners – I had seen life depart quietly, in an instant. It had been the same in the chapel the previous night, when I caught our supper with my bare hands. But this alligator remained as dangerous in dying as it had been in life. Although half-blind, with a needle grinding in its brain, the head pounded so wildly on the jetty that I thought its timbers would soon be smashed into pieces. The tail curved upwards like a scorpion until it almost touched the head of the Indian who had done the murder, then swished back and forth to swat him away – until the energy shrivelled, and faltered, and failed, and the enormous weapon crashed back onto the boards.

Even then the life was not extinguished; the jaws continued to mash together, and the single eye to glare at the world until the *coup de grâce* was delivered. For this, the Indian squatting astride him went quiet for a moment, composing himself as a person might do before undertaking a ritual of great significance, with his head lowered and his eyes closed. Once he was concentrated in this way, he looked up again and took from one of his friends a small hatchet – which was presented sideways, on flat palms – and used this weapon to chop the backbone of the alligator in two with a single heavy blow.

As the yellow eye turned cloudy at last, the Indian rose so that he was standing over his victim, then carefully inserted the point of his spear into the gash he had made between the shoulders, pushing downwards until almost the whole length of the weapon was hidden inside the skin. Next, when he was quite sure there was no more danger, he stepped away from the body and joined his friends to stand in line with them, with their heads all thrown back to make another chant. This was unlike the first, having no hint of threat or excitement but rather a note of sadness – as though, after the passion of the kill, their only feeling was regret.

I have to admit I did not understand at the time why a person might grieve for something he had been determined to destroy; but I did at least begin to think that such a ceremony, for all its strangeness, meant those who took part in it could not be described merely as savages.

When the chant ended, so did our role as spectators, and two of the Indians broke away from their fellows and bounded towards us up the slope of the river-bank. Watching them in their battle I had already noticed how slightly built they were, how nimble and darting; now, as they came close to us for the first time, I saw they were also very open-faced and affable. It struck me that our approach to each other was more like a meeting between friends who had long been separated, than one between strangers who had every reason to feel suspicious. In my own case this had something to do with simple curiosity; in theirs, I could not decide whether it showed a natural kindness, or was derived from previous contact with travellers like ourselves.

As with their hunting, so with their greeting. They made it into a ritual by halting a yard in front of us and holding up one hand with the palm outwards, as I had previously done myself. I noticed the skin of their fingers was rubbed sore where the rope had chafed them; the rest of their bodies were smooth and supple-looking, and their skin a dark reddish-brown, the same colour as the earth thereabouts.

To show we understood their good intentions and shared them, Natty and I then climbed down from our ponies and made the same gesture in return. The Indians seemed very pleased with this and looked happily at one another, and I dare say would have taken us back to their village immediately if we had not delayed them. But Natty had the idea that we should do more.

'Show them the necklace,' she said.

'There's no need,' I told her, very surprised by the idea.

'Show them,' she repeated.

'I . . .'

'Show them,' she said for a third time, and because I did not think clearly enough about what the effects might be, I obeyed. I opened the satchel where it lay against my chest, and drew out the necklace to hold it towards our friends; even though we were sheltered by trees, and the sunlight only penetrated the leaves in odd little flicks, the silver pieces glowed as if they were alive.

'Not like that,' said Natty. 'They'll think you're giving them a present. Put it on.'

Once again I did as she asked, tying the leather string behind my neck, and polishing the silver pieces with a quick movement of my hand as they lay flat against my shirt.

When I looked up again I found our friends had retreated several yards and were gazing at me with anxious faces; one of them had actually dropped onto his knees and seemed to be recommending that others did the same.

'They recognise it,' said Natty. 'They think you've killed him.'

'Do they know him then?' I said – which was foolish of me, but I felt amazed by the confusion I had caused, and was sorry for it.

'They'll be grateful,' Natty said. 'You'll see.'

She took my hand and led me forward, still raising her free arm as before, with the palm towards them. By the time we came close they had shuffled backwards as far as the jetty and could go no further; their retreat was blocked by the body of the alligator.

'We do not mean you any harm,' said Natty, speaking slowly and a little more loudly than usual, as if this allowed everyone to understand. When she had finished she let go of my hand and touched the necklace, running her fingers over the carvings of the animals, touching their hard little eyes and sweeping bodies, then holding her fingers towards our friends as if she was passing them something substantial – colour, or warmth, or a skim of the silver itself.

This seemed to reassure them a little and they began whispering to one another again, bending their heads together as if they did not want us to hear what they were saying. While this continued the clouds gradually lifted from their faces – lifted so thoroughly that when they turned back towards us again they seemed almost as simple and friendly as they had been at first. But there was a different look in their eyes, I felt sure of it.

'They think you're a god,' Natty said.

'Nonsense,' I told her, because it was a preposterous idea.

'Wait,' she said – and as though everything had already been planned, or Natty had seen it in a vision, one of the Indians then stepped forward. This was the tallest and oldest, the man who had killed the alligator and was obviously the leader of the whole party. With the monster's blood still smeared on his chest and face he slowly took one, two, three paces until he was near enough to let me inhale the river-smell off his hair and skin; next, with a little nod as if to ask my permission, which I quickly gave by nodding in return, he extended his hand and gently touched the necklace, stroking his finger-ends over the silver pieces and the animals that chased across them, all the while murmuring under his breath.

Whether he was praying or exclaiming or translating what he saw for the benefit of his friends, I had no idea. But the longer his admiration continued, the more I felt I should help him to a conclusion.

'Black Cloud,' I said. As the words left my lips, I realised this was the first time I had spoken to anyone other than Natty for many weeks. Brief as they were, and although they were the name of an enemy, I felt I had made my first proper connection with our new world.

'Black Cloud,' repeated the warrior, staring hard into my face. He was no longer touching the silver but holding my hand; his fingers felt slimy with river-water.

'You see,' said Natty softly. 'They think you've killed him. You're their saviour.'

'Perhaps,' I told her, but without looking round because my eyes were fixed on my friend, who was now nodding his head very energetically, as if he understood everything.

'Black Cloud,' he said again, 'Black Cloud,' and then another word that sounded like '*mert*', but when I repeated it to myself I realised was '*muerte*'.

'I told you,' Natty went on. '*Muerte*. Death.'

'Shouldn't we tell the truth?' I asked, still facing away from her.

'And how would we do that?'

'We could explain somehow.'

'Why?'

'Because they'll find out one day. They'll see we're liars.'

'Again, Jim. How would they do that?'

'Because Black Cloud will follow us. He'll find these people and they'll know. He'll punish them. We're putting them in danger if we lie to them.'

Natty did not answer this, and I said nothing more; I felt too daunted – though cowardly might be a better word. I let my friend hold my hand for a moment longer; I smiled back at his own smiling face; I felt the hands of others patting me on the back as they also came forward; I let them touch my skin and my hair; I let them caress the necklace, until at last I thought I must show I was satisfied with their thanks, and took a step away so that I was raised a little on the slope above the river.

The Indians accepted that this marked the end of whatever ceremony we had just undertaken, and promptly returned to the work we had interrupted. They untied the rope from the body of the alligator, then used one part of it to truss up the jaws and another part to make a kind of cradle to support the body. Once this was done they watched us lead our ponies to the water and there enjoy the drink they had wanted for so long, then divided into two groups, picked up their trophy, and set off along the river-bank. Every few paces one or other of them turned round to make sure we were following – which of course we were, leading our ponies behind us, and believing these men were the friends we had imagined, the guides who would lead us to others of our own kind, who in time would show us the way home. They made a very pretty picture with the sun dappling on their naked shoulders, and glinting in the moss that hung around us on every side.

CHAPTER 13

In the Village

It was now more than twelve hours since we had escaped from our prison, maybe fifteen, and because we had spent all that time in the wilderness, with every minute stretched by thirst and hunger and anxiety and astonishment, I had not been able to calculate how far we had travelled. Now, as we followed along the river path, I had a moment to think more clearly. Forty miles, I decided; forty miles at the most.

While this helped me understand how our friends had heard of Black Cloud, it also told me that he would find us very easily if he wanted. For this reason I often looked over my shoulder as we led our ponies forward, but saw only leaf-shadows closing behind us, and the beards of moss swaying gently where we had brushed against them.

Our friends had no such fears but chatted eagerly to one another, often turning round to marvel at us, and sometimes calling out in cheerful voices. As their talk continued I noticed here and there a resemblance to French and Spanish, both of them languages I had previously heard among the sailors on the Thames. This confirmed my idea that others like us must have passed this way, not as maroons but as travellers who had plunged into the emptiness to find trade, or missionaries determined to make conversions.

For all that, we saw no trace whatsoever of other men or families on our march – let alone of Europeans. Nothing, that is, until we came to the end of the wood and I smelled a sweet scent I knew was woodsmoke, and glimpsed patches of red and green and white between the branches ahead. As we stepped into the open I saw these were animal skins that had been dyed and stitched together to make tepees: ten, twelve, twenty of them.

We had reached a part of the country where the river, swirling heavily as it worked through a tight bend, had repeatedly collapsed the bank and so produced a miniature plain about an acre in extent, very convenient for a settlement. Water nearby for washing and drinking; the wood for protection and fuel; and on the two remaining sides, the wilderness. In the soft light of afternoon even these two wide prospects seemed peaceful, with the air beginning to cool, and purple clouds swelling along the horizon.

I did not have long to think of such things, because everyone in the village rushed forward as soon as they saw us, with no shyness and no suspicion – the women in dresses made of animal skin, with blankets pulled around their shoulders; the children wearing little skirts regardless of their sex; the men in tunics. In every case their hair was cut short, which meant they were not able to prettify themselves much; a few of the women had feathers dangling from their ears, and their foreheads were decorated with the same single charcoal lines as the men. This was all I could see in the way of ornament; it was enough, combined with their daintiness and neatness, to make me think we must look very dishevelled in comparison.

They pressed around us very eagerly – about fifty or sixty of them – and I could see from the way they pointed and chattered to one another that they were especially interested in my necklace, and in knowing how I had come by it. Nevertheless, their greeting was so much gentler than the one we had received in Black Cloud's village, that I looked around expecting to see a smiling chieftain somewhere, encouraging all their goodwill. But no such person seemed to exist, no obvious ruler at all, in fact, unless it was an old grandmother I spied sitting apart from the crowd and smoking a long-stemmed pipe as though she expected the world to come to her and not the other way round.

However, as our guides continued to lead us forward, receiving a good deal of praise for their courage in killing such a mighty creature as an alligator, it became clear we had yet to reach the centre of the village. This was a tepee much larger than the rest, a really impressive structure that stood twenty feet high, and covered enough ground to make a decent-sized parlour. When we stood outside what I would usually call the front door, which in this case was two large flaps made of deerskin, the hunting party gave a loud shout in unison and then suddenly left us, carrying off their prize towards the river-bank, with the crowd following. As the last stragglers left they took away our ponies to feed and water them. Natty and I continued standing there alone.

A minute passed, in which the village returned to whatever work we had interrupted – not, I thought, because they had suddenly forgotten us, but as a form of politeness. Then another minute, in which we heard scuffling and muttering inside the tepee. Then another, which I think was intended to whet our appetites for what might soon appear.

It turned out to be a man about sixty-five or even seventy years old, who was quite naked except for a headdress of tall white feathers which sprouted from a leather band around his forehead and trailed the whole length of his back. Stooping through the doorway of his lodge, then straightening so we were only a yard apart, he fixed us with his milky grey eyes, folded his arms across his chest, and planted his feet firmly apart. His face was tremendously weathered and lined, which gave him an air of great solemnity and wisdom. At the same time he seemed curiously abstracted, as though not fully conscious of himself.

One or two women called out to him from the tepees behind us, and one or two of the warriors leaped up, shaking their hands at the sky. But nothing seemed to catch his attention. He continued staring, perfectly silent and content. Waiting for something, I thought, and infinitely patient. Gazing from within the halo of his headdress.

This greeting, if I can call it that, lasted another long minute. Then without warning, and for no particular reason I could see, he glanced towards his hunters (who by now had set down their load close to the river-bank), reassured himself that none of them was harmed, and turned to examine us more closely.

Natty and I lowered our eyes out of respect, but also to avoid staring at his nakedness. He would not allow this, and quickly unfolded his arms to extend a hand towards each of us like an English gentleman; his skin felt soft and warm, and moved loosely over the bones. Once this was done, he touched the necklace on my chest, and muttered a few words under his breath.

When he had puzzled like this for a while, looking from the necklace into my face, then back at the necklace again, he held open the flap of his tent and encouraged us to walk inside. Natty blushed as she stepped forward, but our awkwardness quickly ended because, when the flaps closed behind us, our host immediately went to a chest at the side of the tepee and took from it something to cover himself. This was a long cloak that stretched from his shoulders to the ground and was made of the same white feathers as his headdress, all cunningly laid together like a gigantic bird's wing. The sheen of these feathers, combined with the rosy light diffused through the walls of the tepee, made the whole interior glow.

I looked around me as he seemed to expect. The floor of the tepee was covered in rugs and blankets to a depth of several inches, mostly red and brown, and all woven with great skill. And here and there ornaments hung down from poles that formed the frame-work of the tent: strips of plaited grass, and pieces of wood the wind had carved into sickle-shapes, and bunches of dried herbs. But in truth all these things were little more than a blur, because most of my attention was fixed on what appeared to be a bundle of bright striped cloth on the furthest side of the tent. It seemed surprisingly bulky – which soon turned out to be not so surprising after all, since while I continued staring the bundle shook, and balanced, and rose upright to reveal a head, and arms, and feet, all lavishly painted with pink and white and black dyes.

I recognised them at once. They were the colours of an exotic bird I had previously seen in pictures: the hoopoe. At the time, I thought this breed might be native to America, as it is to some parts of Europe; I only learned my mistake once I had already christened this apparition in my mind. His real name was Lives with the Birds, which I thought much too general for the effect he made with his decorations.

The appearance of Hoopoe was enough to make me forget my

manners and stare. His behaviour was even more astonishing, because he paid no attention to his senior the chieftain, but crouched, and peered, and teetered, and shied away, and made bold, and squinnied again as he came close to us, extending his arms sideways and fluttering his hands so the little bells attached to his wrists set up a tinkling music. Where had he found these bells, I asked myself, since they could not possibly have been made in the village? And why was he got up in this way, like a magician, when everyone in the village was dressed so simply? And what . . . ?

But I did not have a chance to continue, because as soon as Hoopoe halted in front of us – though 'halted' is not right, since he continued to swoop and fidget – he delivered his greatest surprise. He spoke to us in our own tongue. Not perfectly, and with a strong Spanish accent, but intelligibly and confidently, in a deep clear voice.

'You are welcome,' he said, suddenly dropping his hands to his sides and standing upright; our faces were level with one another, and his eyes (which were deep brown, but with the whites almost entirely covered with little red veins) flicked rapidly from me to Natty, then settled on the necklace. He began to smile.

I was so amazed by his words, and so pleased to hear them, I almost forgot myself.

'Thank God!' I blurted, and in the same breath began to tell him my name, and Natty's name, and how we had been shipwrecked and captured, and escaped, and then travelled through the wilderness, and found the hunters by the river, and seen them kill the alligator.

None of this seemed to interest Hoopoe greatly; he kept his eyes on the necklace, and did not communicate anything I had said to his chieftain, who had now stepped away from us and collapsed full length on a rug, where he continued to inspect us from the cocoon of his white robe, his head supported on one large and wrinkled hand.

'You have travelled a long way,' Hoopoe said when I finished.

'We have. From England.'

I wanted to say more but the mention of that word, which I had not spoken for a long time, made me pause and collect myself.

'From London,' Natty put in, to cover my difficulty.

This seemed to disappoint Hoopoe. 'Not France?' he asked, briefly looking away from the necklace and meeting my eye.

'Not France, no,' I went on.

'Not Spain?'

'Not Spain either.'

'But she is dark,' he went on, swivelling his eyes to Natty, and speaking as if she was not present or could not understand him.

'Yes,' I said. 'But England, all the same; England is our home. Why do you say France or Spain? Do you know them?' This was a ridiculous idea, but I could not think of a better way to introduce my next question.

Hoopoe rolled his eyes.

'And their languages?' I persevered. 'Do you speak their languages?'

He shrugged, which made the bells jingle at his wrists. 'Spanish a little,' he said.

'And yet you speak ours well.'

The bells jingled again. 'I have met men from Spain,' he said, but reluctantly and with a melancholy expression. 'I have met more from England – and from here, from the north.'

'Ah!' I said, because this was the answer I wanted.

Hoopoe did not seem to notice how pleased I was. 'People are always arriving,' he told me in a flat voice, then made a strange pawing movement with his bare right foot, like a pony. I thought he wanted me to understand that these new arrivals were scooping up the earth.

'And they taught you to speak English here?' I went on.

'In another place, when I was a child.'

'And you have not forgotten?'

'I have spoken with others since then.'

'Others that came here, you mean, and stayed with you?'

'Not that. Passing by.'

'Many of them?'

Hoopoe did not answer this but suddenly screwed up his face and put his fingers in his ears. 'Your language is not good,' he said. 'It is noise.'

I glanced at Natty and smiled, to show her that I wanted to tell him how rough the language of his own people sounded in our ears; but I restrained myself. Instead, I asked whether there were more people in the village who spoke English. When he said there were none, his sadness seemed to lift a little, as though he enjoyed his singularity.

In this new mood he suddenly changed the subject, pointing to the chieftain lying beside us on his blanket, listening to what we were saying but with a nearly vacant expression on his face.

'White Feather,' he said.

'That's his name?'

'In English, yes. White Feather. He has gone ahead of us.'

'I don't understand,' I said.

'His mind has gone forward,' Hoopoe explained, and twiddled his fingers in the air so the music of the bells rained down on us both. 'To our ancestors. They are waiting for his body to follow. We are all waiting.'

Then he changed the subject again, just as abruptly.

'And this?' he said, touching my necklace for the first time; he did this warily, as if he thought the animals carved in the silver might suddenly nip him, and spoke with a dreamy sing-song note in his voice. In the weeks to come I would hear him use this tone whenever he thought he was in contact with some kind of spirit or other.

'Black Cloud,' he said, taking his hand carefully from the necklace and stepping away from me. 'They think you have killed him, the rest of them here. They think you are a conqueror. But this is not the truth.'

I heard Natty shifting beside me, as if worrying about what I might say next, but I ignored her. I nodded. 'It is not,' I said.

'He is alive.'

'We were his prisoners and we escaped.'

'He is following you.'

'We haven't seen him.'

'Certainly he is following you.'

'How do you know?'

'He is Black Cloud.'

'But he has no idea where we went.'

'He will find you. He will track you.'

'Soon?'

'Not soon, no.'

'Are you sure?'

'I am sure.'

'Why not, though?'

'He will not think you are here. He will not . . .' Hoopoe stared around the tepee as if the word he wanted might be hiding among the shadows, or buried under the blankets. 'He will not think we are worthy of you.'

'Because you are peaceful?'

'He thinks you are a warrior, and will go to others who are also warriors. He will look among other tribes first. Not here with us.'

'And so?'

'You will stay here,' said Hoopoe. 'You will be safe here and we shall speak no more about Black Cloud.'

Once again I glanced sideways at Natty. Her face was bright and she gave a little nod; she wanted me to accept Hoopoe's offer.

'You will be safe here,' Hoopoe said again, speaking more definitely now, as though he was reporting something that should not be debated. 'We shall enjoy life together for a long time.'

He looked me directly in the eye, daring me to contradict him. 'Very well,' I said slowly. 'Thank you. We shall stay. We are very glad to stay, and very grateful. But a long time? How long is that?'

He ignored my question. 'It is settled,' was all he said, then raised his hand and held it towards me with the palm outwards. After we had paused like this for a moment, with everything around us seeming to fall silent, he let his hand drop and smiled broadly; his teeth were stained very yellow but not at all broken.

'And now, Mister Jim!' he exclaimed. 'Fiesta!'

Natty clapped her hands, joining our talk at last. 'Fiesta?' she said. 'You will make a fiesta?'

It was a simple question, but our bird-man suddenly shook as if he had been sprinkled with a shower of rain. 'No! No!' he exclaimed. 'I will not make this happen. White Feather will make it happen. I am a doctor, that is all. I am *un medico*.'

He said this last word in the Spanish way, with a good deal of pride, as if he was giving it to us like a present.

'*Un medico*,' I repeated, as respectfully as I could manage.

Hoopoe bowed his head, then walked in a wide circle around the tepee with one hand raised above his head so his fingers brushed through the various ornaments, pieces of bark, and swatches of herb that dangled there. From this we understood that he was displaying his medicines, but the way he did so, with a skip in his step, made me wonder whether he thought his business was all trickery, which he would never admit.

Perhaps I deceived myself in this. Perhaps I judged him by the standards I knew at home, and not by things that belonged here and were strange to me. For when Hoopoe had finished his little tour, which ended with a wave towards White Feather, who roused himself and climbed carefully to his feet and straightened his robe and returned the same gesture, every suggestion of foolery had vanished.

'Now we shall begin,' Hoopoe said, and pointed towards the platform at the back of the tepee where we had first encountered him; this was covered in a thick rug with blankets heaped upon it, and even some cushions which I supposed were stuffed with dry grass.

'Please,' he continued, indicating that Natty and I should sit on either side of White Feather; when we had done as he asked, he fetched one of the cushions and placed himself to my left, with his legs crossed and his hands balanced on his knees, palms upwards.

'We shall wait,' he said, and rolled his shoulders to show we should make ourselves as comfortable as possible.

Although cooking-smells were now drifting through the tepee – along with a good many cooking-sizzles and cooking-splashes and pieces of cooking-advice shouted by women outside – I looked about me as I reckoned Hoopoe wanted me to do, so that I could admire White Feather's luxuries. The walls of the tent were indeed very ingeniously stitched together, and so were the rugs very cleverly made, with stars and zigzag patterns worked into the weave. I was even more impressed, though differently, by a fragment of much smoother cloth, which was jumbled among the others. The colours told me it was a part of the flag of Spain, but badly singed along one edge; beside it lay several short wooden planks that were branded with words written in the Spanish language.

How had White Feather found them? Were they a gift? A bribe? I wanted to ask Hoopoe but the chieftain laid his hand on my arm and pointed towards the flaps of the tent; he did not want my questions. A moment later the flaps opened and two young women appeared, each holding a bundle of clothes; a third hesitated behind them, carrying a large wooden bowl filled with water.

White Feather grunted, but nothing more.

'For you,' said Hoopoe, glancing at me and Natty, then beckoning two of the women forward; both were very pretty, with short black hair and a somewhat Chinese appearance; they showed White Feather the clothes they carried, and he patted them absent-mindedly.

'He is telling you to put them on,' said Hoopoe.

'Now?' I said, a little wildly.

'Now,' said Hoopoe, and waved the women closer still. They dipped their heads as we took what they offered: a new pair of moccasins each, a dress and red shawl for Natty, a tunic for me.

'So . . .' I climbed to my feet.

'Where?' Natty mouthed at me.

I nodded sideways to suggest we move behind White Feather, and there we took off our old rags – our tattered white shirts and black breeches – before kicking them away and dressing ourselves in our new clothes. Once we had done this we quickly washed our faces and hands in the bowl of water the third woman now offered to us; the whole business was somewhat awkward, as anyone might imagine, but Hoopoe and the rest politely looked away from us, just as Natty and I looked away from one another.

In the process I also removed the necklace and slipped it back into my satchel, which I continued to keep close with the strap across my chest. As I did so I thought Natty might say I should continue to wear it where it could be seen – but she only mumbled something I could not hear, and we turned to appraise one another. I thought she looked more beautiful than ever, with her smooth bare arms, and her dress shining. My own tunic was rather less flattering because it was shorter than my breeches had been, and so left a part of my legs exposed; they looked as pale as moonlight.

'Very well,' Natty said, and smiled so broadly it seemed to contradict what she was telling me. 'You look very well.'

I was about to say the same to her, for in truth her red shawl was very becoming – but Hoopoe interrupted me. 'Both good,' he said, twisting round to inspect us. Then he clapped his hands, which showed the women they must go back and help the others with our meal; the next part of our welcome was about to begin.

CHAPTER 14

Paradise

Even before Hoopoe had settled again, and the little tinkling bells around his wrists fell silent, the flaps of the tepee parted once more and a procession of men, women and children started to arrive, all carrying wooden platters piled with different kinds of food. The smells then flooding my head were so delicious, I thought I had never been so hungry since I was a schoolboy.

I restrained myself, waiting for White Feather to take the first mouthful – but when he had done this (so slowly, I thought he might have forgotten that food was for eating) I looked across to Natty on his further side, saw her nod, and together we set to with both hands. Some things tasted familiar: white chicken, and fish, and bowls of maize ground into a paste. Some I had never eaten before: slippery cuts of alligator; coils of grubby sinew I decided were snake.

I suppose our stomachs must have shrunk during our time in prison. At any rate, after gorging for a few minutes I found I could no longer do justice to everything set before me – at which point yet more plates arrived, all heaped with beans, and potatoes, and slices of meat that had been dried out and then dipped in grease to make them palatable again, and prickly pears, and tree roots and flower roots and goodness knows what other kinds of root – some yellow, some white, some reddish; some tasting very sweet, some woody, and some like soil, and eventually, as a climax to the feast, a large heap of rotten fish in which the larvae of hundreds of flies had incubated, which Hoopoe and White Feather picked out and devoured like epicures.

By this time our hosts had despaired of us having a capacity equal to their kindness, so did not seem insulted by our failure to continue eating. In fact they did not seem very sharply aware of anything at all, thanks to the large quantity of liquor they had drunk, which I later discovered was called *mescal*, and is made from leaves of the *agave* plant.

I drank only a little of this, because when I saw its effect I knew it would put me completely at the mercy of our hosts – who were still strangers to us. Hoopoe, however, had no such reason to hold back, and I think may actually have relied on the liquor to boost his skills as a medico.

He certainly reached a different plane of existence as our meal continued, which did not concern White Feather in the least; on the contrary, he seemed to expect it. For as the chieftain browsed with his fingers among the food, collecting titbits here and there and chewing them with a blissful slowness, he repeatedly turned his weather-beaten face towards his doctor and smiled a beatific smile. This, despite the fact that Hoopoe spoke entirely in English, and White Feather did not understand a word.

I will not attempt to remember the whole of Hoopoe's conversation, which was continually mangled by digressions, and also interrupted very often by his leaning forward to touch the satchel in my lap, as though he meant to draw strength from the necklace concealed inside it. But I do recall that he spoke for the first time about his guiding principle in life, which in England we call God but which Indians know as the Great Spirit; it describes the high-minded feeling of cooperation that ideally exists between people of different sorts, and also between people and the creatures they live among.

The last part of this idea was especially attractive to me, since it combined with many of my natural sympathies. But as Hoopoe warmed to his theme, speaking more and more excitedly, with his eyes bright and the bells jingling at his wrists, and asking me to imagine large communities of animals and men living happily together, which he said could be found in grasslands to the north of his own territory, our conversation was cut short. Not, as I feared might happen, by the arrival of more plates of food, but by a troop of young men, some of whom I recognised as members of the hunting party who had rescued us; their leader was carrying a wooden pipe which had a bowl the size of a clenched fist and a stem three feet long; this stem, I saw, was carved with images of snakes and other creatures.

The interruption returned me briefly to the Hispaniola, where I had seen men live permanently in a haze of tobacco smoke. But this device was meant to be shared by everyone, as I realised when the man in charge of it knelt down in front of White Feather, with his fellows also kneeling on either side, then lifted the stem to place it between the old man's lips and lit the substance he had already pressed into the bowl.

As White Feather began to suck on the pipe my recent glimpse of familiar life disappeared, and not just because everything around me was suddenly blurred by clouds of white smoke. To my astonishment, which did not feel like astonishment, because there was no accompanying sense of surprise, shadowy animal-shapes began crawling slowly across the walls of the tepee, and then wriggling among the various objects swinging from its scaffolding. In a moment the scaffolding also started to move, sometimes contracting, sometimes expanding, while at the same time I heard faint drumbeats pulsing in the village outside.

At first I thought all this must be a hallucination produced by what I had eaten and drunk. But when White Feather finished with the pipe and passed it to me, and I drew on the moist stem and felt a dagger of light flash through my brain, I realised the smoke was to blame. The effect might have been extremely unpleasant – I was, after all, losing control of my senses. But as I breathed out again and passed the pipe to Hoopoe I found a smile had plastered itself all over my face, while my mind swerved in unexpected and profound directions. I became convinced, for instance, that the most important thing in the world was to know what was real and what was not, and fell into a deep study to consider the idea further. After reaching my conclusion I thought I should explain it to Hoopoe, but when I tried to speak my tongue tied itself in a knot, and I could not form any words.

By now I had very little clue how much time had passed since we first arrived in the tepee, and therefore no way of knowing how far advanced the night might be. But as the pipe began to circulate a second time, and the women who had brought us our meal reappeared to collect the remains, I caught a glimpse of the heavens before the tent-flaps closed again. The sky was black as a river but sprinkled with so many bright stars it seemed quite wrong to call it dark. And quite reasonable, as well, to think the answer to my question about reality, the answer to every question that men have ever asked about their existence, would be more easily found outside, in a shower of silver, than sheltering here in the fug.

I therefore made an effort to stand up and take myself outside. My legs, however, refused to obey the orders I gave them. This seemed very puzzling and at the same time entirely satisfactory, so I stayed as I was.

I have no idea whether Hoopoe noticed my confusion, but once he had taken the pipe for a third time, and blown smoke to the four points of the compass, which I thought might be some sort of homage to the Great Spirit, he did not pass it to me as I expected; he laid it across his knees and clapped his hands. At this the young men sitting before us all rose to their feet – with less difficulty than I had experienced myself – waiting in silence as their leader retrieved the pipe, then trooping outside with as much dignity as they could muster.

I squinted at White Feather and had the strong impression he approved of their departure, even though it had not been his decision, for at the same time as his men disappeared he gave one of his most genial smiles and also clambered to his feet. Hoopoe, noticing him stagger as he did this, moved quickly to support him, slipping a long painted arm inside his cloak, and in this manner they too reached the doorway and disappeared.

When I stretched out a hand to Natty and asked whether she would like to follow suit, she shook her head. Her face, which I had not been able to see for a little while, since she had been sitting on the far side of White Feather, was very flushed and her forehead creased in a frown.

'Are you quite well?' I asked in a whisper, as I managed to stand at last and we padded across the dizzy patterns of the floor-rugs.

'Why shouldn't I be?' she asked, sounding a little put out and swaying gently from side to side.

'No reason.'

'I'm full of food, that's all. Full as a . . . Full as full can be.' Then she looked at me more intently, stooping forward a little. 'You're very red in the face. Are you sure it's not you who are unwell?'

'I'm perfectly well, thank you,' I told her, also a little disconcerted. 'Perfectly well.'

She leaned nearer still and I smelled the smoke on her breath, in her hair. The pupils of her eyes had swollen and were glossy-dark; I thought if I could only look at them steadily enough I would see my own face reflected back at me in miniature, as though I had fallen into her head.

'What are you looking at?' she asked slowly; her tongue sounded thick and she was half-smiling – a soft smile like a pout.

'Nothing,' I told her.

'Nothing?'

'Nothing you want to hear.'

'Are you sure?'

'So you say.'

'I do say?'

Such banter was almost meaningless, yet at the same time unbearable because it brought us so close together. Any more of it and I would kiss her, kiss her smile and her opening mouth.

But she put her hand on my chest to steady herself, and at the same time pushed me away. The moment ended, as all such moments ended for us, and I turned my back and bowed through the doorway of the tepee.

When we had first arrived in the village we found everything very straightforward: children playing in the dirt, women grinding maize and making oil, boys fishing in the river. But while we feasted everything had been transformed, so now I was entering a kind of theatre, where the stage was lit by torches set on long poles fixed into the ground. In the furthest part of this stage, which was adjacent to the river, other small fires were burning – the barbecues, I thought, where our meal had been prepared; at one end I saw the corpse of the alligator with pieces cut from its flank. In the foreground, and therefore partly obscuring all these things: dancers.

Hitherto I had thought the young men of the village (those not involved in the ceremony of pipe-smoking) must be keeping guard, or perhaps helping to prepare our food. In fact they had been planning a quite different sort of ceremony. While some had brought drums from their tents, a dozen of them had taken off their tunics and moccasins, slathered their bodies in grease, collected their tomahawks and knives and spears, and begun rotating in a slow circle, using the river as their backdrop and the village as their audience.

The moment White Feather and the rest of us appeared from our tepee, these drummers – who were all seated on the ground with their tom-toms gripped between their knees like large flower-pots – began pounding a much louder rhythm. At this, the dancers rotated more quickly and stamped harder on the earth.

I could not help remembering the dance we had seen from our prison, and wondered: have we been lured into a trap? Is all this feasting only a way of fattening us for slaughter? But since White Feather and Hoopoe showed no change in their behaviour, and patted the space beside them as they settled onto a strip of matting already spread on the ground, I soon recovered again. A moment later we were lying full stretch as we had seen White Feather do on the floor of his lodge. The chieftain himself, still wearing his seraphic smile, lay on my right; Hoopoe, however – Hoopoe suddenly jumped up and joined in the dance.

'Let him wear it,' Natty whispered, leaning against me so I felt the weight and warmth of her.

'What?' I said, half-asleep and wide awake at the same time.

'The necklace,' said Natty. 'Let him wear it while he dances.'

'Why would I do that? He might think it's a gift and keep it.'

'No, he won't. He'll understand. He'll only think you're sharing your . . .' Natty paused and there was her smile again, her wide smile and the gleam of her teeth. 'Your power. Besides, it'll be a way to thank them.'

'Thank them?'

'They've given us their food – so yes, we must thank them.' As she spoke she reached forward and opened the flap of my satchel. I helped her, letting our fingers brush against one another as they drew our treasure into the open; the firelight crackled along its surfaces and licked them into life.

'There,' Natty sighed, and lifted the necklace closer, rubbing it briefly against her dress to polish it before handing it back to me. 'There it is,' she said again. 'There.'

And so it was for a second, lying in my hands like a pool of fire that gave no pain, but only a lightness that entered me through my eyes and flooded my whole body.

Then the necklace vanished, because I lifted my hands towards the dancers, and Hoopoe had reached down and snatched it, and put it on, and continued his dance, whereupon Natty leaned against me again and we lolled back to watch him.

To watch him and to dream. For as the dancers continued round and round in a ring, and their shouts grew wilder, and the women tossed more bunches of sweet sage into the fire, and deeper shadows coiled and uncoiled before us, and the rhythm of the drums grew steadily faster, I felt less and less strongly tethered to the earth, and more and more like a creature of the air – as though I was floating above the village and all our new friends, and the river that rolled alongside us, and the wilderness fading into darkness on every side, and was able to see everything below me, to see and to understand certain things that were essential to me, and for a moment seemed almost within reach.

But what things, what certain things? I tried to focus on Hoopoe, and on the necklace, but his colouring had changed from the rosy pink of his name-bird into flame-red, so I could hardly distinguish him from the fires burning in the background to his dance. Besides which, I knew from the way he kept his eyes fixed on the ground, then flung back his head to gaze at the stars, then tossed it forward again, that he was not in the slightest bit interested in me, or in Natty, or in what our questions might be, but only in the old stories that always lived in his head, and the new stories that now rushed into him through the necklace sliding across his chest.

The Great Spirit. That is all my brain would allow me to know that night. Those two words, and the idea that every single thing in existence depends on every other single thing, no matter how ordinary and humble. I imagined it like the painting of a peaceable kingdom, where the lion lies down with the lamb, and the other animals are all content with their station and their place, and the fruit of the forbidden tree hangs uneaten on the branches. I saw it, shimmering and real, then it blew away from me and evaporated. I rubbed my eyes. I felt them sting with smoke from the fires. I shook my head.

'Jim?'

Natty's own eyes were ringed with shadows and her mouth was ajar as if she was panting; in fact she was hardly breathing at all, only taking little sips of air like a fish breaking the surface of a pool.

'I thought so,' I told her. 'You're not well . . .' As the words came and went, the hard shapes of things lurched, then settled again. The fire and the dancing men. The black triangles of the tepees. The stars overhead.

'Tired,' she said very slowly, as if it took all her energy to speak this one word.

But White Feather roused himself then, and to judge by the proud look he gave us, I knew our entertainment would last for a good deal longer yet. I could not decide if I felt pleased or not; I only knew that if I closed my eyes I would sleep for the rest of my life.

Then the dancers stepped backwards and stood in line, all breathing heavily as they got their breath back, and the young women of the village took centre stage instead. Without my noticing they had all changed into clean white robes, with their hair neatly brushed and divided into short plaits.

The drums fell silent and the women began a song they knew, a beautiful and simple song that recognised us as interlopers but also welcomed us, as I later learned from Hoopoe's translation.

> White moon in the morning,
> when two rivals
> share one sky.
>
> White moon in the morning,
> when a stranger stands
> in a new country.
>
> White moon in the morning,
> when two big lights
> polish the earth.
>
> White moon in the morning,
> when a shadow falls
> twice as dark.

The effect of this song, which they sang in unison while standing perfectly still, was so peaceful after the frenzy of the dance that I thought I would soon return to my dream, and walk once more with the animals in paradise. But this did not happen. Perhaps the influence of food and drink and smoke had diminished. Perhaps my tiredness overwhelmed all my other feelings. At any rate, for the next little while I did nothing except continue to lean against Natty while more songs poured through me, often closing my eyes to rest, sometimes looking from the faces of the women to their slim arms, and their bracelets, and their anklets, and the white feathers stuck in their black hair, then away to the river that ran beyond them, then resting again.

Resting, and after a while waking to see the menfolk rise to their feet once more, and to hear the drums returning with a stronger rhythm, which told them to form a circle around the women and to move in a clockwise direction, while the women moved in the opposite way. As these two wheels turned, everyone repeated the same few words over and over, which ended every time with the dancers all clapping their hands together. Hoopoe later translated this for me as well:

> All men must die
> No one knows when
> If the time is due
> Hearts fill with joy.

If I had known this meaning at the time, I cannot say whether it would have made me sad or cheerful. As it was, the words swept me forward with such a feeling of gentleness, I think it might have carried me until dawn and even beyond, if Hoopoe had not abruptly tired of it, shooed the dancers away, and stepped towards us. As one of the women turned to go, he seized her by the hand and brought her with him.

With his other hand he took hold of the necklace, lifted it over his head, and returned it to me.

'Thank you, Mister Jim,' he said, the silver gleaming in his eyes as I returned it to my satchel. When it had disappeared he made a little bow, with sweat beading through his face paint.

'It is full of secrets,' he said.

'It is—' I began, but he interrupted me. I could only imagine he had been debating some difficult matter with himself, and had now hastily resolved it.

'We will sleep now,' he said, glancing away to his friends, who were all trooping back to their tepees with their shoulders slumped and their weapons dangling at their sides. 'We are finished here.'

I wanted to thank him for what he had shown us, but while I was still searching for words he suddenly added, 'This is my wife Sees the Wind,' meaning the woman he held by the wrist. Although I could not make her out very clearly in the torchlight, I should have said she was younger even than me, and like a girl in her white dress.

'She is yours for tonight,' Hoopoe said next. 'It is our custom.'

This astonished me so much I may even have scrambled backwards a little on my blanket like a spider; I certainly felt Natty stiffen beside me and move away.

'It's not our custom,' I said in a fluster.

'Take her,' said Hoopoe, jerking his wife's arm as though he expected me to grasp it.

'I cannot do that,' I told him, and looked at him straight.

'Why not?' he said bluntly.

I could only repeat myself. 'I cannot do that.'

In the pause that followed I hung my head, not able to meet his eye any longer, and half-expecting Natty would say something. Something that strengthened what I had implied about our customs at home. Or something more personal, about her own feelings. In the end she did neither, but gave a long sigh ending in a hiccup that might have been a laugh.

'Truly,' I said yet again, 'I cannot do that,' and to show my determination I climbed to my feet. Hoopoe was scowling, with his eyes bulging a little in their sockets; Sees the Wind was biting her lip and wincing away.

'You do not think she is beautiful enough,' he said accusingly.

'She is very beautiful. Beauty is not the reason.'

'Or too old.'

'Certainly not that.'

'What then?'

'It's . . .' I glanced down at Natty, leaning back on the rug with her arms braced behind her; she was smiling, enjoying my discomfort.

This decided me. 'Natty would not like it,' I announced.

'I think—' Natty leaned forward but I did not want to hear what she thought and now it was my turn to interrupt.

'I mean it would be a betrayal,' I said. I have no idea whether Hoopoe understood the word for he continued scowling. Natty certainly knew its meaning, however, and I thought must be surprised by it, because she did not finish what she had been ready to say.

In this moment of advantage I took a step towards Hoopoe's wife and shook her by the hand, which I thought would be polite. When I had released it again I stooped down and took hold of Natty's hand; it felt much softer in my grip and to my relief did not pull away.

'Now,' I said, speaking in the same decisive voice and tugging

Natty to her feet. 'Show us where we can sleep. We must not speak like this again.'

After another silence Hoopoe allowed himself to relax a little; whether he felt the strength of my argument, or simply dismissed me as ungrateful, I did not mind. I was too adamant, and too tired as well. He stared at me a moment longer, but soon nodded and lifted one arm to point out a tepee that stood on the further side of the village.

'You will stay there,' he said, speaking quite neutrally. 'It will be your home.'

'Thank you,' I said in the same level way. Then I bowed towards White Feather, who all this time had remained lying on the ground, staring at the dying embers of the fire. When he did not acknowledge me, except to twitch his cloak of feathers more comfortably around his shoulders, I led Natty away, and together we made our way to the lodge with Hoopoe following.

I paused outside the tepee and laid my hand on his arm. This caught him off guard and he began to smile. As I smiled back, he once more touched the satchel hanging around my neck; despite what he knew, I thought he was acknowledging that I had some authority, even if it was only borrowed.

It did not occur to me until we had said goodnight, and Natty and I had stepped inside, that he had made us a present of his own home and henceforth would sleep elsewhere himself, perhaps in the chieftain's tent where we had eaten our meal. I felt grateful for this, and at another time would have been interested to see what sort of possessions he owned. But my weariness was now so great I merely groped my way forward until I came to a heap of soft material that felt like blankets, where I fell down on my back. Natty sank beside me and pressed her face into my shoulder.

'Betrayal?' she whispered, as the silence lapped around us. 'What is there to betray?' This could have been an accusation, or at least a question, but it was not. There was laughter in her voice; happiness.

For all that, I told her, 'Friendship.'

'Friendship?' The warmth was still in her voice and I felt it soak into me.

'You understand perfectly well, Natty,' I said. 'It's your idea.'

'It is?'

I opened my eyes as wide as possible, to discover whether I could drag myself more fully awake. I could not. I saw the moon glowing through the skin of the tent, its hard light diffused into an overall glow, and felt the world losing every clear shape.

'You do understand,' I said again, and rolled onto my side and took her in my arms. Whether I held her in fact or in my dream I am not sure.

CHAPTER 15

Her Kill

To the best of my knowledge we lived with White Feather and his tribe for a little over two years, from the late autumn of 1802 to the early part of 1805. But as soon as I say that, I run into a thicket of questions. Why did we stay so long with our new friends? Why did we not merely recover our health, learn how to reach the coast, and a harbour, and a ship to England, then set out once more on our journey?

Did we lose our hunger for home, or were we frightened of the dangers ahead? Were we lazy?

None of these things. We stayed because we were happy to stay; because we forgot ordinary calendars; because we felt as safe as Hoopoe had told us we would be; and because we enjoyed living with our friends.

And having begun this account of our conversion as a catalogue, let me continue in the same way to describe how we managed our affairs:

we continued living in the tepee that belonged to Hoopoe, where I stored my necklace for safekeeping with never a suspicion that anyone might want to remove it;

we wore the same clothes as everyone else in the village and began to understand their language, and soon our bodies grew as lean as theirs, our skins as sunburned, and our hair as ragged (although it was chopped short by Hoopoe's wife Sees the Wind, who quickly recovered from the insult I had given her);

we learned their names – the simple evocations such as Blue Lake and Bright Moon; those describing appearances such as Cat Face and Small Hands; and those describing habits such as Eats Bones and Never Turns Round;

we made particular friends – with Hoopoe above all, but also with others I cannot do justice to here and so will not even name because they exist at the margins of my story;

we shared whatever land-work was necessary: haymaking in summer, planting in spring, and harvesting in autumn;

we learned how to fish, by making contraptions of grass and flag-stems to throw into the river (but never chasing an alligator, except as observers);

we learned how to hunt on dry land, by tracking or by climbing trees to spy for dust-clouds that showed where herds of deer might be gathered;

we studied the stars and learned how to navigate by their lights;

we read the wind.

And in all these ways, as I say, I gradually lost my longing for England – even to the extent of thinking our shipwreck had been a blessing in disguise, because it had brought me to a new life that made me happy.

My father faded from me, as if the moon careering through the heavens above me was not the same that crawled across his square of window;

the marshes where I had wandered as a child, the marshes I had loved – they also faded;

London faded;

the Island faded;

most surprising of all, Black Cloud began to shrink from me. His threats I could never forget, the memory of how he had pounded on my head in our prison and seemed overflowing with violence. Neither could I shake off the things we had seen in the Black Bay, and found by accident in the desert. But the kindness of Hoopoe and the rest made these things remote, like nightmares I only remembered from time to time, with all their colours washed out. Although I knew Black Cloud must be searching for us, I believed that Hoopoe had built a sort of invisible wall around us, which would protect us for as long as he decided it should.

No one spoke of these changes in us but everyone accepted them, in the same way they accepted that the sun would shine on some days and there would be cloud on others. Yet at the same time everyone wanted to teach us more about their lives, and so made every day seem like a step in our education. Our re-education, I should more properly say.

Natty and I were separated for some of these lessons, with Natty being taken by the women to learn cooking and weaving and such-like, while I was instructed by the menfolk in making spears and arrowheads, and the sharpening of blades etc., which she was not encouraged to know.

And we accepted this division willingly enough, for the sake of politeness. But in all matters of hunting and tracking we insisted we remain together, saying we would need to combine our skills when the day came for us to wake from our dream at last, and continue our travels.

I shall mention one instance of our collaborating in this way, as a proof of what I mean and also an example of how our life proceeded under Hoopoe's guidance. It is a single story dating from a few weeks after our arrival in the village, and must be allowed to stand for many.

Our purpose was to kill a bear, which we were told was done at the end of every autumn so that a hide could be presented to our chieftain to keep him warm during the months to come. No matter that White Feather seemed as content with nakedness as he was with clothes: custom was custom, and must be observed.

The expedition was led by Hoopoe, who warned us when we set out, and not for the first time, that of all the creatures in our vicinity bears were the most dangerous, because they were the strongest and had the worst tempers. Up to this point, all I knew of these creatures was what I had learned from seeing their scratch-marks on tree trunks, or watching them work in the river, scooping up their meal as easily as if it was water itself. But this had given me a good idea of their power and savagery, so I paid special attention to Hoopoe as he prepared us for the hunt.

The first question he asked was how we might lure one of these beasts to a place where we could have the advantage over him – which he then answered himself by saying we should appeal to the same force that drove other bears into the open to catch fish: namely, their greed. In particular their greed for honey, which they preferred to everything else.

The next part of this operation was simple enough, thanks to one of the children in the village for whom Hoopoe had a special affection; I think he may have been his son, but did not like to ask, in case it reflected badly on Sees the Wind, who was evidently not his mother. This boy, who was probably ten or twelve years old, had the good plain name of Runs Fast, and spent so much of his life foraging in the wood nearby that he might as well have been an animal himself – always with twigs in his hair, and mud on his face and knees, and some sort of egg or nest or other natural treasure in his hands. He would know where to find a bear and a bees' nest close together, said Hoopoe; we would take him as our guide.

On the morning in question we entered the wood where it grew closest to the village, with Runs Fast immediately proving true to his name by shooting ahead of us. Hoopoe called him back and told him for today at least he was called Runs More Slowly, which the boy did not think funny. To present the scene more accurately I should also say that Hoopoe himself was freshly painted from head to foot with his own red and pink and black and white bird-colours; Natty and I, and the six young warriors accompanying us, were bare-faced, wearing our simple leather tunics and moccasins, with spears and tomahawks in our hands.

At first, and despite his warning, Runs Fast slipped among the trees with such rapid twists and turns I thought we still might not be able to keep him in sight. But remembering Hoopoe's warning, he always stopped when he seemed just about to vanish, and waited for us to make our more laborious way among the leaves and moss-beards.

While we remained in this part of the wood, where we had previously hunted and which we knew how to navigate, we took our bearings from tree trunks and boulders I now thought of as friends. Indeed, at one point I stopped and pressed my head to a favourite oak tree as I had seen others do, and listened for whatever advice it might give me. I heard only the wind breathing in the branches above my head, but perhaps that was all I was meant to hear.

When we came to a different territory, and our familiar trees gave way to laurels growing close together, with their branches often entangled, our path became more difficult.

And soon there was no path at all, only a series of little obstacles we leaped or lunged or fell across, while Runs Fast squeezed ahead, then halted and beckoned us to follow. I am sure we would have persevered without this encouragement, but I have to say it helped me; I thought I was following a spirit of the wood itself, like the innocent in a story.

Eventually these laurel bushes shrank away and we broke into a different kind of country, with small oak trees growing more separately now, and a covering of ferns underneath them that seemed thick and impenetrable at first glance but in fact allowed us to pass very easily. After another half-mile in this green gloom, with Runs Fast always bouncing ahead and showing the way, he brought us where he wanted: a clearing about fifty yards wide, which was surrounded by oaks on all sides. The sun shone very brightly here, and the air had a peculiar freshness and sparkle as it shimmered off the vegetation.

When we burst through the last of the ferns we found Runs Fast standing at the foot of a tree directly across the clearing, pointing upwards to the place where a branch had snapped off; here we saw a gash in the trunk that was coated with dark brown gum.

I recognised it at once as a bees' nest, but did not even have time to say so before Hoopoe and his men bounded forward, slashing at the tree with their weapons and calling for me and Natty to join in. Hoopoe, in particular, went about this work in a kind of frenzy, climbing into the lowest branches and really pounding at the wood with his tomahawk. The bees he dislodged in this way, that soon began to crawl over his face and hands and must have stung him very painfully, seemed not in the least troublesome to him. If one happened to land on his eye he brushed it away, but otherwise kept hacking and smashing as if the bees' wings and stinging tails were only raindrops.

After a few minutes he gave a throaty shout. A moment later he had taken hold of the prize – a dripping mass of honey the size of a large cat, which he hoisted above his head until some of the gold trickled down his arms and into his hair, before he brought it to us on the ground and we pressed forward to admire it.

It was like all bees' nests, which I had sometimes seen before in England, but a marvellous thing nonetheless, with little compartments all very intricately made, and ten or a dozen bees wading among them as if they were drowning in sweetness.

Then the next part of our labour began. One of the men had brought with him a satchel filled with leaves, and these were used to wrap a section of the honeycomb, so that we could take it back to the village as a treat. The remaining piece Hoopoe gripped in both hands (while several bees continued to fly about, as if tethered to their home by invisible strings), ordering us to stand behind him so that he could inspect the clearing and find what he needed.

This was a hollow log lying among the ferns, a trunk that had fallen years before and lost all its branches as well as most of its core. Once Hoopoe had led us to inspect this apparently useless object, which was about fifteen feet long and four in diameter, he told us to drag it towards the centre of the clearing, remove all the remaining fragments of wood, fungi, beetles and other bugs from the inside, block the narrower end with branches, then deposit the half-honeycomb near the centre of the tunnel, making sure we left a trail that led into the open air.

As we did this I understood we were making a trap for our bear and baiting it. Less clear was how we would kill him, once we had managed to lure him in the first place. But I did not like to ask Hoopoe and he did not bother to explain. From the expression on his face, which was perfectly grave and yet mischievous at the same time, I knew he was absorbed in a sort of game, and preferred it to remain mysterious.

I had plenty of time to imagine how it might be resolved. For once our preparations were finished, and the honey carefully installed, and the trail laid, we retreated from the clearing into the undergrowth, where Hoopoe told us to cover ourselves with fern leaves and to lie down as quietly as possible for as long as necessary.

He said this while throwing a suspicious glance towards me and Natty as though he doubted our ability to do as he asked, which of course made us all the more determined. I suppose it must have been early afternoon by the time we had finished hiding ourselves, and I suppose it was another two or three hours before we had any reason to stir, and for that long time I do not think I have ever made less noise in my life. When spiders tiptoed into my nostrils I did not so much as wrinkle my nose. When ants decided to investigate my ears I did not mind. When a tickle began to torment my leg, and grew until it became a sort of mania, I ignored it – and so eventually drove it away. Natty was the same. Although she was no more than a foot away from me, she kept so silent she might have been in England; I did not even hear her breathe.

But I did hear, when the softer light of evening began to sink through the wood, and the songs of birds around us changed from occasional warbles into the more united chorus of boasts and warnings and farewells that occur everywhere in the world at such a time, another sound that made my heart catch in my throat. At first it was very faint, a low rumbling or groaning, such as an old man might make when his joints ache and he thinks no one is nearby to hear him complain. Then the noise grew and developed a note that had less objection in it and more appetite, like the sound a hungry man might make while rubbing his stomach because he expects there will soon be food on the table.

This told me our prize must be close, so I allowed myself the smallest degree of curiosity. I lifted my head a fraction. I opened my eyes a crack. And I saw at a distance of seven or eight yards a bear shoving his way through the ferns and into the clearing, then pausing to sniff the air for a moment before shambling forward again to inspect the trail of honey that glittered at the entrance of our trap.

I had seen drawings of bears before this, and real bears fishing in the river, as I have mentioned. But I had never before been so close to one. I felt amazed. Humbled would be a better word. Although only half my height at the shoulder when standing on all fours, the body was enormously thick and weighty, the head rather disproportionately small, and the back parts unfinished-looking and blunt, which is the case with all animals lacking a tail. The coat: the coat was magnificent: a dense tawny mat like soft thatch that trembled with every step and seemed continually to scatter infinite points of light. So were the eyes magnificent : little bronze fires that burned with a passionate disparagement of the world. So were the claws magnificent, curling as yellow as butter among the fur that covered what I should normally have called feet but in fact were gigantic woolly stumps.

I knew if the creature smelled us it would very easily swat us into eternity: I had heard stories at home of bears in bear-pits which, when they were set upon by dogs, dispatched six, ten, a dozen of their attackers, despite the savaging and laceration they endured in the process. But even if he had detected us – and it was clear from the way the anvil-head continued to swing slowly from side to side that he felt troubled by something as yet invisible in his world – even if he had detected us, I thought we were safe at least for the moment.

With a final cursory sniff of the air, he approached the open end of the log, folded his shaggy front legs, thrust his enormous rump in our direction, inserted his head into the hole, and snorted once or twice. This made the log reverberate very loudly. Having established himself in this way, he then proceeded to squeeze forward by means of lurching and twisting and shuddering and grappling until he was almost entirely hidden from our sight.

Natty jumped to her feet brushing leaves off her hair and face, then ran forward into the clearing. I was confused. Had I misunderstood? Was this something Hoopoe had asked her to do? Did she mean me to follow? I did not wait for her to ask. I simply jumped up and ran forward, positioning myself by the entrance to our trap while she scrambled on top of it.

Now that I was out in the open I thought the clearing looked much larger than it had done while we were hiding; the breeze seemed to blow very slowly across the open space, and the whole circumference of trees began to revolve, spinning together the faces of our friends now peering through the ferns, and the bright green leaves, and the birds, and the patches of blue sky, and the streaks of sunlight, while everything closer to hand remained perfectly still and clear:

the quaking back legs of the bear, whose fur I saw now was really black and only tipped with brown;

the family of beetles walking in line along the tree trunk until they passed between Natty's feet;

the tearing and growling that came from inside the log;

the roaring when the bear realised we were very close, and began to back out from his trap;

and Natty herself. Natty poised above the entrance. Natty with her legs braced and a spear lifted above her head. Natty with her face flushed and her hair tousled and dirty.

'Now!' I shouted, standing my ground behind the bear, jabbing at his hindquarters and feeling the point of my spear lose its way among the deep fur.

Natty did not reply, but kept in the same position with her arms raised.

'Now!' I shouted again. 'Now! Stick him! Strike him!' – with Hoopoe breaking into the open behind me.

'Miss Natty!' he called. 'Mister Jim!' His voice sounded oddly hollow and fluting, as if he was calling his own bird-name, or perhaps the bear's name, calling as one creature to another.

Natty paid no attention and neither did I. As the bear made another gigantic effort and finally worked his shoulders and front paws free from the trunk, I lunged forward with my spear, piercing the fur this time and wounding him. He stopped still, bellowing at the insult, and just as he turned his head, with his jaws wide open and smeared with honey, and his nose also blurred with honey and one of his eyes plugged blind with it, Natty drove downwards; the point of her spear vanished into the broad neck where it met the skull.

It was a clever strike – or a lucky one – and I think must have severed the spine. The bear snapped his mouth shut and a look of great irritation came into his one clear eye, then of great sadness. All his noises stopped, his roaring and growling, and he gave a sigh as if he was settling down to snooze. He lifted his black snout, the nostrils still busily dilating and shrinking. Then he collapsed sideways, with a crash that silenced all the birds in the wood for a moment, and us as well.

I glanced along the stomach; until now I had thought of the

bear as a man and called him a man in my mind, but I saw two rows of brown nipples poking through the fur, each one surprisingly long and crinkled, and each tipped with a little dot of milk.

There must be cubs nearby, I thought; well-grown cubs born last spring. I could not imagine them, because Hoopoe and the rest were swarming around us now, slapping Natty on the back and kneeling to admire her kill, running their hands through the fur and watching them disappear up to the wrist. No one mentioned the cubs, or what might become of them. Natty, who seemed flabbergasted by what she had done, and was leaning against the log to recover herself, did not know they existed.

I found a place to kneel by the head of the bear, where I saw again how much honey was rubbed over the muzzle and cheeks, and how the long teeth were yellow with honey, and how the top lip had snagged on those teeth to make an expression like a sneer. As if death did not matter, because life did not matter.

CHAPTER 16

Our Second Exodus

In this way Natty came to be known as Little Bear and I was Running Bear – not that I had run anywhere during our hunt, and not that Natty's new name gave a fair description of what she had done. The idea was that in killing the animal she had entered its world and become its kindred spirit. I liked this because it combined with everything that Hoopoe and the others had told me; Natty complained it made her sound like a child, when it was perfectly clear she was no such thing.

These conversations lay in the future. Our immediate task was to finish our work in the clearing by fetching long sticks and creepers from the trees around us, and building a sledge to drag our victim back to the village. When we had done this – and when we had skinned the bear so her coat could be offered to White Feather with all due ceremony, and eaten some of her meat (with the rest salted away for eating in the future), and smoked our pipe, and danced our dance – we fell back into our routines once more, which meant the days passed without me bothering to count them.

But I must not give a false impression. As the following two years rolled by, and despite my deep pleasures in the place and its people, I could not forget my old self entirely. Little by little, and then like the sea-tide that would not be turned back, a sense of restlessness grew in me. A melancholy. I suppose I had reached the limit of my capacity to feel at home in the village; I thought I should either embrace it completely and decide to end my days there, or acknowledge whatever remained of my nostalgia for England, and set off to find it again.

Natty and I spoke about these things many times in private before we decided to act on them. The journey ahead seemed so enormous, so full of dangers and threats and surprises and confusions, and these were all good reasons to delay. Another was our fear of seeming to reject Hoopoe and the rest, who had found us as strangers and made us their friends. Yet even while we hesitated we could not prevent our thoughts from taking the direction most natural to them, until at last we felt that our little tent, which had sheltered us so well, and where we had seemed perfectly contented for a long time, was in fact a crucible for plans to escape, or a refuge for painful memories of things far away.

When we could not keep our thoughts to ourselves any longer, and anyway suspected others might be able to see them in our faces, we decided to consult Hoopoe, whom we trusted to know the best way to resolve them. As things fell out, our route to this conversation – which we thought must be taken very cautiously, so as not to offend delicate feelings – turned out to be very direct.

It happened as spring was just beginning, spring 1805 as I know

now, when the temperature was mild enough to make travelling a long distance seem enjoyable. I was about to say as much to Hoopoe when he came to our tent one evening after the rest of the village had already retired, and when I soon expected to be asleep myself. Natty, as I could tell from the quietness of her breathing beside me, had already dropped into unconsciousness.

When I heard Hoopoe clear his throat in the darkness, and opened the flaps of the tepee to find him waiting for me, I thought some accident must have occurred that needed our attention. And so in a sense it had. Speaking softly, and with a sort of embarrassment in his voice, he told me that while out hunting that day in the wilderness he had seen Black Cloud prowling about – but had not been spotted himself. Black Cloud and another man, who was painted with so many colours it made Hoopoe think that his own decorations were drab in comparison.

When I heard this I found myself gazing back through the dark opening of our tent, where my necklace lay in the satchel I used for my pillow; I almost thought it glowed at me, through its several layers of concealment; I almost heard it speak.

What I might say myself, I hardly knew. Hoopoe, who was usually so excitable, seemed very perplexed, pacing to and fro with the bells on his wrists and ankles making soft little chimes until I put out my hand and brought him to a halt.

After staring into my face in silence for a moment he turned away and looked towards the river.

'We must leave you now,' I said, speaking as quietly as possible so as not to wake Natty.

He shrugged, still with his back towards me.

I did not want to continue at once, thinking he might turn round and say a little about how Natty and I had become a part of his family, or some such excellent thing. But when he remained silent and then began pacing to and fro again, I understood that he did not think our friendship should be decisive in shaping our plans. We had said as much the first day we met, and I had not forgotten. Although Black Cloud and the Painted Man were only two, and two dozen of our men could be set against them, their reputation was so fearsome they seemed like an indestructible force.

'Now,' I told him. 'We'll leave you now; as soon as possible. Then they won't hurt you.'

Hoopoe continued walking, his feet making a soft scratch-scratch on the dry earth.

'They may,' he said. 'They may harm us whether you are here or not.'

This idea hurt me and I did my best to knock it aside. 'I'm sure not,' I said. 'It's us they want to hurt, not you. They'll follow us.'

'But we shall not tell them where you go.'

'They'll find out – that's their way. You've said so yourself.'

Hoopoe paused, then tried another tack. 'You cannot be away from your home for ever,' he said.

'I've no wish to be,' I said.

This seemed to encourage him, as though for the first time I had admitted what he already knew.

'We can set you on your course,' he said, with some brightness coming into his voice. 'You must go to the east—'

'Hoopoe,' I interrupted him, without knowing what I might be about to say.

He stopped his pacing and stood close to me. The paint across his cheeks and around his eyes was dried up, which gave him the appearance of great age, like an ancient porcelain figure that has developed thousands of tiny cracks in its glaze.

'You've been very kind to us,' I told him, with a tremor in my voice; it was only a small part of the truth, but I hoped he would feel the great weight of feeling that swelled inside me.

There was no reply.

'You've been kind,' I repeated. 'And I will never forget you. Neither will Little Bear ever forget you.'

Hoopoe nodded, the silhouette of his head bobbing slowly against the paler sky. I thought this would be his only response, and was about to return to our tepee and wake Natty, and tell her everything I had learned. But Hoopoe was not drawing things to a close; he was gathering himself.

'The Painted Man,' he said, looking over my shoulder where the grasses suddenly began seething as the night-wind strengthened and passed over them. For a moment I thought he had seen the eyes watching him, glittering among the dark stems, but he had only imagined them and soon looked away.

'*Berdache*,' he went on.

I repeated the word, which I had not heard before.

'*Berdache*,' Hoopoe said again. 'It is what we call a companion like Black Cloud's companion. Such men do womanish things. This Painted Man does womanish things, and the work of women. But he is powerful.'

'I know that,' I told him, which was only to show that I understood what he meant, not to take it for granted. But Hoopoe doubted me.

'More powerful than you know,' Hoopoe told me, with a snarl in his voice. 'That is why Black Cloud keeps him close. Black Cloud is a powerful man also, very strong in his body and like iron in his mind. But the Painted Man is powerful as well. *Berdache*, yes. He has no heart.'

This was as much as Hoopoe would allow himself to say, and although the sentences were very few, they were spoken so slowly,

and with such deliberation, I felt I had been thoroughly repri-
manded. Chastened enough, at any rate, to imagine Black Cloud
and his companion rising from their bed, and spinning with fury
when they found we had escaped; to think of them taking the
direction that Hoopoe had predicted; to see them disappointed,
and beginning to search for other clues; to feel the heat of fires
they had lit; to hear the stamp and thunder of their feet; to
remember the devastated village; to think Hoopoe and the others
might soon find them rioting towards them.

For a little over two years we had hidden in safety, as Hoopoe
had predicted we would. Now his protection was almost exhausted.
Now Black Cloud would no longer be prevented from finding us.

I had imagined what must follow a hundred times, but never so
clearly as then. And when I remember my conversation with
Hoopoe again today I feel the same fear prickling though me – as
though I am still lost in the wilderness, and still facing the same
question as I did then: why did I not simply fetch the necklace from
our tent and pass it to him? Why did I not say that in due course
he must give it to Black Cloud, which would have been an end to
all our troubles?

Pride, I suppose. Stubbornness. Greed. Some defect in myself,
which proves I am my father's son and also the son of Adam.

More surprising is that Hoopoe himself did not suggest it. But
for this I do have an explanation. I thought then, and still believe
now, that he understood it would give me some authority in our
travels to come. Some authority, and therefore a degree of safety
as well, despite the dangers it would also provoke.

When Hoopoe and I were done, the necklace still lay in the
darkness beneath my pillow. And when we had said goodnight to
one another and I saw him disappear into the shadows, I did not
believe his shoulders were stooped because he thought I had made

a great error of judgement. He was dejected for a much larger and sadder reason. He had reminded himself of someone whose powers matched his own, or were greater than his own, but were devoted to madness and atrocity.

I did not mention this to Natty when I lay down beside her, but only because I did not have to. She had remained asleep throughout my talk with Hoopoe, and was therefore quite untroubled by such thoughts as kept me awake for the next little while. How would we find our way to the east? What strangers would we meet next? Would they treat us with the same kindness we had grown used to? When my eyes closed at last, it was not because I had found the answer to any of these questions, but because I felt overwhelmed by them.

The next morning I expected Natty to tell me we should stay and fight. I had never doubted her courage, and knew it sometimes stood in the way of her better judgement. But whether she feared Black Cloud more than she allowed herself to say, or wanted to spare our friends from troubles we would otherwise inflict on them, she did not demur when I told her what was in my mind. Lying on her back in the early light, staring upwards into the brightening cone of our tent with her red shawl drawn up to her chin, she only said what I had already decided: 'We must go at once.'

I felt so surprised by her straightforwardness I was almost inclined to object despite myself.

'They've been very good to us,' I said again, which sounded much less than I meant, and gave no indication of how much I would miss them.

'Of course,' said Natty. 'But we've always said that can't be the reason to stay. We must leave immediately.'

'Immediately?' I repeated. 'You mean today?'

'Do you think Black Cloud will wait if he knows we're here?'

I shifted my head on the pillow and felt the bars of the necklace slide together in the satchel beneath.

'And the Painted Man,' Natty went on, suddenly sitting upright. 'He certainly won't wait.'

With that, as if she had just now seen the shadow of the monster spilling across the wall of our tent, she leaped up and ducked outside, smoothing her dress as she went. Her disappearance felt very sudden after the long delay of our previous conversations; it seemed almost laughable.

And remained so when I stood upright myself, and looked out to see she had gone to the river, and taken her place among the others already gathered there, who were busily splashing their faces and feet while the morning sun climbed above them.

It was the simplest picture, which I had seen every morning for months on end, and never thought would serve as the beginning of our farewell. But that is what it became: the gentlest of separations, with the women kneeling as they swept their wet hair from their eyes, and the water-drops sliding from elbows and fingers, and the river crinkled by the breeze, and the vast and level country stretching beyond, and the rust-red sky, and the thin straight line of charcoal along the horizon.

As I stared towards that far-off point, I kept myself steady by remembering that ours was the easiest sort of leave-taking, because our sorrow at leaving past pleasures was matched by our interest in what lay ahead. And I continued thinking this for the rest of our final morning, while Natty and I collected a few parcels of food, and our water-bag, and two knives, and my satchel, and a pair of blankets, and then shook hands in the English way with everyone in the village, and thanked them as warmly as possible.

When we reached White Feather, I wanted to make a more elaborate gesture. Although the withdrawn and wandering nature of his mind had made him remote to us, from the first moment in which he had appeared naked in the doorway of his tent, to this last when he appeared in his cloak of bearskin, he had smiled on everything we had done. I would have liked to show my gratitude for this as I stood before him, and felt the weight of his large soft hand on my head, but my words would never have penetrated the mists of his mind, and might have embarrassed him if they had. As a result, the seal of my life under his protection was broken with nothing more than a long look into his empty eyes.

Hoopoe we did not have to leave yet, because he had offered to walk with us for the first hour, and set us on our way. Before that, however, he took us to the river-bank, where he told us we must fill our heads with the music of the water, and its encouragement to continue, and its replenishment, so that in days to come, when we were thirsty and exhausted, we would still have the Spirit speaking to us, to help us as we travelled onwards.

I welcomed this idea very gladly, and when he finished speaking I knelt down and took a deep gulp from the current, then wiped my face and neck and arms. When I had finished this baptism, or perhaps I should call it an absolution, I climbed onto my pony and trotted to catch up with Natty, who had already turned away with Hoopoe walking beside her. When we reached the boundary of the village we looked back to find that everyone we had left behind, including the oldest grandmother and the youngest child, had formed themselves into a fan-shape with White Feather at the centre and their right hands raised above their heads. We made the same salute, then quickly turned away. If I had looked for a moment longer I do not think my resolve to leave would have weakened, but I am sure my last sight would have been less firm and clear, with my friends all flickering as though they might soon disappear from the face of the earth.

CHAPTER 17

A Flock of Birds

Because our ponies had grown fat during our stay in the village, they puffed and laboured heavily as we rode forward, and soon broke into a sweat; Hoopoe, on the other hand, slid alongside us very easily, as if he was our shadow. For the first few miles we passed through familiar places – our hunting-grounds, which I knew as well as my own skin – and felt the breeze like the warmth of my own breath. I had never enjoyed them so much because I knew I would never see them again, and the three of us talked fondly together, as good companions will do, when they know they must soon go their separate ways.

I suppose Hoopoe relaxed like this because he did not want us to think Black Cloud might be anywhere near. But at the same time, and very urgently, he insisted we must never divert from the route he ordered us to follow. He told us that if we continued due east, always keeping the sun on our faces in the morning and at our back in the afternoon, we would eventually come to a large river, the largest of all rivers, a miniature rolling sea, where a boat would carry us south and bring us to a town full of others like ourselves. Here we would find another boat to take us back to England.

He spoke of these things, and especially of the city that would be our salvation, as a true believer might speak of heaven – with reverence and awe. He had not seen it with his own eyes, and had never met anyone else who had been there, but he knew it existed. We must be watchful, that was all; if we were watchful we would be safe, and we would reach our goal.

By the time we felt reassured to this extent, Hoopoe had kept us company for much longer than the hour he first promised, and we had reached a part of the country that was unknown even to him. If I had not suggested otherwise, I think he would have stayed with us for several miles more, because he did not want to reach the point of farewell. But in my first and final challenge to him, and as a sign of my self-confidence, I ordered him to turn back and be sure of reaching the village before nightfall. After a little resistance he relented, and Natty and I dismounted to say goodbye.

I will not linger over this scene, except to say that it forced me to squeeze together a whole range of ideas about what sorts of affection existed between us. It was friendship, certainly, a deep friendship, but not of the kind I might have made at home, with intimacies exchanged, and confidences passed between us, and a great mutual familiarity. In certain respects I felt Hoopoe was quite unknowable to me because of the differences between us. Yet I am sure we felt an unusual bond of trust, as well as interest.

When the moment came we did not even try to speak to one

another but simply embraced in silence, then stood close together while our ponies browsed among the grasses, and the wind complained through the thorn bushes. I remember looking down and noticing that some of the paint from his body had transferred itself onto my hands; I did not wipe it off for a long time afterwards.

Hoopoe then invoked the Great Spirit to guard us on our way, calling us by our Indian names for the last time, Little Bear and Running Bear, then rolled his head and looked straight up to heaven, which made the veins bulge in his neck as the blood pumped through them. I stared at these signs of life for a moment because they seemed very precarious. Then I also threw back my head and stared at the sky, and saw a large flock of white birds, seagulls no doubt, glittering like salt as they made their way to the coast. When I straightened again Hoopoe was already a hundred yards off. He moved fast and straight as an arrow, sometimes leaping over low shrubs, until he disappeared.

Natty was suddenly bustling and efficient. 'We must find a camp for the night,' she said, collecting our ponies.

I took hold of the halter-rein she gave me, and tried to speak in the same way, to prove that despite the sadness of our parting I did not mind us being alone again. 'We need to find . . .' I began, and meant to add 'shelter' or some such word, but gave up as I looked around me. Red rock, red earth, and green scrub unrolling to the horizon on every side. It was beautiful, I could see that, but endless. Terrible in its scale and monotony. Terrible also in seeming to mock all the advice Hoopoe had given us. Keep riding east. The word 'east', the idea of east, did not seem large enough to survive in such a wilderness.

And yet for the next hour or so we rode as Hoopoe had instructed us, with the sun sinking at our backs, and our shadows stretching before us until they had reached a really extravagant length.

Sometimes we reminded one another of what we hoped to find at the end of our journey. Always we chose not to speak of things we had left behind. And eventually, as though it had been prepared for us by Hoopoe, we found a place to rest among several large boulders that seemed to have been carried here and rolled together by giants – the land around them was bare except for a stubble of soft grass.

'Will he have reached the village yet?' Natty asked. By now we had tethered our ponies and watered and fed them, and made a fire to cook the meat we had brought with us. Darkness had fallen, but the moon and stars burned so fiercely, the stones around us seemed almost luminous.

'Oh, yes,' I replied. 'He'll fly home.'

'He's Hoopoe.'

'Exactly, he's Hoopoe.'

'Will they miss us, do you think?' Natty poked a stick into our fire so the flames jumped up; she was frowning.

Now I could not keep the sadness out of my voice, because I missed our friends. 'Why do you ask?'

She stared at her food without eating. 'We could have brought them with us,' she said.

'What?' I said, pushing away my own plate. 'All of them?'

'Hoopoe. Whoever wanted to come.'

'Bring them to England?'

'Why not? It's been done before.'

'But they belong here,' I said. 'They wouldn't survive anywhere else. In London? Imagine it, Natty.'

'I'm trying to,' she said. 'After all, we don't belong here but we're managing.'

'We are?'

'Look at us,' said Natty. I thought this hardly proved her point, seeing how poor we were and undefended, but kept quiet.

'Anyway,' Natty continued, 'we were happy there. We made a home with them. Why shouldn't they make a home with us?'

'It's not the same,' I told her. 'We needed their protection. They don't need ours, even supposing we could give it.'

Natty laughed. 'But they do! If not now, then very soon.'

'From Black Cloud?' I said, but knew he was not all she meant.

'Yes, from Black Cloud,' she said. 'And from others like ourselves.' She was speaking quietly now, as if she thought there might be ears listening in the darkness. But during the pause that followed I could only hear wind breathing over the baked ground, and a night-hawk screaming as it floated along the currents.

'We didn't choose to be here,' I said, in the same hushed voice.

'Nevertheless,' Natty said. 'We're part of it.' She jabbed her stick into the fire again and a fountain of sparks rushed upwards, with a few landing in the grass near where I was sitting; I soon patted them out.

I could not think how to answer this, and the longer our silence lasted, the more difficult it was to break.

'I could leave it here,' I said eventually. 'I could throw it away or bury it.'

I did not need to explain that I was talking about the necklace, and Natty answered immediately. 'We've decided, Jim,' she said. 'That's too late as well.'

'We took it together,' I said.

'I know,' Natty said. 'But if you left it here, and Black Cloud never found it, that wouldn't change anything. We took it, and that's that. We stole it.'

I reached out to touch her, and she squeezed my hand briefly, then let go. 'Is that what you think now?' she said. 'That we made a mistake?'

I did not answer this, but instead delved into my satchel and pulled out the necklace, polishing it quickly with my hand before holding it towards the firelight. The silver sprang to life at once, as though the air allowed the animals to breathe, and stretch, and snap at one another. When we had admired it for a moment, and Natty had run her fingers over the carvings, and lifted one of the pieces to remind herself of its weight, I slipped it back into my satchel. Neither of us spoke, not while we looked, and not when the necklace disappeared again. As we continued in silence, watching the flames gnaw at the sticks of our fire, and the different temperatures of the embers regard us with differently coloured eyes, neither of us could see how to take our thoughts any further. We were thieves, we knew that, but we could not feel it in our hearts. If one of us was damned, so was the other.

I stood up and made myself busy, making sure our ponies were securely tethered, packing away the food we had not eaten, throwing more sticks on the fire, then shaking out my blanket and lying down to sleep. Natty, meanwhile, remained staring into the flames, her shoulders hunched, her Indian dress gleaming darkly in the firelight. I gazed at her, and although she did not return my look, I knew that our minds were very close.

Next morning we made no mention of these things, but ate our breakfast in silence, dowsed our fire, and removed all trace of our camp as though we expected Black Cloud would soon search for us here. Then we put the sun in our eyes, which was our only way to feel sure we were on the right path, and rode into the empty day. And the next. And the next. Perhaps for a week, perhaps two. It is difficult for me to remember, because we were soon exhausted by the sway and stumble of our ponies; by the dazzle and heat; by the wind as it whined or shuffled or rushed through the bushes; by the flat land repeating itself, or bringing us to a little ridge where the dust danced around us in spirals; by the sense of time sweeping around us like water that renewed itself endlessly, and never cared if we noticed or not.

In the midst of this desolation, the least interruption became momentous. When the breeze rose a notch, and blew strongly enough to roll a bundle of thorn alongside me for a few yards, it seemed like a great event. When a crow perched on a cactus and cocked its head to one side, and cawed at me as if to introduce himself personally, it became a thing to ponder for hours.

Eventually, just before sunset on the seventh day (unless it was the fourteenth, or the hundredth), we found something even more extraordinary. After mile upon mile of no trees, a small copse of alders, growing in a hollow of the ground about fifty yards across. Natty and I dismounted and led our ponies between the trunks without even consulting one another; when we lay down on the bed of dead leaves we could not imagine ourselves in greater safety.

We dozed for a while, an hour maybe, and were beginning to think about making our supper, when I heard a murmur in the sky to the west, which I thought must be another flock of gulls returning to the coast. I crept to the edge of our shelter to get a clearer view, and saw at once that the birds flying towards us were not gulls but smaller, with grey-blue backs and wings and russet breasts.

But it was not their colours or their size that made me stop and stare. It was their numbers. For they were gathered into such gigantic flocks they had almost obliterated the setting sun. Clouds, in fact, would be a better word than flocks – clouds that continually broke apart and joined again, sometimes surging upwards in a billowing mass, sometimes sinking towards the earth and crashing through shrubs and bushes, stripping whatever food they could find there.

Then Natty came up beside me and we heard them, the murmur of wings becoming a rush, the rush becoming a roar, the roar turning to thunder, and the thunder breaking into a cacophony of coos and whistles and squeals and flutters and flaps and scratches and scrapes when the first arrivals landed overhead. As the weight of bodies began to accumulate, the trees began to collapse, snapping and splintering with more and more birds fighting for space. Hundreds of birds. Thousands of birds. And thousands more arriving all the time. Millions of birds. All whizzing and whistling as they rubbed together, their feet scrabbling, their wings clapping and colliding and fluttering.

By now I had grabbed Natty by the hand, shooing birds out of my way, battering them, shouting that we must collect our things and our ponies, and quick, quick, get them out of the wood before they panicked and broke away.

They did not panic. They rolled their eyes and snorted and tugged at their reins, but they came with us, then let us climb onto their backs again and ride off with our heads bowed down because a hundred, five hundred, a thousand more birds were still swirling towards us, aiming at us apparently, diving at us with their wings extended on their final glide, until we reached open ground and turned round to watch how it ended.

With branches snapping inside the wood like gunfire, and these broken spars and timbers all turning white as the birds relieved themselves, the wood was no longer a wood but a snow-field. But still with more birds arriving. An enormous scarf of them stretching all the way to the horizon, wavering and undulating and blackening. Flesh and blood, feathers and bone, and all as fluid as pouring grain, cascading into a store that could not possibly hold such a quantity. Any more, I thought, and the wood will explode, what remains of the wood, and we will be showered with feathers and leaves and bones and bark and claws and beaks and little shining eyes.

Yet I still could not turn away, not until the last light had faded from the sky, and the last few thousand birds had squeezed into their places, and the whole immense flock had finished its arguments and conversations, its greetings and goodnights, and fallen asleep. Quite suddenly, in a second or two. Fast asleep. A moment later, and the silence of the wilderness rolled back. A silence that felt complete and boundless, but in fact was stitched together with sounds belonging to other, quieter creatures, which knew the tempest had subsided, and now they could continue with their own more secretive lives.

Natty and I looked at one another amazed, as if we had almost been destroyed ourselves.

'Passenger pigeons,' I said; I had learned the name from Hoopoe, when we had seen them flying in smaller flocks.

'Indeed,' she said. Then added very sensibly, 'Have they made us lose our way?'

'Not at all,' I told her unsteadily; I still could not escape the noise of the birds, or their feathers tumbling together. 'That's the east,' I said, pointing towards the moon, where it rode on a chariot of cloud.

'Our cooking pot,' said Natty, in the same practical way.

'What about it?'

'We left it behind.'

'I know.'

'And our meal.'

I smiled, which she did not see in the darkness. 'We didn't start our meal,' I reminded her. 'But I'll fetch it now.'

I slid off my pony, passed Natty the reins, and ran back towards the wood. Not one of the birds noticed me coming, or cared when I got close. Even when I chose a brace and wrung their necks, not a single one of the rest of them stirred to look at me, or warned the others.

By the time I returned to Natty she had already made our fire, and soon we had prepared our supper and eaten it. Then we settled down in the lee of a large rock – it had a profile, I remember, that reminded me of a witch with a hooked nose. Before I fell asleep, I looked around at the wilderness with no great curiosity; so far as I could tell the ground nearby was covered with the same thistles and scrub I saw every night, and every day as well. And those long shallow ridges in the dust, which were the last things I saw before my eyes closed: I decided the wind must have made them.

CHAPTER 18

The Entertainment

Next morning I woke under a waterfall. No, not a waterfall. I woke in the air – swept up by the angels of heaven all beating their wings together and singing. Then not singing but whispering. Whistling. Cooing. Gurgling. Crooning. Because they were not angels any more, they were pigeons, the same as last night, and now leaving with their mess drizzling beneath them in a continual white rain, first with laborious flusterings and squabblings, then twisting and looping and swaying and swerving until they had formed a gigantic letter S which held its shape . . . and held its shape . . . before it slackened and became a smoke-cloud blowing towards the horizon.

'Do you see?' Natty was propped on one elbow.

I continued gazing at the splintered branches and shattered

trunks; the wood looked as though it had been pounded by cannon-fire.

'Not there,' Natty went on. 'There.'

For the first time I looked at her; she was not facing the trees at all but staring at the ground, at the bare earth I had thought was nothing last night. Now I looked more closely. The little runnels and gullies I had decided were made by the wind were quite clearly hoof prints. Hoof prints and wheel-marks.

I forgot the wood at once: the wood, and the pigeons, and everything behind me. If I was right, and these were fresh, there were people nearby – or had been, anyhow. People with a wagon and horses. As Hoopoe had taught me to do, I crawled forward on my hands and knees, pressing one ear to the ground to listen for the echo of hooves, and the sound of weight passing.

I heard a soft boom, which I reckoned was the sound of my own pulse, then wiped some grains of dust from my eye and asked Natty whether she thought Hoopoe had known about this road.

'It's hardly a road,' she replied.

'Track, then.'

'He knew there'd be people.'

'And the river?' I asked, still kneeling on the ground and squinting up at her.

'What about the river?'

'Do we turn here and follow this track?' I said. 'Or do we keep straight on to the east?'

Natty looked first north, then south, as though the land itself might give us some clue. It was equally deserted in both directions.

'I think straight on to the east,' she said.

'Why?'

'Because that's what Hoopoe told us to do,' she said. 'The river is in the east and it'll be easier for us when we find it – easier than all this desert.'

'Provided it's not too far away,' I said. 'Provided we can find a boat.' I was surprised by my stubbornness and wanted to shake it off; I thought it must be a sign of fear.

Natty picked up her sleeping-blanket, folded it, and carried it to her pony where she arranged it like a saddle. 'Besides,' she said, turning to face me again, 'we've no idea about who we might find on the trail. They might be friends or they might be enemies.'

'They'll be friends,' I said, still determined. 'They'll be pioneers like us.'

'Is that what we are, Jim?' she said, quickening a little. 'Pioneers?'

'In a way.'

'So you think we should follow the trail, then? You think we should forget the river?'

'I didn't say that.'

'But it's what you think.'

'I think a trail must lead somewhere,' I said. 'It can't just end.'

'And you're happy to ignore Hoopoe.'

'I didn't say happy. I didn't say ignore.' I paused. 'It's just that Hoopoe has never been here himself. He's heard stories, that's all. And his stories were all made before . . . before this.' I climbed to my feet and gestured along the trail.

Natty shaded her eyes and stared towards the horizon – a strip of flimsy white, trembling in the heat. I thought: in a moment she will round on me; in a moment our quarrel will continue. But as she opened her mouth to speak we were suddenly interrupted by a new voice, a third voice, very faint and far-off and singing a sea shanty of all things, one I recognised:

Oh the billows roll and thunder
And we think we'll follow under
Where the dead men roam
And the fishes make their home.

It had to be a hallucination; an illness the sun had boiled in my brain. First it had made us bad-tempered, now it made us imagine things that did not exist.

Then Natty heard it too. A cheerful song, not in the least frightening. Exuberant, in fact, and with an orchestra, too; a full accompaniment of groans and rumbles and squeaks and sighs and jingles and judders.

But a madhouse: that was my first impression when they swung into view at last and stopped a few yards away from us. A band of lunatics escaped from their institution, and now as amazed by the sight of us as we were astounded by them.

I stared at each in turn, starting with a Red Indian who was no more red than I am, but smeared in charcoal paint from head to waist except for a white stripe on either cheekbone; he was wearing trousers made of brown leather, and moccasins, and riding a pony about the same size as my own, but black not chestnut and itself smeared over the shoulders with blue dye.

Next to him, sitting astride a mule, was a man who might have been a woman; I could not be sure because the body was entirely concealed by a loose yellow costume, and the face coloured with paler yellow paint (except for the nose and lips, which were red as carnations), and the hair hidden beneath a wig that was also bright red.

Next to this freak was another, but stranger still because her head, her exceptionally large and completely hairless head, bulged as if she had developed a kind of skull-attic to hold her brain.

This deformity, combined with very protuberant and shiny eyes, and lips that were almost purple, made her like a soap bubble, which she accentuated by wearing a voluminous oyster-coloured dress. A dainty and fragile soap bubble, balanced on her pony and holding tight to the reins so as not to drift off towards the sun and expire.

Beside her rode the chorister – or rather, the specimen who had been the chorister, since the moment he saw us his sea shanty died into a gargle, then ceased altogether. Not a chorister now. A heavy and four-square man with a sunburned face, wearing a bushy moustache that curled into his side-whiskers, a sailor's blue coat with shiny brass buttons, and a sailor's three-cornered hat crammed onto his head.

For a while we gazed in silence, assessing and estimating. I thought they must be lunatics as I say: travellers driven mad by sun and loneliness. At the same time I realised we must look equally surprising, bursting out of nowhere with our Indian dress, our hair chopped and matted, our faces scorched, our lips cracked, and our manners almost forgotten.

Savages! I thought; they will think we are savages and kill us and leave us in the road behind them.

Kill us now in fact – because the fifth and last of the strangers to appear turned out to be a dwarfish fellow driving a covered wagon, with a rifle resting across his knees. As he tugged on his reins with one hand he picked up his gun with the other and pointed it straight at us.

Our chorister, who seemed to have eyes in the back of his head as well as the front, instantly woke from his astonishment, snapping his mouth shut and doffing his hat to reveal a deep thatch of inky hair.

'Good morning!' he boomed, as if he was a hundred yards off

and not ten. 'What, may I enquire, brings you to this charming spot in the heat of the day?'

This was so unexpected I sat thunderstruck. The moon-woman drifted a little higher into the air. The yellow clown scowled. The Indian was impassive. The midget driver ran his hand along the barrel of his gun as though it was an animal with a mind of its own, and needed to be kept quiet by tickling.

'We're looking for the coast,' I said at last; my voice sounded small and unconvincing.

'English!' came the reply, like an explosion.

'London,' said Natty, who had pulled herself together more quickly than I had, and spat out the word fiercely, as a kind of defiance.

'London!' The big voice scattered over the rocks on either side of us and the red face turned to the freak riding beside him, whose eyes were bulging so much I thought they might be about to fly out of her head.

'Did you hear that, my love?' the stranger went on breathlessly. 'London! London!' He swung back towards us, once more flourishing his hat in one hand. 'Never did I think I would hear that word in the desert. Blessed word. Blessed plot. But . . .' He shrugged, or convulsed rather, then controlled himself by cramming his hat back onto his head. 'But why are you here? Why are you so far from home?'

'We told you,' Natty replied. 'We're looking for the coast.'

Her voice sounded clipped compared to his own, which was hardly in the spirit of things. But our stranger did not notice. 'Why would you want the coast?' he exclaimed. 'Inland is the only direction. Inland! That is where the future lies! Cities of gold, boys, cities of gold. Golden rewards, at any rate, for such as ourselves.' Still holding the reins of his pony with one hand, he tugged off his hat once more and hoisted it towards the sky as if he expected the clouds to part and the Almighty to confirm this opinion.

'But we are travelling home,' Natty persevered. 'Home to London.'

This word, so magical to the stranger, made him lower his arm and look at us more thoughtfully again, with the clown and driver muttering under their breath.

'Some of us have worked in London,' he went on. 'Some of us have loved London and her fogs and rain. Some of us have loved her very much.' His head sank down, as if a sudden shower had swept across us and softened all the strings in his body. Then he looked up again bright as ever.

'Yes, some of us have loved her and some of us have enjoyed a great reception there. A great reception!'

'As what?' said Natty, still with enough boldness to seem rude – but again the stranger paid no attention.

'Why, as entertainers of course!' he replied, squaring his shoulders so his coat-buttons flashed in the sun. 'We are the Entertainment, the Entertainment, and always ready to do our entertaining, as you can see from the fact that we make a habit of travelling in our costumes. And wisely enough, for are we not even now entertaining you as we speak?'

Natty tried to brush this aside. 'Possibly,' she said. 'But surely there can't be much to entertain hereabouts. Surely . . .'

There was a scandalised pause, then another explosion. 'Not much to entertain? My dear young person, there is the world.' The stranger flourished his hat at the canyon walls on either side, as if to indicate the infinite horizons that stretched beyond them. 'The world, the world, the whole wide world, and us to fill it. Oh yes, we are the Entertainment, and now . . .' He paused, licking his lips as if preparing to address the largest audience of his life, then

rushed onwards again. 'And now, without further ado, I shall introduce you to our number.

'First, and bringing up the hindmost, with an eye to all our
possessions, is the Wee Man.' (Here he indicated the dwarf who
sat scowling in his wagon-seat, and was apparently not at all pleased
to be identified by this name, for he made no acknowledgement
except to stroke the barrel of his rifle even more lovingly.)

'After him, and furthest in this line on my left, is our latest friend
and a most estimable performer on horseback – the Rider. Do not
ask me his origins for I do not know them. On the eastern side of
this great country is all I know, because that is all he has told me.
On the eastern side which he has abandoned – for we met him on
the southern coast just recently and took him into our service.'
(During this longer introduction he pointed to the Indian whose
face and chest were smeared with charcoal, and who did not bow
or smile or make any sign of knowing he had been mentioned, but
regarded us with a calm and steady look which I could not decipher.
His face was like a mask carved out of dark wood, lean and severe
and handsome and watchful.)

'Next, and preserved in what I might call the uniform of his
trade, though costume is a gentler word, and worth his weight in
the same gold that he resembles, is our clown, whom we call simply
Clown.' (Here the hat was wafted towards the butter-coloured,
red-wigged fellow sitting astride the mule, who remained completely
still and so avoided giving any sign that he was associated with
good humour.)

'After that, and closest to me here, and by no means the least of
us, in fact the most of us, our paradigm of beauty and interest,
who also does me the honour, the extraordinary and unexpected
honour, new every morning, of living as my wife, Miss . . . Mrs . . .'
(Here he suddenly lost his way and seemed uncertain about how

best to summarise all his feelings in a single word, then found his direction again and announced very loudly: 'The Spectacle!' At which point the gleaming lady adjacent to him broke into a blissful smile and seemed to inflate so much with pride I thought she might actually rise up to heaven in a gust.)

As this enormous speechification ended we also discovered the name of its maker, which was simply Boss, who once he had made the announcement pressed one hand to his chest to show that although he took pride in his identity, he was also embarrassed to carry the burden of being such a formidable genius. This confirmed the impression we had already received – that he was a ridiculous person. Yet that was not all. For despite his huffing and puffing, and the absurd eruptions of his speech, he had an air of good spirits about him that was in its way very likeable. Furthermore, he had so far brought his troop through the desert in safety, which was a skill of a kind. Such a considerable kind, in fact, I thought his little band of followers reckoned he must be a prophet, and they were his disciples.

Not that any of them had much enthusiasm for the role apart from the Spectacle, who still beamed continually at all and sundry. Indeed, as Boss finished speaking, the Rider, Clown and the Wee Man did nothing that showed they felt any pleasure whatsoever in their association, but only narrowed their eyes and waited for us to speak, and in this way to return the favour Boss had just shown us. Since Natty now sat tight-lipped, staring from one face to another, then settling on the Rider, this task fell to me.

I performed it as simply as possible, giving our two names (our English names, not our Indian names), and saying we had been blown ashore, been imprisoned, escaped, lived with certain people who had become our friends, and now were homeward bound. I thought if I amplified these details I would only provoke other questions, which I preferred not to do. My reward for my discretion was to hear Boss say that he too had been sailing through the Bay of Mexico when a storm struck, and after coming more or less safely ashore was now proceeding inland towards the missionary town of Santa Caterina, following the trail made by others before him. Here, he was assured, the Entertainment would find a welcoming audience, and also a gateway into the more northerly, settled and affluent parts of America. 'We shall be among the first of our kind in this great land,' were the words Boss pinned to the climax of his story. 'And the first in quality for many years to come.'

As her beloved reached this apex of his hopes, the Spectacle woke from the trance of adoration in which she lived, and reached out to pat his hand. This gesture had no effect on the others, who maintained their silence with great determination, but it did at least prompt Natty into speaking again.

'And the Rider?' she asked, without taking her eyes from his face. It was clear that she expected Boss to answer, but in fact the man himself did the honours.

'I met Boss in the harbour,' he said, in good English but with a Spanish accent. 'He needed a guide.'

'Oh, but horsemanship as well,' Boss cut in quickly, like a general who does not want his soldiers to have opinions of their own. 'Magnificent horsemanship. Magnificent.'

'I've no doubt,' said Natty with a little smile. 'And before that?'

'To the east, as Boss said. But my people are not there now.'

'Because . . .'

But Boss was in flood again and would not let Natty finish. 'My dear young lady,' he said loudly, and then, turning to me, 'and my dear young man. Permit a stranger to offer you advice. A stranger, and although not a parent, a man with the sympathies of a father, and a father's solicitude for those young enough to be his offspring . . .'

He gulped, and seemed once more to forget where his words were heading, or perhaps had drowned in them, then surfaced again and carried on. 'My dear young people: do not continue in the direction you are heading. Do not, I beg you. Abandon your original plan and reconsider.'

'Why?' I said, which seemed like the longest word I could fit between his own.

'Why?' Boss repeated, puffing out his chest. 'Why? Do you not comprehend, Mister Jim? Do you not see the dangers that lie before you? If you continue in the direction you are headed, and come to the place we have recently left, you will be ground into mincemeat. Mincemeat which is diced and pounded, then minced again and chopped this way and that and eventually tipped into a hot pan and fried until it turns into grit and then is pounded some more, until it has become dust and is ready to blow away.'

I felt so battered by this description, I could only gasp 'I do, sir, I do understand you!' when really all I wanted to know was how he and the rest of his troop had survived in this place they had recently departed, if it was really so diabolical.

Natty was more straightforward. 'Are you suggesting we join you?' She switched from the Rider and looked directly at Boss as she put the question, then back to the Rider again. I saw him nod, just enough to tip a triangle of dark shadow down his chest; there was so much intensity in even this little gesture, I wondered why he had attached himself to these bubbles. Because of what he had said about leaving his own people, I thought. Because they were the best of all the bad options he had known since then.

If Boss noticed me thinking this, or the quick exchange of looks between Natty and his horseman, he did not show it. 'My dear girl!' he exclaimed, with a fresh burst of enthusiasm. 'My dear girl, why, you are reading my mind. Reading my mind! Of course I am suggesting you join us. More than suggesting. I am encouraging. Insisting. Demanding . . .' His eyes rolled in their sockets as he searched for ways to extend his welcome still further, then a new idea struck him and he put on his hat again, pointing a forefinger towards the sky as though he had suddenly received another communication from above.

'A mind reader!' he went on. 'A mind reader! That will be your business with us; that is why you have been sent to join us. To be a member of our Entertainment and to read minds.'

Boss lowered his hand and began waving it to and fro as though sculpting the air; I think he hoped to suggest something like a tent and a crystal ball and a Gypsy costume. Then, as these things appeared in his mind's eye, he continued more slyly, 'And what other skills shall we see, I wonder? What about Mister Jim here? What about you, sir? What is your . . . expertise?'

He rolled the word around his mouth so appreciatively I almost forgot that to go along with his plan would mean reversing the decision I had made a little while before and heading north, not south to the coast. What did Natty think of this? I could not see; her face was turned away from me because she was looking at the Rider again.

'I can shoot, sir,' I said, but with no eagerness whatsoever.

'Shoot!' came the response immediately. 'Perfection! Why did I not think of that myself! Shooting! You can be the partner of the Wee Man here, who is also a shooter of incomparable skills – are you not, my good fellow?' Here Boss twinkled over his shoulder, but the Wee Man did not blink or budge. 'A regular sharp shooter I should say, the sharpest of them all. Together you will puncture the bull's eyes; puncture them. And dazzle the crowds!'

Boss paused to swallow the saliva that had filled his throat, flung his arm forward to point into my face, then swung it behind him to indicate the Wee Man, as though he was tying us together with an invisible rope. I felt too bewildered by this performance to do anything except nod my head, as though I happily accepted the connection. The Wee Man was not so willing, but at least did me the courtesy of removing the rifle from his knees and dropping it into the wagon behind him. When he turned towards me again he bunched his face and spat out a thick jet of tobacco juice.

'Do not mind him,' Boss went on, leaning towards me in confidence, but still speaking loudly enough for everyone to hear, including the Wee Man. 'He is a gentleman of few words – few but wise.' Then he straightened again and reverted to his usual cheerful self, beaming at each of his charges in turn until finally coming to rest, and most affectionately, on his wife. 'But this is all well, is it not, my love? Very well, and very good. Excellent in fact. Manna in the wilderness. Where we looked for nothing, we have been fed.'

Now the Spectacle spoke for the first time, or rather made a sound. 'Oh yes.' It was nothing more than a whisper, but conveyed a whole universe of agreement and admiration.

The effect was remarkable. Boss seemed entirely to forget where he was and leaned forward in his saddle until he had brought his red face close to her own shining moon, so that he could feast on whatever mysteries he found there to fascinate and reward him.

Now it was Natty who interrupted again, and made formal what she had decided for both of us. 'Mr Boss,' she said, slowly turning away from the Rider. 'We're grateful for your hospitality. We accept. We'll come with you. Though I rather doubt we'll be able to help in the ways you imagine.' She paused, and looked at Rider again, as if she was speaking directly to him. 'I have no skills as a mind reader, and Jim here – I have never seen him shoot. But perhaps there'll be other things for him to do.'

'Natty . . .' I began, stretching out a hand and hoping we could speak quietly for a moment, because I still would have preferred to stay as we were – heading south and alone together.

But she would not look at me. 'Jim,' she said quickly. 'You heard what he said. Surely you can't think it's sensible for us to continue as we were?'

'I have—'

'Do you want to ignore them? That would be ungrateful.' She spoke with a kind of hiss, which would have made me blush if my face had not already been so burned and dusty. Even as it was, I thought the others were bound to notice the difficulty between us.

'This is the desert after all,' Natty went on. 'Aren't you grateful to have friends in the desert?'

I stared at the ground, at the grains of red fine dust blowing among the larger stones, and grey thistle-seeds, and the light lying in fragments. I knew I must say something to Boss but I could not think of anything. I was already defeated. And then defeated again when Natty rode forward and turned her pony and settled in beside the Rider. A moment later Boss signalled for me to take my place at his own right hand, and so we continued together, into the next part of our adventure.

CHAPTER 19

My Confusion

I have known loquacious men all my life. Drinkers buzzing in the taproom of the Hispaniola. Barge-men bellowing on the Thames. Schoolmasters talk-talk-talking. Ferrymen. Stevedores. Sailors. My own father, God bless him, storming continually around the Island with Mr Silver and Ben Gunn and the rest. But these were nothing compared to Boss. From the moment we rode forward again, I doubt whether he drew breath more than once or twice through the whole of our first day together, only occasionally taking a swig from his water-bottle to turn his tongue back into a river. And in this once or twice there was barely a chance to ask the two questions that lay uppermost in my mind, namely: how well had I guessed where we were; and how accurate was my calculation of the time that had passed since our shipwreck? Perfectly accurate I was told, perfectly accurate – we were in Texas, a little to the right of centre; and we were enjoying the year of our Lord 1805; the merry month of March to be precise. To which I murmured under my breath that now two and a half years had passed since we first came ashore in the Black Bay.

I suppose by talking so incessantly Boss meant to distract us from any dangers lying round about, and to this extent was behaving kindly. Yet he took such pleasure in the swoops and swerves of his own voice, which he often accompanied by swats of his hand, or by doffing his hat, or by puffing out his chest, or by twisting to gaze on the Spectacle and asking 'Do you not think, my love?' or 'Is it not so, my love?' without pausing to hear her reply, that I soon let my attention drift, so that I could make a space for myself behind the torrent of his talk, as if I was hiding in a cave behind a waterfall. Here I had the opportunity to think, and to notice the scenery as we continued north from the point where we had discovered the trail, and travelled through more red country, past more red boulders, towards a distant horizon where red at last softened into pearly grey.

In so far as I paid proper attention to any of the thousand subjects that Boss introduced, pursued, forgot, then found again, I remember the following: how he had met all the members of his troop except the Rider in England; how they had decided to try their luck in the Americas; how they had squeezed across the Atlantic without any injury from the war that continued between our country and the Frenchies; how they had come to Florida expecting peace but had found all manner of disturbance between competing interests; how they had settled on Mexico as an alternative – but been prevented from reaching there by the storm, as I already knew; how they had taken refuge in the port of Swaffington, of which I had never heard; how they had found there a great confusion of travellers from the

English, Spanish, French, Portuguese and African nations; how these people worked as missionaries, mariners, milliners, barbers, bar-traders, shopkeepers, cheats and tricksters, slaves and slave-owners; how the need for pleasure was all the greater, because of the hard-ships created by so much coming and going, and chopping and changing, and losing and keeping; how these hardships were our own fault, dear boy, our own fault, because it was our own people who had swarmed though the Caribbean, and our own people who were now creeping west and north into territories that did not belong to them.

I was a little surprised by this self-criticism, because in his appear-ance Boss resembled a strange and peripatetic relation of John Bull. Yet once again he proved to be a man of cross-currents, for he ended his lesson by pressing one hand to his chest in a mournful gesture, and informing me, 'We consider ourselves enlightened but we are not. We are rascals – worse than rascals. Nibblers and gnawers. Thieves and traitors. And our Rider is proof of this. Torn from his home, Mister Jim, torn from his home!'

While Boss paused at this staging-post in his disquisition, he hung his head to reflect on the cruelties he had seen, and the others he expected to find; because I thought this might be my only opportunity to make a contribution of my own, I seized it.

'I've seen some of this myself,' I said, intending to speak a little of Black Cloud and the Painted Man, though not to mention the necklace. 'I know . . .' I began, tucking my satchel inside my tunic, but Boss had no interest in what I was doing, or what I was about to say, or what I had just finished saying, and immediately charged off again.

'And this reminds me to draw your attention to another thing . . .' he began, in the same headlong way as before – but I cannot tell you what this other thing might have been, because my mind was already so choked with his previous subjects, and the heat of the sun on my head was so great, I did not listen. I amused myself instead by once more admiring the tracks of rabbits or racoons in the dust beside me, or the marks of snakes that proceeded sideways, and left behind a figment of themselves in little curling waves. The additional reason for this, which I do not enjoy making specific, is that it distracted me from looking at Natty and the Rider, who so far as I could tell were trotting along quite happily together, sometimes talking like old friends and sometimes keeping silent just as easily.

In this way, half-watchful and half-dozing, I was treated by Boss to innumerable stories of scalping and skewering; and yet more of men buried in sand up to the neck and then left to die of thirst and starvation; and yet more of men disembowelled and tortured with fire, which of course I could have told myself but did not have the opportunity.

As this catalogue continued, and the sun rolled through the afternoon and began to sink in the west, I roused myself sometimes to wonder how Boss himself felt about these stories. On the one hand he described even the most gruesome events with such relish, it was difficult not to think that a part of him enjoyed them. On the other, he seemed so determined to prove our new world was bristling with dangers, and already half-ruined by mountebanks and worse, I thought his decision to stay here was very puzzling. I could only conclude that everything he described was in a sense incredible to him – was in fact a kind of Entertainment.

In this spirit I made my peace, and felt content that we had decided to join his troop when we made our camp for the night, with Boss finding a smooth patch of ground between two large boulders beside our trail, and the Wee Man driving our wagon so as to make a barrier along the third side of the place, which meant we felt snug and protected even before we lit our fire. Once the flames had taken hold Clown filled a pot with some dried meat and beans (all the while wearing a very melancholy expression), and the rest of us sat in a ring expecting that soon everything would follow in order: we would eat, then sleep, then wake and continue our journey.

But immediately there was a disturbance, which was the Rider lolloping into the shadows, finding a clump of cacti, and gathering a handful of their fruit; I noticed that Boss rolled his eyes when the Rider showed them to him in the firelight, but thought nothing of it, except he must have tasted them before, and did not like their flavour.

I had often seen these fruits growing in the country near Hoopoe and White Feather, but it had never occurred to me to eat them, since their bulbous shape and milky skin, which was fissured with small black veins, as though they were some sort of tumour, made them look nauseating. Neither had I seen anyone else in the village taste them: they were reckoned to be dangerous.

The Rider, however, clearly considered them a delicacy. Having displayed the collection he had made, he placed it in a separate pan from the rest of our food and cooked it until the fruit was reduced to a pulp, whereupon he scooped it out with his fingers as though he felt no pain, and squeezed the liquid into a cup. He did not drink this himself but offered it to the rest of us, still perfectly silent.

Boss, the Spectacle, the Wee Man and Clown all shook their heads and continued with their eating. Natty, to whom he offered the cup next, took a sip and immediately spat it out again, which the Rider did not seem to mind, since he only smiled and nodded. When he next gave the cup to me, however, his smile vanished; he looked straight at me, staring until I felt he was searching through my head and finding all my secret thoughts about Natty.

My thoughts about him. My thoughts about them together. My thoughts about the Entertainment and about Boss. My thoughts about everything that had brewed inside me all day, which I did not like to admit.

For this reason I took the cup and drained it in a single gulp; to show him I was the master of my fate, and understood everything perfectly well.

As I passed it back, and saw something like amusement shining far down in his eyes, I heard Boss choke on a mouthful of his food. 'My goodness, my goodness!' he spluttered. 'Now we shall have some sport, shall we not, my love? Now we shall have some sport. Well done, dear boy, well done.'

As I remember it, nothing that came next felt in the least like sport – starting with my impression that the light had suddenly vanished from our fire and my mind as well, and I had gone blind. When my sight returned, accompanied by a hideous banging inside my skull, the world was no longer the wide and spacious place I knew, but pinched very tight around me. As if I could only see it by squinting through the eye of a needle. Squinting and not finding anything real, but only whatever and whoever my brain had decided to invent.

My father, as he appeared the last time I saw him, when he did not know it was me and stood pouring water onto our roses as I sailed past him on the *Nightingale*.

Mr Silver rubbing the map of the Island over the white and prickling bristles of his face.

Smirke bolt upright in the canoe, his face boiling with snake-bites and his swollen tongue babbling of old England.

Black Cloud and the Painted Man swimming below me on their bed of loose cloths. Black Cloud and the Painted Man roaring up together and lunging at me, fiddling open the satchel around my neck and desperate to have their silver back – now! Now! They must have it, they must . . .

I suppose this was when I struggled to my feet and swooped on the Rider, because I had convinced myself he was Black Cloud, and it was my duty to murder him and protect Natty.

I clasp him around the throat with both hands.

My hands tighten.

The breath wallops out of my body as we crash to the ground.

We crash to the ground gargling and groaning and rolling, with the charcoal of his body paint smearing all over me, and the heat of his body burning into me, and the dust grinding in my teeth, and the firelight flickering one moment and starlight the next, and the midget drummer still pounding his drum in my skull, although never loudly enough to drown Natty and Boss who are shouting, Stop! – but the Rider pays no attention and I pay no attention; I keep heaving and strangling and throttling because I have Black Cloud in my grip now, and perhaps the Painted Man as well, and they will not release me, and neither will I release them, until all their life has been crushed out, until they are rags to be thrown away into the wilderness where they will never be buried or remembered.

Until Natty and Boss drag us apart.

Until I am hauled to my feet and away to the wagon, still raving and lunging.

Until I am forced down onto the ground and tied to the wheel of our wagon with ropes around my wrists and legs.

Until my fury burns out.

Until my head sinks onto my chest.

Until I am swallowed by sleep, and drift down to the deepest bed of the deepest ocean where there is no light and no movement but only an immense weight of water holding me still . . .

When I floated back to myself again, I thought dawn must be breaking. There were dim purplish lights swirling through the darkness above me: lights the colour of bruises. I decided to sleep some more to make certain; to let the drummer pack up his instrument and leave me in peace.

Next time I opened my eyes there was no mistake. That glare was most certainly the sun afloat in its blue ocean, and that shadow was Boss standing on the shore to launch his first conversation of the day, which was to give orders about the packing of our possessions, and to quench the embers of the fire, and to water our ponies. All simple things, but all hammer-blows thundering on my skull.

I lay as still as possible, my face in the dust like a dog. Pain: the shimmering brightness of it. And shame. I never chose to drink from the cup. I was given it. I had been tricked.

And what was this darkness falling across me suddenly; was it Natty coming to apologise and comfort me?

It was the Rider: his charcoal paint restored and his severe face immaculate.

'Well,' he growled.

'Untie me,' I told him.

Now here came Natty at last, looming over his shoulder. But I saw nothing contrite about her. Her face was washed and her hair brushed; she was smiling broadly.

I would not speak. I watched the Rider tug at my knots and saw that his fingers were creased and dry-looking.

'You're very brave,' Natty chuckled. 'You should never have finished the whole cup.' She would not look at me but preferred watching the Rider finish his work, and his black hair shining.

Still I said nothing.

'No one drinks a whole cup,' she said.

'How was I to know that?'

'Wasn't it obvious?'

'Not obvious at all. How was it obvious?'

'Because the others wouldn't touch it.'

The Rider grunted to show that I was free, and at once I sat upright, rubbing my wrists where the ropes had chafed them.

'Are you saying it's my fault?'

'Why are you talking about fault? No one's to blame for anything. It was only a drink.'

'It was not only a drink; look what it made me do.'

Natty chuckled again. 'Nobody remembers that. Nobody cares.'

I kept rubbing my wrists, with the Rider now facing away from me and looping the rope into coils.

'Besides,' I said. 'You don't know what I saw.'

Here the mood changed, because the Rider was suddenly tense and listening. Turning towards me again he asked, 'What did you see?'

'Black Cloud,' I said, without feeling sure he would understand.

But he did understand, and he was interested. More than interested. He was on his guard, looking around our camp, then back at me again. How did he know about Black Cloud? Had Natty told him? Was this one of the things they had talked about while I had been unconscious?

'Black Cloud, yes,' he said. 'But where? Did you see where he was?'

'In you,' I told him.

The Rider flinched. 'Where in the world?'

'Nowhere. I saw him here.'

'You are sure?'

I nodded, and the Rider held my gaze for a moment, his eyes refusing me like a cat.

'I'm sure. He was only in you.'

I said this to hurt him; to punish him for taking Natty away. And who knows, it might have led to more words between us, to blows even, but Boss saw what was happening and suddenly busied up. He was carrying pots and blankets to stow in the wagon.

'Headache, dear boy?' he said much too loudly, scattering whatever else had been in the Rider's mind, and in mine. 'I have heard that potion produces a most tremendous headache. Indeed, I remember suffering myself, on one particular occasion, on more than one perhaps, on one or two, and having for hours, I might even say for days, a distinct . . .'

Boss dropped his load into the wagon and took out the saddle for his pony without drawing breath, then rambled away with the stirrups banging against his thighs. He had done what he meant to do; my quarrel was not over, but it was finished for the moment. I stood up and brushed the dust off my legs, and the Rider leaned into the wagon to fetch something he needed for our journey.

But then Natty laid a hand on his shoulder. She laid a hand on his shoulder and he bent his head to whisper in her ear. It was all done in a second, but it was enough. All my anger returned and all my confusion. While I had lain unconscious something had passed between them; I was sure of it.

Natty saw me notice.

'You'll feel stronger soon,' she said, letting her hand drop to her side and giving me her sweetest smile.

I did not reply but walked to the further end of the wagon, where I could stand a little apart. I stared at the earth; at the grains of dust and the shadows of the wagon and the seeds in the grass-heads.

'It's nothing to worry about,' Natty said, following after me and speaking in the same deceptive way.

I still did not answer.

'Jim?'

The world expanded a little.

'What have you done?' I asked. I did not care if the others heard me; although in fact none of them did – they were all still busy preparing for our journey.

'What do you mean, what have I done?'

'What have you done?' I did not want to say any more; I could not find the words.

'Nothing,' Natty repeated. 'I've done nothing. It was you who did something. You poisoned yourself.'

'Not that.'

'What, then? I can't understand you.' Natty reached forward as though she wanted to brush the hair out of my eyes. At another time I would have loved her for this; her gestures of this sort were rare. Now I thought it was deceitful and stepped away.

'That's not true,' I said. 'You understand perfectly well what I'm asking.'

Natty's eyes widened. 'Jim,' she said, with great deliberation. 'I think . . .'

But once again Boss appeared, barging round the side of the wagon to interrupt us, and a moment later had swept us off to our ponies, lifting us on a wave of prattle about the need for an early start, and the heat to come, and the uncertainties of the way ahead, and a hundred other things that did not interest me in the slightest.

'Here we are, then, here we are,' he said, stemming his flood for a moment to hand us the reins of our ponies. 'And now – all aboard! Are you with me, friends?'

As he jumped into his saddle and began fussing over the Spectacle, straightening her dress and wiping the dust from her face, Natty tried to finish what she had started.

'I thought you'd lost your mind,' she told me, bending close to my face; her breath touched my cheek.

'Perhaps I have,' I said.

'That would be . . .' She paused, staring into the wilderness and biting her lip.

'That would be . . . too much,' she said at last.

'It would?'

'Certainly.' She nodded firmly, as though knocking the word into my chest; when she felt sure it was driven home, she turned her back and kicked up one heel so that I could help her onto her pony. The brown skin of her leg, streaked with trails of dried-up water that showed where she had washed herself, almost made me cry aloud. I grasped her ankle, and felt the heat of her skin, and hoisted her up.

Then I scrambled onto my own pony, straightened the satchel against my tunic, and we resumed our journey – with me taking my place beside the Boss, who passed me a piece of bread and a flagon of water, and Natty trotting beside the Rider as she had done the previous day.

CHAPTER 20

Cat's Field

In England one sort of landscape flows very quickly into another: marsh into pasture, plains into hills, woods into water meadows. In the wilderness there are no such quick changes. Threadbare scrub, dust devils and lilac horizons: they are all the same yesterday as today, and the same today as tomorrow. How Boss kept cheerful in the face of such tedium I cannot say. Why we endured his chatter and continued to follow his lead are simpler questions. He was the only guide we had, because he was the only one with enough spirit to consider himself worthy of the role.

I soon lost my sense of time as an orderly thing, and lived once more in a dream of clanks and rumbles, sways and lurches, dazzles and darkness. Did I still think a town might exist somewhere in the country ahead of us? Did I think we might die before we got there?

To tell the truth I did not care much in either case; I felt too consumed by the sight of Natty and the Rider still moving along very smoothly together; too distressed by the speed and depth of her absorption in him; too preoccupied by their occasional laughter and their contented silences.

And still too preoccupied a day later, a week later, then ten days later, whenever it was that the trail broadened at last, and we found the country tensing as it will often seem to do before vanishing under bricks and mortar.

Boss soon began to share my sense of expectancy, lifting his hat from his head and then cramming it down again, his red face turning scarlet and his back straightening as though he had swallowed a poker. All this was wonderful – hilarious, in its way – and so were the greetings that erupted when we saw our first living and breathing strangers. A farmer leaning on his rake in a field. A clerical-looking gentleman riding in a buggy. A cowboy lounging against a tree. Each of them in succession were hailed with such a stentorian 'Good morning!' I thought they might be frightened straight back into oblivion.

For my own part: I felt perfectly astonished to see such people and such proof of civilisation. Wide fields began to appear, with hedges and gateways. Then the smallholders who owned them, rattling along in carts or ambling on ponies. Then well-to-do men and women who had no other purpose in life except to survey what belonged to them, and enjoy it. Creamy skins and feathered bonnets! Fancy waistcoats and clean hair! The shine on watch-chains and eye-glasses! The newness of everything felt so great it was almost painful – especially because no one returned our stares, our waves, our greetings, with anything like the same enthusiasm that we showed to them. They seemed pleased to see Boss himself, because he promised them some entertainment. But I was mistaken as an Indian, and judged accordingly. I am sure Natty and the Rider felt offended in the same way, although I did not ask them.

Then the roofs of a few buildings broke the skyline, and we knew we had reached the town that Boss had predicted for us.

The first houses we saw were more like fortresses than homes, with high palisades all around, and thick walls made of rough logs and planks, and small dark windows in which the only signs of life were a shadow passing among shadows, or a shutter pulled to and bolted. The effect, despite all the warm opinions that Boss continued to pour forth at every turn ('Charming, charming', 'most ingenious', 'very practical and robust'), was to make us feel the place was closed against us.

Boss never so much as suggested this, and after a while I had to admit he was right to persevere, because these fortresses gave way to less forbidding homes, with gardens front and back, and windows where families gathered to wave at us. A little further, and the welcome was even more enthusiastic, with doors opening, and men and women stepping out to stare, and children asking Boss who we were, and where we came from, and what we meant to do, some in English, many in Spanish, a few in French, and others in languages I had never heard before.

To each of them – and over their heads as well, so their parents heard and their neighbours, and regardless of whether they understood him or not – Boss explained in his loudest voice that we were the Entertainment, oh yes, indeed we were, and shortly we would be performing for the delight of everyone, and he would be most obliged, really very sincerely obliged, if they would take it upon themselves to spread the word, since a diversion as remarkable as this, a spectacle as spectacular, was the first of its kind in the New World, and might never be repeated as long as a world of any description continued to exist.

Admiring this cascade, and watching the children pluck up their courage to come close, and tell one another how strange we looked, or in the case of myself and Natty how dirty, I felt like a hermit dragged off his solitary pillar. A moment before I had been surrounded by wide horizons; now everywhere I looked there were walls and turnings and obstacles and faces – faces with work to finish, and friends to meet, and plans to make, and all of them peering about, and laughing, and scowling, and frowning, and sneering, and commenting, and criticising, and appreciating, and gossiping, because here was their home. Home with a wide road, and now even tidier houses on either side, wooden houses, houses two storeys high, and a church, and shopfronts, and glass shining in these shopfronts, and an open door with fiddle music, and horses tethered along a rail, and more shops, and a shaded walkway where people clattered to and fro, and a hotel, and another church, and another hotel, this one much smaller, at the furthest end of the main street, where the bustle died down again, where a tortoiseshell cat slept in the sun, where a yard opened before us, where Boss led the way and our wagon groaned in behind us, and we pulled at our reins, and slithered to the ground, and handed over our reins to the stable boys, and stroked our ponies on the nose, and patted their shoulders and thanked them, and looked at one another, and knew that for the moment at least we had reached the end of our travels.

We stood in amazement, Boss speechless for once in his life: at the row of stables ahead of us; at the fresh straw that lined the stalls; at the patterns of sunlight that came through the tiles of the roof; at the saw-marks on the beams overhead.

Boss recovered first and told us – with a great deal of hand-rubbing and back-slapping, and a tender embrace of the Spectacle – that the place was well found, very well found, before leading us away from the stableyard and in through the back door of the hotel. With his shoulders square and his hat shining on the back of his head, he looked as though he stayed here every night of his life, and was the best of friends with the manager, and had personally arranged for the paraphernalia of tassels and drapes and picture-frames and pictures that greeted us.

'Business!' He pounded on a desk that stood in the lobby, and shouted as though he meant to be heard across the whole of America.

In the pause following this eruption, several doors slammed shut on the storey above (I imagined guests crouching behind them, wondering what tornado had blown into their shelter), and a piano in the neighbouring room tinkled to a halt.

Then silence, and the suffocating sense of being *indoors*, as though everything had suddenly closed around me and squeezed the breath from my lungs: the dark yellow stripes of the wallpaper, and the milky candle-bowls, and the carpet that showed little blue waves rippling endlessly towards an invisible shore.

What was the need for it all? What sort of wrong turn had mankind taken, when it abandoned the life of simple things and open air? I gasped, and found I had clutched the arm of Clown, who quickly shook me off. Was I the only one choking like this? Apparently. Even the Rider seemed perfectly at ease, gazing at the picture of a sunset fuming on the wall beside him, while Natty kept her shining eyes fixed on his face.

Then doors creaked open again upstairs and feet shuffled along a landing. The piano trickled back into life. Shadows shook in the alcove behind the lobby-desk. And the hotel owner Mr Vale appeared: small, stooped, wearing a green eye-shade, and apparently as mournful as his name, which hung above him on a neat wooden sign.

Boss hailed him with tremendous vivacity, giving orders about how many rooms we needed, and what kind, and for how long.

'You, Wee Man . . .' he said, scanning our faces in turn as though to remind himself how many disciples he had gathered around him in the desert, and feeling impressed by the number. 'You, sir, I think must sleep outside in our wagon to protect our possessions. Are you content?' (He made no pause.) 'I see you are content. You, my love . . .' (He beamed at the Spectacle, who clasped her hands together and rose onto tiptoe as though the tether that kept her tied to the earth was being sorely tested.) 'You shall of course remain with me, in the matrimonial bower. Now . . .' (He pointed at Clown and me and Natty and the Rider.) 'You and you and you and you will all have a room to yourselves. A room each I should say. Extravagant, I grant. Extravagantly extravagant. But we shall have great profit from our Entertainment, great profit, Mr Vale, and pay you when we have made that profit, which will be tomorrow night. You accept our terms, I am sure. Very good, very good. Excellent in fact. We shall be very generous to you. Generous to a fault. We are generous people. We are brave hearts.'

What else could Mr Vale do but agree? He winced. He tugged at his eye-shade as though it was the peak of a cap. He winced again. Then he meekly passed Boss a handful of keys and murmured that he accepted us gladly into his hotel, before returning to the shadows from which he had been summoned.

Even as I watched all this my mind was hurrying to understand what Boss had done. He had not put Natty and the Rider into a room together. But at the same time he had not exactly forced them apart. He had given them a room each, and with that sort of separation he had also allowed them the chance to move from one to the other, to be together in secret.

I wanted to think more about this, while at the same time

dreading what conclusions I might reach, but Boss was in flood again. 'Come come, now,' he called. 'Come come. With me now, with me. Go to your places, and find your beds, and close your eyes, then rise up again, and wash your faces, and meet me –' he jabbed at the carpet rippling beneath his feet – '*here* in an hour, so we can proceed with our business.'

He did not wait to explain what this business might be. He merely jerked his head a few times when he had finished speaking, to show that what he had said was the law, then stamped up the stairs that rose at the end of the lobby, dragging the Spectacle behind him. She had a way of covering the ground with small and rapid steps; these, combined with the baldness and smoothness of her large head, and the glamour of her dress (though now very dusty), made her seem not like an earthly thing at all, but a visitor from the clouds whose natural tendency was to return there.

I dare say I ran this little fantasy through my mind as a way of preventing myself from thinking how Natty had reacted to her instructions. When I turned away from the Spectacle I found her hoisting a blanket-roll onto her shoulder; her face was flushed.

'We're the lucky ones,' she said.

'We are?'

'A room of our own? We're very lucky. When did we last have a room of our own? Not since before we stepped on board the *Nightingale*. And goodness knows how long ago that was. We have luxury here, Jim, luxury.'

I suppose this was well meant; it seems so, when I think of it now. At the time it felt like a dismissal. A denigration of all the time we had spent together. A humiliation. And because I did not want to show as much in front of our friends, I immediately swung off and followed Boss upstairs.

Quick as I was, I thought everyone must surely have seen what was in my mind; I felt their amusement and their pity and their curiosity all burning into me as I disappeared, and stumbled when I reached the top step.

Natty laughed when she saw this – I heard it, but I did not look back. I pressed on down the corridor and shut the door of my room smartly behind me. In one part of my mind were thoughts I detested: Natty and the Rider trotting side by side, talking together, turning to one another in the darkness while I was drugged and ignorant. In another part: voices telling me I had nothing to fear, I was inventing things, I was exhausted, I had been away from home too long. Both sides feinted and dodged, advanced and retreated, locked and gripped, with nothing to prove which was the wiser, and no one to resolve them.

I shook my head and told myself to concentrate on here and now, on this room, which was the first I had seen for a lifetime. For two years and more. To look at the plain plaster walls and the plain ceiling. The single window. The curtains made of brown sackcloth. The heavy afternoon light soaking through. The bare table beside the bed. The white pitcher and basin, on another table by the window. The metal bed, with its stained bolster and yellow shawl stretched over the mattress.

I threw myself down expecting to lie awake until Boss needed us, and to torture myself by grinding my thoughts together – but I did no such thing. I closed my eyes. I lay in darkness for a moment, and then I slept.

When I awoke again there was no more sunlight seeping through my curtains, and no more gentle day-noises, but shadows blackening my room, and laughter and singing from the saloon below. I scrambled to my feet, splashing water into the basin to wash my face, pulling my tunic straight, tucking my satchel inside it, then tumbled downstairs into the lobby.

But there was no sign of Boss and the rest, only Mr Vale simpering behind his desk. Although it was dark outside, he was still wearing his eye-shade.

'I expect you are wanting your friends,' he said; his voice was a whispering drawl, and when he finished he wiped his mouth as though his American accent was an embarrassment to him.

I told him I was.

'They are in Cat's Field,' he said.

'Cat's Field?'

'At the edge of town, where tomorrow they will perform the Entertainment. They are rehearsing; they will be waiting for you.'

'I know they'll be waiting for me.'

'Because you are a performer,' he said, looking me up and down and apparently surprised to see me still wearing my dusty Indian costume.

'You could say that,' I told him. Then I suggested, 'Perhaps you'll direct me?'

'I will do better than that.' Mr Vale laid a hand on my bare arm. 'I will take you.' He stared into my face and blinked rapidly, as if dazzled by even the small amount of candlelight that shone around us.

Although I found this disconcerting, because it made him so plaintive, I said I was grateful and asked him to lead the way. He seemed grateful in turn, rubbing his damp hands together and muttering, 'I shall, I shall,' before giving a loud holler – a surprisingly aggressive noise – which produced a lanky boy I had not seen before.

'My nephew,' said Mr Vale. 'He will mind things while we are gone.'

This made it seem we were about to set out on a great undertaking, but the nephew did not mind. He merely bowed as we passed into the darkness and wished us goodnight, in a voice even more sibylline than his uncle's; when I looked round he had already slipped behind the reception-desk as though he owned the place.

This little ceremony was so strange, so insignificant in the scheme of things yet so elaborated, I felt I had merely stepped from one kind of confusion to another. Everything I saw seemed larger than life; every behaviour was like a performance. And remained so, when we turned out from the stableyard into the street, and found its shopfronts and houses patched with lamplight, each of them showing a little scene of families eating, or men smoking, or grandmothers watching the bustle and traffic of the street. Real people, I kept reminding myself. But everyone just an inch away from the wilderness, and the night-breeze prowling over the empty places, and the moonlight that stretched to infinity.

We had walked only two or three yards when I discovered that Mr Vale, who had seemed very shy when we first met him in his hotel, became almost as voluble as Boss when he left it. With the acceleration of a man running downhill, and before I could ask any questions of my own, he launched into a history of the town (brief and turbulent, as I hardly needed to be told), of local characters (farmers, cattle-men, precious beauties, rustlers and murderers), of the weather (hot, and sometimes hotter), and of memorable emergencies (fires, mostly), all of which he remembered with equal excitement. And once he had painted the scene in this way he built the frame around it, giving a disquisition on the whole of Texas, and explaining in the year of our Lord 1803 it had been sold by Napoleon to America in the same bundle as the neighbouring state of Louisiana, but still contained a great many interested parties from France and Spain, not to mention Indians from tribes living round about, and might therefore be considered a very competitive sort of place, full of large areas of nothing which were apparently valuable to all and sundry.

Such a comprehensive lesson had a curious effect on me, and not just because it was so unexpected. It made me feel that Mr Vale's strenuous efforts to establish himself in the town, and so become a citizen of the New World by means of hard work, were really a sort of oppression – because they had smothered his true nature, which I now saw was open and easy.

This made me warm to him, despite the great difference in our appearance and age and manners, because he reminded me of myself – of the happiness I had felt with Hoopoe and White Feather, which had diminished as soon as I left them. Although I did not say as much, in my heart I knew I would have preferred to be back with those dear companions, lying under the stars with nothing but their light and the winds of heaven for my covering.

When we came to Cat's Field at last Mr Vale made me stop still and admire it for a moment. I did not need much encouragement: the field was about fifty yards across, cleared of trees and bushes, and now illuminated by a circle of torches on long stakes that Boss and the others had driven in the ground. I suppose these torches were burning some sort of tar or pitch, for really the whole area was bright as day, only more beautiful because the air had turned a soft yellow, which seemed to gild everything it touched.

The Spectacle sat on top of a platform at the dead centre of the ring, like a pupil at the centre of an eye, except a pupil is dark and she was glowing in a pure white sugar-puff dress that she had previously kept clean in the wagon. This alone would have made her radiant, but she had also coated the skin of her bald head and bare arms with some kind of glittering powder. Everything strange about her appearance, everything that might have been alarming, was softened and stilled and polished. Now her entire reason for being was to display herself, which she did by no more extravagant means than sometimes turning her head from left to right, and sometimes twisting her body a little, but always with a blank expression on her face, so some new cascade of light was continually pouring across her cheek, or down her neck, or along the exposed skin of her shoulder. As a performance it was next to nothing; as an effect it was wonderful.

'Beautiful, beautiful,' whispered Mr Vale.

This was too quiet for Boss to hear, but he would have paid no attention in any case. He was prowling to and fro across the ring in a bright red topcoat and silk top hat, holding a riding whip in one hand, occasionally glancing at his beloved in order to feel amazed all over again by her incandescence, but otherwise concentrated on Clown, who wore the same yellow costume and face paint as usual, but had coloured his eye-sockets a blacker black, and his nose a redder red, and his mouth a deeper carmine. The two of them were apparently playing a game, a very silly game as it seemed to me, which required Boss to pretend that he meant Clown some harm (by sometimes slashing at him with his whip), which Clown could only escape by apologising for himself with some ridiculous whining and cowering; his costume was soon coated with dust and his expression so wretched it suggested he was about to be tortured to death like a gladiator.

As for Natty and the Rider: I could see no trace of them at first – although once I had scoured the darkness beyond the lights I found them beside the Wee Man's wagon on the furthest side of the ring, almost lost in shadow. They were leaning together again, with their shoulders touching; although Natty was still dressed in her Indian costume as before, the Rider had equipped himself with a headdress made of long white feathers that swept upwards from his brow, then folded into a sort of tail that twisted down his naked back and shone very brightly against the charcoal smeared over his skin.

I told myself there must be a reason for their closeness: they needed to discuss their performance. But the explanation was not good enough – not for such intimacy. I could not look away. I wanted to, but I could not.

Then they broke apart because Boss was tired of making his victim sprawl in the dirt and beg for mercy, and gave a much fiercer snap with his whip. At this, Clown hobbled off and the Rider swung onto the bare back of his pony, riding slowly towards the centre of the ring with Natty walking at his side.

It was a very un-theatrical sort of entrance compared to some that I had seen in circuses at home, with no drum rolls or barking from the ringmaster – but the effect was powerful all the same. The Spectacle stopped her writhing; Boss stepped backwards and stood on the further side of Mr Vale, whose shoulder he gripped in a passion of encouragement; and I – I folded my arms across my chest, and shook my head to clear it of what I had seen, and composed myself to watch.

I thought at first that Natty's job was simply to stand and admire the Rider while he galloped around her. But as she came into a patch of brighter light I saw she was carrying a collection of properties, including a dozen or so wooden rings about a foot across, which she then laid on the ground in a circle within the larger O described by the torches.

When this was done she advanced towards the centre of this circle, where I could not help thinking her dark skin and her nimbleness made a pretty contrast with the Spectacle. But if this had been one part of Boss's plan, it was soon made insignificant by another. For once Natty had reached her place, the Rider dug his heels into his pony and began galloping around the perimeter of the ring at top speed.

Remember, all this took place in a very confined area – about fifty yards across, as I say – so the pony had to be very neat in his movements, and the Rider also very handy, which he managed by somehow making himself smaller and more efficient, tucking in his elbows and gripping tightly with his knees. For one or two rotations his whole purpose seemed to be no more than that, to move as fast and tidily as possible, but then he became more ambitious. Letting go of the reins and swooping first to his left and then to his right, he skilfully snatched up all the hoops that Natty had laid on the ground, flinging each one back to her with a whoop so that she could catch them; as she did this she gave a little cry, shaking her head to make her hair swarm around her face.

I have made this business of throwing and catching sound simple; in fact it required an almost miraculous sense of balance, with the Rider seeming really to hang in thin air every time he bent down to pluck a hoop from the ground. And the same when he ran through the rest of his repertoire. First he continued to gallop in a circle while Natty placed the wooden rings back on the ground so that he could fetch them up again – this time on the point of a small spear that she gave him; then he took the reins of his pony in his teeth and climbed onto his back to ride while standing upright; then he sat himself down again, but only to slip off one side, bounce his feet hard on the ground, and leap astride again before doing the same the other side.

I suppose his pony was tired when the Rider had finished all these tricks, and was moving more slowly; this was as well, in view of what happened next, and came as the climax to the whole display. After Natty had passed the Rider a small bow and a quiver full of arrows which he slung around his neck, she returned to the centre of the circle where she lifted in front of her face a target painted with brightly coloured rings – blue, red and black. While the Rider continued to gallop around the outer limit of the circle, Natty then began to spin on her heels, which allowed the Rider to have the target before him at all times, and to fire his arrows at whatever speed he chose.

This turned out to be as quickly as possible, fitting one arrow to the string of his bow as soon as the last had flown, so for a minute or two the whole area of the ring was continually shot through. It was a wonderful feat of skill, but not one I could enjoy in the least. If Natty had lowered the target even a little she would have been killed; if the Rider had missed his mark – the same result.

For all this, I clapped just as loudly as Boss and the Wee Man and Clown and Mr Vale, when the performance was finished; and when Natty rested the target on the ground, and showed her face glowing and smiling, the Rider slowed to a trot, and then to a walk, and we gathered together in the centre of the ring where Boss lifted the Spectacle down from her platform, and I congratulated everyone on their brilliance, which I said would surely dazzle our audience tomorrow.

The Rider was breathing fast, and when he took off his head-dress I noticed his hair was saturated with sweat. He did not reply to me, which I thought showed he was hiding something in his mind. Natty was also short of breath but not so guarded. She pressed her hand to the base of her throat, her eyes wide.

'Did you see?' she asked me.

'I saw.'

'Every one safe and on the target!'

'Every one.'

She did not hear me echo her like this; she had already turned away to fling her arms around the Rider. He closed his eyes, holding her tight and resting his cheek on her hair; how long they stayed like this I cannot say, for I immediately began helping the Wee Man to extinguish the torches around the perimeter of the ring, so we would have enough fuel to light our performance the next day.

Boss came to join us then, which I am sure was meant to comfort me. 'We must find a role for you in this little drama,' he said. 'Do you not think, Mister Jim? A role of some kind, a role – but you say you are not a shooter after all?'

'No, sir, not, to be truthful.'

'No matter.' His voice was much softer than usual and he laid a hand on my arm. 'Something else, then.'

'I should like that, sir,' I replied, without looking at him. 'If you think there's anything suitable.'

'I am sure there is.' He took his hand away and placed it in the small of his back, rubbing the base of his spine while he stared into the surrounding darkness. 'Now, what can it be? Let me see.'

CHAPTER 21

The Performance

When we left Cat's Field I already knew how I would spend the next few hours. A sleepless night hearing Natty sneak from her room to the Rider's, or him creeping into hers; a day pretending to be pleased with the Entertainment; an evening smiling at strangers.

But nothing happened as I expected. When I reached my room I heard Natty pause on the landing to say goodnight to one and all, then go to her bed alone; when my head touched the bolster I spent a minute wishing it was more comfortable – or less: that it was bare earth – then dropped into a sound sleep; when I woke again and took myself downstairs to breakfast, I found Boss holding forth to Natty on one side of the table, with the Rider and Clown sitting in silence on the other.

I stared at them, thinking my torments would now surely begin again. But the sight of my friends sitting together like this was a kind of rebuke. I had no evidence for my distrust, no foundation for it. And I knew in my heart I would be wise to end it; if I stayed as I was, I would not be myself; I would be a kind of jailer, locking myself in a prison on my own devising.

For this reason I took my place beside Boss and gave the appearance of being entirely content, asking him whether he had given any further thought to my role, as he called it. He looked nonplussed for a moment, no doubt taken aback by the change in my mood, then collected himself and told me he had, indeed he had, and it would be no ordinary role. It would be a vital role, an indispensable role, because it required me to help Natty with her work in the ring, as she passed the Rider whatever equipment he needed.

In the same enthusiastic way, Boss then announced that as soon as our meal was finished the whole troupe of us would take it upon ourselves to spread the news that we were performing at sunset. I thought this was fair enough, and for the rest of the morning I walked through the streets squawking about the Rider and Clown and the Spectacle, then returned to my room at noon and decided the best use of my time was to go back to sleep. I had started my day with an effort of will, to forget my jealousy. It pleased me to think I could end it by proving this had become a habit.

The next thing I knew, Natty was knocking on my door saying the rest of our party had already left for Cat's Field, and she had stayed behind to walk with me. This was so unexpected I thought it must be a lie; more probably, she had fallen asleep as well, and only now woken. But I was so pleased to see her I did no more than thank her and say we should hurry, and with that we set off as though there had never been any difficulties between us, none at all.

Once we had left what I must call the centre of town – which is to say: after we had walked two hundred yards from the hotel, and found ourselves in a much more uneven street, among a large crowd of townsfolk now all drifting in the same direction as ourselves – Mr Vale caught up with us. Although still very talkative once away from his desk, his purpose this time was not to give another history lesson but to ask some questions.

'You know what is expected of you?' he began.

'Oh yes,' Natty said, apparently determined to be as casual with him as she was with me.

'And you, Mister Jim?' Mr Vale was walking sideways, blinking under his eye-shade.

'I hope so,' I said, and then, because I thought he was only trying to be friendly, I continued more affably: 'We've got the least to do so we have the least to worry about. It's really the Rider who carries most of the burden, as you know.'

This was all said very easily, to remind Natty how much I had done to govern my feelings, and show I had forgiven her.

Mr Vale quizzed on regardless. 'And Boss?' he said. 'Is he word perfect?'

'More than anyone,' I said.

'I suppose he must be.'

'The Entertainment is his existence,' added Natty.

'I suppose so,' Mr Vale said again, and stared through the jostling heads to where our road ended in the field. The torches were already lit, but did not yet seem to burn very brightly, because the last oranges and yellows of the sunset still flared on the scrubland beyond them. I closed my eyes for a moment and breathed its sweet smell of sage. I was almost myself again; I was almost happy.

Natty was more distracted. 'What are you saying?' she continued with Mr Vale. 'What do you mean, you suppose so?'

'Nothing,' he said, with a startled little flinch. 'Nothing at all.'

'Surely you'd expect nothing less of Boss?'

'Quite so, quite so.'

'What, then?'

I was so struck by Natty's tone I almost interrupted and told her to leave him be. But then Mr Vale twisted round and faced us directly.

'It is just . . .' he said.

'It's just what?' Natty came to a halt, ignoring the crowd that pressed around us.

'I have heard stories,' Mr Vale said.

'What stories?' Natty said.

'Our town is not so large,' he said. 'Not so large yet, at any rate. It cannot keep a secret.'

Mr Vale smiled, but not with any good humour; previously I had thought his wincing only proved his shyness. Now I was not so sure, and my happiness started to shrink away.

'What are you trying to say?' I asked him. 'If you have something to tell us, tell us straight out. We won't mind.'

'I fear you may,' he replied. 'It is concerning you, after all. Both of you. But especially you, Mister Jim. Especially . . .' He stretched towards the satchel, which I had forgotten to tuck inside my tunic and so hung around my neck in full view; although his fingers did not connect with my skin, I felt a quick sensation of moisture, as if I had been splashed by a raindrop.

'How do you know what's here?' I asked. 'You haven't seen it.'

'No, but I have guessed,' he replied. 'It was easy to guess, knowing what I know.'

'Which is?' said Natty, now very impatient.

'They have been asking about you,' Mr Vale said again.

'Who?' Natty and I said together, although both of us knew the answer already.

'An Indian man. Two Indian men, in fact.'

'Can you describe them?' I asked.

'I have not seen them.'

'But others have?'

'So I believe.'

'And what did they tell you?' Although I tried to speak calmly, so as not to scare Mr Vale into making any more evasions, he winced as though I had slapped him.

'My informant is a serving man,' he said, suddenly speaking fast. 'In a hotel at the opposite end of town. He saw them arrive – a strong-looking man and another, younger. Both Indian and one of them painted all over, face and arms and legs. A wild pair, my informant says, and when another guest in the hotel tried to shoo them away, wilder still. They pushed this gentleman to the ground and stood over him with a knife. They asked if he knew you, and said they would find you, wherever you were, because you had taken something that belongs to them. They would have killed him, if they had not been restrained. Though only restrained for a moment, I should say. They shook everyone off and disappeared.'

'Disappeared where?' I asked.

'I have no idea.' Mr Vale swallowed. 'They asked for you again before they went, Mister Jim. Not by name, but they asked – did anyone know, had anyone seen, was there any news . . . That. News of that.' He reached towards my satchel again, but still did not touch it.

'And what were they told?' I said, holding my nerve.

'Nothing,' he protested. 'My acquaintance had not seen you, and I had not mentioned you. Why would I do that? I run a respectable house. I do not discuss my guests with anyone.'

'But you mentioned others in our party?' As Natty said this she laid a hand on Mr Vale's shoulder, which made him shrink down between us.

'Others in your party have been mentioned,' he murmured. 'It is understandable, is it not? They are unusual. You are all unusual.'

'We're not blaming you, Mr Vale,' I said. 'We're trying to know what you know, that's all. So we can decide what to do.'

I said this while staring over his head at Natty, silently asking for her advice.

'We can't leave,' she said, taking my cue.

'You mean we can't leave at all?' I said. 'Or we can't leave now?'

'Now. This evening. They need us here. We can't just abandon them.'

'Why not? It's our lives.'

'We can't.'

'It's our decision.'

'We can't.'

I glanced down and saw her fingers had tightened on Mr Vale's shoulder; as her knuckles whitened he wriggled free. Was she slipping away from me again, turning back to the Rider? Was everything I had been thinking, all the reassurance I had given myself – was it just foolishness?

'Shall we walk on?' Mr Vale asked. He was suddenly much more composed, as if he had begun to enjoy our discomfort and not feel frightened by it.

'We are still deciding,' I told him, then looked at Natty again. I knew what she would say next, and tried to head her off.

'There'll still be enough tricks if we're not there,' I told her. 'They don't need us. They managed before they met us and they'll manage again.'

'But not the best trick,' she said. 'Not the trick with the arrows.'

'No one will miss what they've never seen before.'

Natty shook her head; she was also more like herself again, more settled and determined. 'Don't you feel we owe a debt to Boss?' she said. 'He took us in, after all.'

'We chose to join him,' I reminded her, then paused because I was about to speak his name. 'And anyway – what if Black Cloud comes to the show and sees us? What if they both do?'

'They can't hurt us there,' said Natty. 'We're among friends and they'll defend us.'

'But we've seen how dangerous he is.'

'It's two men,' she came back. 'Two against the whole lot of us. And the crowd.'

'The crowd won't care,' I said. 'And anyway, have you forgotten what those two are like? They're cold-blooded murderers, Natty. They're savages.'

Natty shook her head. She could not forget the Rider; she would not leave him now.

I turned away from her then; I did not want to hear her stubbornness any more, or her excitement. I looked instead at the strangers still trooping past us, the families herding together, and the children running ahead, then back. One of them, a little fellow half my age who was missing a front tooth, broke off his conversation with a friend and asked me: was I all right? Did I need any help?

I told him no, and thanked him, and turned back to Natty. 'Very well,' I said heavily. 'But this is your decision, not mine.'

Natty sighed. 'Sometimes, Jim,' she muttered, folding her arms.

'Sometimes what?' I said.

'Nothing.'

'You know I only want to keep you safe.'

'I understand that.'

'What, then?'

'If you don't know now, you'll never know.' Natty seemed about to speak some more, then changed her mind and marched away to the end of the street, where the lights of Cat's Field simplified her into a silhouette. Here I caught up with her and was about to continue asking her what she meant when Mr Vale arrived.

'Off you go now,' he said, rubbing his hands together. 'You have nothing to fear. I shall be your eyes. Your ears and eyes both.'

I did not answer, dismayed to think my life might depend on someone so fickle and insinuating. Instead, I grabbed Natty by the hand and half-dragged, half-raced her to the edge of the field.

'There you are, my dears, there you are!' Boss shouted as we came into the light, and his racket ended our talk. 'We have been looking for you everywhere, thinking every conceivable sort of thing must have befallen you. Stage fright, perhaps. Or spirited away! But no, here you are safe and sound. Safe and sound. Beguiling the time, I dare say, following the trails of whim and fancy! But with us now as promised – our latest recruits!'

When this outburst ended he flung out his arms and embraced us both, squeezing my face so hard against his red coat I felt the buttons scrape my skin. If there had been a moment to think properly, I should have said we were sorry, and warned him about Black Cloud, but Boss rattled on as soon as he released us, and I knew I would never divert him now. He was on the brink of his triumph; he was unstoppable.

'Here!' he boomed, like a cannon firing. 'Here you will both be a part of our celebration. A great and glorious part. A part of our creation of civilisation, I should say. Our creation of the finest Entertainment in America. Perhaps of the only Entertainment in America!'

This last word – 'America!' – turned into a bellow that brought a loud cheer from the crowd. 'First in America!' Boss shouted again, in case anyone had missed it. 'Finest in America!' And when he felt sure that everyone had indeed heard, and agreed, he gave a deep bow and apologised for whisking us away, but business called, business called, and a moment later we were off through the crowd and across the circle of lights and among the rest of our friends again, with the Wee Man lounging against the tailgate of his wagon. Was everything ready? Boss wanted to know without drawing breath. Was everything perfect?

Natty and I left him to his questions, and still not speaking to one another we faded into the shadows on the further side of the wagon, where we found the Rider standing by himself, already wearing the headdress he had used during his rehearsal. He had wiped all the charcoal off his body, and was decorated with two white streaks on his cheekbones.

'You are here,' he said.

'Ready and willing,' said Natty, and gave a little smile; she had forgotten her anger the moment she saw him.

'And late,' he told her, which was more peremptory than I expected.

Had he already heard something about Black Cloud; was that why he spoke so sharply? I chose not to ask. As Natty put on her headdress, which was a single white feather standing up from the headband, and he stood close to her to straighten it, I looked away into the distance to watch the sun sink at last – a final blaze of gold and purple. Then the Rider stepped back from Natty and we faced the crowd together.

Eyes and ears, I remembered Mr Vale saying, eyes and ears – and decided I should use my own very carefully now, in case he failed us. But it was hard, because Natty and the Rider loomed so large in my mind, dragging my thoughts where I did not want them to go. And hard because of the crowd. The children scrambling at the front. The men and women jostling behind them. Here was an ancient pioneer with a scar on his forehead and sunken cheeks. And here was a priest with a brown cassock and a face as dark as an olive. And here was a pretty lady with corn-coloured hair, and a husband who never took his arm from her shoulder. And here was a Negro still wearing the striped apron from work. And here was Mr Vale as good as his word, twisting and snooping. And here was . . .

The Rider snapped his fingers in front of my face. 'Look,' he told me, and I saw Boss taking long strides towards the centre of the ring, with the Spectacle bobbing along beside him; a tremendous burst of applause and cheering broke over them both.

I thought I must check the crowd once more, just a glance to be safe.

Which is how I came to see – not a face.

A flurry.

A crease in the air, and gone.

It might only have been a child fidgeting.

I turned back to the ring. Boss was handing the Spectacle up the steps of her platform, where she arranged herself at the centre of light so her dress sparkled like star-beams and her head gleamed like a miniature planet.

The audience applauded more loudly than ever, and as its roar subsided Boss seized on the chance to regale them, shouting above their hubbub, introducing himself and the rest of us, explaining how we would entertain them, and how they would want to reward us when he was done, oh yes, reward us most generously.

I hardly listened to a word of it.

Was he here already, Black Cloud? Would he strike at us now in the open?

Boss finished his welcome and Clown stumbled towards him

trailing his whip. The audience foamed over again. His yellow costume! His red nose! His staggering and sliding! The whip tingling his ears!

I scanned the faces again but always nothing.

Not there.

Natty sighed; I was worrying too much. The Rider was more interested, leaning towards me; I smelled the horse-sweat on his skin. What had I seen exactly? And where?

Surely I had been wrong again, wrong about Natty and him. The Rider was a friend to both of us, nothing more.

But Clown had staggered offstage and there was no time for that. Now it was our turn, our show, and Boss was waving us forward. The brightness! My body turned almost to liquid. Every footstep, every smile, every frown felt so enormous it could surely be seen from the moon.

'Come on!' Natty managed more easily, and was already arranging the hoops, the bow, and the quiver she had filled with arrows, while the Rider took his pony to the edge of the ring and began to walk slowly forward, then to trot, then to gallop, with the feathers of his headdress fluttering out behind him.

'You see,' said Natty, marvelling under her breath. 'No need to be so careful, Jim, no need at all. We're perfectly safe here. Safe as houses.'

CHAPTER 22

Our Mistake

Natty passed me the wooden hoops and I set off around the ring to place them on the ground as I had seen her do. It was easy work but it distracted me, and so did the crowd – the children shrieking and laughing, their parents suddenly like children themselves, and loudest of all a drunken old cowboy whose face was pitted with smallpox scars. All he wanted to know was: why was Natty so dark? Was she an Indian – she looked a bit Negro? And what was the Rider up to? Why was he galloping round like that? And what kind of Entertainment was it really, just watching an Indian ride about in circles?

I should have let it pass but looked up and told him in my smartest English voice to watch his tongue, just to surprise him, then cut back to Natty again as the Rider swooped towards us, collected the spear she gave him and settled it in his right hand. Our performance began.

The Rider was circling much faster now and crouched forward like a cavalryman, using the point of his spear to hook the rings from the ground, then flick them to Natty again. It was done in a moment and even the fool cowboy was impressed, saying how clever this Rider was, how nimble, and that was one good thing about Indians, their way with horses. Then it was time for the next trick, and Natty had passed the Rider his bow and the arrows, with the crowd roaring him on. Then roaring again when Natty lifted the target to cover her face, then again when the Rider galloped faster still, and the tail of his headdress swam out behind him, and he took the reins of the bridle between his teeth and fitted an arrow to his bow and drew his bow tight. Then loudest of all when he fired the first arrow, and it struck the target near the centre so Natty (who was only a foot or two away from me, and revolving on her heels to keep in line with the Rider) gave a gasp and lurched backwards a step.

By the second arrow, and the third, and the fourth, I felt dizzy myself, because I was turning on my heel as well, keeping pace with Natty. But not so dizzy that I stopped looking. Not too dizzy to forget the crowd, with their gasps and squeals and squeaks and sighs and laughs and open mouths and closed mouths and hands pressed over their mouths. Not too dizzy to forget Mr Vale and check he was keeping his word, being our eyes and ears.

I had just whizzed over his face and seen his blink and twist and blink, then passed to his neighbour, a quiet face and a soft cap, when suddenly I was back with Mr Vale again. His voice drew me, and his jumping up, and his pointing: 'Ah!'

I looked – and saw a ripple like the rings in water where a fish rises. And in the heart of the rings I saw a face.

A smear of skin.

Then nothing again.

But a shadow.

I kept on staring. At the gap between faces where this face had been. At the cheerful smiles and wide eyes. I swept on, then back, then on again to the next small gap, then on again to the next . . . And there he was. Black Cloud and no doubt; Black Cloud and the Painted Man. His mouth like a pike. His shoulders gold in the lamplight. The rise and fall of his chest, as though he was panting.

Natty had not seen him. 'Keep turning,' she hissed, because I must keep pace with the Rider, who flashed through my sight and away. I ignored her. I folded my arms over my chest to conceal the satchel hanging there, as though I expected Black Cloud to snake out an arm twenty feet long and snatch it from me.

But he was not looking at me. I was not important to him any more, because I was already as good as dead. He was concentrating entirely on Natty. He had seen a way to destroy her first and he would take it.

I understood this when I saw him making a space for himself, rolling his broad shoulders and sticking out his elbows. Lifting his bow with an arrow already set to the string. Levelling his eye along the flight. Aiming at Natty. This was the plan, perhaps made here and now, perhaps earlier when he had crept up to watch the rehearsal. The plan to make it seem as though the Rider had misfired and killed Natty. And it was a good plan, because the crowd would think there had been a mistake, an accident not a murder, and this would allow Black Cloud to melt away, but only when he had fired a second time, and struck me down in the panic. When no one would notice him ripping the satchel away from me.

A good plan, but the Rider saw it.

Without seeming to take his eyes off Natty, and with his pony still galloping, and his stern face creased with the effort, and the lights still dazzling, and the crowd still booming, he swept closest to Black Cloud when the danger was greatest. When the arrow that would have killed Natty was about to fly. At exactly the same moment, he swivelled round on his pony and let loose his own arrow, which hummed towards Black Cloud and struck him in the shoulder, or seemed to strike him, or at any rate shocked him so much that he jerked backwards, and released his arrow quite uselessly, high above the heads of the crowd, where I saw it dwindling into the star-flow and, if everyone had been quiet, would have heard it clatter down useless onto the stones of the wilderness.

Was this a part of the Entertainment? The crowd thought so, and began shouting even more loudly, and clapping, and encouraging the Rider – while others knew better what they had seen, and screamed just as loudly 'No!' or even 'Murder!' although it was not clear who or where the victim might be, because nothing was clear now, nothing at all, not even to those who had seen most, not even to me, who watched Black Cloud drown in the crowd and drag the Painted Man after him, sinking away and leaving the ripples to cover the place he had been.

No, not even clear to me, who in the second that Black Cloud vanished was suddenly spun round and lifted up from the ground, because the Rider had finished his business with the bow and arrows, finished with the Entertainment entirely, and hauled me onto his pony so I was seated behind him, gripping him around the waist, pressing forward with everyone screaming and shrieking and flapping their hands until we reached Natty and dragged her up as well, and sat her in front of the Rider and then, squeezed together as we were, and with the pony grunting beneath our combined weight, we drove forward again and broke through the crowd, out into the wide open air and the hush, not knowing whether we were still in danger or not.

I looked behind me, still holding tight to the Rider and feeling his skin damp with sweat. Everything in Cat's Field was chaos. The clear O of the ring had disappeared, with the crowd barging and weaving because they knew what had happened, or had no idea, and in either case thought that an arrow was about to strike them, any one of them, any moment. Bonnets and hats, bare heads and whiskers, fists and faces all jumbled together. Most in the torchlight, some in shadows, some in darkness. And at the centre, with his arms high above his head, Boss in his bright red topcoat, bellowing fit to burst and ordering everyone to keep calm, to return to their places, to wait for the show to continue, to please make their dona-tion before leaving, if leave they must.

Bellowing and then beseeching, with a note I had never heard in him before, a note of panic, because in the midst of everything the Spectacle had stayed at the top of her platform, catching the juddering lights, thinking perhaps this stampede had come to admire her, to be close to her, to love her, and so must be greeted with another wave of her hand, another smile, another caress of her moon-scalp.

'My love! My love!' Boss shouted, as another shuddering wave ran through the crowd.

'Dear heart!' he bellowed again, as the platform supporting the Spectacle began to tremble. 'Have a care! Have a care!' But it made no difference. The platform began to sway. It began to tilt. It began to fall – and the Spectacle his beloved, still splashed by the glow of the lamps, slithered and shuffled and scrabbled and finally tumbled from sight, with her white dress and its many spangles and stars striking the darker faces and shoulders and arms and legs and feet of the crowd beneath her like an explosion of sea-spray.

I did not hear Boss after this because the noise smothered him. But I saw him crumple, then also vanish as he plunged down to make his rescue.

Then I saw nothing more, because the Rider had torn off his headdress and Natty's as well, and dug his heels into his pony, who carried us as quickly as he could through the wilderness. In a dim landscape of rocks and bony trees, with the stars our only light.

'Do you think he's still here?' I asked, speaking over the Rider's shoulder so Natty could hear me.

The Rider himself answered. 'He is here.' His voice seemed slow even when he spoke fast. 'He has come a long way.'

'But you wounded him,' I said. 'Or you killed him.'

We were trotting now, heading round in a wide arc towards the town, and our poor suffering pony bounced the words out of us.

'Not killed,' the Rider replied. 'He is not dead.'

'You're sure?'

'Besides, there is the other man.'

'Will they follow us?'

'They will – for the necklace.'

I hesitated for a moment. How did the Rider know about the necklace? I had not shown it to him. Natty could not have shown him. But she had told him, she must have. And perhaps other secrets as well, about our life together.

'And for other reasons,' the Rider went on.

'What other reasons?'

'Don't ask him that,' Natty said; she was leaning forward and clinging to the pony's neck. 'Ask him where we are going.'

The Rider did not mind her interrupting. 'To fetch the other ponies,' he said. 'We cannot stay here.'

'Suppose they're waiting for us?' I asked. 'At Mr Vale's?'

'They will not be there,' said the Rider; it was as though he had seen everything that lay ahead of us and it was all preordained. 'They will ride off, then come back when they are ready. You have robbed them, remember.'

'Can we give it back?' Natty asked, the same question as always.

'The insult remains,' said the Rider. 'You cannot change that.'

'I know.' I felt full of apology and the Rider heard it, but it did not lessen the sting of his words.

'You know?' said the Rider. 'I do not think so. You say you are sorry but you do not regret.'

'I am sorry, I am,' I pleaded, like a child.

The Rider did not rebuke me again. 'I understand,' he said. 'You want the necklace. You like it. You think it is yours now – it is always the same with treasure, it is . . .' But he had said enough, because there was nothing more to be gained, and for the next several minutes we continued in silence over the dark ground, coming at length to a point where we could enter the town at a good distance from Cat's Field, and reach our stableyard along empty streets.

We rode very cautiously all the same, creeping from shadow to shadow and still not speaking. But thinking. In my case thinking: the Rider has left the Entertainment and joined us now. But is it just his way of staying with Natty? No, he is our friend equally; we have him to ourselves now.

When we reached the stableyard and dismounted, and went to untie our own ponies from their stalls, Mr Vale lurched out from the back door of his hotel.

'You startled us,' said Natty. 'That's not kind.'

Mr Vale ignored this. 'I ran back,' he wheezed, raising his eye-shade and wiping his forehead. 'I could not let you go without another word.'

'You mean you want us to pay you?' said Natty.

'No, nothing like that!' exclaimed Mr Vale. 'I'm not concerned about that – your Boss-man will pay, tonight or another night. There will be other Entertainments. Not with you, but other Entertainments.'

He made the prospect seem dismal and hung his head; although I was desperate for us to be on our way, I took pity on him.

'You want to see, don't you,' I said. 'You want to know the reason for all our trouble.'

Mr Vale looked up and gave me a weak little smile. 'A glimpse,' he said. 'That is all I want.'

'Here, then.' It sounded impatient but Mr Vale did not mind. And when he saw me hand the reins of my pony to Natty, walk straight up to him, and open my satchel and hold it towards him, his smile turned into astonishment. I did not take out the necklace. I only offered for him to look inside the satchel, and when he bent forward I teased it away, so he would know not to touch. Although the stableyard was lit by nothing more than lamps burning inside the hotel, the silver caught their glimmer and flashed into his eyes.

'Aaaah!' Mr Vale gave a long sigh. 'Thank you, Mister Jim. Thank you.'

'Well, you have seen it now,' I told him.

'I have seen it.'

He shied away and before I had closed the satchel I looked at the Rider.

He held up his hand. 'I do not need to see it.'

He was so definite I did not ask again, only nodded and tucked the satchel inside my tunic. Besides, Mr Vale was all busy-ness now, scurrying around the yard, handing Natty our two blanket-rolls, and a flask, and a parcel of food, all the while muttering under his breath. 'Such brightness,' I heard. 'Such brightness, such brightness.'

And then, 'Not for that butcher. Never for him. I looked for him, though. I waited. I looked for him. And you two only children still. No blame, I am sure, no blame, no blame. But you must be on your way, no matter what. On your way now!'

It was an extraordinary performance, as though seeing the silver had driven him out of his wits. At another time I might have thought I should stay and comfort him, to bring him back to himself. In the event I did not even thank him for what he had given us.

'Are you ready?' I called softly to Natty.

'Ready,' she said, handing me back the reins of my pony, and with that we rode out into the street, where I turned to look at Mr Vale for the last time. He had retreated to the threshold of his hotel, and for once in his life was standing straight, with his long arms hanging down loose. I was glad to leave him, but thought he was brave to make this place his home, when he knew that one day he would die here, and be buried in ground that was not his own.

CHAPTER 23

Nowhere Else

As we left Santa Caterina the Rider found us a trail winding towards the east. A very faint mark, which starlight made nothing at all, yet it came alive when the breeze blew the dust from footprints and wheel-marks, and for the next hour or two we made good progress. I thought once the town had vanished he might explain why he had thrown in his lot with us, but he said nothing and I let him be. It was enough to know that he wanted to find a way back to his own people, and enough to have his kindness as well. Whatever his feelings for Natty, or hers for him, when we made our camp later that night he was equally attentive to us both, and built our fire and cooked as though he had never forgotten his old customs.

When the sun rose next morning he continued in the same quiet way. Handing out food from the parcel given to us by Mr Vale, then leading us forward along a track that now only he could see clearly. As far as Natty and I were concerned, everywhere was the same wilderness. Red rocks, and dusty grass, and cacti holding out their waxy arms, and little stunted trees. The same landscape as ever, in fact, but more blistered and shrivelled than before, with the tracks of our fellow creatures very faint in the earth beside us.

In such a desert I needed all my curiosity to care for anything, and might not have done so without a good deal of help. But the Rider did more than encourage me. Under his instruction I found that a speck at the highest point of heaven turned out to be an eagle – a flake of gold that only revealed its valuable colours when the sunlight flashed along its wings. When he uprooted a dreary shrub and shook it so all the dirt blew away, I discovered a miniature universe of green shoots and insects, most of which were tasty to eat. When he pointed to a scribble on our track, that looked like a sand-ridge blown together by the wind, it suddenly curled into a snake and hissed at me and squirmed away to hide under a stone.

I suppose my childhood had given me an appetite for all this staring and studying; although our marshes were much more fertile and watery than the wilderness that now enclosed me, they were also a place where enormous skies made the ground seem dull, until the eye narrowed and sharpened and moved carefully to see what there was to see.

For this reason, I sometimes still imagine I am living alone and unremembered in America, with only the Indians for my company. But when I look around at my present life I check myself, because now I understand we cannot easily deny our origins. And although it has taken me a lifetime to accept this, some part of me knew it even when we made our second camp on this part of our journey, with the Rider once again building our fire and choosing where we should sleep. A crumbling boulder protected us from the breeze and its shadow was all the blanket I needed for warmth.

Then a part of this shadow moved, and I saw the Rider pull the knife from his belt, his black hair hanging around his face and the firelight rolling over his bare arms; a moment later he slackened again, when the shadow stepped forward and turned into a man.

Into three men in fact, Indians whose faces were smeared with ash, and whose bare arms and legs were thin as sticks. This alone made me think they were no threat to us, but as they shuffled closer and came into the light of our fire, I could see they were too weak even to look at us for more than a moment.

When we had given them something to eat from our pot, the Rider spoke to them in his own language and they rallied a little, answering questions that he then translated for us. Very soon he told us we had been invited to their camp.

'How's that?' I wondered.

'They are lonely,' the Rider said, which I thought was a strange notion.

'But surely they're not alone out here?' I said. 'Surely they have the rest of their tribe?'

Natty interrupted. 'They don't belong here, that's what he's saying; they've travelled from somewhere else.'

The Rider nodded, then picked up a stick and laid its tip in the flames until it began to blaze. He seemed fascinated by this, and kept his eyes fixed on it.

'They have travelled,' he said at length. 'That is all I know.' Then he looked up. 'They have come here to be safe.'

'They don't seem very safe to me,' I said.

This sounded facetious and the Rider frowned at me; I rebuked myself, and began to understand what he meant. These people were not as I had imagined we might become ourselves in this new phase of our existence, content to wander from place to place and accept the world as we found it. They had left their home against their wishes; they had been evicted. This was why their bodies were smeared with cinders. They were grieving.

Despite this, they were determined we should follow them to their camp. To make us welcome, the Rider said, but also because they thought we should not stay in the open.

'Because he's here?' I said at once, meaning Black Cloud.

The Rider shook his head. 'Not now. He has been here, though. He came this way, perhaps on his way to Santa Caterina. But his ghost is here.'

'Is this what you think? That his ghost is real?'

'I think we must do what they say.' The Rider's face was a mask, and I could not decide whether he believed the danger was genuine, or merely wanted to show courtesy. I decided the latter, and did not persevere with my questions. When we had finished our meal, I therefore helped him put out our fire and gather up our things, and all six of us set off together.

We left the path our Rider had found through the scrub, heading across stony ground towards the north, and because the moon was now high and cloudless we saw the landscape quite clearly. It was a wretched country, with a stiff breeze blowing grit against my bare legs, prickling my arms and face.

'Why here?' Natty asked the Rider in a hollow voice, which was also my question.

'They have nowhere else,' he said.

'But they've chosen the worst of all places,' she went on. 'The very worst.'

The Rider did not answer this, and for the rest of our trek, which could only have taken half an hour but seemed much longer, we kept silent as we led our ponies up the gently rising slope, seeing the earth grow poorer with every step and the plants more desiccated, until we came to an obstacle that seemed to represent the entire spirit of the place. A makeshift barrier of thorns about six feet high and spiny as a hedgehog.

I could not see how to go any further, and for a moment even wondered whether we had been led into a trap, where Black Cloud was about to fall on us. Then without any warning the thorns began to shake, and to shudder, and eventually to open – showing a little scratchy gap through which we could pass in single file.

We found ourselves in a compound about fifty yards long and the same across, with thorn-walls bristling on every side and the central area trampled flat, which made for convenience of a sort, except the dust was very fine and hovered in the air like mist. Why so much dust? Because there were so many people. People churning and tramping even though it was the middle of the night, while others lay on blankets in the open, or peered at us from the dozen or more tepees that stood scattered about, or stood close to the boundaries that hemmed us in, with their hands pressed to their faces as though they could not believe what they saw.

There were about a hundred of them, every one smeared in ashes like our companions, and every one equally dejected. A few children tottered to their feet and stared; one or two dogs ran about; occasionally a thin face turned to inspect us, then cringed away again. But no one spoke, and no one rose to greet us.

'Why did they bring us here?' I asked Natty.

'You know the reason,' she said. 'To make us welcome.'

'But this isn't making us welcome.'

'It is custom,' the Rider broke in. 'They have to ask us – it is their way.'

'Even though they're so miserable?

'Even though.'

As if they had understood my questions, and to prove the Rider right, our guides then pointed to a rail where we tethered our ponies, and led us towards the centre of the compound. Here the largest of all the tepees had been erected, a dingy affair smeared with filth and charred by flames.

The Rider told us we should wait while the guides disappeared inside to fetch their chief. When we had listened to a few whispers hissing to and fro, the flaps opened to reveal an ancient half-skeleton, half-man, wearing a tunic of moth-eaten bearskin and a necklace of bear's claws. A crown of drab brown feathers was perched on his head, and his face was coated with the same pale ash that covered the rest of his people.

As our three guides took their places – one on either side and one behind him – he pulled himself up as straight as possible and confronted each of us in turn; his face was very weather-beaten and leathery.

The sight of the Rider made him frown; Natty almost made him smile; and I made him curious, so his eyes passed quickly from my face to the satchel around my neck, which he then reached out and opened before I had the wit to prevent him. When he saw the necklace inside he half-lifted it, allowing a few of the silver pieces to slip between his fingers, then withdrew his hand and stared at me. What was he thinking? I could not tell; his face was expressionless. But I do not believe he recognised the necklace, except in the sense that he knew it was valuable.

At last he roused himself to speak – a greeting I assumed, but I only heard grunts and growls, with the Rider acting as my interpreter; he said the chief's name was Talks to the Wind, but he had no gifts to welcome us.

'We know that,' I replied. 'We have none of our own, and don't expect any in return.' Then, with the Rider speaking one beat behind me, we continued as follows.

'Tell him we come in friendship,' I said.

'Talks to the Wind is grateful. He offers you his protection.'

I doubted this would be possible, because the whole tribe seemed so wretched and feeble, but I did not say so. Instead, I asked where they had come from.

'The east,' I heard. 'Many days' march.'

'Why?' I said.

'The White Man,' said Talks to the Wind.

'I am sorry,' I told him, and bowed my head. 'We would not all do the same.'

Talks to the Wind nodded impassively.

'Where will you go?' I continued.

'Where we can.'

'And where is that?'

'Where we are allowed.'

'But the country is so big! Endless.'

'Each of us has his place. We belong in the east near the ocean. We do not belong here in the desert or anywhere to the west.'

Talks to the Wind rocked on his heels when he had finished speaking and stared into the darkness. I turned to the Rider. 'You are from the east,' I said quietly. 'Did you know these people already?'

'I know they exist,' he told me. 'I left when they left – we took different ways.'

'But you are going back.'

'If I can.'

'And they cannot go back.'

'It seems so.'

The Rider fell silent then, and at the same moment Talks to the Wind raised a hand to show he had finished speaking as well, whereupon two of our guides helped him back into his tent, while the third led us away to another part of the compound.

Here was our place for the night: a patch of bare sandy ground where I lay down without a word, and immediately closed my eyes. More than sleep, I wanted to blind myself to everything around me – but could not. The voices of the camp continued in my head for a long time, as if I was still upright and awake. A child sobbing and a mother in tears. A dog whining. Wind hissing through the thorn-fence. Before these things disappeared and I shelved away into my dreams at last, I thought I had never heard such desolate sounds in the whole of my life, and would be grateful never to hear them again.

CHAPTER 24

Healing the Sick

Next morning I woke thinking we should leave Talks to the Wind as soon as possible, and return to the trail that would take us east to the river that Hoopoe had told us we must find. But when the sun rose above the barricade surrounding the camp, and the shadows of its thorns scratched my eyes open, we seemed bound to delay again – because most of the tribe were crowding around us. Why had this not happened the night before? As they continued staring and I saw how gaunt they were, with their eyes half-closed and their bellies swollen by hunger, I thought they must simply have felt too stupefied to bother. But when we had finished our breakfast and wandered through the camp for a while to shake off our audience, I knew there was another reason as well.

The place was strewn with relics – offerings of some kind, I guessed, and all very grotesque. Rabbit skeletons dangling on poles. Desert foxes hollowed out by the wind. Collections of feathers, stuffed into leather bags and left on little platforms. Skins, stripped from small creatures such as mice and rats, then twisted together to make ropes and stretched between poles, or draped around the doors of tepees. Matted balls of hair, which were collected on a large red blanket, and laid on the ground beside the tepee belonging to Talks to the Wind.

'What are they?' I asked the Rider, but he only told us we must present ourselves to the chieftain in order to make our farewell. Then, when he had led us to the tepee, he surprised me by putting one arm around my waist and the other around Natty so that he could whisper to us both in confidence.

'Sickness,' he said. 'That is the explanation for all these things.'

'Sickness?' Natty repeated anxiously. 'You mean fever?'

The Rider nodded.

'Shouldn't we leave at once, then?' she said.

'We cannot,' said the Rider. 'We have something we must do first.'

'What sort of thing?' I asked; suddenly I felt as alarmed as Natty, with the dusty air thickening in my throat.

'I did not see last night. It is not just custom, bringing us here. It is something more. They need our help.'

'What help?' I asked.

The Rider let his hands drop away and stared straight ahead, as though he could see through the walls of the tepee and envisage the scene inside. In the pause that followed, everything that had previously seemed mysterious about the camp began to make sense to me. These famished men with their sunken eyes and ashy hair. These women with their sallow faces and slumped shoulders. These children with their pot bellies and flies in their eyes. They were not just hungry. They were suffering another sort of hurt as well, and had invited us here because they thought we might heal it. We were not only guests but physicians.

I turned to the Rider and found him looking at me very gravely. 'Mister Jim?' he asked. 'Have you finished what you are thinking?'

'How do you know what I'm thinking?'

'We are all thinking the same thing,' the Rider said; then he bent down and opened the flaps of the tent, holding them apart so the three of us could enter together.

I stepped into twilight – thick, swimming twilight scented heavily with sage – and paused for a moment to let my eyes adjust. There was Talks to the Wind, wearing the same moth-eaten furs as yesterday and the same sad little crown, sitting on a mat of woven grass. What else? Dangling from the crown of the tepee: charms made of feathers and wood and even scraps of metal. Scalps too, dried up and crinkled like seaweed, one with its ears still attached. To the right of Talks to the Wind: a bench with a bowl of corn, uneaten, and half a dozen clay pots, some with steam drifting from their mouths. On the ground: dark brown rugs patterned with creamy lines, which made the air swirl around me although it was perfectly still.

And at the centre of the tepee, an elderly woman cushioned on a deep bed of blankets. Dead, I thought – then at a second glance not dead, but sick. Very sick. A narrow face with greying hair in a plait. The plait coiled on her head and stuck through with a wooden pin. Her eyes wide open but seeing nothing, gazing into the crown of the tepee where sunlight soaked through like rust.

'Come,' said the Rider, leading me forward; I knew at once what he wanted.

'I'm sorry,' I said, turning to Natty, who gave me a baffled look and shrugged her shoulders.

'He does not want your sorry,' the Rider said, nodding towards

Talks to the Wind as he sat down beside us, keeping his eyes fixed on my face.

'I can't help him,' I said. 'I wish I could but I can't. I have no medicine.'

'You have your medicine,' the Rider insisted, as though he had not heard me.

'I don't,' I told him. 'I wish I did.'

'That is not true,' said the Rider. 'You can heal.' He spoke very stubbornly, as if he was making a plain statement of fact, and reached out to touch the satchel around my neck. 'Here it is,' he said.

I looked down at his fingers, long and thin with skin so supple they almost seemed to shine. 'How will this help?' I asked.

'You will find a way,' he said, and laid a hand on my shoulder, drawing me forward until I was standing beside the woman's head, close enough to touch her.

'This is Fire Wife,' he said gently. 'Wife to Talks to the Wind.'

I was not expected to answer, only to look at the thin face and the cracked lips; at the veins pulsing beneath the grey temples; at the specks of sand in the corners of her eyes, and paler sand-trails creeping into her ears, which showed where her tears had run down.

When I had seen all these things, and felt them weigh on me, a chant began outside the tepee, regular as a heartbeat.

'Mister Jim,' said the Rider, speaking even more quietly now.

But I did not need his encouragement any more. I reached into my satchel, removed the necklace, and slipped the cord around my neck. The slim oblongs of silver clicked as they settled, and the torchlight scattered their brightness into the half-light around me. Then I lifted my hands and laid them on the woman's forehead, one upon the other.

Natty thought I was about to press down and gasped, 'Gently, Jim, gently!' I did not answer. I kept my hands on the woman's forehead, feeling its heat enter my fingers, and asked the Lord to bless her. Then I said His prayer – 'Our father, which art in heaven' – and heard Natty join in behind me, her voice growing steadily louder until we reached the end – 'the power and the glory, for ever and ever, Amen' – when I lifted my hands and made the sign of the cross. Three times. Once on the woman's forehead. Once on her mouth. And once above her heart.

It took two minutes or less – and by the time I had finished, the chanting outside the tepee had risen to a crescendo, so the walls actually seemed to vibrate. Talks to the Wind remained as he was, his eyes sliding away from my face and fastening on his Fire Wife again. The Rider was also still as a stone, with his head down and his hands clasped.

Then the chanting stopped as though the people knew my healing was over, and my hands returned to touch Fire Wife on her forehead again. Her skin was much cooler now, and softer. Instantly – like that. I felt it and I believed it. So did Natty, when she came to stand at my shoulder. So did the Rider, when he lifted his head and saw the change in her. So did Talks to the Wind, when he climbed painfully to his feet and clapped his hands together.

As for Fire Wife, I would like to say her journey back to us was very easy. But it was not. She did not look into my face and smile. She did not turn her head to find her husband, or stretch out to clutch his hand. She did not speak. She merely blinked, and blinked again, then writhed and trembled so desperately that all four of us had to hold her still, in order to prevent her from heaving off her bed and crashing onto the ground.

What had she felt, I wondered, as she burst out from her dark underworld? Surprise. Terror. Disbelief. Amazement. Regret. Regret most of all. A moment before, she had been ghosting through a country without suffering. Now she felt sadness again and remembered the reasons for it.

Yet her distress did not last. As Talks to the Wind continued to hold her still, and spoke to her in his own language, and I suppose told her the story of the miracle we had seen, and pointed to the necklace I was still wearing, she began to quieten and breath more easily, and at length even smiled to herself or perhaps at me. This smile was so radiant it brightened her whole face, and remained in her eyes when it had faded from her mouth.

Now it was my turn to feel a sort of paralysis. I could not respond at all. I stepped away. I told her (which she did not understand) that what I had done was nothing.

This, despite the cheering and shouting that now started outside the tepee. Despite the Rider, who clapped me on the back very proudly. Despite Talks to the Wind, who told me that I was his son, and embraced me, and held me so close I almost choked on the mustiness in his bearskin. Despite Natty, who I would also like to say was pleased by what she had seen – but cannot.

For when all these congratulations were finished, and I had slipped the necklace back into my satchel again, she took me aside to speak in private.

'You see?' she whispered.

'Natty—' I began, but she interrupted me.

'You've made her fall in love with you.'

This was so surprising I could only stammer at her. 'That's ridiculous! She's grateful, that's all, she's not in love with me.'

Natty brushed this aside. 'Either that or they think you're a god. Like it was with White Feather.'

'He certainly did not think that; he couldn't think of anything.'

Natty ignored this as well. 'Whatever sickness this woman has,' she said, 'we must get away from it as fast as possible.'

'We must—' I said, but got no further because Talks to the Wind stepped between us, and took hold of me, and made me understand that I must come outside with him now, so he could show me to the people and tell them what I had done.

I followed him as he wanted. I stooped through the doorway of his tepee and I faced the people, and I heard their shouts and the clattering din as they banged their spears together. When I held out my hands to show I wanted to thank them, and not to receive their thanks, they did not understand, and only cheered me more loudly.

CHAPTER 25

The Thicket

In happier times we might have looked for feasts and dancing – for songs to celebrate our miracle. But partly at my insistence we did no such thing; Fire Wife remained in her tepee, dozing to recover her strength, and the rest of the tribe dismantled the offerings they had strewn around the camp, thinking they had now done their work.

Natty was very pleased by this lack of fuss, and wanted us to be on our way immediately. The Rider, however, persuaded her this would be discourteous and insisted we must stay a day longer, because there was no danger of our becoming sick ourselves unless misery was infectious. By the time it was sunset again, and we had smoked a pipe with Talks to the Wind, and then another pipe, and heard his stories of the land they had lost, and how they lost it, I thought the Rider was wrong. 'Our lives are broken.' These were the words that Talks to the Wind spoke to me before we turned aside to sleep, and they settled in me as definitely as any illness has ever done. 'I am tired,' he said, 'and my heart is sad. I will fight no more for ever.'

Others before me have written about sorrows such as these, about the ruin of the whole Indian nation, and it is not my business to record them in greater detail here. But in case I seem unfeeling, let me also remember the words that Talks to the Wind said next morning, when the Rider told us we had done our duty to custom, and could now be on our way. We had already received our instructions about where we would find our trail again; we had been embraced by Talks to the Wind and embraced him in return; I had shaken the hand of Fire Wife as politely as any English doctor; and now the warriors of the camp had pulled open the gate in their thorny barricade to bid us farewell. I thought Talks to the Wind might follow this with a final ceremony of thanks. Instead, he straightened his battered old headdress and looked out over the stony country.

'I saw the White Man,' he said, pitching his words into the emptiness. 'I saw the White Man and was told he was my enemy. I could not kill him as I would kill a wolf or bear; yet like those things he came upon me. Horses, cattle and fields he took from me. Still he gave me his hand in friendship; I took it; whilst taking it, he held a snake in the other; his tongue was forked; he lied to us and stung us. I asked for a small piece of this land, enough to plant and enough to live upon; in the far south of our country, a place where I could scatter the ashes of my people, a place where I could lay my wife and child. This was not granted me. Now I am here. I feel the iron in my heart.'

I need hardly say that he sounded much more broken and halting than I have made him here, because the Rider was required to translate phrase by phrase. I know, too, that I have misremembered some words. But the essence of the thing I have preserved, just as I have also remained true to the promise I gave myself at the time: it would never be forgotten.

For all that, I could not help thinking that if I turned back as we rode away from the camp, I would find it had already disappeared. Knowing what I know now, safe in another country, I see this was prophecy of a kind. Talks to the Wind and the rest of them could not have stayed more than a few days longer in that barren place. Where they travelled next, and how they managed, I have never liked to imagine.

Our own circumstances were much more fortunate, but since this makes such a painful contrast with everything I have just described, I shall cover our next few miles very quickly. As soon as we found our trail to the east again we remained in dry country for two or three hours, which our ponies did not like at all, as they told us by repeatedly shaking their heads and blowing through their noses and sometimes stopping altogether. When this patch of desert ended, however, which it did quite suddenly, as if the whole landscape had been transformed by a miracle much larger than anything we had witnessed the previous day (as Natty could not resist pointing out, and I did not deny), we entered richer terrain, with tall trees and lush grasses, and streams running with sweet water.

When we made our camp I wondered aloud why Talks to the Wind refused to send hunting parties here, and so help his people. Natty told me that in her opinion the whole tribe was so dispirited they had lost the will to make the best of their existence. This sounded like a wretched sort of truth and I changed the subject, asking the Rider whether Talks to the Wind had spoken to him about this part of the country. He said they had not discussed it;

so far as Talks to the Wind was concerned, it belonged with other things he could no longer call his own.

As it transpired our journey next morning was more peaceful and easy than any we had previously known. Sometimes we saw the scratch-marks of bears on tree trunks, or the prints of their paws on dry earth, but no creature ever came to frighten us. More often we found turkeys which we could easily chase through the scrub and overtake and kill for our food. Indeed, these birds were so careless of the need to protect themselves, with their gorgeous plumage and tremendous beaks and wattles, it seemed no human being could possibly have come into this region before us. I thought that if they had been allowed to prosper in their solitude, and remain untroubled by hunters, they might eventually become quite stationary in their complacence, and live like potentates.

We were only three people, but three hundred or even three thousand could not have exhausted that part of the country. For mile after mile and hour after hour we travelled through open pastures in which life teemed tumultuously. When we tired of turkey we hunted deer. When we tired of deer we ate rabbit. When we lacked for sweetness we found honey. When water tasted dull we sucked the juice from wild apples. And when we tired of eating and drinking altogether we had entertainments of other kinds. In the warm daytime, enormous flocks of cranes sailed overhead and cried down to us, encouraging us on our way; in the evening foxes and opossums appeared beside the trail to watch us ride past, and wondered what kind of friend we might be to them. The change from everything we had seen with Talks to the Wind was so marked, I felt I had entered an entirely new world, rather than a different chamber of the one I already knew.

When we had glutted ourselves in this way for a week or more, and thought our adventures would never present us with any more obstacles because the whole of America had become our garden, the Rider told us our progress would shortly become difficult again. I asked him how he knew, and he said he remembered stories from earlier days – from the time he had lived in the east – which I took to mean that we would soon have to endure a few days of drought or some such inconvenience.

But it was not another desert that faced us when we reached the end of our land of plenty; it was the opposite. An even greater abundance of trees and plants. Laurels mostly, that first grew in small clumps and then joined into a continuous forest, with some specimens as wide as barns, and others the height of church towers. Although we were pleased to have some shade after the days spent riding in the open, we were also very frustrated to find ourselves so impeded. The branches cut our bare arms and legs, which were not protected by our Indian clothes, and slashed our faces. They frightened us too, as invisible creatures scuttled from their lairs or eyed us from the shadows, making me think our enemies had caught up with us again, and were about to take their revenge.

'How long will this last?' I called to the Rider after a few difficult hours; he was now leading us in single file and did not look round, but lifted aside another whippy branch and then ducked forward.

'In our stories we called it the Thicket,' he said. 'We used that word. In English.'

'The Thicket?' I repeated. 'That doesn't sound very bad. A thicket isn't very bad.'

'It might not be,' he said, shielding his face from a new onslaught of twigs. 'We shall find out.'

I thought this sounded a little melodramatic, but the difficulties of moving forward were now so great I let it go, concentrating instead on ducking and dodging, but nevertheless making slow progress until the sun began to set at last, and we found ourselves beside a colossal old laurel tree that had grown into a dome-shape, with a ceiling of intricate interlaced branches.

Here we tethered our ponies and made our fire and ate, and here we lay down to sleep when the first stars began to peer between the leaves. The sense of protection was so great, and the quiet so profound (once the birds had finished saying goodnight to one another), that as I closed my eyes I thought perhaps the Rider had been pessimistic. The Thicket, I told myself, was certainly a hindrance but we had survived worse; it would annoy us again tomorrow, then it would be gone.

I was still confident next morning when we continued on our way. In fact after a mile or two I began to think our ordeal might be over sooner than I expected, because the spaces between the trees had gradually become wider, and the way ahead more obvious. Just when I was about to say as much, the Rider held up a hand and brought us to a halt; we stood in a little glade, our ponies breathing heavily.

I could see at once that far from being about to leave the Thicket we were in fact about to enter it; everything we had fought through to this point was only a preparation. There was no trail whatsoever in front of us now – no trail, no track, not even the smallest winding path. Just a confused mass of leaves and tree trunks and branches all coiling together and looping through one another's arms and plaiting and matting and interweaving. To make matters worse these were ghost-trees, permanently enveloped in a swirl of mist and steam and dew and raindrops and fog.

Natty was the first to break our silence. 'Is there a way round?' she asked the Rider. The conversation between them now was always plain and direct.

The Rider shrugged. 'Our stories did not say.'

'You mean they don't mention it, or there isn't one?'

'They said there was no way round,' said the Rider. 'They told us the Thicket runs all the way to the sea.'

'That means to the south,' she said. 'What happens to the north?'

'It runs all the way,' said the Rider.

'All the way where? To the North Pole? That's not possible.'

'It is our story, Miss Natty.' The Rider sounded a little crestfallen, as though he had been caught out in a lie. But he was not backing down.

'And what does common sense say?' Natty went on. 'How long would it take, do you think, if we went to the north?'

She was so impatient now, I thought the Rider might refuse to answer. But he shrugged. 'A week?'

'A week is no time,' I said. 'We should definitely go round; we should go to the north.'

Natty wanted none of this. 'A week!' she said. 'A whole week!' and began urging her pony forward. 'We will never get where we want, if we delay any more. We should stick where we are; look what we've come through already.'

She pushed past me and I tried to grab her arm, but she slipped away. 'No, Jim,' she said, moving alongside the Rider and facing towards the Thicket. The trees breathed at her, their mist seeming more like fire than moisture; like smouldering, greenish fire; like wet flames.

There is no way through, I told myself again – and began turning aside to change our direction. But Natty saw this and would not follow. She suddenly pounded her heels into her pony and made him dash straight ahead. A little charge: five strides, six, seven, then she disappeared.

The mist billowed and settled again.

A bird screeched, then stopped.

And that was all; she had gone.

'Natty!' I shouted, but the trees turned my voice into water.
'Natty!' I called again.

'She will not come back,' said the Rider. He was astonished but also angry – because he knew what must happen next. I knew as well, but I did not accept it. Not until he beckoned to me and I came up beside him. Not until we nodded to one another, and the trees seemed to inch a fraction apart, and we rode forward together, and the mist swallowed us.

In this way began the strangest part of all my travels, when I had never felt so much at a loss. Everywhere I turned I found the same wandering smoke-trails, the same drifting steam, the same rubbery bowls of fungus, the same drip-drop of moisture, the same trickles of dew, the same muffling, the same halting, the same warm leaves slapping my face, the same groping and stumbling, the same slithering into slimy holes and bogs, the same suffocation.

'Natty!' I kept shouting continually. 'Natty! Natty! Natty!' And always I heard my voice soak away from me, or else meander among the shifting lights, weakening as the echoes multiplied. This only made me shout more wildly. 'Natty! Natty!' But it made no difference. There was another soft submergence and – if any answer at all – giggles and prattles and screams from the invisible birds that perched overhead in the invisible canopy.

'Here,' said the Rider at last; he was still close beside me and pointing forward, the moisture gleaming along his finger.

I saw no trace of Natty anywhere, just more tree-ghosts flouncing and flirting.

'On the ground,' said the Rider. 'You see?'

He leaned out from his pony and touched a monstrous old tree trunk sprawling beside him.

I looked harder, wiping my eyes.

A dab of dew had been brushed away from the bark. And another, on the next tree. And there on the spongy ground was a run of black hoof prints.

I turned to the Rider to thank him but he did not notice; he was leaning forward over his pony's shoulder, examining the marks more clearly and deciding to follow them.

And follow them we did for the next . . . the next few minutes I want to say, except time ran so strangely I could not measure it. For as long as it took, that is all I can say. For the next little bewilderment, in which my existence was made of water-gurgles, and bird-trickles, and moss-slaps, and the suck of our ponies' hooves as they plunged through the sopping ground.

I knew we would find Natty eventually; I felt sure the Rider would manage it. And I thought when we set eyes on her again she would seem like a wraith, then turn back to herself as we approached. In fact it was much more sudden than that. One minute we were squeezing through a gap where a great whoosh of moss had leaked into a silvery trunk and made it glow death-pale; the next we found her in a small clearing at a standstill. Her pony was grazing and she seemed at ease, with sunbeams lancing through the mist and sparkling the dew on her hair.

'What's taken you so long?' she asked. 'I heard you calling.' She was half-smiling, as if we had caught her in a game of hide-and-seek.

'Why didn't you answer then?' I said very curtly.

She lifted her head towards the Rider. 'Did I keep in a straight line? I tried to keep in a straight line. So I wouldn't lose our direction.'

In the past I would have expected the Rider to forgive her at once and show he was a part of her game. Now he went forward without a word, reached out his hand as though he was about to congratulate her, and instead cuffed her around the head.

It was not a hard blow but she felt it hard. I knew this although she touched her face as casually as possible; her skin was flushed – a faint rose colour beneath the brown.

'You put us in danger,' the Rider said.

'But I didn't think—'

'You should have thought.'

'You found me easily enough.' Her voice was steady, but there were tears in her eyes.

'Not easily, no.'

'But you did find me. And you'll find our way through the rest as well, I know you will.'

'If we are lucky.'

Natty slowly took her hand from her face; she wanted to wipe her eyes and would not allow herself.

'We will be lucky,' she said. Her voice was trembling now. 'You will make us lucky.'

Because the Rider's back was turned to me, I could not see his face. But from the way his shoulders sank down a little, and his head, I knew his anger had already begun to leave him.

'I will try,' he said.

Natty lifted instantly, like a child. 'So you see?' she said, looking to me for support and giving another of her smiles.

I stared at the ground, at the water-bubbles fizzing in the hoof prints made by our ponies.

'Oh, Jim!' Now she was exasperated, as if she had not been to blame for anything.

But I would not look up. 'You should never have done that,' I told her.

'Poor Jim,' she said. 'You don't want to lose me, do you?'

I faced her then. 'Never, Natty,' I told her, so angrily it might equally well have been the opposite.

She did not seem to notice. 'And you?' she said to the Rider. 'Do you never want to lose me?'

There was no answer, which was the final part of the Rider's punishment, and proof of all I had come to believe since I cured myself of my jealousy. Although Natty had thought she was safe a moment ago, now she suddenly crumpled again. She put her hand back to her face as if he had struck her a second time. And when the Rider moved forward into the trees she followed him without speaking, just as I followed her. In this way, winding and creeping, with branches continually blocking us, and the earth always melting away, we did not know she had been forgiven a second time until evening approached, and the trees thinned out a little, and the ground became more like solid land, and the Rider looked over his shoulder and said we were through the worst.

We paused for a moment to take stock, shaking our heads as if waking from sleep. But not waking in fact, because what lay ahead of us seemed like another kind of dream-country – a dry river-bed covered with shale and boulders – and, on the opposite bank, rising ground. Although this was still covered with forest, the trees here all grew a good distance apart from one another, and the way between them was easy. I thought that if we could reach the summit we would certainly see our river, and begin to make our way south.

But that was all for tomorrow. Tonight we were tired and hungry, so we made our camp and ate our supper and told one another we felt grateful to be alive, without any mention of what had passed between us.

Then I walked back to the edge of the Thicket, to enjoy the things that had alarmed me during the day. The mist had dispersed by now, leaving the trees absolutely bare and hard. Yet when I looked at them more closely I saw a thick layer of dew covered every branch, every leaf, and every hank of moss. They did not seem like solid things at all; they were watery enough to flow away at any moment.

I had come here to congratulate myself on our escape. To find everything that had frightened and mystified me, and to stare it in the face. Yet the longer I gazed into the Thicket the more certain I felt that I would never be free of it. The ghost-trees could never draw me back – but they seemed to reach out, and suggest their dangers had the power to follow me. Did I want to stay lost in them, however much I said otherwise? And if so, did I also secretly want Black Cloud to find us? I had no idea. I only knew that I had it in me to say: enough. And then to float away. To disappear.

Such thoughts as these kept me watchful through the small hours of the night, but when I opened my eyes next morning and saw the sun had already risen, I found they had vanished, as night-thoughts will in daylight. Natty and the Rider were already busy loading our ponies, and within a few minutes I had gobbled down some breakfast and we were on our way.

An hour later we had crossed the dried-up river-bed and climbed the facing hill.

Two hundred yards away, seagulls were rising in clouds.

There was a deeper blue in the sky.

There was a cane-brake, then a belt of mangrove trees.

And beyond them – there was a river.

I checked that my satchel was safe around my neck and felt its weight. I clicked my tongue. I shook my reins. I called 'Good girl, good girl' until my pony had broken into a gallop. I saw the country vanish beneath me. I saw all three of us in line abreast, and I thought we would soon be home.

PART III

THE RIVER AND THE SEA

CHAPTER 26

Achilles Williams

The Mississippi.

The almighty Mississippi.

But first the cane-brake, growing twenty foot high, where the leaves flashed as bright and sharp as knife-blades. They made it look impossible to breach, but once we pushed inside we found so many animals had already decided it was their home and created trails for us to follow, we moved quite easily, with birds on every side telling one another about our progress. One was a fellow the size of a sparrow, with a yellow-and-green tail twice the length of his body, who owned a completely circular nest of leaves and a front door as round as an eye; I saw him flutter inside as I came close, then study us with his own much smaller eyes as we trampled past.

Then the next obstacle. This was the belt of mangrove trees that began where the cane-brake ended, all growing so close together, in such tangled falls and clumps, I thought we must have stumbled into a second Thicket. And as these branches forced us to move more and more slowly, I lost my sense of what might happen when the river did finally appear. Would we stand on the bank and hail a boat as she passed? I had imagined something like this ever since Hoopoe first gave us our plan; now I could see it was a ridiculous idea. No boat could stop in such a wilderness – the banks were too overgrown, and too snarled with fallen logs and other obstacles.

But the river. The almighty river. When I say I saw it at last I am putting everything the wrong way round. I did not see the river. The river saw me – shining through the mangrove trunks, and so vast that even to my eyes, which from childhood had stared at the wide Thames from my bedroom window, it seemed not to be water at all but a stretch of the yellowing sky. Gigantic clouds were buffeting one another; calmer patches opened and stilled; the whole panorama surged and buckled under strange tensions.

I stopped beside Natty and the Rider, standing on a slippery platform of roots, and now that I could see more clearly I changed my mind. The river was not like the sky. It was like the sea, with the opposite bank more than two hundred yards away, and as distant-seeming as another country. A sea that began hundreds of miles to the north, and ended hundreds of miles to the south. A sea that obviously felt disgusted with the idea of stretching between two such distant points, and therefore bunched itself into countless coils and curves and doublings-back. To describe it as a gigantic snake is an absurd kind of understatement. When I looked to either side of me I saw only a few dozen yards of open water, before the current curved out of sight and was hidden by a bulge of green land.

'Look,' said the Rider, pointing off to our right beyond the tops of the trees.

'What?' I was still dreamy.

'Can you not see?'

Natty was looking as well and eventually she nodded, saying 'Yes' – but only slowly, which made me think she was lying to please the Rider.

I blinked and focused again – and made out a faint column of smoke.

'We will go there,' said the Rider.

'Where is it, though?' I said; I could not decide if the smoke was on our side of the river or on the opposite bank; the twists and turns made it hard to tell.

The Rider smiled, a rarity for him, and muttered something I did not catch, which I thought might have been 'For the last time.' Natty could not have heard him either for she said nothing, but put her head down and began stumbling forward once more, over the tangled roots.

For the next two or three hours we kept close to trees – so we could have the river in sight and hail a boat if one happened to pass – but sometimes veered into the corn-brake if the way ahead was too difficult. On both courses we made slow headway, and by mid-afternoon had become a melancholy crew, tramping in single file with our hands covered in scratches and our faces swollen by insect-bites. Our ponies seemed equally unhappy, with swamp-stains up to their knees and flies fizzing around their eyes.

In such a depleted state it was easy to feel that all the effort of the previous weeks was about to prove pointless. 'Hoopoe was wrong': that was the phrase I found myself repeating over and over, and still had in my head like a kind of pulse when our ponies stopped dead.

We had come to the edge of a clearing where trees had not only been cut down, but stumps pulled from the ground, and a ditch dug for drainage, and a jetty built into the river – a surprisingly strong-looking jetty, made of mangrove trunks with the branches lopped off. Beside this jetty stood a cabin, just as surprising and just as well built. A cabin with a pitched roof and shutters bolted tight, and a chimney at one end made of mud-bricks, and smoke – sweet-smelling woodsmoke – rising straight up to heaven.

None of us spoke for a moment; we just stared, watching the smoke rise and the light fall, and the mosquitoes dancing in their cloud-formations, and the huge brown river swirling beyond the jetty.

'Are we safe?' This was Natty, breaking the hush at last.

The Rider slid to the ground, handed her the reins of his pony, and walked forward without making any reply.

Someone heard him nevertheless, someone I thought must be a bear when he appeared round the side of the cabin some thirty yards off, because he was completely enveloped in fur – hat, jacket, trousers, even his shoes. But he was a bear carrying a rifle, an ancient flintlock that he held like a pikestaff, and pointed at the Rider's chest.

I found his face among the skins – a white man, so far as I could tell, but speaking in a rumbling language I did not immediately recognise as English.

'Stop right there!' he called, but kept marching forward himself until he was only a yard away from the Rider. Here he halted, and spat out a shining jet of tobacco juice; some of it landed on the Rider's moccasins.

The Rider grimaced, raising both hands as a sign that he came in peace.

'Stop right there!' the bear-man repeated, although the Rider showed no signs of moving. 'Stop right there so I can have a good look at you. You too.' Here he waved the point of his musket towards me and Natty, ordering us to let go of our ponies.

'A goooood look,' the stranger said, now taking one hand off his gun to push back his hat, revealing a larger part of his face. I thought he must be fifty years old, but so weathered he might have been eighty.

'Indians,' he said, sneering at our costumes and hoisting his gun to indicate that he thought we were nothing more than vermin. But just as his finger tightened around the trigger his companion wandered into the clearing and distracted him.

This was not a second wild man or even a wild woman but a goose – portly and white with clean orange feet – who apparently had more sense of occasion than her owner, for she ambled forward like a princess about to address an assembly of courtiers. At this stately appearance, we all stood straight and still.

The goose acknowledged this with a hiss, then waddled up to the Rider and pecked at the dark tobacco-stains on his moccasins; this seemed to reassure the stranger, because he now lowered his gun and spoke more kindly.

'She likes you,' he said.

When the Rider said he thought so as well, the stranger lowered his gun still further and gaped in amazement; his teeth, I noticed, were all made of wood.

'Speak English, do you?'

When the Rider said he did, the stranger's puzzlement turned into a smile. A reluctant smile, but a smile none the less. 'I ain't expected that,' he said, and clicked his fingers to bring his goose to heel as though she were a dog.

'See how obedient she is?' he went on, more amiable still. 'Best friend a man could have, a goose. Necessary in these parts, too. In these parts you find all sorts roaming around – so me, I'm always ready, thanks to her. Gives me all the warning I need. New arrivals, you name it. It's on account of her I saw you coming.'

As the Rider listened to this he turned to me and Natty and gave a little shrug; it was the first time I had seen him at a loss.

'Is it just you living here?' I asked – but the stranger ignored my question.

'English again!' he exclaimed. 'And better English, if I ain't mistook.'

'Both of us,' Natty chipped in.

The stranger rested the butt of his gun on the ground and leaned forward, narrowing his eyes. 'I had you for Indians,' he said at last, when he had scrutinised us from head to foot. 'You're wearing their clothes.'

'We're not Indians,' I told him, my voice sounding very formal and strained.

'What do you reckon you are, then?'

Natty chuckled. 'I can tell you what we were,' she said. 'What we are is more difficult to explain.'

The stranger was too astonished even to smile. 'You a girl?' he whispered.

'I am,' Natty told him without flinching.

'My, my.' The stranger backed away again and rubbed his chin. 'My, my. A girl. I ain't seen . . . not in the wilds, anyhow . . .' He raised an eyebrow at me, then peered at Natty harder than ever.

'A Negro girl,' he said, under his breath. 'A Negro!'

'That's right,' said Natty quickly, as though to head off whatever else he might say on this subject. 'Or a girl with a Negro mother at any rate. That'll do for me. And here we have an Indian' (she held out her hand to the Rider), 'and here we have an Englishman' (she held out her other hand to me). 'We are a whole universe in miniature.' She let her hand drop. 'And you,' she went on. 'I suppose you're an American?'

The stranger was so surprised he forgot to answer. After

scratching his chin for a minute he stepped backwards, rubbed his hat to and fro, chomped his jaws, found he had no more tobacco in his mouth, ground his face to a halt, and sighed a long sigh.

'Mr Williams,' he said eventually, and stretched a leathery hand towards us. 'Mr Achilles Williams. But you can call me Achilles. Most folks do.'

With this we all returned his greeting and told him our own names – but I could not help wondering about the other folks he had just mentioned. So far as I could tell no one else lived hereabouts, just the goose and a few chickens strutting in the dirt, and a goat tethered to a stake near some outhouses on the further side of the cabin, where our ponies had drifted away to graze.

Achilles did not notice me staring around like this; now he had decided we were friends, he only wanted to know more about us. 'Where you from then?' he asked, still leaning on his gun like a walking stick.

'London,' I told him. 'In England.' In the corner of my eye, I saw the Rider take a step away, gently shaking his head.

'London,' Achilles repeated wonderingly. 'London, England. You sure? Big old place, I heard. London.'

'Very big,' I said.

Achilles needed to think about this for a while longer; he dipped his free hand into a furry pocket attached to his furry coat, took out a plug of tobacco, bit off a corner, half-offered us the remains, returned them to his pocket when we declined, and began chewing.

'Well,' he said at last. 'I've seen all sorts coming through here, but never from London. That sure is the most marvellous journey.'

Natty and I agreed with him; it was a marvellous journey.

'So – why?' Achilles asked. 'What brings you here?' As I knew I must, I then told him how we had been shipwrecked, and wandered inland, and how we now wanted to travel south as soon as a boat came to rescue us; as I did so, I noticed the Rider staring off into the trees, peering into the shadows and frowning.

Achilles listened without interruption, quietly nodding and chewing. Indeed he became so placid as I continued, I began to think we would stay in his clearing for the rest of the afternoon, perfectly easy and relaxed. But as I came near the end of our story, and was passing quickly over the miracle we had seen with Talks to the Wind, our host interrupted me by banging the stock of his rifle on the ground.

'I know who you are now,' he said; and although he sounded relieved I felt a prickle of fear.

'You do?' I said.

'Your friends told me,' he said. 'They were here asking for you – I clean forgot. Said there'd be two of you, though, not three. That's what threw me.'

Natty moved to my side but we kept quiet; we did not want to alarm Achilles and set him against us; we did not want to alarm ourselves.

'Well,' he carried on regardless. 'They called themselves friends anyhow, but friends come in all shapes and sizes, I guess. These two were a big Indian fellow and another littler one. A strange one, this little one, I'll grant you. All covered in paint like a fire-cracker. Said they were looking for you. I didn't—'

'When were they here?' I interrupted.

The stranger pulled his hat down over his forehead, then pushed it back again. 'Hard to say. Two days back. Three maybe.'

'And where are they now?' This was Natty with the Rider crouching beside her, one hand touching the knife in his belt, his eyes still on the trees.

'Gone,' said Achilles, who had not noticed any of this.

'Where?' I asked.

'Who knows. Just gone.'

'What did you say to them?

Achilles laughed. 'What should I say? Hadn't seen you then, had I? Hadn't had the pleasure.'

'Did they say they'd be back?'

'Not that I heard,' said Achilles, but speaking more slowly now, peering more narrowly, because at last he had noticed the change in us.

'You're not in any kind of trouble, are you?' he asked.

'You could say that,' I told him.

'Killed someone?'

I shook my head.

'Taken something then?'

'Maybe.'

Achilles sucked his teeth. 'Indians,' he said contemptuously, as if the Rider could not possibly understand him. As if the Rider did not even exist. 'Always thieving things. Gypsies, all of them – thieves and scoundrels.'

I was about to object to this but lost my chance, because now that Achilles had decided we were not as simple as we seemed, he suddenly quickened his pace. He would not admit to thinking we should take cover, exactly, but he wanted us indoors all the same, even the Rider.

'Standing out here won't do us no good,' he said, tucking his rifle under his arm. 'Standing out here with me forgetting my manners. So come right along in. Come right along and get out of this damn daylight.'

He turned on his heel and began marching briskly across the clearing. 'Though I tell you something,' he called over his shoulder. 'They'll not be around tonight, those friends of yours. Not tonight and not for a day or two yet. They went north. Seemed to think they might find you there.'

'You're sure?' I asked, as we strode behind him.

'Certain.' He laughed again. 'Took off at a great lick – they had ponies too, like you. 'Cept theirs were painted, or the little one's was, at any rate. Smeared all over with red, like him.' Achilles slowed down again as he said this, and brought us round the side of his cabin where the goat threw us a blethering cry.

'Surprised they didn't meet you,' he added as an afterthought. 'Reckon they must've passed you on the way.'

'Very likely,' I said, and thought of the thousands of shakings and rustlings we had heard in the cane-brake. Any one of them might have been Black Cloud; we might have passed within inches of him and not known it.

'No harm though,' Achilles went on, before I had time to think any more about this, or feel the heat of our near-miss. 'The hand of the Lord is a powerful hand. Now . . . here . . . tie up your animals here.'

He pointed towards the outhouse, and without any more to-do we collected our ponies, found a place for them among all manner of old sticks and wheels and timbers, fed them oats from a sack, encouraged them to begin a snorting sort of conversation with Achilles's goat and his goose, then left them and stepped inside the cabin.

The cabin. In truth, it felt more like a box, with three windows shuttered and only the fourth one open, giving a view of the river. This was done for safety, I thought, and would have made the place very dark if Achilles had not devised an ingenious solution, which was to buy, or borrow, or barter, or steal a large number of mirrors and hang them on every wall, or lean them against pieces of furniture, or dangle them from the ceiling where they might catch such slivers of sunshine as bounced off the surface of the water and came though the river-window. As a result, the whole interior of his home was continually flickering and shifting.

This made what I saw next seem all the more disconcerting. While Achilles had assembled a good number of ordinary objects such as a bed and a table and two chairs, his prize possessions were a prodigious number of dead creatures preserved as if still alive, and pinned or nailed or glued onto wooden boards. Small creatures like mice and rats that had been dried in the sun. Opossums and otters. The heads and feet and hooves and skulls of larger animals, including the head of a wolf. Also fish swimming in little dry boxes, and bugs and beetles, and butterflies, and moths, and sea birds and land birds – among them, a brother of the same fellow that had recently looked out at me from his round nest of leaves in the cane-brake.

Achilles had taken great care with his preparations, and was very proud of the displays he had made, and made a special point of noticing how inoffensive they smelled. Natty and the Rider did not seem entirely convinced by this, and detached themselves to stand near the window and admire the view; but I allowed him to take me on a tour, and so became acquainted with many dozens of bear paws, snake skins, fox masks, turkey wings, and rabbits' feet, listening to the story of their lives and especially of their deaths, with the goose (who had now followed us indoors) pottering along-side and enjoying the talk as if it had no implications for herself.

I prefer not to describe in great detail the other kinds of treasure I saw during this diversion, which confirmed my sense that the cabin was as much a museum of loneliness as it was of nature: the scarred workbench where corpses were pegged out ready for dissection; the wooden bowl containing dozens of white knuckle bones; the collection of sticks marked with notches at regular intervals to show the passage of – I did not know what; boats that had stopped at the jetty below the window, perhaps. Or days that Achilles had lived by himself in the wilderness. Or years.

By the time my inspection was over I had decided that something in Achilles had collapsed, and although this made him seem revolting in certain ways, he was pathetic and touching in others. Especially when he had banked up his fire and cooked us supper, which was good plain muddy fish from the river, and begun describing his work for the river-boats. He did this standing in his window, with reflections of the current shuddering across his face, and when he took off his hat I was able to see his features whole for the first time – his deep-set eyes framed by hanks of dirty grey hair, and his jaw tightly clenched when not engaged in chewing or spitting. A face made severe by hardship, but also hollow with sadness.

'Yes, the boats,' he said ruminatively, as if answering a question one of us had put.

'Are there many?' I asked.

'A good many,' he said. 'But then again, none.'

'What do you mean?'

'I mean there's none for days, for months even. Then several all together suddenly. They like to keep an eye on one another.'

'Because the river's dangerous?'

'Just so. Always twisting and turning. Always filling up with mud and trees and I don't know what. One journey, the captain will find an easy way through – the next time he comes, that way don't exist no more. The current changes everything, see. Fills up and takes away. Fills up and takes away.'

'So we don't know when the next one will arrive?' I said, feeling it was dull to be so tenacious, but anxious to hear the answer.

'Oh, soon,' he told me. And then with a shrug, 'Or not so soon. I just have to be ready is all.'

'Ready for what?'

'To tell them!' Achilles exclaimed. 'To tell them if there's a passenger!'

'A passenger for where?' I asked, which might have seemed a strange question – but I did not yet know the name of the town on the coast which was our destination.

'Why, for New Orleans,' Achilles said, with a wistful note in his voice, as if remembering a place he loved but had not seen for a long time.

I looked at Natty in the shifting lights and we repeated the name to one another. New Orleans. Then I went back to Achilles.

'And do you have many passengers?' I asked, hoping he might say more about Black Cloud and reassure us that we were safe.

He faced away from us towards the sunset, staring at the long stripes of purple light that now lay across the current as if he was suddenly absorbed by the debris of logs and leaves that disturbed the surface. When he turned back he had forgotten what we were saying, and instead asked whether we had everything we needed for our comfort.

This was kind I am sure, but I did not understand what else he was implying until a few minutes later, when the sun disappeared below the horizon, and the birds in the trees around us fell quiet, and we spread our blankets on the floor of the cabin and bade one another goodnight. He was wondering whether we would sleep comfortably within four walls after so many nights in the open; whether we would feel safe here during the next night and the next, with our enemy still at large.

For this reason, my dreams when I fell asleep at last were filled with visions of myself standing on all sorts of piers and jetties and land-banks, while all manner of ships and luggers and barges and wherries sailed past me without hearing my cries. The effect was so dispiriting that when I woke up I immediately thought of my father; I had been reminded in dozens of different ways how much I longed for his forgiveness.

If I had been left to myself for a moment longer, I might even have begun to rehearse the words I would speak to him when I saw him. But there was no moment of that sort, no time of any kind; when I opened my eyes I found Natty was already on her feet, staring through the window at the river.

She called my name and I jumped up.

A drowned boat was gliding towards us, rising from the river-bed of my dreams.

A phantom, with scraps of morning mist clinging to her hull and blowing around her deck-house, and shadowy figures packed together on deck or working at the oars either side of the bow.

And Achilles was dancing and shouting on the jetty, waving his furry hat above his head.

And a bell was clanking, which told us we had been noticed.

CHAPTER 27

The *Southern Angel*

Although I did not explore the *Southern Angel* until our journey was under way I shall describe her now. River-men called her a keelboat, an open craft with a covered stern, over which projected a slender tree trunk (about sixty feet long) that served as a steering oar, operated from a small cabin occupied by the captain; in addition, she was directed by four much smaller oars working either side of the bow, at the rate of about five nautical miles an hour going with the current. Her purpose – which I discovered in the course of our journey – was to travel from the upper reaches of the Mississippi to New Orleans in the south laden with cargo, then to unload before being very tediously rowed and poled and pulled upriver again, until she regained her original berth. Whereupon the journey began all over again. A voyage downstream and back sometimes occupied as much as nine months (the first part of the exercise being the much shorter journey) and gave employment to any number of men, generally very muscular fellows, since the labour was very great.

When steamboats arrived on the river, which was some years after my time, these keelboats were variously sold or sunk or turned into homes for those who had worked in them. And while this change will have spared many men from being almost blinded by the sweat of their brow, I regret their passing. Natty and I felt our lives had been saved when we saw that grand old barge floating towards us through the dawn, and no matter what frights we had to endure after we came on board, we continued to look on her as our salvation.

In truth the *Angel* was a very humble kind of vessel – a floating tabletop about twenty-five yards across and seventy long, with no keel to mention (despite the name 'keelboat': the shallow river made such a thing impractical); and a warren of cupboards and lockers for storage below-deck; and above-deck a small village of tents, huts, shacks and pens where travellers kept watch, or slept, or played at cards, or quarrelled, or made up, or helped to navigate (by volunteering advice about sandbanks, logs etc.) alongside the sheep and cattle they were transporting, and their families in various states of excitement or distress or boredom, and a whole forest of farm implements, bundles of furs, bales of cotton, sacks of rice, crates of potatoes, parcels of cloth, a gang of slaves, and – I remember this very clearly – an upright piano. To call the *Angel* a chaos is to do her a disservice, since everything she carried was necessary to someone. Yet the confusion of all these things, and the continual murmur of human talk, blended with assorted bleats and whinnies and grunts and whistles and sighs, and the regular booming instructions issuing from her captain – who seemed never

to sleep, and able to make his voice carry to the ends of the earth
– gave an appearance of muddle that was at first perfectly flum-
moxing. I thought I had escaped the hush and solitude of the
wilderness only to arrive at a kind of aquatic Babel.

To arrive, and almost certainly to die. Or so it seemed, because
as Natty and I stood beside Achilles on the jetty, and joined him in
waving at the *Angel* as her oarsmen steered her towards us, I could
not see how even their best efforts might prevent her from splintering the jetty into matchsticks and crushing us in the process.
Her speed, which had seemed so lackadaisical in the distance, was
suddenly too great, and the power of her oarsmen too slight.

And yet, as I debated with myself whether I should turn and
run, and so save my life, a fierce jousting began between the *Angel*
and the river which changed the picture entirely; some of her
oarsmen abandoned their rowing and instead picked up long poles
which they plunged into the water fore and aft, then heaved on
with all their weight, issuing a spate of oaths that in their way
seemed as torrential as the river itself, until with a hideous creaking
and groaning in her timbers, the boat came under control. Once
this was done, a rope snaked out from the prow towards Achilles,
who tied it around a convenient tree trunk before retrieving a
second rope from the stern, which he also made fast, and so achieved
a miracle of mooring. The reaction on board was nothing less than
this deserved – namely, a flourishing of the gangplank, followed
by a great burst of applause, and laughter, and some hollers of
congratulation, and advice about how much more comfortable
Achilles might be if he had not come dressed as a bear, and questions about who had put them to all this trouble in the first place
and would now join their company.

In some ways, as I have already said, Natty and I felt almost
light-headed with relief. Here was an end to our life of

land-wandering and here was our redemption. Here was our final escape from Black Cloud, whom I imagined still trekking north to look for us while we were about to glide south. Here was our moon-faced captain leaning through the window of his cabin, with one gigantic hand resting on the rudder of his boat, and the other beckoning for us to hurry up and come aboard.

Yet in the middle of my happiness I was sad – to the point of feeling blind to everything except the past. I remembered the beauty of desert places and the dazzle of starlight when I lay on open ground. I heard the wind-song again, lulling me through miles of dry scrub. I saw the footprints of animals in the dust, marking their companionship with me. I saw them, and knew I would never find the same ways again, or the power of such simplicity.

Worse was to come. After I had collected myself, and told Natty we must fetch our ponies quickly, because they were all we had to use as payment for our journey, then run to untie them from their lean-to by the cabin, then returned to the ferry where I found her waiting with a bundle of our other possessions, then put my hand to my chest to make sure the satchel was still safe and sound – when I had done all this I noticed, which in my haste I had previously failed to do, that the Rider was not on the jetty beside us.

I understood at once. The Rider thought he had fulfilled his obligations. He had done his duty. Now he had his own direction to take, which was not the same as ours. Therefore he had ridden off from us without a word, because he knew we would otherwise try to prevent him, and keep him with us.

Natty saw this as well and the sorrow of it struck her like a fist. 'Ah!' she gasped, as if she was actually wounded, and with the blood draining from her face she stumbled away from the jetty towards the middle of the clearing. Here she stopped with her back to me, facing into the trees.

'Hurry up there!' shouted the captain, reaching a hand though the window of his cabin to bang against its wall. 'All aboard! All aboard!'

Achilles at least felt stirred up by this; he seized the reins of our two ponies, passed them to men waiting on the gangplank, explained they were the payment for our journey, and smacked them on the rump to send them forward; when they had clattered onto the deck they were tethered in a line with other ponies at the stern of the *Angel*.

For my own part, I ran towards Natty in the clearing and, as I came close, heard her whispering, 'Come back! Come back!' The tears running down her face and her wet mouth were shocking to see, but she was not aware of them. When I put my arm around her shoulder she did not notice that either.

All the same, I like to think we imagined the same things then, the same things in the same sequence. The Rider, keeping himself and his pony out of sight in the cane-brake until the great hulla-baloo of the river-boat had taken us away from him. The Rider hiding for a while longer, then skimming northwards over the treacherous ground. The Rider melting away as he shook our din from his head, along with the nonsense of the Entertainment.

'Natty,' I said. 'We must leave him be.'

She stared into the trees without speaking, and tears dropped off her chin onto the dusty ground. As their stain began to darken, Achilles's goose waddled forward, mistaking it for a titbit; in other circumstances this would have been ridiculous.

'Natty,' I tried again and squeezed her shoulder.

Still no reply, but I heard more shouting from the boat behind us, and feet pounding along the jetty, which I knew must be Achilles coming to fetch us.

I kept still for another few seconds, watching the leaves tremble and the tufts of moss swaying as though they had been disturbed when something passed through. But that was all I saw; and all I heard was the breeze sighing on its way to the horizon.

Achilles was not so patient. When he lumbered up to us he waved his great furry arms in our faces.

'Now, you two – get! He's gone, that Indian, gone. That's what they do, and there's no point trying to change it. Gone, gone. So you just take yourselves out of here and you be gone too. Go, now! Go – or you'll never find your way home!'

I think he would have continued in this way for much longer if he had not run out of breath – whereupon he continued flapping his hands as though we were biddable like his goose, and might be directed in the same way. This performance was so violently at odds with our mood I thought Natty might strike him, or rush into the wilderness regardless, which made me tighten my grip around her shoulder.

Whether this helped I cannot say. I do know, however, that when she finally did as I wanted, and ended her watching, my own sorrow at leaving the Rider was offset by the idea that I might bring her some comfort, which she would value.

Not that she had any chance to show it, because as soon as Achilles had shooed us back across the clearing and we had boarded the *Angel*, we were caught in a great flurry of business – the gangplank pulling up, ropes shivering, our captain shouting his orders, the faces of our fellow passengers surging towards us – travellers and traders and Indians and Spaniards and Frenchmen and free Americans and slaves – and voices clamouring to know who we were, and where had we been, and then just as suddenly losing interest in us so we could move off along to the starboard rail and say our farewell to our latest friend.

Achilles stayed on his jetty until the *Angel* swept round the next curve of the river, and waved his bonnet in the air with such affection I thought we might have known one another all our lives. We had been in his company for no more than a few hours, yet the drama and strangeness of his existence had made him loom before me like a giant. Was this a kind of distortion, I wondered, watching him continue to wave on the river-bank, with his goose honking at his side and shaking her snowy wings? Was it because I had spent so long in the wilderness, and seen so few people for so long? Or was America full of such grotesques, all remaining their unfettered selves until civilisation found them, and diminished them, and made them ordinary again?

These thoughts occupied me for as long as it took Natty to dry her eyes, and when she had composed herself again, and Achilles had disappeared from sight, we were ready to address more practical questions.

The question, for instance, of where we might find a part of the deck to call our own, which we decided should be a few yards in front of the captain's wheelhouse.

And after that, the question of how best to occupy the great expanse of calm and floating time that lay ahead of us.

To start with at least this seemed easy, for the simple reason that every part of our new existence was very interesting to me, and the river especially. A passionless, remorseless, ineffable, inexhaustible, implacable monster – at once absolutely determined to reach its conclusion, which was the sea, and yet completely witless in its endless wriggling and writhing, so as we drove south we were often required to steer east, or west, or even northwards again, and sometimes wondered whether we were in fact travelling on a river at all, and not merely scraping from one sandbank to the next, where the captain and his oarsmen were always required to shunt us forward with their poles.

On the shores of this great expanse we saw the same mixture of moss and leaves, moss and branches, moss and swamps, moss and roots that we had struggled through to reach Achilles's cabin – but now blissfully separate from us and therefore enjoyable to watch. Occasionally our wash would disturb a flock of egrets that flew up from the mudbanks like handfuls of torn-up paper. Sometimes two rotting logs turned out to be alligators who slid into the water to follow us for a few yards, loathing us with their hard yellow eyes. Sometimes what I thought must be a solid wall of foliage shook or thrummed or even split apart, and another invisible creature took to its heels.

And between these eruptions?

I would like to say peacefulness.

I would like to say rest.

But the enormous unrolling panorama, like a picture with no beginning and no end, soon soothed me into a state where I only appeared to be half-asleep, lolling against the rail that ran round the whole circumference of our deck; in fact I was busily awake, with my mind wandering wherever it chose.

In particular I found myself imagining the Rider as we continued to float further and further away from him. I saw him with his eyes shining, his head cocked at a familiar angle, but of course travelling alone now. Riding on northwards until the cane-brake ended and he came to a ferry and crossed the river, where he approached the country of his fathers.

As these scenes flashed through me I began to see other men trekking towards him, Indians like himself, some members of his own tribe, some from tribes who lived adjacent, and all passing him on their way west as he continued east. They came in ones and twos, in families and groups – the children and the older squaws with bundles in their arms, the warriors with their weapons trailing and dogs panting at their heels. They came in silence, and they came chanting in time to the beat of a drum. They came when the sun rose and when the sun set. They filled the pathways under the trees, and the dry trails that crossed the scrubland. They came with the dust billowing around them in muddy clouds, and they came under clear blue skies.

When I brought myself back and found I was still propped against the rail of the *Angel*, I looked up and thought the trees on the bank beside me were no longer things I would find remarkable. Surely they would have already become monotonous? But as I stayed to watch them, and the river shuddered beneath me, and spray sometimes splashed across my face, I realised they were a part of everything I had been thinking. More than a part, in fact. They were its origin. The quietness of the forest, the absence of anything moving except birds and animals, the absolute lack of any human presence – a village, or a hunting party, or a curl of smoke from a fire – were all proof that the people who once lived here had departed. I dare say some remained, and if my eyes had been sharp enough I would have seen their faces watching from beneath a fringe of leaves, or their hands lifting a branch. But even if I had been able to distinguish such things among the flickering light and shade, I felt sure I would have found very few of them, and thought these few were insignificant when compared to the hundreds of miles of green silence, with empty clearings in between, and long vines trailing through the still and heavy air.

And our crew and fellow passengers? Did they hear this silence, or think what it might mean? Not at all. They had their own lives to lead, which I thought was shameful and at the same time perfectly understandable. And while Natty and I did not feel in the least bit inclined to join them, because we had so quickly and happily fallen into our old ways, it became more and more difficult for us to ignore them as the *Angel* continued her journey.

I should say they were a fair sample of every sort this new world had magnetised, or soaked up, or lured, or bought from the old one – beginning with the captain, who seemed to have been produced by a marriage of the moon and whiskey, which he consumed in large quantities with no visible effect. He kept himself apart in the little box of his wheelhouse, but sent the whip of his voice snaking back and forth all day over the heads of everyone on deck; commanding us to stand still, or to shift to the starboard or the port in order to influence the direction of the *Angel*; or to retie a pony that had broken from its rail; or on one occasion to admire two alligators which had caught and dragged into the water a deer they were determined to tear into a meal of two equal sizes; or to encourage the oarsmen; or to upbraid them for allowing us to run aground; or to congratulate them on levering us loose again; or to blame himself, or more often to praise himself, for his own work with the rudder which he continually heaved this way or that as the river demanded.

Compared to this fountain of energy and advice, the others on board seemed lesser mortals. Most of them were pioneers in their way, as I have already suggested – farmers and prospectors and men following a whim. Among them were also a few Indians, some wearing the costumes of their tribes, some squeezed into ordinary town clothes such as striped trousers and black hats, beneath which their hair protruded in braids or plaits or greasy hanks. In either case, they sat apart from other passengers, who declined to recognise them except to insist they move aside, or to spit in their direction. Occasionally this led to fights between parties who wanted to occupy the same spot; more often the Indians gave way at the first sign of difficulty, sloping towards some unpopular part of the boat; I saw the same quietness in the slaves who were travelling with their owners, or stood in a gang beside the ponies in the stern until they were needed.

Because Natty and I were still wearing our Indian clothes we were treated with the same indifference or scorn I have just described. Initially I found this very objectionable, and wanted to protest in a clear English voice that the manners of the wilderness were infinitely preferable to those in parts that called themselves civilised. Soon, however, I decided we should avoid every kind of confrontation, and move even closer to the stern of the boat, by the pony-stand and the slaves. I can hardly say it was peaceful there, since it brought us nearer still to our vociferous captain; but it was a neglected spot, and therefore suitable.

CHAPTER 28

Lost – and Saved

As we found our refuge in the stern of the *Angel* we looked around at those nearest to us in a friendly fashion, to show we were willing to be good neighbours, and introduced ourselves to a young man and woman not much older than ourselves. They seemed out of place in this part of the boat because they were pale-skinned and smartly dressed: the man in a suit of dark worsted; the woman in a plain woollen dress with a tartan shawl pulled over her head, but not to conceal the yellow ringlets that reached to her shoulders; both of them fresh-faced and eager-looking, or that was my first impression.

While we began to exchange pleasantries, such as how pretty the sun looked while it died across the water, or how noisy the trees along the bank had become now the birds were preparing to sleep – I decided their enthusiasm was in fact a form of anxiety. Their clothes were too small and pinched them around the waist and under the arms. Their smiles came and went too quickly. Their voices were very dry, which meant they swallowed at the ends of their sentences, with the young man often rubbing his long fingers across his forehead. Even when the darkness had settled around us more definitely, and the captain hung a lantern in his wheelhouse which caught all four of us in its net of light, I saw his hands trembling when he spoke.

I would have preferred not to mention any of this, but Natty showed a strange recklessness – propelled, I think, by the sadness she still felt at leaving the Rider. When we had exhausted our pleasantries, and were peering at the river swarming away into the gloom behind us, she told them our names and the outline of our story, then asked for theirs in return.

Joshua and Anne Marie, they told us; their home was hundreds of miles to the north, near where the *Angel* had begun her journey, in a settlement built at the confluence of the Mississippi and the Missouri.

All this was mild enough, but then Natty became much bolder. 'Are you in danger?' she asked. 'You seem troubled.' I am sure she tried to seem solicitous, since she felt she understood unhappiness very well in her present state of mind. But Joshua was not to know this. Before answering he took hold of Anne Marie's hand and squeezed it until his knuckles whitened.

'What's that to you?' he asked; his voice had the soft American drawl.

'We're travellers too,' Natty told him. 'We have our own worries.' I thought for a moment she might be about to talk about the Rider but she drew back. 'You can't help it,' she said. 'Everyone who is far from home is in difficulties of some kind. It can't be avoided.'

Joshua leaned towards Natty, seeming glad of her enquiries. 'Very well then, Miss Natty,' he said. 'I suppose you could say troubled, yes.'

When he said the word 'troubled' Anne Marie also repeated it like an echo, and as if this suddenly gave him permission to speak his mind, Joshua then lost all his reserve. Looking from me to Natty and then back again, with his eyes glittering, he said, 'We have run away from home. Our parents – our fathers, at any rate – do not approve of our friendship. But we have turned our backs on them. We are making a new home in New Orleans.'

'In New Orleans,' said the echo, also leaning forward until her pretty face was flushed with lamplight. I saw now she must be a little younger than Natty, and much paler in her complexion. I felt touched by her innocence, and tempted to add that we had also been driven into the world by our fathers, but Natty was ready with her next question.

'How long have you been travelling?' she asked.

'I reckon we've lost count,' said Joshua, and gave a little chuckle, as if he could not believe the size of the country he lived in. 'Maybe a month. Maybe six weeks. Strange way to start a life.'

'Strange how?' asked Natty.

'Floating along,' Joshua said. 'Just floating along.'

'I can think of worse,' said Natty. 'We're bound for New Orleans ourselves.'

'How's that?'

'Well –' Natty began, but the captain interrupted her, shouting even more violently than usual, and suddenly pointing behind us over the wake of our boat.

Most of the other passengers paid no attention but continued their conversations in little groups and knots, or their sleep on the hard boards, or their meditations where they lounged against the bales of skins and other commodities. I found myself thinking how serene they all looked, how peaceful. And if not peaceful: how helpless. How like a ship of fools.

Perhaps this occurred to me because I already knew what the captain had seen – although when I turned to look where he was still pointing into the darkness behind us, I could make out very little. Beyond the fringe of our lights, a million mosquitoes bounced in the air like grains of sand in the mouth of a spring.

But there was a sound in the air, faint yet persistent. A bell, ringing continuously, then a murmur of voices muffled by the last bend of the river, then shouting.

It was another boat. Were the crew in difficulties and needing help? If so, why did it feel as though they were hunting us down? Were they pirates?

Our captain thought they must be, to judge by the way he now began roaring at his oarsmen to work faster. 'Go to it, you idlers,' he shouted. 'Go to it! You have the fallen angels coming up behind you, and if you want your wages go to it!'

But I knew better than him. I knew it was not pirates, or not the kind he imagined.

I touched Natty on the shoulder, meaning she must stay sitting with our friends and not show herself, then worked my way further aft through the few other passengers collected there, and the groups of slaves, and then the line of ponies, until I reached the tail end of the boat where I had a clear view of the river. The mud smell rose in my face, warm and close.

But this was not the reason I held my breath.

I held my breath to listen.

There! The shouting came again, blowing towards me like smoke so I could not hold it. Then again, and this time with a sprinkle of lights showing through the trees that marked the last river-bend. Now I heard it properly, and snatched it.

The words were my name. My name and Natty's name.

Black Cloud. He must have learned what to call us from people along the way. He must have returned to Achilles and hailed a second boat to follow our own. Had Achilles not said they came suddenly in groups, then not at all?

And where was Achilles now?

I did not like to imagine him, or the dead creatures staring down with their blind eyes, and the mirror-light swaying across the silent walls of his cabin. I could only think about Black Cloud finding a lighter boat than our own. A boat closing very quickly, which would soon be alongside us.

The captain still did not know this; he still thought it was pirates. The other passengers did not know it either, because they could not hear our names in the voices echoing across the water. But they knew there was danger all right, great danger – and were now suddenly milling around the deck, with the women mopping their faces and exclaiming, and the men promising to stand firm, and showing the weapons strapped to their belts, and boasting how they would use them if necessary.

Natty left our friends and came to stand beside me. I felt the warmth of her shoulder soaking into my own, just as I had felt it years before on the *Nightingale*, as we cut towards the Island and saw the fires burning in the darkness.

'It's him, isn't it?' she said.

'It is.' I reached for the satchel around my neck and felt the weight inside it and heard the pieces of silver sliding softly together.

'What shall we do?'

'At the moment? Nothing. There's nothing we can do.'

They were the same words I had spoken in the Black Bay, gazing at the waves as they pounded the *Nightingale* and slithered across her stripped and tilted deck; the same that I had said again in our prison in Black Cloud's village.

Natty remembered. 'Nothing again?' she said.

I looked behind me towards Joshua and Anne Marie, who were embracing one another, and at the other passengers still churning beyond them; they looked like figures in purgatory, waiting for judgement.

'We will fight him,' I said, which was all I could think of. 'We have what he wants but he mustn't take it. I won't give it to him.'

It was ludicrous — the sort of thing a child might say — and anyway Natty did not hear me. She was fixed entirely on the scene behind us: the boat closer still, the bow-wave creaming the mud-coloured water, and the torchlight dripping off the arms and shoulders of the oarsmen, fizzing into fragments where it struck the ripples in the current.

Only a hundred yards behind us now. A trim little boat. A dainty boat. Half the size of the *Angel*, with a compact cabin at the centre and just two passengers on deck. Two passengers standing between the oarsmen, and sheltered by a pale awning.

Eighty yards.

Seventy.

'Mister Jim!' The voice was hard as a hammer-blow and perfectly expressionless. 'Miss Natty!'

That was all. The same sounds pounding the air over and over. 'Mister Jim! Miss Natty!'

Now the captain heard them too. 'What are they saying?' he shouted, thrusting his shining head and shoulders through the window of his wheelhouse. 'Who's put us in trouble?'

I kept my eyes on the devils behind us and kept quiet.

'People have put us in trouble,' repeated the captain. 'Jim and Matty.'

'Natty,' said Natty, which I thought was a confession, but she quickly muddled this by adding, 'We heard him say "Natty".'

The captain blew out his cheeks and made a loud puffing sound. 'Natty, then. You wouldn't have seen them, I suppose?'

'No,' I said, without even turning to face him, because I knew he would see straight through me. 'How could we know them? We've only just come aboard.'

I gave a little laugh, but the captain was not so easily fooled. 'You wouldn't *be* them, I suppose?' he persevered. 'You two?'

'No,' I told him again, and did him the courtesy of half-turning, laughing more loudly. In the corner of my eye I saw Joshua and Anne Marie, who remembered our names; they had stiffened into waxworks.

'Probably it's a trick,' I told him. 'To make us slow down so they can jump aboard and rob us.'

The captain considered this for a moment, glaring down at me, then away.

'Maybe a trick, maybe,' he muttered under his breath, but I ignored him. The boat was fifty yards off now, and the deck-lights dappled more brightly over the oarsmen at the prow – six tall Negroes on either side, stripped to the waist and plunging so hard into their work the spray leaped towards them in melting claws and teeth. Between them, two other men stood in loose tunics and leggings. One was massive and four-square, his big hands cupped to his mouth to make a trumpet for his voice; the other was much smaller and slighter, his face bare to the breeze and his fire-paint glimmering.

Forty yards.

Thirty.

Twenty-five.

I was spellbound. Transfixed by the drumbeat of the voices. By the waves sloshing against the prow. By the jinking lights. By the men themselves. By Black Cloud and the Painted Man – the two of them stretching forward together, suspended over the prow of their boat as if they were flying, with the swirls and spirals of their decorations swarming across their faces, and their eyes bulging, and their teeth bare, and their skin shining, and their hair glossy as polished metal.

Ten yards.

There was no wound on Black Cloud, nothing to show the Rider's arrow had ever hurt him. There were only his hands dripping with river spray, and his stony eyes, and our names no longer our names but groans and gasps, and his fingers like talons, and the satchel almost within his reach – almost, almost.

Five yards.

Four.

Three.

He had paralysed me. I had no choice, no will of my own. I hung there like a bird skewered on a thorn.

The captain's shouts were whispers.

The other passengers did not exist.

And I knew how it ended. I saw our two boats splintering together. I heard the soft bang of Black Cloud pouncing onto the deck beside me. I felt the weight of the necklace lifting from me, and my whole body lightening and floating and fading as if my heart had been torn out of my chest.

Except my heart was not torn out.

My heart was still thundering.

And I was still here, living and breathing.

With the satchel still safe around my neck.

With the captain's moon-face still looming through the window of his cabin, still bellowing at his oarsmen.

With the oarsmen now shouting back: the *Angel* must fly! Fly to the left! Now! Now! To miss the sandbank ahead!

And she did fly – with the captain hauling on the polished old beam of the rudder so it almost struck the following boat on the nose and knocked Black Cloud from his perch. With a shudder that ran through the whole length of our hull. With a screech, and a squeal, and a big splash over the port rails.

I lost my balance and grasped at Natty. It broke the spell. It freed us. I crouched down and braced for the catastrophe.

But nothing happened.

There was only the river sweeping us forward, the thick brown water churning and purling and twisting and gurgling, while I looked off the stern of the *Angel* and saw the pale bulge of the sandbank looming in the current behind us like a whale, an albino whale, then sliding exactly beneath the prow of our enemy, and rising up, and bringing his boat to a dead halt, and holding it fast with a scraping wrench of timbers and pitch. And still holding it fast.

In a second we were out of reach.

In two seconds safe.

In five or six vanishing round the next bend of the river.

But I saw everything I wanted to see – and did not want to see. I saw Black Cloud snarling. I saw his eyes swelling like a gargoyle. I saw his talons tearing the air. I saw the Painted Man collapsing onto his knees, raging, cursing. I saw their lamps dwindle. And at the same time I heard the river still splattering against their hull, and their timbers keening, and our captain roaring, and our fellow passengers cheering, because there was nothing behind us now except darkness and silence.

And when this silence broke?

I expected a barrage of questions but very few came. The captain told us he would like to meet this Jim, and this Natty or Matty or whatever her name was, and give them a piece of his mind – then he seemed to forget us. A few other travellers drifted up to congratulate us on our escape, and some wanted to know our story so they could marvel at our luck, but of course we did not tell them. Otherwise, everyone assumed we were not the culprits after all, and left us alone. We were just the latest episode in the long story of their journey, and now our moment was done. We were negligible again. We were Indians again, and free to sink back into the shadows.

We did sink back.

We returned to our place on deck and lay still.

We listened to the river.

We heard the splash of the oars, and the breeze as it ruffled the awning over our heads.

We prepared to sleep – and would have done so, if Joshua and Anne Marie had allowed it. But they had seen Black Cloud at close quarters and felt the heat of his rage; they had trusted us with the story of their adventure, and now they wanted the whole of ours in return. I gave in to them as I felt good manners required, but when I explained why Black Cloud had followed us, and showed them the treasure we had stolen from him, I realised my pride must be another reason.

As I drew the necklace out from my satchel, turning my back towards the captain so that he would not see, Joshua was silent for a moment.

'Dear Lord,' he murmured at last. 'You have your start in life.'

'Do you think so?'

'I know so,' he said, awestruck. 'Look at that. It is your future.'

I did not reply, but let my eyes run over the beauty where it lay between us on my blanket. I had not let myself admire it for several days now, and its power struck me afresh: the silver pieces glowing as I polished them quickly with my palm; the carvings breathing and shivering and hunting and flashing their dark eyes.

I could easily have thrown it away to Black Cloud a moment before. I could have returned it to where it belonged. But I had kept it. I had covered it with my hand as if it were my own. Just as I now covered it with my hand again, when I thought Joshua had stared for long enough. Covered it, then returned it to my satchel, and slipped the satchel around my neck, and said goodnight to Joshua and Anne Marie, and turned my back on them, and lay down to sleep a little distance apart.

CHAPTER 29

The Interlude of a Foggy Night

Although the canvas that covered us kept the sun from shining directly into our faces, we woke at dawn next morning. My first instinct was to look off the stern, but there was still empty water behind us, with light twisting the surface into innocent scribbles and dashes. Natty and I watched without speaking for a while, feeling content with the silence. Joshua and Anne Marie were silent too, when they came to their senses. Either Black Cloud had scared them too much to speak, or our treasure had made them wary of us.

No matter, I thought, they need not be a part of our adventure – and turned to the only distraction at hand, which was the river. Mile after mile it yielded up wonders. On that first day alone, the first after our emergency, we passed several enormous mud-heaps on the starboard bank, built to a great height above the surrounding jungle. There was no sign of life round about, and when the mysterious and silent shapes fell away behind me, I did not know whether I had seen burial mounds, or temples, or simply a statement of existence.

I also remember a small party of Indians we surprised after swinging round yet another bend; they had plunged into the shallows in pursuit of a bear and were busily hacking at its head with axes, but this only provoked the animal to greater explosions of fury, which seemed (before the current swept the entire scene from our sight) more likely to end in the death of the hunters than a meal for their village.

A mile or so later, when we passed the village itself, I saw how welcome this meal would be. While the children ran out to wave at us, the mothers and elders hesitated beside a smoking heap of rubbish; they were almost skeletal with hunger, and responded to my cry of friendship with empty stares from empty eyes.

My fellow passengers paid little attention to such things, but continued to doze or chat and play at cards, and variously to amuse one another. For my own part, I expected to encounter more melancholy scenes for as long as there was daylight to see them, but at sunset they were hidden from me because a thick fog suddenly descended on the river. If we had been in a lane near my home at the Hispaniola we would have been compelled to stop, for fear of wandering into the marshes. Here we did not have the luxury of a delay – the river would not allow it. Here we steered as close to the bank as our captain felt was safe, while our oarsmen kept their oars continually buried in the water in order to slow down as much as possible and in this way hope to avoid any serious accidents.

Even so the current continued to drive us forward at a steady

pace, our lights making so little impression on the universal grey-
ness – except to turn it into a kind of soup – that we soon felt
entirely removed from the world. Our voices were fog. Our breath
was fog. Our footsteps to and fro on the deck were fog, and left
dark prints to show where we had been. Our clothes and hair and
skin were fog.

In such a peculiar state, where we felt at once safe (because we
were hidden from enemies that might be following us) and vulner-
able (because we could not see the way ahead), Natty and I decided
we would pass our second night on the *Angel* in much the same
way as we had passed our first – by settling down near the stern
of the vessel with Joshua and Anne Marie for company. Because
our talk the previous night had ended a little awkwardly, I hoped
we would eat our supper and fall asleep without much ado. But
Joshua, who seemed emboldened by a day spent wandering among
our fellow passengers, decided we would not close our eyes immediately and instead listen to a story. He had heard it, he said, in his
home on the Missouri, and when I repeat it now I shall use as many
of his words as I can remember.

'There was . . .' Joshua began, then paused to make himself
more comfortable, sitting shoulder to shoulder with Anne Marie,
while Natty and I remained on our blankets close by. 'There was,'
he eventually began again, 'an old river-man known to my father
since they were both youngsters, fifty or more years ago. Name of
Allbright. Charles William Allbright. He was a good worker, often
away for weeks or months at a stretch, on keelboats much like the
Angel. As an oarsman to begin with, then mate, then captain. He
was always first to wake and last to sleep, if he slept at all. But
always cursing the natural lot of man, as well, and dreaming of
easier ways. How he found a wife remains a mystery, even to those
who knew him best. How he kept this wife was another puzzle,

seeing she was very pretty and they lived so much apart, with him afloat on the river and her abiding at home.

'Still, there was never much trouble between them, no hard words or jealousies. And the early part of their life rolled by happily enough. Rolled like the river you might say, carrying all before it. Until a spring ten years ago, when I was still a boy but old enough to understand most things.

'Old Captain Allbright was setting off south for the umpteenth time, taking the same route we're travelling now, sliding down to New Orleans. Enjoying the flow of the current, and the cooler air at this time of the year, because he knew that coming back would be hard and slow, and maybe not in time for Christmas and the holidays with his pretty wife.

'A dozen miles out from home, only a dozen miles, one of his crew spies this barrel floating in the water. An ordinary barrel, all beat up but sturdy enough, with iron hoops and a bung tight in the hole. And always sitting bolt upright, bobbing when the current bobbed. Looking like it was paying attention, my father said. I remember that especially.

'The crew all thought so, at any rate, and they told their captain as much. They didn't enjoy being watched, they said, not even by a barrel, which had no business seeming so alive, as if it had eyes and a brain, and no business keeping up with them either, and staying level all the time. But Captain Allbright, he didn't mind it. It was a barrel, see, that was all. Just a dumb barrel. So how could it be watching them? That was their minds playing tricks. And how could it be following? That was only the wind and current.

'The men knew their captain cared for them but they weren't having this. They said the captain was wrong, it did have a mind of its own, this barrel, and to prove it they made a few tries to sink it – and every time it just floated up again, whenever they gave it a wallop. Ducked and dived and floated up again.

'They didn't like that one bit. And they disliked it even more when things started happening, unlucky things, with that barrel still bobbing alongside them watching it all.

'First they had a brush with a big old tree trunk. Hit them fair and square and stove in the prow on the port side and killed a man. Killed him when the water burst in. Drowned him when he was sleeping, quick as you like.

'Then another man dead, this time in a storm, a raging storm that followed them just like the barrel was following, and sat overhead like it meant to frighten them all to death, if it couldn't throw down one of its sparks and see them off that way. Which it did. Threw down one of its sparks and hit one of the oarsmen. Set him on fire like a stick.

'Then a third man dead, when this storm cleared away. Accident with a rope this time, tying up to some jetty somewhere. Could have done it asleep with a crew like that – but no, not paying attention, not concentrating. A slip, and the next thing you know there's a man overboard, drowned in the water with a rope around his heels, and that barrel still bobbing along beside them, just bobbing along.

'So that was three of them dead in three weeks, which was too much bad luck by anyone's counting, much too much. And the men went to the captain again and said there must be an explanation. But what could it be?

'Why, they knew the explanation already. The barrel. That was it. The barrel that stayed with them like it was Jonah himself. Or the Devil. So after that they pure and simple had to sink it, despite what the captain said. Sink it or better still catch it. So they could get rid of it, like. Burn it or break it up or anything. Just as long as they didn't have to watch it any more, or think it was watching them.

'And this time they did catch it. They caught it with a lasso, some cowboy did that, one of the passengers. He caught it, and he hauled it in like a catfish, except it was turning over and over in the water like it wanted to get away, which catfish never do. But it couldn't get away, see, it was caught tight, so pretty soon they pulled it on deck and opened it up, and . . .'

'And . . .' said Natty, because Joshua had paused as his father must have paused when he first told his son the story.

'And what do you think?' said Joshua. 'They all stood around on deck while someone flipped off the end of the barrel, and the water poured out, and they heard something. Something crying.'

'From inside?' said Natty, because Joshua had paused again.

'From the captain,' he went on. 'From Captain Allbright, my pa's friend. Him who said it was nothing, this barrel, but who turned out to be . . .'

'A liar.' Natty leaned forward and the lamp that hung closest to us sent its light into the fog-jewels sprinkled through her hair, making them shine.

'Worse,' said Joshua.

'Worse,' echoed Anne Marie.

'A murderer,' I said, without quite knowing how this might be so.

Joshua lifted his face.

'No need to look guilty,' he said, which puzzled me.

'I'm not guilty,' I told him, 'Why should I be guilty?

'We're all guilty of something.'

I wanted to make him pause again, so I could ask him what he was talking about exactly. The necklace – or something else? But I wanted the end of his story even more.

'So what was the captain's?' I said. 'What was his guilt?'

'His baby,' said Joshua. 'They thought there was nothing in the barrel, but there was a baby. The captain's baby. A little boy. He knew it was his, because of the marks and moles on him. And dead as a nail and naked as the day he was born, which can't have been long before, because he was still very small, and all folded up like he was still in his mama.'

'Who killed him?' asked Natty, which I might have done myself, had I not been distracted by Anne Marie, who I noticed was now very bright-eyed and cheerful, urging her beloved to finish.

'No one had killed it,' Joshua said. 'Or rather, nature killed it. Not a father or mother or any human hand.'

'But why the barrel?' I asked, finding my tongue again. 'Why all the unhappiness and the bad luck?'

'I shall tell you,' said Joshua, and leaned backwards against the rail.

'The baby –' he said, when he was ready. 'The baby had been born alive as far as anyone knew. A beautiful baby son born to Captain Allbright and his pretty wife, that is. But he died soon after, being too good for this world. Whereupon the captain returned to his work on the river thinking to occupy his mind. But not thinking, or not thinking enough, how his wife might need him to stay at her side and comfort her.

'So that was it. They buried their boy, and soon after the captain said goodbye and he set off south on his keelboat. And what did she do, the lady Allbright? She visited the graveyard, and dug up their one and only, and put him in a barrel, and sent him after his father.

'She wanted to punish him I guess. Well, she managed that and no mistake. She punished him by sending her sorrow after him, and she punished him by keeping too much alone while he was away and by wandering in her wits. By letting sadness hunt her down, in fact, just like the captain was hunted down. In the end, when he picked up his baby all dripping and cold from the barrel, what do you think he did?'

Joshua asked the question but did not want our suggestions. 'He spoke to his oarsmen,' he went on very quickly. 'He told them to steer for the river-bank, and when they got there he went ashore, and said he was going home now and they must choose someone else to be their captain.'

Joshua paused once more and this time Natty took the chance to cut in. 'So he found his way home after that?' she said. 'And did he live happily ever after?'

'My father never spoke about it,' came the answer.

'The country's very difficult,' I said. 'We saw that ourselves.'

'But you found a way through,' said Joshua. 'It is possible – you proved it.'

'We had help,' I told him. 'It wasn't the same for us.'

'And yet we all have some guilt chasing after us,' said Joshua, as if logic told him this followed exactly. His voice was sombre now the heat of his story had faded, and all the nervousness I had seen in him yesterday was gone.

'Why do you say that?' I asked, and saw Natty frowning because she heard the change in our voices.

'Well,' said Joshua, peering into the fog which had thickened so much it even wound around the lamp hanging outside our captain's wheelhouse and made the wick hiss as it burned. 'I saw those men following you. We all saw them. They did not –' Joshua hesitated, and swallowed with a little click – 'they did not look as though they wanted to shake your hand. Or anything to do with friendship.'

'Not exactly,' I conceded. 'But that doesn't mean I feel guilty.'

Joshua shrugged again, as though he had already achieved what he wanted and could afford to back down. I had thought him so humble when Natty and I first saw him, sitting with his girl beside the slaves. Now I felt sure he had played me, and for a reason I did not yet understand.

'Very true,' he said eventually. 'Perhaps you don't. But never mind – we've passed some time together, haven't we? We've eaten our supper and we've digested it, and we've dispensed with an hour that might have been tedious otherwise, and now we can fall asleep.'

As he said the word 'asleep' he dropped his head, whereupon Anne Marie instantly closed her eyes and put her head against his shoulder.

'Indeed we can,' I replied, rather formally, because I did not want to think my day had ended with a quarrel.

Natty felt the same, to judge by her own quick 'goodnight' – then she shuffled a few yards away across the deck and patted the space beside her, to show I must follow. I did as she asked, and lay down with the satchel between us, where I thought it would be safe. I kept my eyes open as the silence settled around us again, but all I saw was the fog swirling above me like marbling on the pages of a book, and all I heard was the river muttering to itself as the *Angel* toiled forward into the darkness.

CHAPTER 30

Ashore Again

After his bold story and the bolder moralising that followed, I thought Joshua might chase me into my dreams and accuse me there as well. But it was Black Cloud who did that – I should have known. Black Cloud once more crouching forward in the prow of his boat with his eyes bursting and talons grasping. When I woke next morning I had frightened myself so much I lay with my heart pounding, telling myself 'I am still alive! I am still alive!' – and opening my eyes wide. Breathing the scent of the ponies tethered a little way off. Hearing the splash of the river against our hull. Feeling the soft glide of our progress.

I was myself again, looking round to find the fog had blown away and our boat was moving much faster than I thought, with the current stronger and our oarsmen making up lost time. Where was Natty? Here, beside me. And where were Joshua and Anne Marie? Gone away – because they had woken before us, and seen our journey was almost done, and moved to the prow of the *Angel* so they could watch their new lives rise up to greet them at the first opportunity.

I felt in no hurry; I liked the relief of my awakening too much, and the warmth of the early sun, and I did not want it to end. Why was this, when I had waited so long to reach my destination, and travelled so far? As I climbed to my feet and watched the river tying and untying its threads behind us, I thought I must be nervous of feeling disappointed the moment I stepped ashore. There was a simpler reason as well. Black Cloud would never forget us. He would find us in New Orleans. And if not in New Orleans, then on board whatever ship took us home. And if not there, then at home itself. And if not at home, then at the ends of the earth, because we were his prey for ever.

What was my defence against him? Watchfulness, that was all. Like the poor Christian soul who believes the Devil lies in wait at every turn, and knows this Devil is his own creation and cannot be banished. The same watchfulness that helped me survive the wilderness, and now kept me safe on the *Angel* as I gazed at the river-flow, and the debris of straw-wisps and leaves, and the last rags of mist, and the sun-sparkles, and the trees massed on either side of me: the silent battalions I had seen ever since we first came aboard, sometimes shivering into life when a flock of white birds rose from the black shadows, but otherwise blank and endless.

Black Cloud was nowhere in this and everywhere – in the water, in the blue sky, in the trees, in the vapour. If I cupped my hands to my ears and listened as carefully as possible, I heard the river pattering against the prow of his boat and remembered how quickly he was gaining on us. If I narrowed my eyes and concentrated on the trees masking the bend we had just travelled round, or the one before that, I saw his silhouette glimmering through the leaves. If I closed my eyes entirely, he rose to his full height before me, his fire-shadow at his side. Black Cloud with his decorations swarming over his arms and bull-chest. The Painted Man with his narrow shoulders like a boy.

'What are you doing?' Natty wanted to know, when she eventually came to join me. I told her I was on watch, making sure we were still safe. Once she would have reproached me for saying this, in the days when she thought the Rider could rescue her from every difficulty. Now we were alone she was gentler again, and accepted that we must look out for one another.

'He will come, you know,' Natty said, laying both her hands on the stern-rail so the spray and sunlight mingled on her skin.

'Natty, not again . . .' I began, but she carried on regardless.

'We could drop it in the river.' Her eyes moved from my face to the satchel around my neck, as if she might be about to lunge and tear it away from me, settling the matter there and then.

'But we decided. He'd never believe us – he'd think we'd hidden it somewhere.'

'We could hand it to him.'

'He still wouldn't be satisfied. He'd still want to kill us.'

Natty frowned into the sunlight, gathering herself to say something she knew I would not like to hear. 'You only talk about him. You never say why you want it yourself.'

I let her charge sink into me, keeping my eyes fixed where the huge muddy river met the purplish blue of the skyline.

'We're like our fathers,' I said eventually, as if I was half-asleep.

Natty nodded slowly. 'Our fathers,' she repeated. Her voice hung in the travelling air, and I could not decide whether she had finished her sentence.

'We can't help it,' she went on. 'Except we haven't done as much as they did.'

'As much damage?'

Natty spread her hands on the rails and turned them over, showing the pale skin on her palms, and the darker creases. 'I don't know,' she said, then pushed back from the rail and stepped up close to me. Her mouth was ajar, which let me see the wet tip of her tongue; I am sure if we had stayed this close for a second longer, for only a second, she would have kissed me.

As it was we hesitated, and then it was too late: a shout suddenly rose from the deck behind us. We turned to look, and our fellow passengers were throwing their hats in the air and congratulating one another; they had seen the beginnings of a town float into view among the trees on our starboard side.

A moment before, I had wanted to stay in my dream. Now everything was changed. Natty grabbed me by the hand and together we ducked round the side of the captain's wheelhouse, then towards the prow of the *Angel*. We wanted to see the future as much as everyone else; we wanted our journey over and done with.

But as the crowd brought us to a standstill they told us this was not New Orleans, it was Baton Rouge. Baton Rouge which I am sure is a fine old city today, with all manner of churches and theatres and paved streets, but then was still very uncivilised. As I watched the meagre shacks drifting past, and the boats loading and unloading, and the sailors glance up from their work to wave at us, and admire us for travelling so far to see them, I thought the advice I had previously given myself about feeling disappointed was sound after all.

Then the last buildings drifted away and the trees returned again. But as we watched these last shreds of the great forest disappear, and the silvery marshes beyond them, I knew that enough had changed for us to see everything with new eyes. Who were we to blame others for being rough and ready? Our feet were black with dirt; our clothes were made of skin and twine; our hair straggled around our faces; our minds were filled with memories that did not belong here. We were savages. We had neglected the habits of our tribe.

That is why we felt more and more adrift, the nearer we came to our destination. We were grieving for everything we were leaving behind. The scrubland had almost starved us. The dry valleys had parched us. We had been nearly blinded by wind and sunlight and dust. We had almost been broken by swamps and bogs and fog and dew. But we had also found these things wondrous, and shared the sorrow of the people who lived among them. In my last view of the wilderness, it did not surprise me at all that my eyes were filled with tears.

After that: cleared ground with farms and plantations. Big smooth lakes opening in between, bordered with fragments of the old woods. White cotton fields and rice fields, and slaves working there. Saplings and ornamental bushes in rows. Pleasure boats beginning to shimmy around us, inspecting us, as well as working boats minding their own business: barges and luggers, smacks and schooners all about to collide with one another but all finding a safe passage, like bees in a swarm.

I did not look closely at any of this. In fact I could hardly look at anything, never mind that I had just told myself to stay watchful. Instead, I returned to our old place at the stern of the *Angel* and sank back into my river-dream for the last time. I saw myself jumping ashore, or else onto one of the other boats that passed us – onto one that was labouring upriver the way we had just come down. I raced back through the mangrove swamps and the cane-brake, through the Thicket and thorn-village, through the endless miles of flat and empty land. I imagined myself vanishing into the immense and level western part of the country, where I was accepted among the people and knew their ways and spoke their language. I believed I would live there according to the laws of simplicity, with my mind open to the sun all day and at night filling with starlight.

Was Natty a part of this vision? I was on the point of imagining that, when my dreams were scattered.

'Look!' she was calling. 'Come here!' – and I went back to join her, where she was pointing towards the shore.

Set back from the river, sometimes only ten feet off and sometimes a hundred or more, was an embankment rising about twelve foot high. An astonishing construction, which gave the clearest possible impression that from here onwards mankind had settled the ground. The country was under control.

Such was the destination we had longed for; such was our entry into New Orleans.

At Baton Rouge I had seen enough doors and windows to remember what a town looked like. But here were so many more of the same, and so mightily extended into towers and turrets, chimneys and steeples, quays and wharves, warehouses and lodging-houses, they seemed to deserve another name entirely. The sky darkened and narrowed. The sweet smell of vegetation turned into smoke. The silence became noise, and slow time quickened into hurry and bustle.

The change was extraordinary. In London I easily forget that streets used to be swamps, and tall buildings were once empty air. Here the newness of things was paramount – the newness, and the ingenuity.

It was this more than anything else that abolished my visions of a different life. As Natty continued to point out this church or that shopfront, this stevedore unloading or that sailor standing to watch him with arms akimbo, our captain rattled our bell and announced our arrival to the whole community. While the echoes reverberated I wanted to rinse them out of my head or ignore them, yet at the same time an older part of myself, the earliest and least destructible part, reminded me this was the world I knew best. This was what had made me, whether I liked it or not. Sluggishly at first, and then more hungrily, I began to devour the sights that appeared along the shore.

The men and women whose voices drifted towards us in a stream that mingled English with French, French with Spanish, Spanish with Portuguese. The houses where a hundred different styles played a continuous game of Trump, so Gothic arches leaped towards pagoda roofs, and fanciful metal balconies looked down on plain wooden doorways. The ships – the ships more and more, as we came towards the centre of the town – which had sailed here from the four corners of the world and now had their hulls so closely packed at the wharves, and their rigging so intricately criss-crossed, they made a gigantic net to catch the sun.

'We'll get home from here,' Natty said, her eyes gleaming.

'I'm sure we can,' I told her.

She thought there was a note of doubt in my voice. 'Surely you're not still thinking we might be caught?' she said.

I noticed she still did not mention Black Cloud by name.

'Nooo,' I said, stretching the word to make myself seem relaxed, but not creating that effect. Natty screwed up her face and pointed off the stern.

'There,' she said. 'What can you see?'

The river ran more nearly straight this close to the town, and had also widened with every mile we came nearer the coast; I was faced with an immense stretch of water.

'Nothing,' I told her, which was obviously not true. I saw rowing boats hovering in the sunlight like water boatmen; smaller craft ferrying passengers; tall trading ships and passenger ships – their sails furled or unfurled, their decks empty or congested, their crews anxious to leave or happy to return.

'Well,' I corrected myself. 'Not nothing.'

'Exactly,' Natty said. 'Not nothing. But not Black Cloud following us.'

She had said his name at last, because the very idea of him now seemed remote, and the thought that he might hurt us impossible. Impossible even when I forced myself to search more carefully through the confusion, crawling from prow to stern of every boat on the river, from crow's-nest to cabin door, and still found no trace of him.

It was enough, for the time being at least. Without replying to Natty again I looked forward and watched the captain bring us alongside a wharf which had our name, *Angel*, written on its timbers in billowing red letters. This was his place, where he was always allowed to return. Now it was our place, where we would begin the next stage of our existence. I squared my shoulders and made myself ready to step ashore.

Because I have learned more about New Orleans in later years than I could possibly have known at the time, I will allow myself to interrupt my story at this point and give a brief history lesson.

The city stands on the eastern bank of the Mississippi, which is vastly wide at this point as I have already said, and also very deep, and therefore suitable as both port and harbour. Forty years before we arrived, the population was a few thousand and no more – men and women who had lived under French protection, and flourished because they had surrounded themselves with a line of fortification, and also built the embankment we had seen (which they called a levee) to keep the river at bay in case of floods. And, I might add, in case of storms, which I knew to my cost were frequent and violent in those parts.

As their prosperity increased, so of course did the interest of others in owning it, and rights of possession passed to America in 1803 at the same time as Louisiana and Texas. When Natty and I arrived, we therefore found ourselves in a place that had only recently learned how to call itself whole, while remaining legion.

This paradox was reflected in the design of the place, since New Orleans had grown up around a large square that lay close to our wharf (and contained on its fringes a cathedral, a town hall, and other important buildings) but soon gave way to a most bewildering labyrinth of alleys, snickets, dead ends and short cuts. In this respect, the grand old town can best be described as a theatrical stage ('Entertainment' would be a more suggestive word), on which order and confusion were always at loggerheads, not least because the mix of nations on which it was founded seemed continually to attract more friends and family, traders and travellers, gawpers and tricksters, lawyers and priests, honourable men and dishonourable ones, admirable women and deceivious ones, slaves and profiteers, all bringing with them a torrent of stuff as mighty as the Mississippi itself: sugar and skins and hides and lead and flour and wheat and corn and tobacco and rice and cotton and cotton and cotton.

To end my history lesson, I must also say that when Natty and I had confirmed our arrangement with the captain in respect of our fares, and even received a handful of coins in exchange, I quite forgot this view of the wide world for a moment, and returned to my own much smaller part in it. I mean, I pushed back through the crowd of passengers all eager to set their feet on dry land, and went to bid farewell to the ponies we had just sold.

Harder hearts than mine have insisted that the love that exists between mankind and animals is inferior to the feelings we have for others of our own kind. I have often had reason to disagree, but not that day. After I had stroked our ponies' faces, and tugged their ears, and thanked them for carrying us safely for hundreds of miles, through deserts and swamps, they gave me no more in return than a nudge with their noses, and a nibble at my tunic to see whether I had brought them any food to eat. They could not understand that we were parting. Perhaps they had even forgotten the journey we had made together. I walked away knowing my affection had in a sense not been shared by them – and might mean nothing at all.

This thought disturbed me a good deal, since it compared so unfavourably with my sense of how Natty and I might speak of our adventure one day. But when I rejoined her among the crowd and stood ready to disembark, she was too distracted to notice how preoccupied I felt; she merely waved at the ponies, then hurried to tell me she had spoken to Joshua and Anne Marie, and we had been invited to join them in their search for a place to stay. Here she said (or rather half-shouted above the hubbub that now surrounded us) we could lie out of sight until we discovered how to begin the last part of our journey towards England and home.

All this sounded very easy and convenient, but as I waved a final goodbye to the captain I lost my nerve for a moment. The city that lay ahead of us was not so much a city as a sort of massive convulsion. A bait-box. A pullulation. Women dressed in flowing gowns and women capped and bonneted; women trawling for sailors, and women shopping for their next meal; Yankees and Spaniards; Negroes and Chinamen; Mexicans and Scotsmen; Englishmen and

Indians – Indians in tall hats and suits, and Indians slathered with paint and half-naked; mulattos both curly-haired and straight-haired; quadroons of every shade of brown and black and ebony and yellow and even tawny orange.

To be blunt, the effect of all this crowding-together was to make me feel we had arrived somewhere extremely *odd*. As compensation, I can add that if had been any other sort of town, our own appearance would have been a part of this strangeness, since we arrived wearing our Indian clothes and a thick coating of dust. As it was, I do not think we seemed in the least peculiar, and were therefore not in the least obvious.

On the contrary. When I pulled myself together and set my feet on the gangplank, and felt its boards bounce beneath my weight, I believed we were once more about to take our place among the ordinary children of light.

Things That Happen

Joshua led the way with one arm around Anne Marie, I held Natty by the hand, and even before we reached the central square and the labyrinth on its further side – which is to say, while we were still leaving the docks that lined the river – I felt so many elbows poke me in the ribs, apologised to so many different strangers of so many different colours for blocking their way, thanked so many others for standing aside, or patting me on the back, or ushering me forward, I thought that after my long exile from the world I had been reminded of each and every part of it in the space of ten minutes.

Our hotel was a clapboard affair recommended by the captain, where the porches and balconies were all wonderfully decorated with wrought iron, sometimes as barriers to prevent its guests from

falling out of their windows, more often to show the city's exuber-
ance in miniature, and to prove something about the ambitions of
its owner. About his very great scale and weight, I should say. We
found him overflowing the desk in his lobby, with his shirt open
to the navel and his sleeves rolled up despite the fact that he was
positioned directly beneath a large fan, which he operated by
pumping a pedal with his right foot.

'What can I do for you folks?' The voice of this man-mountain
was a dubious little treble.

'We're looking for rooms,' I said as firmly as possible. I thought
that by speaking first and in English, I might reassure him that I
was not as I appeared.

'For rooms?' repeated the mountain. His name, I now saw from
a board that swayed in the breeze above his head, was Thomas A.
Brydges; he looked me carefully up and down, staring at my Indian
clothes, and seemed not in the least reassured.

'Would that be one room or two rooms or three rooms or four
rooms?' he asked.

'Two rooms,' said Natty confidently, which I was pleased to
hear.

Mr Brydges rolled his shoulders, sending a flutter along the flesh
of his arms, then looked aside into a dusty mirror that hung on
the wall beside him, as if to remind himself he was as powerful as
he thought, before facing us again and demanding to know how
we would pay. By now we had all drawn into a semicircle in front
of his desk and felt so pleased to be in the breeze of the fan, and
the current of food-smells that floated from an adjacent kitchen,
we would gladly have handed him whatever he asked for – except
that all Natty and I had in our possession was the handful of coins
given to us by our captain.

At this point Joshua surprised us again. Having seemed so meek when we first met him on the *Angel*, and then so mysterious and moralising, he now became very efficient.

'Here are five dollars,' he said, pulling the sum from his pocket and slapping it down on the desk. 'Is that your tariff?'

Mr Brydges gathered himself with more trembling and shaking. 'For one room, yes,' he said truculently. 'For two, no. Five dollars will pay for one room for a week.'

I thought that Joshua would now explain to me, politely or otherwise, that he would accept this offer and in the same breath say goodbye to us. But with a glance at the satchel hanging around my neck, and no doubt a thought about the value of what lay inside it, he said, 'Very well, two rooms for three days, and change of fifty cents due to me. Three days are all we shall need. Because in three days we shall find employment and a home elsewhere.' He bent forward over the desk so the jacket of his suit stretched tight across his shoulders, then continued in a confiding way, 'You see, we have come here to make our fortune.'

Mr Brydges, who must have heard this sentiment a thousand times before, was nevertheless impressed by Joshua's determination. Sufficiently impressed, at any rate, to forget he must keep tramping on the pedal connected to his fan, so the slicing sound ceased above our heads and warm air fell down on us like a cloth.

When he began pumping again, the effect pleased him enough to accept our offer. Joshua did not seem surprised. 'Thank you, Mr Brydges,' he said quite calmly, and with that he straightened his back, extended his hand palm upwards, received his change, pocketed it, and so began his career as a businessman. A moment later we had climbed to the floor above, taken rooms next to one another, arranged to meet a few hours later in the evening, and shut our doors.

Natty and I crossed to the bed and lay down together with as little fuss as we had lain down side by side in the wilderness. Although less than two months had passed since we last slept under a roof – in Mr Vale's hotel – I thought it might as well have been a year, because our feelings for one another had changed so much. Or rather, our feelings had not changed, but the way we showed them had changed. My jealousy had burned away and our good companionship had returned; beneath these things, and as the source of both, everything was the same as ever. Unsayable and unsaid. Waiting until we reached England to find an expression, as Natty had stipulated.

For this reason all we did next, when our heads had cleared and our land-balance was restored, was to look about us. To find our windows showed the blank brick wall of a house across the way; to hear our peace broken every so often by the shouts, cries, sobs, moans and laughter of others in the street below; to be grateful we had privacy enough, and comfort enough, and clean water in a pitcher, and a shiny white wash-bowl; to feel the strangeness of all these things, and to know we were perfectly content.

This is all the description I shall give of our time in that room, except to say that after we had slept for an hour or so we woke refreshed, and cleaned our faces, and ran our fingers through our hair, then knocked on Joshua's door and told him we were about to return to the docks, where we would ask how best to make our way to London.

To London? Wherever we went and however we put the question, the response was always to laugh us nearly back to our hotel. To London? No boats ever sailed to London. To London? Did we think London was just over the horizon and could be reached in a single stride? When we replied that we did indeed know the answers to these questions, having lived in that city some time before, having come from there in fact, we were laughed at even more loudly. As far as these sailors were concerned, we were two Indians who had been driven mad by losing our homes, or by the sun, or by drinking.

All this – until we approached our umpteenth whiskery old captain, and this time found our replies were taken as proof of spirit not lunacy, and so waited on the quayside until he had climbed down from his wheelhouse to examine us more closely.

'New York is the way to go,' he told us. Initially, while he had been regarding us from his ship, which was a twin-masted clipper a little smaller than the *Nightingale*, I had thought his beard was wild as a hedge. Now I could see it was carefully trimmed, but so profuse it had almost crawled across his eyes, which perhaps for this reason had become very fierce. Despite that eagle stare, or perhaps because of it, he did not seem to mind us being dressed for the wilderness, and if he noticed Natty was an unusual sort of sailor – which he could hardly fail to do – he never mentioned it.

'You look lively,' he said, when he had studied us both from head to toe. 'Do you know anything about ships? And about sailing?'

We told him we did, without saying that all our expertise had ended in a wreck.

'And do you know about hard work?' he went on.

'More than we care to know,' I told him, which was facetious but true enough.

The captain folded his arms and made his decision. 'I'll take you to New York,' he told us. 'If you'll work for me.'

I promised him we would, and then wondered how soon we might set sail.

When he told us next day I almost said we could not join him after all, because it surprised me so much: I had expected a longer delay. But once I had gulped once or twice and felt Natty tap me on the shoulder, I informed him that this would do very nicely, and we would return the next morning if he liked, and acquaint ourselves with the ship. As soon as he agreed we bade him farewell and went on our way rejoicing.

We made these arrangements very swiftly and simply in contrast to our previous travels. So much so, I felt we were at last keeping step with destiny, and fulfilling whatever purpose Fate had in store for us, rather than pushing against the grain of things. Yet I must also admit that in passing over certain details (such as the names of our ship and her captain, which were *Mungo* and Yalland respectively; and the colour of her sails, which were a dark liverish brown; and the number of her crew, which I estimated to be a dozen or so; and her business, which was to carry cotton) I also intend to suggest a less comfortable aspect to all this speed.

I felt driven forward by a force I could not control. In the wilderness, where a particular day had often seemed identical to the one before and the one after, I had generally thought of time as a slow current. On the river it had been the same, and literally. Now everything was hasty, with appointments to keep and meals to eat, and every one of them tied to a particular moment, so we were continually in danger of being too early or too late. I could not help thinking again how much peacefulness I had left behind me, amidst the danger.

Having said that, I also believed our first task was to return to our hotel. But as soon as we got there and found Mr Brydges inflating himself under his fan, I discovered that haste was the least of our difficulties.

'Ah-ha!' he sighed, as we tried to slip past him and reach our room without starting a conversation.

'Yes, Mr Brydges?' said Natty, pretending to be taken aback.

Our host kept twitching his foot to operate the fan, making our hair fly around our ears.

'What is it, Mr Brydges?' I asked again.

'Pleasant afternoon?'

'Very pleasant, thank you.'

'Sunshine?'

'Always sunshine.'

'Ah-ha.' Mr Brydges worked faster at his pedal, which began to squeak like a bat.

After a moment I asked, 'Was there anything, Mr Brydges? You wanted something, I think?'

At last he looked at me directly. 'A man called for you,' he said, in his finicky little voice.

Natty and I knew at once. Knew as we had known at a similar moment in Mr Vale's hotel in Santa Caterina. Knew so well we wanted to run – but at the same time not. We must hear all there was to hear; we must not seem alarmed.

Natty found a way. 'What sort of man?' she asked.

'A strange one,' said Mr Brydges, relaxing his footwork and smiling because he knew he had something we needed, which gave him power over us as long as he kept it to himself.

'One man?' I asked.

'I can see you know him then,' Mr Brydges replied. 'And you are quite right. Not one man. Two men.'

'Indians?' I continued.

Mr Brydges now abandoned his fan entirely and tilted against one side of his chair to spit a bullet of tobacco juice into a bowl placed beside him on the floor.

'You could say that,' he said when he was working his fan again, more gently than before.

'We know them, Mr Brydges,' Natty and I said together. My intention, which I am sure must have been hers as well, was to show we were still in command of the situation; that we were not in the least alarmed.

Mr Brydges was unimpressed. 'Friends of yours, are they?' he asked.

We were less unified in our response this time, and replied in a jumble, 'Not quite'; 'Not exactly.'

'I thought so,' Mr Brydges murmured, nodding his head.

I waited for him to continue, and when he did not I asked, 'You thought what?'

'I thought they were not your friends,' he said, and raised himself a little in his chair to bring the current of air away from his head and onto his chest, where his shirt-front began to panic and open, revealing skin as white as chicken meat.

'I thought they could not be friends,' he said again. 'Although they said they had travelled a long way to meet you. A long way and a long while.'

'They spoke to you in English?'

'What passes for English round here. I understood them well enough.'

'Did they say they would come back?' Natty had recovered from our confusion a moment before and now spoke very intently. I thought this might annoy Mr Brydges, and provoke him into behaving even more like a cat with a mouse; in fact, and to my great relief, it had the opposite effect.

'They did not say anything about that,' he said, then paused and gave another tremulous roll of his shoulders. '*They* did not say,' he went on, with a little smile of self-congratulation, 'because *I* did not say you would be here to meet them. In fact *I* did not say you would be here at all. Would be or ever had been.'

'Oh, thank you, Mr Brydges,' I burst out, with so much relief I embarrassed myself somewhat.

'Yes, thank you,' Natty added, with more dignity.

'Things that happen in my hotel!' Mr Brydges said, swelling even more enormously in his chair. 'Things that happen!' This phrase, which he clearly felt to be very rich in meanings, gave him so much food for thought he let it hang in the air between us for a while, before narrowing his eyes and staring at us more closely, to make sure we were as grateful as we should be. Once he had satisfied himself on this score, he drew a plug and a knife from the pocket of his trousers, cut off a piece of the tobacco, popped it into his mouth, and began to chew.

After he had continued in this way for another minute, he felt able to repeat his judgement a third time – 'Things that happen in my hotel!' – and then to elaborate it. 'They happen,' he said, 'when I let them happen. The folk I allow in, I allow in. Them I don't, I don't. Them two, I don't.'

He stopped chewing for a moment, which allowed his chins to settle onto his neck, and I thought this might be a signal for us to speak again, and say once more how indebted we were to him. But I let the moment stretch until it became a silence, at which point he waved one hand loosely like a flipper to show he thought our conversation was over and done with. We were free to go.

I could not resist asking one more thing.

'Do you know where the two men went, Mr Brydges, after you had given them that answer?'

My Brydges looked through the open door of his hotel into the street behind us. When I turned in the same direction I saw such dazzling sunlight it felt like blindness.

'No idea,' he said, still gazing off. 'They went away. That is all I can tell you.'

Now it was my turn to stare, until my eyes got used to the brightness and I was able to see the dust blowing up from the street and the feet of the people who walked there – the moccasins and sandals, the riding boots and ladies' boots, and the bare toes as well, all pattering out their different rhythms.

'Jim?'

Natty was shaking my shoulder because I seemed to have fallen into a trance.

'Yes?' I blinked and looked round, first at Mr Brydges, who had slumped back in his chair and closed his eyes, then at Natty. Her face had a sheen of sweat which might only have been heat, because Mr Brydges had again stopped working his fan.

'We're still safe,' she said to me.

I kept still a moment longer, listening to the voices of the hotel around us, and the murmur outside as the town continued with its bustling. Yes, apparently we were safe, and could stay safe if we also kept to our plan. If we went to our room and lay low, then slipped away to our boat in the morning. We would be gone by noon. Sooner perhaps. Black Cloud would never find us now. We were almost invisible; we were almost free.

By the time this thought had taken hold of me, and we had left Mr Brydges in his doze and returned to our room, we had pushed Black Cloud to the side of our minds and were cheerful again. We had not forgotten him, but we chose not to think about him. Instead, we preferred to lie on our bed and listen to the bed-springs remind us of other travellers who had rested here. To sleep a little. To talk about England and the changes we would find waiting for us. And to do all this so easily, with such a growing sense of our liberty, that when the afternoon began to darken, and the air cooled, and a smell of rotting vegetation drifted up from the river and in through our window, I could almost believe I was back at the Hispaniola, with the Thames a stone's throw away and the Mississippi a distant memory.

Then Joshua knocked on our door, an hour or so after darkness had fallen. We knew it was him; Anne Marie would not have dared.

He was tired after his day, he told us, tired of exploring and asking for employment, and now also tired of resting and recuperating. Would we care to step outside with him and his beloved, and find something to distract us before we retired for the night?

Although he spoke courteously like a gentleman, I would like to say we demurred because we still felt nervous of the world, and conscious above everything of the need to protect ourselves. Instead we told him we were due to board the *Mungo* next morning, and would not see him again after that – which provoked him into an even greater fit of friendliness. He insisted we come with him immediately; he also insisted we make a proper goodbye, which he told us was the least we owed him for the cost of our rooms.

I stood at the door of our room while we talked, with the chatter of other guests bubbling up from the lobby below; when I turned to Natty to see if she agreed, I found her sitting on the edge of the bed and running her hands through her hair – as if she had already decided to accept, but heard the voice of reason telling her not to. Joshua, in contrast, looked more enthusiastic by the minute. He had thrown away the tight old clothes he had worn on the *Angel* and was wearing a smart black jacket and trews, which made me think he had already got the measure of the town. Likewise Anne Marie, who now appeared in the corridor behind him wearing a yellow dress that almost matched her hair.

'Well?' said Joshua.

'We've only got what you see,' I told him.

'No other clothes at all? Only those old Indian things?'

'That's right. No other clothes, and no money either; only a few coins.'

Joshua held up his finger, tapped the side of his nose, then swung away without a word, which left Anne Marie twisting her hands and muttering 'Oh! Oh!' under her breath.

She did not have to suffer for long. Joshua's footsteps had hardly faded along the corridor before he was stamping towards us again with a crumpled white shirt and dark trousers, and an equally crumpled green dress, draped over his outstretched arms.

'Take these,' he ordered, thrusting them towards me. 'They need a shake-out, but they're good enough, I think. We have plenty.'

'Plenty,' echoed Anne Marie though with such a blank look on her face, I thought she might not have known the meaning of the word.

'We can't repay you,' I told him.

'No matter!' Joshua said gaily. 'We are beginning! We shall soon have clothes galore, won't we, my darling? Clothes galore.'

'Galore,' came the echo.

'Besides . . .' I went on, but changing direction. 'We're happy with what we have.'

Joshua looked me up and down, then drew his fingers slowly across my tunic.

'You're happy . . . ?' he said disdainfully. 'With that?'

'It's mine,' I said, and looked over my shoulder at Natty on the bed; she was touching the grimy hem of her dress, avoiding my eye. 'And hers is hers,' I added. I did not want to explain everything implied by this – how we had been given our clothes, and by whom, and what they had come to represent. I did not think Joshua would understand; not this new Joshua, and perhaps not the Joshua we had first met either.

'They don't look like yours,' he replied at length, which was polite compared to what I knew he was thinking. Then he went on more straightforwardly. 'Anyway, do you plan to wear them for ever? When you're back in England even? Are you going to be Indians in England?'

'Definitely not,' I told him a little stiffly. 'We'll change at some point.'

'Well then.' He widened his eyes. 'Why not change now? I told you – we are beginning. And tonight is the beginning of the beginning.'

This was all it took. I knew I should hesitate. I knew I should thank him and say no. But I had already begun to fall. So I merely nodded at him, and told him I understood what he meant, and received the clothes from his hands, and thanked him for his generosity.

Natty too. She stood up from the bed to claim her dress, and held it against herself and said she was sure it would fit, and yes, it was a pretty green – although yes again, very crumpled.

'Quite the belle,' said Joshua, smiling as though we had done something clever. 'Now,' he went on, 'you two get dressed, and we'll wait for you downstairs. Five minutes, all right? Five minutes.'

He grasped Anne Marie by the hand, turned smartly on his heel, shut the door behind him, and clumped away along the bare boards; by the time his footsteps melted into the laughter downstairs, we had already begun to change.

CHAPTER 32

Our Evening Together

Our new clothes, which for a while seemed so unnatural to us – so tight, so bright, so peculiar in their ingenuity – made us feel interesting to everyone as soon as we left our lodging; I tucked my satchel inside my shirt and buttoned it up tight. In fact no one paid us the least attention, because everyone was too preoccupied by their own affairs. We were just four more faces among a multitude of strangers, and this soon restored my sense that we were invisible. By the time we had found our way through the backstreets and across the main square, then sat down together to make our celebrations as Joshua wanted, I felt certain that Black Cloud could not possibly harm me.

I should call the place we had chosen an inn, but it bore so little resemblance to the inn I knew best – the Hispaniola, which had been my home until I met Natty – that some other word would do better. It was a single high-ceilinged room, with a gallery (fed by stairways on all four sides) for additional seats such as you might find in a church, dozens of tables and chairs, candles gleaming, an endless bar, waitresses wearing black dresses and shirts like French maids, and an enormous, sweating, heaving crowd of people whose sole purpose was to consume a tremendous quantity of liquor while producing an equally tremendous din of shouts and whistles and comments and accusations and arguments and secrets and convictions. Not so much an inn, therefore, as a kind of den. Uproarious, outrageous and chaotic – as though everyone present was convinced the world would end tomorrow morning, and tonight was their last chance to enjoy themselves before the catastrophe.

Joshua, as I have said, was not at all interested in last things. In fact no sooner had he found us a table – beneath a long window overlooking the river – and hailed a waitress, and filled our glasses with whiskey, than he once again toasted the start of our lives, and how we would henceforth share them together. From this I understood him to have decided that our leaving tomorrow was an incredible idea, ridiculous in fact, and hoped to persuade us of this before the evening was done. Wishing us wealth and happiness, he waved his glass in the direction of my satchel – which he knew must be concealed inside my shirt – to show how well he understood its contents would help us achieve our joint ambitions. I glanced away at Natty and she gave me a little nod; in this way we agreed that tonight we would not protest any longer. We would play along with Joshua's ideas of our partnership, then disappear quietly in the morning.

For this reason I preferred not to encourage a conversation about our future together, and instead waited for Joshua to finish his cajoling, then spoke of nothing in particular – of the astonishing variety of people who thronged around us; of the great degree of drunkenness; of the tobacco smoke that swirled through everything like a fog; of the habit, apparently common to all Americans, of spitting on the floor whenever possible; of the myriad accents and languages and voices – and, when we were tired of these things, of the view through the long window beside us. This window opened directly onto a wharf that ran along the waterfront and so acted as a landing-stage for every vessel that tied up here, as well as being a temporary store for merchandise: bales of cotton, piles of logs, sacks of rice, and wicker crates in which (whenever the moon swam from behind the clouds that had blown in from the bay) I could see the claws of lobsters and crayfish waving slowly behind their bars.

I suppose we continued drinking for an hour or more. I also suppose that such a spell of shouting above the hubbub, of rubbing eyes and clearing throats, was long enough to make me pay less careful attention to things than I usually do. Less attention and yet more attention as well. I remember, at any rate, that after a while I became remarkably interested in those meaty claws waving at me in their traps. Very interested too in the men who sometimes strolled along the wharf and stared into our own faces as we stared out at them.

Especially in two men I saw too late, when they were walking away from me with their heads bowed and their shoulders touching. Or rather floating away from me, not walking. Drifting over the decking as if they were weightless.

'What is it, Jim?' Natty was sitting with her back to the window and had seen me staring off, but I could not answer her at once; I was not sure.

I stood up and bent forward, leaning my hands on the table so I could look further out through the window. The two silhouettes had vanished.

'No one there,' I told her after a minute. 'I couldn't see.'

Natty leaped up at once, pushing past me so she was no longer blinded by the lights of the taproom. I imagined the difference she must feel, with the breeze whispering through the rigging of the ships, and the river slapping against the struts of the wharf.

Then Joshua was up as well, resting his hand on her shoulder, on the strip of green between her bare neck and her short sleeve. He knew what we were saying – he had seen Black Cloud off the stern of the *Angel*; but I thought he might still be full of bluster and say we had no reason to worry. Again he surprised me. Once he had turned Natty round to face the room, and made sure he had my attention as well as hers, he unbuttoned his black topcoat and held it open as carefully as he could manage, so no one else in the room saw what he was showing – a silver pistol tucked into his belt.

I sat him down as quickly as possible, saying once more that I was mistaken, certainly mistaken; there was no one. 'Please,' I went on, looking at Natty now, and waiting for her to sit down as well.

This time she believed me. With a final glance outside, she sank into her chair, took a big gulp of her drink, smiled – and a moment later we were happy again, toasting our coming success in ships, or trade, or ferry-boats, or running a store, or any of the thousand other opportunities that awaited us in the grand new city. The two shadow-walkers might never have existed.

By midnight we had drunk enough to believe that all our triumphs would come to us immediately, perhaps even before daybreak. But when we stepped outside, amidst a barrage of good-nights and encouragements from others who dispersed at the same time, with the waitresses saying we were welcome to visit again tomorrow, we felt the collapse that every drinker knows when they are knocked on the head by a blow of cold air. The square before us was a desert of silvery light, with the shadows of balconies and chimneys lying on the stones like iron. Late walkers clattered home-ward, their echoes quickly vanishing into the tall sky. A dog barked, and was answered by another far off. A moth thrummed in a lamp. Then the vegetation-smell and the mud-smell and the salt-smell poured over us.

I suppose it was the shock of this change – which in truth felt like another kind of intoxication – that persuaded me we should not go back to our hotel at once, but rather stroll to the river and watch it run past. Why the others agreed so readily I can only guess: perhaps Joshua and Anne Marie wanted to make a senti-mental connection with their new home, just as Natty and I wanted to begin our farewell to it. In any event, when I led the way round the side of the inn and climbed down a few steps onto the wharf, the others followed me without question.

Although the surface of the wharf was only a few feet lower than the solid ground, I might as well have stepped into a different world. Here, with the shallows gleaming between cracks in the decking, and the suck and push of the water much louder, I had escaped the boundaries of the town – escaped the whole of America in fact, and everyone in it. If I stared upriver I saw the vast mirror-sweep of the current bending out of sight, and knew that beyond its margin of trees lay the wilderness I loved. If I turned to my right I saw the same universe of water vanishing between mud-islands towards the sea, which I imagined marking the horizon with a line of silver foam.

Two kinds of nothing, and myself at the centre. Two kinds of emptiness, but also two kinds of fellowship. For a moment I had my wish. I felt planted deeply in the world, yet removed from it. I was safe. I was invincible.

CHAPTER 33

What is Mine

I finished my star-gazing and turned back to my friends, expecting I would say something about the warmth of the night or the beauty of the river before we wandered back to our hotel. Expecting, too, that I would find everything as I had seen it a moment before, with Joshua gripping Anne Marie around the waist to prevent her from lurching into the water, and Natty staring into a stack of crates where another consignment of lobsters was stealthily signalling to her.

But nothing was the same.

Nothing.

Natty, Joshua and Anne Marie were all in a line with their backs to the river, bolt upright and apparently cold sober. Two other figures were guarding them, standing no more than five yards away and lit from behind by lamps in the tavern window.

I did not need to ask who they were. The Painted Man was crouched with a knife in one hand, his weight shifting from one foot to another and his decorations rippling across his shoulders – red and gold and ochre and white, as though he was winged with fire. Or winged with blood. Black Cloud was slowly shaking his head and stepping forward to show himself more clearly. His face was a skull carved from stone, the lips full and dry, his face yellowish and heavy-looking. He kept coming. Another step, then another, until he was only a yard away. Close as when his eyes had bulged at me from the boat following the *Angel*. Close as when he first strode into our prison and hauled me to and fro pounding his name into my head.

Black Cloud. Black Cloud. Black Cloud.

The silence between us was immense, and as the moon floated out from a cloud-bank I studied him inch by inch: the greasy black hair swept back from his forehead; the nose like a hawk's beak; the sunken cheeks; the sleek muscles swelling in the neck and shoulders; the thick body; the hands and feet too large, as though all his energy had flowed out from the centre and congealed there, giving him an unearthly strength.

'Mister Jim.' It seemed the air itself had spoken, and all the floating pieces of my brain suddenly rushed together.

'You learned my name,' I heard myself say. The steadiness of our voices astonished me; we might have been friends meeting after a little separation. 'And you speak my language.'

'It is not difficult,' he said. 'English is arriving everywhere.'

'I suppose so,' I said, still hungry for every detail of him – the bristles prickling along his cheek and jawline, the flaking cracks in his lips, the bronze in his skin, the stubby eyelashes. This was my avenger. This was my death. And my privilege was to see him precisely. Yet it was also my privilege to know how wrong I had been. In all my dreams he had been exceptional, almost a god. Now I knew he was an ordinary man, his voice shrunk with thirst and his eyes bloodshot with the dust blown into them by the desert winds. It was not his strangeness that frightened me any more, but the opposite. He terrified me because he felt so familiar.

'Why did you take so long?' I was playing for time, but Black Cloud seemed content with this; he knew I could never escape him now.

'Two years is not long,' he said, with the trace of a smile in his voice. 'No time is long to me. I looked for you, then I went back to my house. I left my house and I looked again. Then I went back to my house and looked a third time. I almost found you – but . . .' He raised his right hand to his left shoulder and pulled aside his tunic to show me a wrinkle in the skin, where it had healed over a wound.

'You see?' he said. 'Your friend was clever and you escaped. But I knew where you would go.'

'Then why not come here first?' I asked. 'You could have waited for us.'

'I could not wait,' he said. 'You have what is mine.'

'Which is?' I said, but this was too much like foolishness and Black Cloud was suddenly impatient.

'You know the answer,' he snapped. 'What is mine.' As he spat the last word, he stooped to press his forehead hard against my own and I felt his heat seeping through my skin as though his thoughts were burning into my brain.

'Mine,' he kept saying, his sour breath swarming over my face. 'Mine, mine, mine.'

Then he straightened again, and as his heat diminished I put my hand to my chest. Black Cloud focused there for a second, but he still did not know the satchel was inside my shirt.

I gabbled at him some more to throw him off. 'You have travelled a long way,' I said. Preposterous again, but for a moment good enough. He spun towards the mouth of the river, where the night-wind wandered about the islands of the estuary; he seemed to be listening for something he could not hear, looking for something he could not see; then he lost patience again and turned back.

To rob me, I thought. But just as I expected to feel his hand thrusting inside my shirt, and the tug as he wrenched the satchel from its strap, a shudder ran through the muscles of his neck and along his arm into his fingers. I looked down and saw the quick shine of a knife. When the tip of the blade cut me I felt a hot dash of blood.

'Jim!' I heard Natty cry. She had seen this blood; it was darkening my shirt.

'It's only a scratch,' I told her, then wished I had not. Black Cloud would hurt me again now; he would cut me more deeply.

Instead, he rocked back on his heels and indolently lifted the knife away, throwing back his head and showing his large yellow teeth, smearing me with the fish-smell on his breath.

'A scratch,' he said lazily. 'You are right. A scratch.' He did not care because he knew he could kill me whenever he wanted.

My wound started to sting me then and I hid my face. I wanted to clear my mind. To think. I should give him the necklace as Natty and I had so often said we must, then I should plead for our lives. But as I stayed hunched over, with my eyes shut and my blood booming in my ears, I still refused to do this.

'It's not yours any more. It's mine,' I whispered. 'It's—'

Black Cloud would not let me finish. He bounded forward, seized me by the hair as he had done in our prison, and jerked me upright so fast I felt the skin tightening all over my face.

'That is a lie,' he snarled. 'A lie, Mister Jim. You are no better than the rest, though you think you are. You are a liar.'

I could not reply. Where was Natty, I wondered in a kind of daze; she would know how to answer. When I glanced up I saw that she had stepped so close to the Painted Man his knife was hovering an inch from her throat. Her eyes glittered and the lamp-light streamed over her green satin dress.

'Here!' she said to the Painted Man, seizing the moment by daring him to hurt her, nudging forward until the point of the knife actually touched her throat – which made Joshua reach out and grab her arm to hold her back. As he did this I remembered the gun in his belt, the silver shining pistol. Why not use it now? Why not shoot the Painted Man, then turn on Black Cloud and shoot him as well, and so finish everything?

Because he was cunning, that was the only explanation. He was planning to let Black Cloud murder me and Natty, then kill the murderers himself, so that he could collect the necklace and begin the life he wanted.

I lunged towards Natty to protect her but that was my mistake. As I stretched out my hand, the satchel slipped from beneath my shirt and Black Cloud saw it at once. 'Is it here now?' he gasped. 'Now?' He did not wait for my reply, only tucked his knife back into his belt and gripped my shoulder, holding me steady while he grabbed the satchel and ripped it away from me; as the strap broke it made a sharp little twang and burned the skin of my neck. Then he shoved me aside like rubbish; I no longer held any use for him.

'Ah!' He flipped open the mouth of the satchel and when he plunged his hand inside I heard the separate pieces of the necklace chiming together, slick and heavy and warm. His eyes widened as he felt the weight. He held it. He drew it out and hoisted it to eye level, grasping it by the knot which had once rested on the nape of my neck, and before that on his own, so all the pieces swung free and the whole design became clear. As they caught the light from the window behind him, and reflections from the river in front, the creatures carved along the individual pieces once more began to crawl and glide, sliding into and through one another, endlessly moving and always still.

I forced myself back to Natty again but she was safe suddenly; the Painted Man was no longer interested in her, any more than Black Cloud was interested in me. He wanted to stand as close as possible to Black Cloud, who was lifting the necklace even higher above his head now, letting the silver light splash down onto them both equally, glittering over their skin and dribbling into their eyes and noses and mouths.

This was our chance to escape! But it never occurred to me. In the clear light pouring over our enemies, all I could think about was how soon they would finish their gloating, and lead us away from the wharf and into the shadows where they would murder us. Where they would slice the scalps from our heads so our spirits would not rise again, and slash the tendons of our legs so we would never run through the world in our afterlives. Where they would fling us into the river and forget us.

'Jim!'

Natty was calling to me now but calmly, almost matter-of-fact.

'Jim,' she repeated. 'Look!' For a moment I thought I had jumped from one dream to another. Black Cloud and the Painted Man were still as I had seen them a moment before, with their backs turned to the wall of the inn, but they were no longer admiring the necklace. They had let it go. They had dropped it onto the wharf beside my satchel. And all their quickness had drained out of them – all of it, just in a few seconds.

I had been wrong again about Joshua. He had never wanted to harm us; he had only been waiting for his moment. While Black Cloud and the Painted Man were gazing at their treasure, and while

I was lost in thoughts of my own murder, he had decided it was time to undo the buttons of his topcoat and pull the silver pistol from his belt. Now he was pointing it towards our enemies.

My ears were already tingling with the explosion I thought must follow; as their bodies collapsed onto the wharf the tremor passed through the timbers and upwards into my feet, flooding through my body until it had filled me and set me free.

Natty snapped me awake.

'Joshua!' She was standing side on, silhouetted against the tavern window and holding out her right hand. She was asking for his gun; she wanted it herself.

I glanced at Black Cloud and the Painted Man, expecting to see them coiling all their strength together, convinced in their rage that nothing could harm them. But they were stock-still. Aghast that all their miles in the wilderness, all their scouring and listening and watching, had been made worthless by something so paltry. By the little silver mouth of a pistol.

Except I was wrong. They were not stunned or anything like it. They knew their knives and the strength of their own bodies were nothing compared to a gun, but they were still entirely themselves. When I looked at Black Cloud again, thinking I might hold his gaze and show him that I was his equal, he slowly shook his head. I was worthless to him. I was dust blowing in the wind.

Joshua and Natty did not see this; they were arguing. 'I can't give it to you,' he was telling her, still pointing the gun at Black Cloud. But as I began listening to them again I did not believe him; there was too much confusion in his voice.

'You can,' Natty told him. 'You'll give it to me right now.' It was the same note I had heard in our first conversation together, when she called me onto the towpath outside the Hispaniola and said I must come with her to meet her father. She would not be denied; Joshua would not be able to withstand her.

And sure enough, when she leaned across to prise the gun from between his fingers, Joshua surrendered it without a struggle, almost as if he was glad to see her take it. Then she gripped the gun with both hands, aiming at Black Cloud's heart, and nodded towards me without taking her eyes from his face. Like Joshua I did what she wanted – but in my case because I understood, and I loved her. I stepped forward and picked up the necklace where it lay on the wharf, and I heard Black Cloud groan. A soft roar, as if all the breath was leaving his body at once. The Painted Man covered his eyes with his hands.

'It is mine now,' I said, and slipped the cord over my head so the silver pieces spread out across my chest again. Their light flickered into my eyes and half-blinded me, but I saw Black Cloud's face clearly enough. His eyes were absolutely black and expressionless; he would not give me even the smallest part of himself.

'Change places,' Natty ordered, tossing her head to show our prisoners they must stand on the edge of the wharf with their backs to the river, while Joshua and Anne Marie withdrew into the shadows of the inn.

I understood again, and this time I knew I must not obey her. But I was too weak, and Black Cloud and the Painted Man were indifferent to her now. They shuffled over the wharf, and when they came close to Natty she plucked the knives from their belts and threw them casually into the darkness behind her; one fell on a soft bale of cotton and made no sound, the other clattered on the bare decking.

Only then did I try and reason with her. 'You mustn't do this, Natty,' I told her. 'They're men, the same as us.'

'They're not the same,' she replied. 'They would have killed us before, and this is what they deserve.'

'No, Natty,' I said. 'We must give them to the law.'

Natty raised her eyebrows. 'The law? Why ever should we give them to the law? The law will decide we're thieves, Jim – that's what the law will do. It will decide we're guilty and put us in jail, not them.'

'But we have what we want!' I said. 'They can't hurt us any more.'

How much of this Black Cloud understood I cannot say; in the corner of my eye I saw his mouth twisting into a sneer.

'We'll tie them up, then,' I said, floundering now and with no other arguments left. 'We'll leave them here, or take them further off. And we'll still be gone in a day – we'll still be safe.'

Natty was not listening to me. She had fixed her eyes on Black Cloud and decided, or very nearly decided. 'There will never be an end to it,' she said quietly, speaking to herself. 'There will never be an end to it, except this end. This.'

She spoke the last word very oddly, breaking it into two pieces so the 's' was separated and turned into a hiss. I think she was about to fire – that she would have fired anyway. As it was, Joshua suddenly jumped forward from the shadows.

'I'll do it,' he said, 'I'll do it. A woman should not do it.'

I believe to this day he planned to disarm her, to take the gun and lead our prisoners away to jail. But Natty gave a sudden jolt of anger, as though her great effort of self-control was over, and she had let herself loose.

'A woman!' she said, arching her shoulders like a cat. 'Being a woman has nothing to do with it.'

This was the moment when all her arguments were settled. After that, she fired the gun very quickly – once, twice – then Black Cloud leaned back on his heels but kept standing, glancing down at the blood on his chest before brushing it away with his fingertips.

Then he did the same for the Painted Man, with a kind of nursing tenderness.

I heard my own voice squeezed out of me – a gasp. Then another gasp from Joshua and Anne Marie together, which I thought sounded like admiration. From Natty herself there were no words, no sound at all. Just the gun slowly lowering, still clasped tight in her two hands, and the barrel releasing its coiled breath, and the sound of the shots rippling away from us over the river until they struck faint echoes from the mud-islands in the distance.

'You stole from me,' Black Cloud said, glaring at the necklace for the last time. 'You took what I loved. I have tried . . .'

But that was all. He had more breath left in his lungs, and chose not to waste it on us. Instead, he slung his arm around the shoulders of his friend and together they turned their backs and stepped off the wharf, their bodies making a single splash as they slipped through the surface of the river.

CHAPTER 34

Forgiveness

No one noticed what we had done. No footsteps pounded over the square behind us. No voice cried out. No lights flared between the dark houses or in the long window that overlooked the wharf. The city was asleep or cared about other things. Rigging on the ships docked upstream, and crumbled mountains of merchandise beneath them, were all still as a picture. And we were still too, standing at the centre of the picture. Turned to stone by what we had done.

What *we* had done.

Natty had made the final decision. Natty had pulled the trigger.

But we had all played our part.

Joshua with his hanging back, then blundering forward.

Anne Marie with her timidity.

And me. Me with my thieving and my stubbornness and my weakness.

I swung away from the edge of the wharf and turned round and made myself stop exactly where Black Cloud had stood when he spoke his last words to me. I saw the bullet strike him again, and the blood. I saw him fall. I thought: I am alive. Then I thought: I have done the same as my father. I have killed a man.

I closed my eyes, expecting my father would immediately step into my head and confront me. But it was not him I saw. It was Mr Silver with his white bristles and his lank hair and his old blue sailor's coat. He grabbed me by my shirt-front and the snake-tattoo writhed along his arm. 'What more do you want, my boy?' he hissed, his voice wet-sounding and lascivious. 'What more do you want? You have Natty safe and your treasure too. That's everything, surely. Everything. Well then. Go to her now and comfort her. Look, she is sad. Sad, because the rest of you were gutless. Gutless. Comfort her if you love her.'

That is all the time we were allowed together; as Mr Silver gave me a shake, like a terrier shaking a rat, he faded. And it was not Natty who drove him away but Joshua – Joshua gathering his wits and bounding forward, twisting the pistol from Natty's fingers, tucking it into his belt again, buttoning his coat, seizing Natty with one hand and Anne Marie with the other, then rushing towards the stairs that led up to the square and calling for me to follow.

There was no mention of what we had done. No shock, or remorse, or blame, or guilt, or relief, or pity, or praise. Just quickness and caution, which had me tucking my satchel out of sight inside my shirt, then following up the steps as though this had always been my intention and I went quite willingly.

All the way through the square, and then into the tangle of streets around our hotel, Joshua kept his arms around Natty and

Anne Marie. Swooping and sweeping them onwards. Silent. His coat-tails flapping behind him. Glancing into shadows left and right, into the arcades and blind alleys, across empty balconies and verandas, into the hollow doorways and windows.

He heard me coming after but never looked back. Was he avoiding my eye? Did he think I was most to blame? I pressed my hand to my chest and felt the shape of the satchel once more inside my shirt, its strap securely knotted, and the necklace sleeping inside it. Then I pressed my hand to my wound, where Black Cloud had scratched me. For the first time I thought this must be all he had ever intended to do – to give me a flesh wound and make me remember what I had done, not to kill me. If we had let him finish admiring his treasure, he would have left us alone. Taken what was his and left us. We had never had a reason to murder him.

'Come on, Jim!' Natty called to me. 'Be quick!' – and my thoughts left me. Everything was scurry and dash now, ducking and darting, until suddenly we were back where we wanted to be, at the hotel and still undetected. The lobby empty, with the blades of the fan standing still over our heads, and the piano silent beyond the door into the parlour.

I have often wondered since: what if Joshua and Anne Marie had thought we would see them again next day and thereafter? This had been their plan, after all. In which case I can imagine us wishing each other goodnight, even embracing. As it was, friendship had become impossible. We were ashamed of one another. We stared at the carpet, and its white zigzags racing through the blue like waves. For my own part I felt glad. I never wanted to think of them again, or remember what they knew about us. And they must have felt the same, because as soon as they got their breath back they left us, Joshua seizing Anne Marie by the hand and hurrying her upstairs to their room. Still with never a word spoken, we heard the door click behind them, then there was silence again.

I offered Natty my arm but she would not look at me.

'Will you be able to sleep?' I asked.

She nodded. She had drifted away from me and I needed to call her back, to be practical and sensible. 'We'll go to the *Mungo* in the morning early,' I reminded her. 'At first light.'

Now she glanced up at last, her eyes vacant. I could not decide whether she had suddenly grown much older, or was much younger – like a child again.

'You'll come with me, won't you?' she said.

'I shall,' I told her. 'Nothing has changed.'

She smiled. 'I had no choice, you know.'

'That's not true, Natty.'

She stared into the mirror hanging on the wall beside Mr Brydges's desk; she might have been a cat, to whom a reflection of itself means nothing.

'All right, then,' she said. 'But did I make the wrong choice, Jim?'

'You killed him,' I said.

'I killed them both.' She faced me directly. 'And now they'll never follow us again.'

'They may. But if they do, it'll be our choice.'

Natty held my gaze. 'And is it your choice, Jim? Will you let them follow us?'

Once again, I could not decide whether she spoke innocently, or as someone who understood more than I did.

'We'll find out,' I said. It was the best I could do.

Natty bowed her head. 'Very well,' she said. Then she reached for my hand, turned it over, and began to trace the lines on my palm with her fingertips. In the gloom she could not possibly have seen what she was doing, and I soon bunched my hand into a fist, catching her finger in the trap.

'And what about this?' She touched my shirt with her free hand, where the blood had already begun to dry. I shrugged, and told her what I had told myself: it was nothing.

Then I led her away from the lobby and upstairs to our room, with Natty wriggling her hand free from my grip, finding the key in my pocket, and afterwards locking the door behind us again. In the time it took me to take off my shirt and bathe my wound, she crawled into bed and fell asleep. I slipped in beside her and lay as quiet as possible – like a figure on a tomb, except I could feel the weight of the satchel pressing against my heart.

I do not remember that night; my sleep was a sort of darkness, an abyss, and next morning I wished it would swallow me again, because when I came to my senses I saw Black Cloud still alive and sneering at me on the wharf-side; I saw the Painted Man laughing in his cascade of silvery light; I saw the two of them stepping into thin air, and floating face down over their underwater kingdom.

Then I opened my eyes and found Natty perched on our window-sill in the sunlight.

'At last!' she said, with a kind of impishness, and came closer to peer into my face; she had put her Indian dress back on, ready for our journey. 'Are you wearing those same clothes as last night?'

I could not answer.

'Better for working on a boat, I suppose. But really, my green dress . . . I'll keep it for England.'

I still did not answer.

She relaxed against the window frame again and pouted. 'Not even a "good morning" from you, Jim? I've been waiting for you to wake up for such a long time.'

I was tongue-tied – this chatter was all guilt, I thought; guilt and anxiety mixed. I stared at her. Then still without speaking I pulled back the cover and stood upright, running one hand over my face and flattening my hair. I had work to do. I had our possessions to collect, my old Indian clothes and Natty's dress. I had to place them on our bed and roll them inside the blankets we had used in the wilderness, and in this way carry them safely home.

'So this is my punishment, is it, then?' Natty went on. 'If so, how long will it last?'

Again there was no answer from me, and now she lost patience, rocking on her perch by the window. 'You are not being fair, Jim,' she said.

'What do you mean?' I said, breaking my silence at last. I had been folding her dress, making it small and neat and placing it inside the blanket; now I looked up and felt the blood pumping into my face.

Natty was not in the least abashed. 'Am I the only one who needs punishing?'

'I haven't said anything like that,' I told her.

'You might as well,' she said. 'That's how it seems.'

'You think I need punishing too?' I was struggling to keep my voice steady. 'Believe me, Natty, I am being punished.' I raised one hand and banged myself on the chest, striking my satchel as I did so. 'Here.'

It was only a word, but I said it with so much heat, Natty started from her place in the window, resting one hand on my arm.

'Listen a minute,' she said. Suddenly she was herself again, and I stared down at the bed; at my dusty Indian tunic, stained with sweat and covered in thorn-scratches; at my moccasins almost worn through.

'Neither of us needs punishing,' she went on. 'That's all I'm saying. We have to do the next thing now – we have to be free.'

'But we can't forget,' I said.

'That would be our choice,' she said, and squeezed my arm. I glanced up; she was smiling, and her right cheek looked flushed, a rosy colour in the brown, where the sun had warmed it. I could not resist her then, as I had never been able to resist her when she gave me her kindness.

'Do you know what I think?' she said, looking straight into my eyes. 'You still haven't understood.'

'Understood what?' I asked. There was a kind of emptiness in my head, which I was so anxious to have filled, I knew I would accept whatever she said to me next.

'Black Cloud was a murderer,' she said. 'He deserved what happened – him and the other one, both.'

'But we don't know that, Natty,' I replied. 'We never saw that. We saw his village but not him in it – or only at the end. We heard stories about him, that's all. Rumours. And we made up stories ourselves.'

I turned to my work again, rolling the blanket with the clothes inside. Natty watched me in silence.

'Besides,' I added when I was done. 'Is that why we killed him? For being a murderer? Or did we kill him to save ourselves? Because we'd stolen from him?'

Natty would not answer directly. 'Jim,' she said with a sigh. 'Does that matter any more?'

'You know it does. It has to.'

She shook her head. 'He would have killed us, anyway, whatever the reason. We had to be first if we wanted to stay alive.'

I stared around the room – at the light touching the bed-frame and the ewer and the basin; they seemed to be looking at me, waiting for my answer.

But I did not have answers any more. I had used them all, and

Natty had replied to them all. And yet she was not triumphant; she was gentle. 'Come now,' she said, and stretched towards me, taking hold of my hand and laying it against her cheek. 'Here,' she said. 'I am here.' And that was all. We were done.

We were done, and the day began again. I shrugged, as though I had only that moment awoken. Natty went back to her place by the window. I finished my folding and tidying. The sun shone more brightly. The breeze blew. The curtain lifted and bloomed. And a moment later we were downstairs in the lobby, flying past Mr Brydges's empty desk, out into the warm street. Ten minutes more and we had reached the docks – weaving our way through the sailors, the passengers, the stevedores, the gawpers, the idlers, the pickpockets, the touts, until we found Captain Yalland at his place in the stern of the *Mungo*, and heard him calling down to us as if we were old friends and his most valuable sailors.

'All aboard!' he boomed. 'Almost too late . . .' And so it continued: climbing the gangplank and shaking the captain's hand (which felt callused like a claw); meeting our shipmates (a dozen of them, who made us welcome enough); admiring the ship (which I thought would turn into a greyhound when she was slipped from her leash); finding our cabin (a coffin, with two bunks squeezed on top of one another); stowing our possessions (but not the satchel, which I kept safe inside my shirt); returning to the deck to begin our work (which began with loading and varnishing, then involved mending a sail, then continued with more loading).

By lunchtime it was finished: Captain Yalland was satisfied; our cargo was all aboard; everything was ready; and we would sail at once. 'Time and tide!' I heard him muttering to himself, as climbed onto his platform and spun the wheel, dreaming of the high seas and not a moment too soon.

I might have been back on the *Nightingale* almost three years before. A gang of shipmates heaved at the capstan to raise our anchor; other men shouted fore and aft as they pushed us away from the quayside with long poles – and then we were off, the first sail breaking out on the foremast and the breeze filling it with a delightful clean smack; the waves chattering against our prow as the *Mungo* entered the lanes that ran along the midstream of the great river.

By this time I had found a place beside Natty in the stern of the ship and seen the docks fall away behind us, then the tatty outskirts of the town, then the slimy marshes where no houses could be built. The first soft lights of evening began to shake out their colours here – salty green, and purple, and brown. The same colours as home, and the same mist rising. But in a mile – in no time at all – shadows had stepped into this mist and turned into faces which were the opposite of home. Of my original home, at any rate. The faces of White Feather and Hoopoe; Boss and the Spectacle; the Rider; Talks to the Wind and Fire Wife; Mr Vale and Mr Brydges flustering under the blades of his fan. But not Black Cloud and not the Painted Man. I could not find them, although I saw their village and their house standing empty, with dust blowing in through their open door.

All this ended when the land ended, or rather sank into a shoal of mud-humps that seemed to race towards us under the water. These seemed likely to stop our journey almost as soon as it had begun, which the captain evidently feared as well, ordering me to stop my idling and move forward and stand in the prow of the *Mungo* where I could keep a lookout. I would like to say I did this efficiently, but when it came to it, and I shielded my eyes and set to work, so many obstacles appeared to me that I found myself shouting almost continuously that we should turn to port, or to starboard, or to port again, and was soon told to quieten down, and only call out if I saw any dangers that were really and truly about to sink us.

After this I allowed myself another spell of thinking, for the mouth of the Mississippi is an extraordinary sight. And also, I decided, a sight of extraordinary melancholy. A colossal mass of water spreading to the distant horizon, in which every slop, twist, pulse, ripple and surge is stained with mud the current has carried from inland. Here and there, bringing the only variety to the scene, were examples of the ruins the captain had spoken about – the masts of ships that had foundered, and were now poking above the water, all decorated with weeds and barnacles and seagulls perching on their topmost points. In the whole of my life at sea, I had never seen so many signs of destruction, gathered so closely together. When I had counted more than a dozen of them, and warned the captain about each in turn, I began to think that ruin and wreckage were all that any of us can expect in life.

Then we were through these disasters, slicing the foaming ridge of the bar and reaching the open sea, where mud-stains sank away and the water stretched blue to the horizon. Breeze blew off the land to our port side with a sugary fragrance. Our mates hung out all our sails and the *Mungo* leaped forward as I knew she would. Birds that a moment before had seemed like spirits of the damned now skimmed around us like angels. The whole atmosphere, in fact, was so suddenly freshened and woken, I felt I had also quickened in myself, and was regaining time I had spent in the country behind me.

I was thinking ahead as well. Captain Yalland had told us when we left New Orleans that our journey would take us straight into the bay – somewhat above the course we had followed in the *Nightingale* when travelling in the opposite direction – then round the tip of Florida before turning north until we reached the harbour of New York. And this was indeed our route, but with two diversions I must briefly describe. One was a stop on Booby Island, for no better reason than to amuse ourselves by observing the many thousands of birds for which the island is named, and also the alligators that swim around them in sullen rage, watching in case a bird falls asleep, or dives straight into their jaws, in which case it is gobbled down with a prodigious thrashing of wings.

Our second stopping-place was the Tortugas, where we were told we would buy some turtles; it was easy work we heard, which involved bringing them on board, turning them upside down, and stacking them as easily as if they were gigantic bowls. In this way, we would guarantee a supply of fresh meat for the rest of our voyage.

When we reached the appointed spot, and I expected to be sent ashore to capture some of these creatures, I found there was no need. The turtles came to us, not of their own accord, but brought in canoes and other sorts of small craft by the Indians who also live on the islands, and make their pittance by selling the turtles to sailors as they pass by.

It was a curious operation, at once delicate and sad. Delicate because the dry slopes of the islands, which rise very steeply from the deep water of the bay, and are sprinkled with only small patches of grass and mangrove, first appeared as dusk began to fall, and seemed as uncertain as the hills in a dream; sad because the Indians who live there are very emaciated and pathetic. Our captain, who in other respects seemed an admirable fellow, full of good sense and good cheer, treated them with no kindness at all, shouting from his deck that their prices were too high, that he did not need their help, that they were not much better than highwaymen, and in the end flinging down a few coins without caring whether they landed in the canoes or not – whereupon a basket was filled with turtles and raised on deck.

As soon as this was done Natty and I were ordered to set more sails, which pleased us because it brought to an end our miserable exchange with the islanders. We were still clinging to the crossbeam of the mainmast as the Tortugas shrank into the sunset behind us. I am sure the captain would have preferred it if we had returned to the deck immediately, and occupied ourselves with some new practical matter. But despite the perils of our position we chose to stay aloft, and to contemplate for a moment longer the brown tusk of the mainland that was vanishing behind us.

'Will I be forgiven?' Natty asked, cutting straight to the quick of things. Like me, she had hooked her feet into the rigging and was resting against the crossbeam. The waves were so far beneath us we could not hear them breaking against the prow of our ship, but the breeze was strong – strong enough to make a purring sound in the sleeves of our shirts, and bring tears into our eyes.

'Not in general,' she went on. 'Will *you* forgive me?'

This was softer than I expected, and I could not reply for a moment.

'You know the answer to that,' I told her at length.

Natty nodded towards the satchel, where it hung inside my shirt.

'You didn't begin this,' she said. 'Our fathers began it.'

I turned my head and looked at our wake stretching behind us, where the water lost its whiteness and became a latticework of smaller waves. Although the sun had now almost completely set, its last light had turned the whole surface of the ocean into beaten silver, solid-seeming and apparently perfectly smooth.

'I know,' I said, as though I was talking to myself. 'And yet our lives are our own.'

'So I'm not forgiven?' Natty was smiling but not in her eyes.

'I didn't say that.'

'What, then?'

'We have to forgive ourselves.'

'And how shall we do that?' Natty asked.

'By deciding we're innocent.'

'Is that what you've decided?'

'I'm still deciding.'

Natty pressed further forward, so her body hung over the cross-beam as though she had fallen from the sky. Only her own weight held her in place.

'Then I'll do the same,' she said. 'We'll decide together.'

'It's what we have always done,' I said.

And there our talk ended. We did not mention Black Cloud by name, or the Painted Man; everything we said was about ourselves. Or so it seems now. At the time, as we watched the land disappear at last, I felt sure we were concentrating on everything else, our friends as well as our enemies, the country as well as its inhabitants.

I suppose it might therefore be said that we had deceived ourselves, when we climbed down onto the deck again and returned to our work, and felt lighter in our hearts. But I like to think we had only done what all men and women do. We had preferred the future to the past. We had turned our faces forward, as we now did in fact, staring along the slender deck of the *Mungo* as she raced ahead.

CHAPTER 35

My Father's House

I have no wish to linger over our journey back to England. That belongs in a different sort of history – one that involves ships and shipping, sailors and sailing, and not one concerned above all with land.

Suffice it to say we made good time to New York, and did not suffer unduly at the hands of the weather-gods, or those men-of-war belonging to the English or the French navy, whose tussle, I was surprised to hear from Captain Yalland, had continued the whole of our long time in America, including since we left Mr Vale, who was the last to speak to me on this subject.

And suffice it to say as well: while Natty and I lacked the expertise of our crew-mates, and their stamina in crawling across rigging, or repairing woodwork, or mending sails, or any of the thousand other tasks required of sailors everywhere, we did not acquit ourselves badly, and did not break our fingers or our heads, and arrived at our destination with enough credit for our captain to recommend us for a similar position on a different vessel, which would carry us across the Atlantic and so to our homes.

This second part of our sea-voyage has as little to do with my adventure as the first (except it was the means of bringing it to an end for the time being); for this reason I shall also treat it very briefly, saying only that the *Antigone* was more sturdily built than the *Mungo*, and our cabin was more spacious (in that it more nearly resembled a vault than a coffin), and the conditions we encountered were not nearly so easy and peaceful as those we found on our way north from Florida.

This was because an early blast of autumn arrived in New York at the same time as we did ourselves, and when we left it again the heavens decided we should have a taste of what winter would bring in due course. Although we were spared icebergs, we nevertheless had to endure a month of freezing winds, of waves like mountains, of snow in our sails, and of sickness and stumbling that made our crossing very uncomfortable. I did not quite get to the point of thinking we would be sunk a second time, and on this occasion lose our fight with Neptune, and lay our bones to rest on the bed of the Atlantic, but I most certainly did feel raged-at by the country we had left behind. America had not made us welcome, except in unexpected ways, but it seemed very unwilling to let us go. It is a contradiction I have noticed in many of the places that are dearest to me, and the people.

Be that as it may: we survived our ordeal, and when we came into the mouth of the English Channel this foretaste of winter was banished, and beautiful autumn weather settled over us. Soft breezes, calm waters, sunshine, and gulls that I thought were speaking to me in a language I recognised.

I thought this homecoming would inspire a great surge of gratitude and excitement. I believe I may even have practised such feelings during the stormiest part of our crossing, when our safety seemed at risk. But I have to admit that when the red cliffs of Devonshire first glowed onto our horizon, bringing at the same time a delicious scent of damp earth, I did not immediately sink to my knees or believe I had found the only place I wanted to be.

On the contrary. I felt my heart fill with sadness, which I only began to understand as our progress continued towards the east, and we came to Start Point, then wafted along the coast of Dorset past Lyme and Weymouth, Lulworth and Swanage. Apparently I had lived among too many people deprived of their homes to feel easy about finding my own. I could not separate their pleasure from my sorrow.

This is the truth I most often told myself – which was in fact a sort of dissembling. For there was a second and more intimate source of my confusion, which I could not so easily admit.

I cannot describe it without hesitating even now, although I shall try.

When we had rounded the coast of Kent and come into the mouth of the Thames . . .

When the daylight had begun to fade . . .

When our captain knew we would not reach London before nightfall . . .

When we had hauled to and decided to spend the night at anchor in the estuary . . .

When Natty and I had eaten our meal, and fixed a lamp to the mast, and come to stand by the starboard rail of our ship . . .

When we stood in silence and heard the waves slither against the hull, and the timbers creak, and the breeze rasp through the grasses of the marsh . . .

When we remembered that Natty and I had been together every day since she first arrived outside the Hispaniola a little over three years before . . . Every day except the handful she was held prisoner by Smirke on the Island . . . Every day . . .

When we knew that tomorrow . . .

We shrank closer together and felt the warmth pass between us, stretching the silence for as long as we dared.

'Have you spoken to the captain?' Natty said at last.

'No,' I told her. 'Spoken about what?'

'About our plans.'

'Do we have any plans?'

'You know we do.'

'Remind me what they are, then.' I turned to look at her; soon after we left the Tortugas we had both been given plain sailors' clothes to wear, and now she had also borrowed a jersey from one of our crew-mates, and the rolled-over collar hung away from her bare neck.

'Don't pretend,' she said. 'You know perfectly well what we have to do.' She spoke half-smiling, to soften the force of her argument.

'I know what will happen,' I told her. 'For a little while.'

'Exactly.' She nodded. 'You must go and see your father. I will go and see my father – and my mother. We must tell them what we've done. They must hear our story and know we're safe.'

As Natty finished speaking, the clouds shifted above us and a gust of moonlight showed the expression on her face. She did not look as steadfast as she sounded; her eyes were slippery with tears and she was biting her lip.

My arms closed around her and she gave no resistance; she lifted one hand to wipe her eyes, then pressed it in the small of my back.

'My father,' she said, muffling her words into my shirt-front. 'I'm sure my father . . . My father won't be there.'

In my stupidity, which came from thinking about ourselves and not our parents, I could not understand.

'But your father will forget the silver very soon,' I told her. 'He'll understand we couldn't save it.' I paused for a moment, soothing her hair and feeling it spring back as soon as the weight of my hand was lifted. 'Anyway,' I went on eventually. 'We can show him the necklace. He can see that, and then he'll only be glad you've come home.'

'My father will be dead,' Natty said – or rather whispered, as if she was telling me a secret.

'You can't say that,' I said, which was not quite to contradict her. 'You don't know that.'

'We've been away too long,' she insisted. 'I feel it.'

'And your mother?'

'Oh, my mother . . .' Natty did not finish her sentence and did not need to.

'No,' she added with a sigh. 'You must go to your father – he's the one who must see the necklace first. When you've done that, come and find me.'

This comforted me but I was still impatient. 'How soon after?' I said – and immediately regretted it. I could hear the same wheedling note that I had used to her once before, when we were locked in our prison.

Natty pushed away from me then and her eyes were dry. 'Jim,' she said. 'There will be time.'

Time for what, I wanted to ask, and time beginning when, but I resisted. Instead, I looked down to the current flowing beneath us: the remorseless grey water; the wig of seaweed catching against the anchor chain, remaining there long enough to collect a fringe of dirty foam, then swinging loose.

As it disappeared, Natty continued in a gentler voice. 'As you believe, so shall it be,' she said, and raised her hand to my face once more, stroking my cheek. In the giddiness of feeling her touch I did not perfectly understand. And still not, when she turned away without saying another word, and blew out the lamp hanging near us on the mast, and led the way below-deck.

When we reached our cabin I climbed into my bunk, the top bunk, and waited until Natty was lying on her own bed below me. Now, I thought. Now I shall ask her what she meant: 'As you believe, so shall it be.' But I did not. When she called 'Goodnight' I replied in kind and that was all I heard – except, for a long while afterwards, the river scraping against the hull beside my head, and the waves making sudden slaps and leaps.

When I closed my eyes at last, I felt sure I would not sleep for long, and would certainly be awake with the sunrise; I thought the confusion of my feelings required it. But the moment I opened my eyes next morning I knew the *Mungo* was already under way, and Natty had left her bunk. When I scrambled on deck and found her at our usual place in the bows, I asked her why: had the captain not needed me? She told me he had decided to let me lie, as a reward for coming home at last, and had also agreed I should go ashore when we came near the Hispaniola.

'I thought I should settle this with him,' she told me, 'because you were not here to ask him yourself.'

I did not rise to this bait. 'Thank you,' was all I said, and turned to look away from her.

It was a grey morning with rain-clouds smudging the northern horizon, and the breeze struck coldly as it brought us upriver. For the first few miles the country would be called dull by someone who did not know it, since it was made entirely of marshes and hardly seemed a part of the earth at all. Everywhere I looked I saw only miniature soft cliffs, streaked with slime; shining mud-heaps; a ribcage of decaying timbers, wrapped in a cloak of sea-lavender.

All apparently cheerless; all apparently ugly. Yet to my eyes the greatest beauties in the world, with the most beautiful creatures living among them – the geese that craned up from their grazing to honk as we passed them by, and the godwits and sanderlings that blew away from our shadow and turned the air silver, and the curlews calling the sound of their own sad name over and over.

As we drew onwards, and the traffic of other boats increased around us, the land became more solid and fertile. Here, with as much curiosity as I had felt while cruising along the Mississippi, and seeing all manner of novelties for the first time, I found cottages standing among cornfields that had recently been harvested, and hamlets with people leaving their homes for work, or standing in groups talking, or pausing with their hands on their hips to watch us pass. Where I could not see things exactly, because they were too far off, I imagined them. The dusty leaves on the elm trees fringed with soft little teeth. The plum-coloured brick-rubble used to fill a hole in the surface of a lane. The knapped flints on a church tower and the clever pattern of their black-and-white facets. The blue caps worn by men in the fields, and their green and yellow waistcoats, and their boots laced with string, and the fringed bonnets on the women, and their clogs, and their long dresses stained with mud along the hems.

As each bend of the river brought us into more populous country, and the ragged shoreline lifted into pasture, and the bare mud-banks into hills covered with trees, such a feeling of tenderness swelled inside me that I struggled for breath. These were my fields, I told myself – or rather felt in the veins of my body. My fields; and my salty inlets winding between them; and my fishermen's sheds; and my bridges across my streams; and my ponies drinking from my troughs, eating my grass.

Then all that gliding ended. All that gliding, and absorbing, and praising, because Natty left my side to ask the captain for his permission to set me ashore.

I must now change the way of telling my story, for the simple reason that everything previously settled was suddenly uprooted, and everything continuous was broken. I saw the next several minutes in fragments, and could not easily join them together.

A sail was reefed. The *Mungo* slowed to a walking pace. The rowing-boat strapped at our stern was lowered into the water, with a crew-mate working the oars to keep her steady. I thanked the captain and collected my bundle from our cabin. I found my way back to the daylight. The grey daylight, and the cold air. I walked to the stern. I said goodbye to Natty.

I could not believe it was me speaking, me living and breathing. When I wrapped my arms around her she stood very still, and I felt the bones of her shoulder blades. When I bent to kiss her she turned aside so I only brushed her cheek, which the breeze had made dry and cold. I told myself to keep moving.

What could I think, in such a rush of things happening? I had no wish to think. I had no capacity, because the weight of my heart had dragged everything out of my brain. Out of my body, too, so letting my hands slide away from Natty, turning away from her, climbing over the rail of the *Mungo*, finding the rope ladder that hung there, reaching the rowing-boat, sitting in the prow with my bundle on my knees, untying the tow-rope, watching my crew-mate heave at his oars, reaching a little tumbledown jetty protruding from the shore, climbing the slippery steps, feeling them heave beneath me after my long time at sea, grasping the dry rail at the top, hearing mates on board the *Mungo* holler that my oarsman must hurry or else be left behind, seeing him set off and tether the rowing-boat and climb the rope ladder again, then watching the *Mungo* unfurl her topsail and accelerate away: so all these things were quite separate from me, perfectly foreign and incomprehensible.

Until I saw Natty standing in the stern of the ship. She was too far off already, not herself but a silhouette. And yet from the way she waved one hand above her head, and continued waving until she vanished round the next bend of the river, I told myself I knew well enough what she was feeling. If I had not done this, I could not have withstood the silence that followed, or begun to make my way.

It was an hour's walk, or perhaps half an hour. I do not remember. I remember instead the prints of gulls' feet in the mud as I jumped over gullies and creeks. I remember doubling back on myself sometimes. I remember the ground improving, and a towpath made of sandy-coloured stones. I remember a church bell tolling, a dark red sound blossoming over the fields. I remember touching the satchel inside my shirt, and my father coming more and more powerfully into my mind.

I saw him accepting the necklace when I held it out to him; I heard the pieces slide together as he bowed his head and put it on, then watched them separate and hang in place against his chest. I watched the animals begin their dance inside the silver, bringing their brightness to the English air.

And at the same time I remember my mind stalling, because I had no idea what I might say to my father, how I might begin to explain what we had done.

Not even now, after so long to get ready.

Not even when I saw the Hispaniola on the horizon, with its roof sloping down to the ground on the landward side, and the outbuildings where we kept our puncheons.

And still not when I drew close enough to notice the smudges of green on the clapboard walls, and the brick chimneys where the mortar was almost rotted away, and the windows turning their blind eyes.

And still not again when I reached the front of the house and found the rose-bushes my father had planted there all smothered in weeds, and a part of the towpath fallen into the water, and the window of my own room, the window I had looked through to see Natty for the first time, cloudy with dust.

I took a breath and settled myself; I stepped off the towpath and onto the weeds around the front door.

Locked.

Then round the back, to the other door. Broken glass on the step. Green glass and brown glass. Gin bottles and beer bottles.

This door locked as well.

I stood still for a moment, staring back across the marshes in the direction I had just travelled, and felt the weariness in my legs, in my whole body, so I had to sit down and rest against the house, which took my weight without a sound.

This was the worst possible homecoming, then; the worst. It was not Mr Silver who had died. It was my father. Died and left the house deserted. I could never tell him what I had seen, or show him the treasure I had brought, or ask for his forgiveness. The worst.

I looked up and a face was staring at me. A thin face above a thin neck, with his coat blowing about his ankles. Not a face I knew. One of my father's customers, perhaps.

'You won't find a way in there,' he said, and laughed to show he thought I was a fool for trying.

'What?' I asked, squinting up at him.

The man opened and closed his mouth; he was old, and did not have any teeth. He might have been a scarecrow, standing stark against the enormous sky, deluged with its grey light.

'Do you hear those bells?' he asked, as if this was an answer to my question.

I did hear them, still tolling faintly in the distance, as I had heard them when I first came ashore.

'What of it? I asked.

'A famous victory,' he said, and smacked his lips. 'We have conquered the Frenchies.'

I began to think he was witless. 'A victory?' I said.

'A famous victory with Admiral Nelson,' he went on. 'The news has just come. That's why they're ringing the bells. For Trafalgar.'

None of this meant anything to me. I scowled, and banged on the wall of my home with a clenched fist.

'Why is it locked?' I asked, dragging him back to here and now. But he would not easily follow.

'Locked and gone away,' he said.

'Who's gone away?'

'Mr Hawkins, of course,' he said, suddenly reproachful, as if I was talking nonsense. 'Mr Hawkins is gone away. Or been led away, rather.'

'Led away? Led away how?'

'Led away by a stranger and months ago. Led away by a stranger and not seen since.'

I cannot say how – I have no memory of standing up – but next thing I was on my feet and floating towards him.

'Tell me!' I ordered.

He cringed and lifted one hand to protect himself. 'Tell you what?'

'Tell me everything you know.'

He flinched again, and I saw myself as he saw me, my face salted by the cold Atlantic, with the fire of the wilderness still burning inside me.

'What's it to you?' he asked, his voice shaking.

'I am his son,' I told him. 'I am Jim Hawkins come home. I am his son.'

Acknowledgements

I'm very grateful to my wife Kyeong-Soo Kim, and my friends Tim Dee and Alan Hollinghurst, for the help they gave me while I was writing this book. I'm also indebted to the following:

American Indian Portraits: George Catlin, ed. Stephanie Pratt and Joan Carpenter Troccoli (2013)
American Places, Wallace Stegner and Page Stegner (1981)
Changing National Identities at the Frontier, Andrez Resendez (2005)
Chronicle of the Narvaez Expedition, Alvar Nunez Cabeza De Vaca (1555)
Ecological Imperialism, Alfred W. Crosby (1986)
Empire of the Summer Moon, S. C. Gwynne (2010)
The Essential Lewis and Clark, ed. Landon Y. Jones (2000)

The Eternal Frontier, Tim Flannery (2001)
The Fall of Natural Man, Anthony Pagden (1982)
Ghost Riders, Richard Grant (2003)
Guns, Germs and Steel, Jared Diamond (1997)
The Indians of Texas, W. W. Newcomb (1961)
La Salle and the Discovery of the Great West, Francis Parkman (1869)
Life on the Mississippi, Mark Twain (1883)
The Magic World, ed. William Brandon (1971)
The Mammoth Book of Native Americans, ed. Jon E. Lewis (2004)
Native American Voices, ed. Steven Mintzl (1995)
Native Americans and Anglo-American Culture 1750–1850, ed. Tim Fulford and Kevin Hutchings (2009)
North American Indians, George Catlin (1989)
The Red Man's Bones, Benita Eisler (2013)
Rivers of Blood, Rivers of Steel, Mark Cocker (1998)
Travels of William Bartram, William Bartram (1791)
Wildlife and Man in Texas, Robin W. Doughty (1983)